NUA

| AUTHOR | HUNT, J. | CLASS | F |
| --- | --- | --- | --- |

| TITLE | Notes from utopia |
| --- | --- |

*About the author*

Jemima Hunt was born in London in 1968. She divides her time between London and New York.

# NOTES FROM UTOPIA

Jemima Hunt

FLAME
Hodder & Stoughton

07951041

Copyright © 2000 by Jemima Hunt

First published in Great Britain in 2000
by Hodder and Stoughton
A division of Hodder Headline

The right of Jemima Hunt to be identified as the Author of
the Work has been asserted by her in accordance with the Copyright,
Designs and Patents Act 1988.

10 9 8 7 6 5 4 3 2 1

A CIP catalogue record for this title is available from the British Library.

ISBN 0 340 75152 5

Typeset by
Avocet Typeset, Brill, Aylesbury, Bucks
Printed in Great Britain by
Mackays of Chatham PLC, Chatham, Kent

HODDER AND STOUGHTON
A division of Hodder Headline
338 Euston Road
London NW1 3BH

To my mother, father, sister and the boy.

I would like to thank the following people: my agents Stephanie Cabot and Eugenie Furniss, Rebecca Carter for her interest and support, all those friends who have read *Notes from Utopia* along the way and my editor, Kirsty Fowkes.

# Chapter One

"Saul Siseman, known for his *Hello Kitty* work, seen alongside his *Canal Street Chic* work." Saul read the caption beneath the photograph.

"The picture's kind of cool," he added.

Saul, an artist who was never surprised to find himself featured in the style section of the Sunday paper, was reading aloud to Utopia. They were lying on the bed with the air-conditioning on MAX drinking espresso, which always reminded her of melted chocolate. It left that same sweet aftertaste, its urgency faintly erotic. She took the paper from him. She felt him watch her read it. The photograph showed Saul in a metallic New York Fire Department coat standing, glass in hand, beside one of his installations commissioned by a Madison Avenue department store. It was made from a collection of nuts, bolts and junky machine parts welded together to form a clothes rack. Utopia had been in the studio when Marcus, the creative buyer, first came to call.

"Fabulous," he had enthused. "We'll take two for New York and another ten for Tokyo. But you must incorporate a few stainless steel buckets and more wire. The Japanese go crazy for wire."

Utopia had watched his tanned face bead with sweat. AC was exclusive to the bedroom as a way of cutting costs.

She handed back the paper and took another sip of coffee. At times like this she would find herself questioning her involvement with the curly haired boy stretched out beside her, a boy who kept a framed photograph of his mother by his bed. Early on in their sexual encounters, in a state of arousal, she had knocked her head on the bedside table and turned to find herself eyeball to eyeball with Mother Siseman.

"Does she have to be there?" she asked, suddenly self-conscious.

"She's always been there," he said, which did nothing to reassure her.

Utopia saw it as a cultural thing and something she would never understand. Did English boys invite their mothers into their bedrooms? Not the ones she knew. She made a point always to flip the photograph on its front before joining him in bed.

She reached over to put down her cup and he ran a finger down her spine. It tickled and she laughed. Saul was a good few inches shorter than her own five eleven, but once in bed this was easily forgiven. He looked like a garden statue with perfectly proportioned limbs, and muscles that carved his arms and rippled across his back. He earned a living wielding a blow-torch and she liked his hands-on dirtiness and the hardness of his body. She was impressed that he had built a living space out of a printing press warehouse. The ability to install a kitchen, knock up a bathroom and sand the floors was seductive. Macho without the machismo, she reckoned. Saul was very good with his hands.

"Do it again," she said without looking round.

Saul said nothing but moved across the bed to press his body flat against hers.

As far as they had a routine, Sunday – today anyway – was set aside for trawling the fleamarkets, all-day brunching and too many coffee refills. But Saul had to recruit a new assistant in order to complete the order by September. "What a fucking drag," he had complained, as the rat-a-tat-tat of the alarm clock woke them at eleven. "The only time I could do her was today."

The sound of a fist hammering against the metal lattice-work that protected the studio's glass front broke the spell.

"Shit," he said letting go.

Rolling over, Utopia watched as he swung his legs over the side of the bed and reached for his jeans. She stretched her arms above her head. Her spine cracked and felt longer. "Who did you say she was?"

"Andrew's sister's roommate. She's a painter."

His head disappeared beneath his T-shirt. On it was written *Zac's 11th Ave Hardware Outlet* and there was a picture of a hammer and sickle.

"Does she know how to weld?"

"Wants to learn," he said, as his face popped out. "The TV's working again. I fixed it."

Then he left her.

Utopia leaned out of bed to shut the door. She pulled at the sheet to bury her chin. She didn't want to watch TV. She looked out of the bedroom window at a yard hemmed in by four dirty buildings criss-crossed with fire-escapes. A supermarket trolley, piled high with empty cans, sat waiting to be picked up. Someone was going to do lucrative trade. Visible along the top was a flicker of sky. She blinked at the glare, thought how happy she was to see blue then remembered why she was here and felt hopeless and sad.

In January, five months ago now, her mother had died and everything stopped. Nothing made any sense because she no longer knew what was important. All that lay ahead were empty hours with nothing to fill them. She had found herself useless to make decisions, simple things like what to eat, where to go, who to speak to when she picked up the phone. Try to keep busy, was what everyone said, but she had left her job so had no reason to be busy. "Take it one day at a time," she read in a book called *Coping With Loss*. In expectation of what? She had been robbed of her mother. All that was left was the loneliness of fear and lethargy of loss.

She did nothing but sleep.

Her father had put up a stoic front and returned to work. What else could he do? He had his students to teach, the department to run and Cynthia, his secretary, to make him cups of tea. Utopia's sister was a barrister and lived in her chambers when she wasn't in court. "Can't talk now," she would say, when Utopia finally managed to get through. Her sister was very good at shutting out the rest but she was also an expert at telling lies.

And then there was P. It was P who kept her afloat.

"There's no need to rush it," he would say, arriving home with favourite things.

She had made a list. Margarita sorbet, avocados but not too soft, magazines, crumpets, runny honey, wine – lots of it – and new CDs. "I've got nothing to listen to. I hate everything here," she had vented her fury at her collection of plastic discs.

"Fine. I'll go shopping," he said.

Later when he returned with with music recommended

by the boys in Tower Records, crispy novels and films from the video shop, she felt guilty and wretched but couldn't explain why. P made a point of trying to rent comedies if he thought they would be funny. They usually weren't. But they would try to laugh anyway, usually at each other.

Even he grew concerned.

It was the sight of her in the same pyjama bottoms, the same hooded sweatshirt she had been wearing for weeks. It was the way she wore the frayed cuffs tugged over her hands so that the wispy bits trailed on the floor. It was the fact she saw no reason to leave the flat. He didn't have to say it. She could read it on his face. He thought it was a sign she was becoming unhinged. Eventually, at her aunt's persuasion, she made an appointment to go and talk to her GP. She left with a prescription for six-month's supply of Prozac, which had sat at the bottom of her bag until the writing wasn't legible and she threw it away. To be honest, she would rather smoke a joint, have a drink and defend her despair.

Then one day it came to her. She had been on her way to have lunch with P. "I want you to leave the flat *now*," he had telephoned to say.

It was what she needed to hear. She changed out of her pyjamas and into a skirt, put on a pair of shoes for the first time in weeks and went to catch the bus. Buses she could handle. Buses she liked for the way they freed the imagination. She was not going underground. Tube journeys were suffered with panicky silence but the meandering progress of buses made for gentle reverie. Glad of the company of strangers and their chatter as they headed into the fray, she pictured herself in a foreign city. A place where she would have to make decisions. A place so big it would steal her attention with no time to think about anything else.

A snap decision, the effect was immediate. It was the

physical relief that floods the body when something lost is suddenly found. Sitting on the number 19 as it jerked its way down Rosebery Avenue, she was conscious of having found a sense of direction. She went to find P. When she found him, she embraced him so hard she thought she would break.

"What happened?" He laughed.

But it was not until the following week that she revealed her plan because by this stage she knew she could not be dissuaded.

A cloud scudded into view and thoughts of P faded. Instead she was joined by her mother. They were fragmented images, like peering through glass misty with breath. Her hair like wet tarmac spun in a knot, her mother was playing the piano. Sometimes she played Gershwin, sometimes Bob Dylan, but late at night, and when alone, she played Mozart. It was music that used both sides of the brain. "It brings me peace," she used to say, a comment which, as a child, had made Utopia think of angels.

Her mother described New York as a Holy Grail. It was 1967. She was nineteen, had waist-length tawny hair and wore mini-dresses cut from Vogue patterns. *Bonnie and Clyde* had just opened at the local Rialto. "I knew then I had to get away," she told Utopia. She was half-way to America long before she crossed the Atlantic. She hatched a plan with her best friend Maureen, they saved up for a year then caught the ocean liner from Southampton to New York one blowy April morning.

They ran into storms and the five-day crossing lent itself to eight. It was her mother's first voyage. There had been a fancy-dress ball. Dressed as a cowslip in a champagne slip and a mask painted with the face of a cow, her mother won first prize. She had her photograph taken and danced all night with the officers, who took it in turn to be next. Both girls were invited to sit at the captain's table for the rest of the journey.

By the time they arrived, her mother had finished all one thousand and five pages of *Gone With The Wind*. She and Maureen spent two nights at an all-women hotel with a view from the roof, then set off again. It took a month of hitch-hiking and buses to reach San Francisco but they made it. They found a room on Haight Street, shared a bed, ate ethnic food and went to Freedom Rallies in Golden Gate Park, Be-Ins and Earth Days. They learned to distinguish the smell of pot from patchouli, and her mother was given a chocolate chip cookie, which might have been spiked. "We think it had marijuana in it," she said. "But I was never quite sure."

She fell out of love with a hippie called Ken, a jealous man who fed her the cookie, and they caught the Greyhound back to New York. Maureen returned to England, but Utopia's mother wasn't through. "Something held me back," she said. At the advice of a girl she met in the hotel, she pinned up a card on a noticeboard at Columbia University advertising her skills as a typist. Seventy words per minute. Fast. Utopia's father, a Fulbright scholar who was completing his Ph.D. in American literature, spotted her name and number and booked her for a dissertation that needed to be typed overnight. And that, in short, had been that.

Bright-eyed, on the verge of getting serious, her parents had fallen in love during a period of civil unrest and student activism. They hadn't been together long in New York when they decided to catch the bus to Washington DC and stand with anti-Vietnam war demonstrators outside the White House as they chanted, "Hey, hey, LBJ, how many kids did you kill today?" before the National Guard moved them on. This, their one act of protest, was a story Utopia had heard many times but she loved the image of her parents holding hands as they soaked up the spirit of the times. It was a day out that owed as much to romance as protest. Clear skies and flower power. It was their sense of feeling part of something she was fascinated by.

Not only had her parents met in New York but they stayed long enough to name their first-born Liberty, the second Utopia. They could as well have been New York One and New York Two. "Nixon babies," her father liked to joke. Utopia was the name of the campus café where the noticeboard lived. It was a venue where sit-ins were organised and pamphlets passed out. Four Black Panthers, foot-soldiers whose names weren't known, had been spotted by her mother at a corner table. The café had become part of family folklore and was guaranteed an airing during Christmas toasts.

"Here's to Utopia, where you could get eggs, coffee and change for a buck." Her father would raise his glass while the family groaned.

Her parents' era was one Utopia tried to recreate as she roamed the city in search of landmark names and addresses. There was the maternity hospital on East 93rd, their first apartment on West 95th, their apartment with rats behind the skirting-boards on 84th and Columbus, and the Montessori school she and her sister had attended on Central Park West. Mythologised through time, they should have been larger, Bohemian somehow. They looked too neat and conservative with their watered window-boxes and heavy dark doors. Even so, gazing up at these brownstones and granite façades triggered a glut of emotions.

Everywhere she went, she thought of her mother.

There was also the photo. It was a snapshot, black and white, which she carried with her in her wallet. It was of a headscarfed mother wearing a second hand fox fur as she pushed two little girls in a pram through Central Park's meringue-topped snow drifts. It was an event Utopia couldn't recall because she was too young at the time. It was her mother before she knew her, a person she could only guess at. A person the same age as she was now.

When her father landed a lecturer's job at University College, London, several years later, her mother had been loath to leave. It was a regret Utopia had grown up with alongside her sister, but they had packed up and left within the space of weeks. Veiled in gloom, it had been January, with sub-zero temperatures and mountains of ice lining the roads. There had been angry voices, closed doors and figures moving boxes, men she held personally responsible for the collapse of their world.

"I hate you," she had shouted at the packers, charging at their legs, clinging like a monkey.

Their mother had wrapped their possessions in sheets of newspaper and rags. Her silence had been interrupted only by instructions for them to say goodbye to the cat and the German lady next door, who gave them tangerines wrapped in napkins. The sisters' tantrums went unheard. It was not a happy time. In retrospect, neither parent had sought to leave while both clamoured for escape. Utopia had long felt that each somehow blamed the other for prompting their departure. All these years and they had never been back.

Perhaps she was dreaming.

She pulled back the sheet and exhaled the air from her lungs.

She was twenty-four and alone in New York. No one at home had been convinced she should come but she hadn't listened. She had shaken her head like a wilful child as they came up with alternative plans. Her father suggested she spend time with Granny in Kent. Pink-faced walks along the beach, and breakfast, lunch and dinner to set your watch by. P found her work reading scripts for a friend. Liberty wanted her to sign up for therapy with a woman in Swiss Cottage. Eight sessions for starters, to clear the cobwebs. Those had been her sister's words, "clear the cobwebs". Liberty's insensitivity never failed to appal her. "Do you really think I'd go to your therapist?" Utopia had reacted in disbelief.

No.

She had made up her mind and there was no turning back. She saw New York as the place where she would regain control of her life, something she had lost with her mother. If the city had been her mother's so could it be hers. Whatever that meant. There had been reluctant nods all round. In compliance with her father's wishes that she stay with friends, she had rung an ex-colleague of his who lived on Riverside Drive and asked for a bed. "I'll leave a key with the doorman," said the man's kind wife. "Take the elevator to the fifth floor and make yourself at home. There's iced tea, spreads and crackers in the fridge." It was then that Utopia had packed her bags and boarded the plane.

"This is the last call for Virgin flight zero five from gate thirty-two. Calling Virgin flight zero five . . ."

She sat up.

She poured the last drops of espresso into her cup and braced herself for a caffeinated heartbeat. Ba-boom, ba-boom. From the studio came Saul's voice interspersed with giggles. What were they doing? she wanted to know, but pride prevented her from opening the door. Her guess was that the assistant was a Marlboro-smoking, East Village girl with a tattoo with a story and a boyfriend with a Brooklyn studio. She also couldn't help but speculate that whoever she was would end up here in Saul's bed. She had only known Saul a couple of months but she wasn't naïve. She had fallen for the exact same show of flirtation herself and not that long ago.

She pictured the scene.

At the end of a hard day's welding, at around, say, nine or ten, Saul would suggest walking over to Chinatown for a bowl of prawn noodles and a couple of beers. Afterwards they would come back to the studio for the assistant to pick up her bag. Saul would produce the bottle of tequila and shots would be lined up on the table. Head back, one, two, three. Roar. Saul would ask a couple of questions about her work, look intensely at her as she flattered herself he was interested, and then midway through her monologue he would kiss her. Softly at first, self-consciously hesitant, but then again and this time like he meant it.

Well, it wouldn't take an expert to get from there to the bedroom, the fuck box, the oak-panelled cabin used once upon a time as the foreman's office. Saul was a charmer and more than equipped to cater to the many channels of New York life, gay, straight, male, female. Utopia's own affair with him had been initiated with the fervour of grand passion yet she still knew him occasionally to spend the night with Bonnie, his ex. "She's lonely. These things happen, you know", he once bothered to explain.

Lying in bed like the mistress hidden from view, Utopia felt irritated with herself for obliging his artistic promiscuity. If she was expendable, why she was here? She heard the rattling of the glass door as it opened, more muzzled voices, more tittering. The bedroom door flew open.

"Yee-ha," he whooped, as he threw himself on to the bed and on to her.

She suppressed a smile as she bore his weight.

"Where're we having brunch?"

"I'm meeting Marina."

"Is that an invitation?"

She said nothing.

Sensing her mood, he kissed her. It was an act of defiance and she laughed as he yanked the sheet up over their heads. His trail of kisses continued down her neck to her breasts and over her stomach. He reached her legs and parted them. The vigour of his tongue consumed her. Small strokes at first, finding his way, then faster and faster. She rose. Nervous inhalations. She liked the way he licked her, pushing inside. She succumbed. She dissolved and lay there as he crawled up her body to find her face. He smiled through half-closed eyes. "You like that, don't you?" he said.

They kissed. Their kissing deepened. Then he tore back the sheet and snatched at the clock. "Jesus Christ. Twenty minutes until Marcus swings by."

Utopia groaned and threw an arm across his chest. It was a typical show of Saul-style affection, unpredictable and rushed. She lay naked before the reedy-air conditioning with the sheet bunched between her legs. "You do know he wants to get into your knickers, don't you?"

"So?" he baited her, fluttering his lashes in the way that he did. "Who says I don't want to get into his?"

"No one. That's what I'm worried about. You're a tart."

"Whore," he corrected her. "Sculpture whore."

"Whoring sculptor, more like."

Then he was up, clambering off the bed to prop up the photograph of his mother, Regine. She had flashing eyes and a pelican smile. A former Miss Pennsylvania, she was a confection of big hair and creamy silk. She was divorced from Saul's father and emotionally married to her son. They spoke twice a day. She called him Saul-ee. The last time Utopia had met her, she had been smoking very long, very thin Cartier cigarettes and on her way to the fridge asked Utopia if she knew the current dollar-sterling rate of exchange. "Saul-ee, baby, there's nothing in here," she had complained, when she reached it. "You want me to order in some groceries?"

Utopia had remained diplomatically mute.

"It looks like there's a wind machine in that photo," she said now.

"There is. She had it done professionally. I'll go make coffee."

Crawling to the edge of the bed in search of clothes, Utopia found Max the cat sitting on them, purring like an engine. "Oi," she grunted, wrenching them out from beneath him. "Bloody cat."

Everything Max touched acquired a fine ginger fur. He never stopped moulting probably because he never left the building. He was an indoor cat. But, still, he had it better than most. According to Saul, most New York cat-owners only fed their cats biscuits so that their shit was easier to handle. This being New York, where nobody had time for anything much, it wasn't hard to believe.

She had lost her knickers to a pile of dirty laundry.

She found a pair that weren't hers, tried to ignore the fact that they weren't hers and tossed them back in. Then her stomach rumbled and she realised she was hungry. If Saul's priority was Marcus, hers was to see Marina, a friend of only two months although even she sometimes lost sight of this. It was to do with the way Marina had imparted her life story the moment they met. Initially taken aback,

Utopia had soon felt flattered to acquire so much from this fashionably dressed woman with her air of self-possession and gusty laugh. A woman forced to break off conversation and press cheek to cheek with a succession of faces streaming past.

Marina was an honorary New Yorker. Well, she had been in Manhattan ten years. She was one of those inheritance girls. She had blown hers by the age of twenty-five on what she called the three Cs, coke, Curtis the dealer boyfriend and Cheyne Walk, a house she had been forced to hand over to her father. She escaped England and never went back. "It's a little island full of little people," she said, a barb directed at her father, who drank and had gambled the family fortune away. Marina's face changed colour, it turned puce, like an alarm, when the subject came up, which wasn't often.

It was Marina's worldliness that impressed. A sense of entitlement preceded her like an outstretched arm, there to open doors. Alongside her Utopia felt that anything was possible, a conviction she couldn't often summon by herself. Admittedly, it hadn't taken long to meet Saul and find an apartment and arrange a life of sorts but there were still days when she felt so daunted by what she had taken on that paralysis set in. She was convinced she had nothing to say, that it was all a big mistake, and the city streets terrified her. These were the days when she would go and meet Marina for lunch at her favourite sushi spot just off Park.

"It's *all* going to happen," Marina would tell her, sucking her chopstick because smoking was banned.

And as Utopia watched the grains of rice grow slowly dark in the puddle of soy sauce, she would reflect that she preferred the company of older girls as she did older men because her appetite for more responded to their experience of more. She looked to Marina and their eleven-year difference as something of a role model and everyone needed role models.

She found her knickers underneath a pillow and stole a clean T-shirt from his drawer. It read *Triumph* on the front. She could hear him gargling. He did it for hours. First he disinfected his throat with minty green mouthwash then he flossed with cinnamon floss. Hygiene was an American obsession. She was thinking about the ads on TV for scented tampons and the products engineered to wipe out all known germs. Germs were the enemy. The way Saul leaped out of bed to shower straight afterwards she thought was funny, though also slightly strange. "You don't have to do that," she would tell him in vain.

She picked up her bag from the sofa and shouted goodbye. He didn't hear her. She slammed the glass door with a satisfying crash.

# Chapter Two

The midday sun was dazzling. Utopia jammed her Aviators over her eyes and stared at the steps leading down from the police building opposite in the event one of the celebrities said to live there might appear. What used to be a police headquarters was now a fortress of deluxe apartments. She considered the whole thing an urban myth. Saul had only once witnessed a shadow pass an upstairs window. Some movie star stretching, he reckoned. The night cleaner yawning, she reckoned.

Flanked by two stone lions with their tongues hanging out, the only occupant of the steps was the bored-looking doorman. He was wearing a coat with gold buttons and a cap pulled low. He was peering up and down the street in search of a vehicle heading his way, a stretch limo perhaps or a fashion shoot's location van. It wasn't unusual to find a convoy of them lined up along the street as models darted in and out shadowed by boys with reflector screens and girls with brushes. The building's blank stone provided a perfect backdrop for Summer Sizzle and the New Length. But not today. Not on a Sunday.

Little Italy was swarming with misshapen Long

Islanders, grizzled Sicilians and women carrying loaves of bread. Smells from the bakery drifted in the heat. Outside the Cuban diner on the corner old men were playing dominoes. Utopia skirted the crowds and thought about Saul. They were the same questions she was left with every time she said goodbye.

What was he thinking? What did she feel?

Going nowhere in particular, their passion lacked purpose. They never discussed it, and yet did it matter? Her affair with Saul was about sensation, she told herself. It was proof that she could have fun. Wasn't it enough when there had been so much analysing of everything at home?

She was fascinated by what made him tick. She was amused by his navel-gazing. The Polaroids pinned up around the studio of himself naked underneath a streetlight made her laugh out loud. They managed to combine the knowing gaze of a male pin-up with the fear of an animal about to become roadkill.

"Do you ever get tired of looking at yourself?" she once asked, just testing.

Saul had stared at her, murmured something she didn't catch, then had switched on the blow-torch and gone back to work.

Passing an empty phone booth, she remembered the coffin.

About a week ago at around two a.m. Saul's photographer friend Kurt had come banging on the door. Obviously expecting him, Saul disappeared on to the street carrying a wooden coffin. Up until then, it had been propped up in the corner of the studio like an off-duty sentry box. "Next project," he said, as Utopia followed to observe.

A roadworks operation was underway on the street and the workmen had left behind a bomb-crater-sized hole. The block was deserted, and Utopia watched as Saul descended with the coffin into the pit. Positioning it at the bottom, he ripped off his clothes and climbed in. Kurt was rigging up the lights.

"How shadowy do you want the pictures?"

"Just do it."

"You want I Polaroid first?"

"Just fucking do it."

Kurt shot two rolls of Saul encased in his makeshift coffin with the roadworks signs and barriers crowded behind. Utopia wasn't sure if the look was urban terrorist or vampire, although the plan as later told was to blow up the pictures life-size and hang them in the windows of the studio.

Despite her familiarity with Saul's art, the memory of him naked in the ground made her smile as she crossed Broadway and headed down Prince. Saul she understood somewhere along the line, it was Kurt she didn't. She didn't trust Kurt. It was a feeling that he was laughing at her expense or that he would rather have Saul to himself. He refused to call her by name, always the English chick, which would have been fine from anyone else but from Kurt it sounded rude. It made her feel as though she was just passing through, Saul's fuck for the night, one of many. Kurt was a one-time NYU student and had lived in the city for years. Utopia had been in New York three months. This, she sensed, lay at the root of his contempt.

He was German. Tall and handsome, he had a bleach-blond skinhead and bright blue eyes, their glitter of cruelty like a shark's. He also had a fetish about death. She didn't know how else to describe someone who bungee-jumped off the Grand Canyon, collected Vietnam war memorabilia and had only one knee-cap – the other had been lost to an upstate highway when his bike collided with a truck. Saul expressed nothing but adulation for his neighbour. "Sure he's crazy. Man, those scars are out of sight," he had said more than once.

But it wasn't just Kurt's lack of interest in her that made her uneasy. It was the sight of Saul beady-eyed with silvery skin when he got in from a night upstairs that did it. Saturday nights Kurt like to stay in for a smoke. Heroin, as it turned out.

"Did no one ever tell you it's the purest drug you can take?" Saul would say, as he cranked up the music.

But what could she say?

It was impossible to disrupt their weekend rituals. "Just come with me," Saul would urge. She didn't want him to deny what she knew he was doing. She didn't need him to tell her things he thought she wanted to hear. The mysteries of Saul's universe were part of the attraction: the beeper in his pocket summoning him away, the foreign voices on his ansaphone, the anonymous faces that appeared round the studio door, the way his eyes glazed over when she probed too deep. She felt special because she was there when the others called and that was enough.

And she couldn't feign innocence.

It was a Saturday night about a month ago now. They had been to a bar down on Houston to shoot some pool. A band was playing and they hadn't stayed long. Kurt's girl-friend was out of town so it was just the three of them. The night air was hot like swimming through tar. They arrived back at Grand Street and decided to go upstairs to Kurt's. Saul was out of ice and out of liquor. Prostrate on Kurt's sofa, the solitary fan making patterns in her hair, Utopia watched Kurt gather together his gear. She had guessed as much although nothing was said.

Saul was fixing drinks. He was in the kitchen smashing the bag of solidifed ice-cubes with a baseball bat. She could hear the sound of ice chips sent skating across the floor. He appeared with glasses of vodka crescented with limes. Sweat dripped from his brow and bubbled down his neck. Kurt was seated at the coffee table and had produced a brown lump which he was burning on a piece of foil. He had taken off his T-shirt to reveal a square of chest hair like a stick-on patch. Utopia watched as he inhaled the smoke through a silver tube, filling his mouth, his lungs. He exhaled slowly. Saul kneeled down beside him.

"You want some?" he said.

She shook her head.

"You sure?"

She looked at him then at Kurt. She had tried most things before but never this. Kurt handed Saul the tube then burnt the foil as Saul followed the smoke. She watched him exhale then smile, the tightness around his eyes relax. Moving off the sofa, she went to join them. "Go on then."

Saul passed her the tube. "Hold it in," he told her, as he placed the lighter beneath the brown.

She sucked as the foil crinkled. It had an acrid taste and a hot flush filled her to the top of her head. She let go, lit from within by a syrupy warmth. Everything went white and she had to lie down. She lay on the sofa, floating, with Saul beside her stroking her hair and she remembered thinking, I'm slipping away. Later beside the lavatory bowl, the thought came again but it was hard to care.

"Just relax," Saul was whispering.

They were there all night, rolling joints and listening to

music that had no words. In the brightness of morning they floated downstairs and went to bed.

It was some time before she told Marina what had happened, because she had a presentiment of what she would say. Marina had exploded. "That's right. Just fuck it all up. Jesus Christ. I mean, how old are you?" Her brother had been a junkie. She had lived with the fear of his death for years, though he had since managed to quit. Realising that Marina was right and that it wasn't somewhere she wanted to go, Utopia now refused to accompany Saul on his trips upstairs. For once, once was enough.

"You're late," Marina called out.

"I know."

Utopia fielded a path past backs and bags.

The café, a SoHo mecca, was crammed with Sunday brunchers. Stylists were studying the papers' fashion pages. Couples were sharing the arts sections while solitary coffee drinkers sat reading Russian novels. Marina, the entertainment editor of one of New York's glossy fashion magazines, was poring over *Vogue*. Despite it being Sunday with the temperature scaling ninety-five degrees, she was sporting full make-up, spike-heeled sandals, white fish-net tights and a towelling, baby pink Chanel skirt suit.

"Glad to see you've dressed down for breakfast," said Utopia, scruffy in flip-flops and cut-off shorts. She had managed to drag a comb through her hair, though not brush her teeth. The lingering taste of his breath, the faint smell of his bed pleased her. It was that Saturday-night-Sunday-morning shroud. The sense that it wasn't quite over.

"You know me, darling. My wardrobe doesn't stretch to a pair of jeans," said Marina, pushing her Jackie-O's up from her face like a celebrity widow.

Utopia had met Marina over the phone. There had been no letter of introduction or referral via mutual friends. She had found Marina's name printed on her magazine mast-head and rung to introduce herself. What she really wanted to do was find out if she could perhaps come up and meet her. But she had managed only half a sentence when Marina had interrupted her with what can only be described as a scream. "What a sensational name," she had shrieked. "Yes, darling, we *must* meet. And I know – let's make it tonight."

Utopia couldn't believe her luck. That very same night they had rendezvoused at the top of the Empire State Building. It had been a book-launch party. Utopia was worried she was going to miss her, but that would not have been possible. In a fuchsia dress, a feather choker and her Vanilla Biscuits on her feet – this was her little play on the shoe designer's name – Marina was unmissable. She had green eyes as translucent as a cat's and an expression that fell somewhere between a sneer and a smile. You could never quite tell what she was thinking but you were dying to find out. Utopia was impressed by her ample mouth, proud nose and high, hollow cheeks. Her mother was Catalonian, she later discovered.

"Utopia." Marina savoured her name, rolling it around with her tongue. "With a name like yours you'll have the city at your feet in seconds. And, darling, I'm signing up as your manager so that I get my cut for discovering you."

They drank vodka gimlets and watched the city lights speckle the darkness. Their friendship had been an instant hit. The way Marina embraced her was redolent of the city at large, she felt. And Marina seemed to enjoy her role as confidante to her new friend with the promotable name. She was generous in her affections and thrived on making new acquaintances. "New blood, new blood," she would chant, as she entered a room. "Now, come on, let's be quick and find someone new to talk to before we all die of boredom."

Utopia cherished the asides Marina would hiss from the corner of her mouth wherever they went. "Lausanne is beauty director because she slept with the publisher," she would say. Meanwhile her appetite for starriness was insatiable. She was a mistress of hyperbole, adored LA and was on home-phone-number terms with all the big publicists. Her celebrity stories were incisive yet worked entirely to protect Hollywood's A list. Celebrities knew what they were getting with Marina and it made them feel good. She knew how to give enough spin to be sexy without taking an angle or pulling the rug from beneath and disclosing what in fact she knew. Marina was a pro.

She was also a consummate actress. She had a slot on Fox TV as a movie news pundit. Perched on top of her desk, legs tightly crossed in a mid-thigh-length skirt, she delivered sycophancy disguised as sensationalism with a twist of camp. "Thanks for listening and remember where you heard it first. From me, Marina Lansdowne, entertainment critic, Fox TV," she would say, with a lick of her lips. Then she would smile and shake her head, though not a strand of hair moved.

"Can I get you a coffee?" asked the waitress, fastening her hair with a chop stick before pouring.

Utopia stared at the menu's italicised French. "Have you ordered?"

"The works. An omelette with lox and sour cream, home fries and a toasted sesame bagel. I need it. I drank enough last night to forget how I got home."

"Oh dear," said Utopia, as she reread the list of pancake flavours. She decided on blueberry. "Where were you?"

"Bar in the meat-packing district. You don't want to know. You?"

"Saul's."

"Right. Well, I'm back to LA on Wednesday to interview that English actress named Star of Tomorrow. More about her nauseatingly perfect marriage, pseudo-analytical interpretation of her film role and how she's just set up her own production company. The same old crap."

Utopia sipped her coffee. "Doesn't sound like you need to interview her at all."

"That's exactly it. I don't."

"But you love it really. You're just as fabulous as she is."

"Oh, darling, please. If I was earning what she's earning then yes. A few happy millions and I could be just as fabulous."

Marina loved talking money. How much she earned, how much her boss earned, how much the editors of New York's other competitive glossies earned and, more importantly, how much she would cost if she were ever to switch jobs. It was like a mantra, proof of her worth.

"So, any news of anything?"

Utopia shook her head. She didn't want to think about it but it was too late now.

With two years on a magazine in London behind her, she had arrived in New York hoping to find work. She was beginning to lose faith. She had spent her first month on the telephone. Cold-calling shrill-voiced girls, girls who sounded as though they had secrets she could only dream of, to be put through to editors she had never heard of was galling. There were times when she wanted to give up and forget the whole plan. However, since being befriended by Marina whose Martini cures put it all into perspective, it had grown easier. Besides – what could they do other than hang up on her, which occasionally they did.

And early on her persistence seemed to pay off. Her first

round of calls had led to a host of appointments and up she
would troop to the editors' vanilla ice-cream offices to
explain why she was here. She found herself looking
forward to these trips for their glimpses of magazine life.
The miles of white smiles, hundreds of manicured nails and
immaculate streaks were friendly. The editors she met loved
her name. "It's just so kooky," they chimed. They offered
her coffees and sodas and tips on where to go bowling on
Saturday nights or buy half-price cashmere.

Now nothing.

Now every call went unreturned.

Though it wasn't all gloomy. She had landed a job for a
month. On Saul's suggestion, she went one day to the
Broadway offices of the magazine *Note*. She went to say hi
but left with a month's work sub-editing while someone was
out. It was run by a roomful of baggy-jeaned boys, and
women with rainbow-coloured hair, and was a chronicle of
downtown life. It ran stories about musicians, drag queens,
futurists and famous children. It had been fun while it
lasted. With an office that resembled a nightclub – music
pumping and a stream of skateboarders and vamps
dropping off flyers and arranging guest lists – *Note*
invested most of its energy in sponsoring parties. There
were aftershow parties for up-and-coming bands, indie
movie premières, special-issue celebrations and legalise-pot
events.

But in the end, the world of club listings and porn stars
had lost its appeal. Maybe she was growing up. But with
Marina's example to follow, she aspired to more. She had set
her sights on going uptown to Madison Avenue. If only
Marina could offer her a job, she would dream in bed alone
at night. But life was never that simple. According to
Marina, her magazine was now so tight that she was having

to do all her own travel arrangements and fill in her own expense forms.

Heaven forbid.

"I know I sound like a scratched record but why not do a couple of shifts at Trudi's if you're feeling the pinch?" said Marina, adjusting her fringe which parted like plumage between her fingers. "Everyone waitresses in the city."

Trudi was a friend of Marina's who owned a teashop, Home Comforts, in the East Village. It was a haven of ex-pat life. A bottle of HP sauce sat on every table. There was a lingering smell of gravy and grease stains on the curtains. It was an establishment Utopia avoided as best she could. The only time she had visited was as a guest of Marina. A bulldog had growled beneath their table while a game of satellite football had blared from a ceiling TV.

"I'll think about it," she said. "How's the D-man?"

D for disinterested. Degenerate. Dorian. It was Marina's name for the man in her life. The bane of her life. Marina shook her head. "Why aren't I the type of woman men leave their wives for?"

"I thought you were."

"One rich divorcé's all I need. Just one. We had drinks on Friday and Dorian told me I should be dating other men. Can you believe that? I told him to go fuck himself. As if I need him to tell me to date. He's screwing his neighbour. You should see her. Some Swedish model with legs up to her ears. He really is so fucking predictable. They even met in the elevator. Going up? Going down. Jesus Christ."

Utopia watched Marina cut into her omelette. A river of yolk cascaded over her fries and marooned her bagel. "Why do you still see him?"

Marina licked a smear of egg from her top lip. "Because he's the only man who can make me laugh when he reads aloud from the telephone directory. Didn't your mother ever tell you that secret?"

Utopia shook her head as Marina began spreading butter on her bagel so vigorously that her bangles shook.

"And this is New York, darling. You're not in London now with all those overgrown public-school boys running around."

Utopia wondered if it mightn't be preferable to have a few more of them knocking about but said nothing. The New York gender ratio of five women to every man was too boring to discuss right now. She picked up the *Times* and turned to the style page. "Have you seen Saul?"

Marina took the paper. "Does he have to go out looking like the Tin Man?"

Utopia laughed, but only for a moment. Marina pursed her lips and it was her mother sitting across the table from her. It was the face her mother pulled whenever Utopia had news to tell. Things she didn't want to hear.

Marina wasn't a huge fan of Saul. She knew of others who had been in his bed. She disapproved of his drugs. "But don't let me spoil your fun," she would say, and Utopia didn't. It was the only advice from Marina she made a point of ignoring in the same way that she had shut her ears to her mother's instructions.

She watched her friend light a cigarette and exhale a lungful of smoke. She smoked like a movie star, with grace and without guilt. Utopia had put out her last cigarette at Heathrow before boarding the plane. She had been sitting in the departure lounge with P. Mute with doubts, it was all she could do to watch tobacco burn. They had sat couched in smoke with only the sound of P's tapping foot and her occasional cough. Sick with nicotine, she had decided that a fresh start meant fresh lungs and so far she had been good to her word. Giving up one would mean failing the other. She inhaled Marina's second-hand smoke in remembrance of that first cigarette of the day.

God, it smelt good.

The café door swung open.

Marina smiled at whoever was blown in. It was Miles. His eyes travelled the room, straining to find a face he knew. He spotted Marina and staggered over, running a hand through cornstalk locks. "Hey, you," he said, pulling up a chair.

Utopia drank in his features. Miles had a tousled look and a sleepy air. He wore mirrored sunglasses, which he never took off. He looked like a boy who knew how to have a good time.

"Up long?" said Marina.

"Been at an audition. The new Andy Warhol movie they're shooting."

"You're not Andy Warhol?"

He smiled. "A singer."

"So you play yourself."

"Clever, huh?"

They all laughed.

Miles fronted a band called Mouthwash. It was a glam-rock band. His performance involved a lot of posturing, frenzied screams and dramatic pauses as he contorted his frame around the mike. Marina had taken Utopia to see his last show.

"He's part of the factory scene. He gets to sleep with Edie Sedgwick."

"Lucky you."

"Yeah. I haven't seen you around for a while, though," he said to neither in particular.

Bunched shoulder to shoulder, Utopia found it difficult

to believe she had only been here three months. There was something about the city's high-speed velocity and its village-like density that meant crossing paths with the same people again and again. From the you-must-meet-so-and-so person at every gathering to chance meetings on the street, introductions through Marina had come thick and fast. There was always a card or someone's number in the pocket the next day. Few of them she saw again but the ritual pleased her. It provided a feeling of belonging. She had come to New York for the company, not to be alone.

"Christ. Is that the time?" said Marina, uncurling her mobile phone.

Utopia leant forward as Marina squeezed past and headed for the ladies'.

Miles was spooning an iced latte and tongueing the froth. He was scanning the room with radar-like precision. He would bolt as soon as the target was cleared. "What have you been up to?" he now asked, having completed his initial circumference.

Utopia looked at him, or rather at herself and everyone else in the room, in the reflection of his glasses. She felt reluctant about giving too much away. There was something about Miles' absence of doubt that magnified her own into terrible close-up. "I left *Note* last week. I'm trying to find another job."

"Let me know when you can do a story on the band. Did I tell you we're going to be in Italian *Vogue* in September."

He hadn't but she wasn't surprised.

"I wore a pair of paper pants."

Utopia could imagine androgynous Miles pouting for the camera with his hips thrust forward, staring eyes and hair falling over one side of his face. Sex on Legs, Marina called him. "I'll look out for it," she promised.

Marina returned from the ladies'. It was sandwiched between two noticeboards collaged with adverts for downtown life. Utopia would always study them just in case.

*Sign up now for transcendental Tai Chi.*

*Drummer wanted for all-boy, cover band. Must be fan of Tammy Wynette and Karen Carpenter.*

*Bi S.W.F seeks room in West Village apartment — non-smoker, cat-lover, Spanish speaker, lactose immune.*

*Looking for the answer? Guru Sai Baba Junior meets with disciples every Tuesday night 8 p.m. at St Mark's Hall, St Mark's Place, for yogic inspiration. $5 per session. Your choice of incense.*

"I've just been reminded there's a perfume launch party at seven."

"Oh."

"Everyone's going to be there. It's at the Statue of Liberty."

Miles had joined a table tucked away at the back of the room. Three blondes in snug white T-shirts had enticed him over. He was playing air guitar and cultivating his rock 'n' roll persona. Utopia gestured for Marina to take a look.

"Yes, I saw Mr Sex is doing the rounds."

"Well, we are just brunettes."

Strictly speaking Utopia was a mouse. Her mother, too, had been a mouse before going grey but Liberty was blonde. That was the point. Ever since she could remember, Liberty had used her colour as proof of her virtue. Sunshine girls were never blamed. The battle against blondes, a treacherous breed, had been necessary for survival from an early age.

"Why don't you come with me?" said Marina. "I was meant to be taking Dorian but I don't see why I should."

"Really?" asked Utopia, elated. A party on a Sunday night would provide a buffer zone before the horror of Monday.

"Won't he be disappointed?"

"D is for disappointment, darling," Marina fired back. "It also stands for Dumped. Let's get the check. You need to get out more."

# Chapter Three

As the boat pulled out of South Sea ferry port and into the Hudson river, the city's skyline was suspended beneath a bleeding sky. Stationed by the railing, Utopia focused on the helicopters buzzing between skyscrapers like greedy flies. It was difficult to relate what she saw to what she knew.

Was she really living in the city she could see before her?

She gripped the pole. Beside her, Marina was a model of composure in a red dress that plunged and rose at all the right places and a pair of three-inch Vanilla Biscuits. "You look fantastic," Utopia told her again.

It was only a party but she was nervous.

"So do you, darling."

Flattery was the key to Marina's job but it managed to instill confidence in Utopia over her own choice of dress. It was white, knee-length with a leaf motif. She had picked it up at some sample sale or other, and though it was a favourite, she had begun to feel that it wasn't nearly glamorous enough and that she was earmarked an outsider.

It was getting dark.

Before long you will be a shadow, she told herself. Relax. Around them swarms of immaculate women gossiped and twittered, strutted and preened. The ferry was one of a fleet transporting magazine and fashion glitterati out to what Marina assured her was the party of the week.

It was the launch of the perfume Liberté.

The boat changed tack.

Suddenly before them rose the Statue of Liberty. She was lit up in milky dazzle. Monster spotlights strobed the sky. The island was lined with rows of flares. Without warning, a fizz of sherbet pink exploded and littered the night with shooting stars.

The boat lurched.

It parked alongside a jetty and the gaggle of women teetered down the gangplank. More fireworks laced the sky. Greetings flew as fast as air kisses. *Quelle spectacle. Bellisimo.*

There was no doubt about it, this was a full-scale fashion orgy.

Marina led the way as the two of them headed towards the crowd. The flares were ill-equipped to light the island, and it was virtually impossible to identify people in the darkness. "I have to find my boss and my photographer," she said. Her magazine would be running pictures of the celebrities on the people page. It was essential Roberto the photographer didn't miss anyone. Under existing conditions this was not an easy task.

"Champagne?"

A waiter supporting a tray of champagne flutes appeared from nowhere. "Just what the doctor ordered." Marina took a glass in each hand. "Come on, darling, I've got to find Roberto. I hope he's not missing all the action."

A group of paparazzi had gathered by the jetty, their flashes creating a firestorm of light with the arrival of each famous face. "Over here, over here," they called out to a girl, who tripped down the gangplank like a creature released from captivity. She smiled, waved and kept on walking.

"I'll kill Roberto if he's missed her."

"Marina," a male voice called out.

At last here was Roberto. He was a handsome Eurocrat, Italian or French, and had a camera slung around his neck.

"Darling," she greeted him, planting a lipstick kiss on his stubble and wiping it off.

"Have you got everyone?"

Then from out of the gloom stepped a French actress so recognisable that Utopia couldn't remember her name. She was wearing a floor-length dress and her head was ringed in a halo of light. She was the face of Liberté and it wasn't hard to see why.

"Quickly," said Marina, as she pushed Roberto from behind.

He called her name, she turned and he caught her in his flash. It was a look not of surprise but of professional poise. Lips slightly open, chin subtly raised and eyes that gave nothing away. Marina moved in. "Your dress is beautiful. Who's it by?"

"Givenchy," she whispered.

The actress stage-managed the entire exchange without yielding eye-contact, observed Utopia. The end of conversation was signalled with a regal bow of her head and off she floated into the night. Marina returned to Utopia. "Darling, I've got to get captions."

"Yes. Of course."

"Let's meet back here later," she said, and with that she was gone and Utopia was alone.

She felt suddenly self-conscious and giddy with champagne. She wanted to blend and appear blended. Something to eat might help, she decided. Nearby a group of women stood holding glasses and a few were fingering expensively shaved vegetables. Utopia headed towards them. "Do you know where I can find something to eat?" she asked a statuesque brunette with a diamond cross shining at her neck.

The woman paused then curled her lip as though Utopia had asked if she had any spare change.

No one said a word.

Utopia took a second or two to realise that she had been snubbed. She opened her mouth and was on the verge of repeating herself before she reconsidered. She marched off quickly in the direction of the water.

What had she done wrong?

She began following a row of flares as she fought off a desire to run and hide since there was nowhere to run to. She stopped to draw breath. Manhattan was now a mass of twinkling lights. The helicopters had mutated into fireflies with flashing tails. She closed her eyes. The breeze coming in off the river gathered swell and she imagined that she was standing in front of a garden sprinkler as its arc of spray slowly doused her.

She opened her eyes.

What was she doing, loitering at the edge of the party like this, she forced herself to consider. There were editors here whom she had met before and could talk to again. Wishing that she could operate more like Marina, she dragged herself away from the water.

She headed for the party and drummed up a second wind.

She entered the crowd and looked for a familiar face. They were an indistinguishable bunch. A short woman with a handbag wandered past. Utopia did a doubletake. Was it? Yes, it was. It was Simeon, the associate editor of the new celebrity lifestyle magazine she had been to see. With swollen lips – "I've just had them done and they're kind of sore so you'll have to excuse the ice cube," she had said. She had gone on to spend half an hour explaining how the magazine would do an "At home in Montana" story. How the story should convey the pioneering spirit of the actress captured in her rural homestead and choice of bed-linens, kitchen ware and local art.

Utopia had been taken by this image of herself curled up on a Navajo print sofa with the movie star in question as they sipped organic juices blended earlier in the open-plan kitchen. She could hear their discussion as they explored the meaning of motherhood and the beauty of those wide open plains, a place where children could roam free, away from the pressures of Hollywood and the perils of stardom.

She followed behind. She was almost sure.

"Simeon?"

The woman spun round. She stared.

"Utopia."

"You what?"

"Utopia Holmes. I came to see you."

"Aha, I remember now. From London. How's it going?"

Utopia nodded as she struggled with what to say. There was to be no admitting her failings while clearly the continued search for a job had to be got across.

"It's good."

"D'you try calling Marie in beauty?"

Who was Marie in beauty?

"Utopia. Where've you been? I've been looking for you." It was Marina, wide-eyed, perspiration highlighting her features. "Come and meet Felix. He's a sweetheart and he knows everyone."

Mouthing goodbye, Utopia found herself dragged off by Marina. Chattering faces whisked past her, slivers of cheekbone and waves of hair. She was flying. There was the tinkle of jewellery against glass and pockets of laughter. There was an aura about the gathering she felt must surely rub off. Expensive and all-knowing, these women had means and ways she was curious about.

They had stopped.

"Utopia. Felix."

Utopia was conscious of her feet touching the ground. In front of her was a man with very short hair, his head like a baby bird's. The lenses of his glasses glinted in the light thrown off by the flares. He had a boyish face and dancing eyes. He smiled. "Hi."

Marina had disappeared.

"English?"

"Yes. From London."

She realised exactly who he was. Not only was he a friend of Marina's but Saul knew him too. He was a jewellery maker who collaborated with other designers. He had profiles written about him in magazines. Marina had shown her a story somewhere. She remembered a portrait of him with his arms round an enormous white husky dog with a black nose.

He tugged at his cuffs, which she noticed were decorated with oval links. He had a stillness about him as though he were oblivious to the hordes.

"And this is Jean Weiner."

Utopia blinked. She hadn't noticed anyone beside him but he had a companion. Utopia didn't know how she could have missed her. The woman was taller than her and was dressed in a lime-green coat. She had a beakish nose and a gash of lipstick the colour of roses.

"Utopia Holmes," she introduced herself.

"Press or fashion?" asked the woman, her voice exploded from somewhere deep within.

"Press. I work on magazines."

"Which ones?"

"Well, I was an . . . er . . . arts editor in London. *Music Today*."

"Never heard of it. Arts editor, though, huh?"

"Yes," she lied.

She had actually been hired as slave girl for a job tied up with running around for a bloke called Keith. Her boss. It was her job to organise his friend's stag nights in Essex hotels, blag VIP passes for Wembley Stadium shows, keep his wife sweet while Keith told lies, and book tables for lunches that fed into dinners. But it wasn't long before she had also found herself compiling pop reviews, doing girly interviews with whichever girly singer had charted that week, and editing the "High Notes" page – a guide to the month's music news. At all of this she had proven herself and yet ultimately had been forced to leave.

It was Keith's endorsement of a catalogue of disasters that prompted her departure only months before the investors pulled the plug. Hiring Keith's brother Gary as managing editor had been the final straw. Deadlines were overlooked, accounts misspent and the magazine was hitting the news-stands weeks overdue. A final attempt at salvaging diminishing sales had been the introduction of a fashion page. But designers had refused to lend clothes and the only models available to them were old dogs, as Keith put it.

"Jean is features director of *HQ*," said Felix.

Utopia took a mental gulp.

*HQ* was the only magazine said to rival *Vogue*. It was the only other magazine Marina would ever work for. She trawled her mind for a suitable one-liner. She felt her mouth fall open. "Gosh."

"Do you know it?" asked Jean.

"Oh, yes."

"Have you worked in New York?"

'I just spent a month at *Note*.'

"*Note* is a New York institution," assisted Felix.

Utopia held her breath.

"Right," continued Jean, still examining Utopia with that quizzical frown.

Utopia shifted her weight to the other foot. She felt under scrutiny. She had a hunch they were headed somewhere although she had no clue where.

"I've got something next week that might be good."

Utopia exhaled.

"Meg's out and Winola was going to fill in but if you've done the arts desk and you're from London . . ."

"Meg?"

"My assistant. She's out next week. I don't know if you're available but if you are?"

The sound of a boat's engine drifted across the water.

"And I thought we were going to be here all night," said Felix.

But Utopia couldn't believe what was being said. Was Jean serious? She had never been so available in all her life. "Oh yes. Very available."

"I'll need you tomorrow. You know where we are, right? 1188 Broadway. Twenty-ninth floor. Are you interested? If you are . . ."

"Tomorrow? Yes. Absolutely."

"Great. OK. So tomorrow, then. Nine o'clock." she offered a slightly skewed smile and her hand.

Utopia shook it vigorously. "Thank you."

"And you, Felix, lunch. And I don't mean in the next millennium."

Staring at the blank space left by Jean, Utopia stood

stricken with disbelief. She looked round for Felix but he was being chastised by a baby-voiced woman for never calling. Marina was nowhere to be seen. But she had done it. She knew she had. She had been summoned to the twenty-ninth floor of magazine heaven.

"Well done," Felix congratulated her, as he took her elbow and they headed towards the ferry.

Other stragglers and guests joined them on the crunchy gravel path as it wound its way to the jetty. Marina caught up with them. She was breathless. "You OK, darlings?"

"You'll never guess what . . ."

But Marina wasn't listening. She was peering over her shoulder. "Where's Roberto? I hope you haven't been bored. We've got to drop the film off at the magazine then drinks at Roxanne's. It's a penthouse on fifty-seventh. *Playboy* used it for shoots in the seventies. The view is to die for. You are coming aren't you, Utopia?"

"She's coming," said Felix. "She's ours now."

# Chapter Four

Utopia inspected her face in the bathroom mirror. It was the smallness of her features, nothing dramatic, which left her feeling cheated every time she looked. She had peeping, muddy green eyes, a small nose and a meagre mouth. It was the type of face pronounced plain one minute and a classic English beauty the next. Both descriptions bothered her as being conventional.

What were her distinguishing features?

"Everything about you," P would always say. But then he would. That was his job.

Post-adolescence, the prospect of conformity still frightened her although she fought it less. She no longer dyed her hair, nor had she maintained the piercings. There had been three in each ear and a nose stud. But subliminally that desire to be different, to be louder, taller, faster, still ticked. Her grandmother always said she should have been an actress. Not true.

Beneath the urge to show off was a shyness. It was Liberty who was the tougher of the two. Her own bluff was all bluff. Her fearlessness was born of fear and her self-confidence was rooted in doubt. She was a Virgoan. It was dissatisfaction that spurred her.

Come on, you can do better, said the little voice.

At the age of twenty-four, she had been forced to dig a bit and these truths had become apparent. Liberty, in contrast, was a plodding Taurean. Not only was she sure of her path but she came armed with a dictionary of therapy-speak. She had discovered therapy at university under pressure of finals and maintained it as a weekly date. She created dramas like riddles so as then to solve them where Utopia avoided them with a survivor's instinct.

There was no need further to complicate life.

She applied mascara to her invisible lashes.

Her eyes were still hidden behind the puffiness of another muggy night. Her mother's theory was that a woman's face didn't fall into place until midday which meant her eyes had four hours to go. Her attempt at grooming was a disaster. The move uptown to a world of discrete power dressing and caramel lips demanded a degree of perfection which was, frankly, impossible to achieve. Black linen trousers and a sleeveless white shirt would have to do, she concluded, dissatisfied.

Her stomach gurgled.

She was awash with coffee and nerves. It was the uncertainty of what lay ahead that frightened her. It was still impossible to believe that last night's party and her meeting with Jean had taken place. She had woken this morning, long before the hands on her clock triggered the alarm, and tried to recall last night's conversation with Felix.

They had been standing on Roxanne's balcony overlooking Central Park pretending to feel refreshed. He was from small-town Massachusetts, he told her. He had escaped to New York aged eighteen to study at Parsons School of Design and never went back. Nantucket Island was great for vacations though, he said. He had a clapboard house with a porch on the dunes. Utopia saw it as the house in *Annie Hall* where the lobsters escape across the kitchen floor and Diane Keaton screams. She liked the idea of spending summer on a porch.

"I hang my double hammock, play Ry Cooder and make mint juleps. There's nowhere beats it," he said.

Utopia paused. "Is Jean a good friend?" she asked.

It was the question that had been bugging her all night.

"I see her at parties. She's a personality. She's always got a million ideas about wanting to change stuff."

"I see," said Utopia, not convinced that she did. Things like this didn't happen in London, not to her anyway.

"This is New York, " he added, and she laughed.

"I'd noticed."

To say that she had been discovered at a Statue of Liberty party was the type of thing written up in columns, boast disguised as confession. It confirmed New York's best loved cliché, the one about discovery lurking just around the corner.

She couldn't believe it was real, that was all.

The heat was mounting. She switched on the TV. The Channel One news barometer read ninety-five degrees. How she was going to prevent a waterfall of perspiration from sludging her face before she hit midtown, she didn't know. She had been to more than one appointment somewhere up near 42nd Street and been forced to sponge her face in the ladies' before waiting in reception.

She had never been the type to glow. At school she had been envious of the girls who stayed dry while others like herself dripped during games. There was a connection between levels of secretion and the secrets of womanhood, she felt. Sweat was unseemly. Her mother, a model of femininity, had never perspired. Not even after tennis on a warm July day. It was her father whose hair sat matted to his scalp, his T-shirt stained with a map of Britain across his back. Her hopes of outgrowing this phase had been disappointed. She continued to sweat and to wonder why.

She applied deodorant.

She began the habitual search for her keys across the sideboard, behind the bread bin, in front of the window, on top of the fridge. What she found was a postcard of a red telephone box. Scooping it up, she slammed shut the apartment door, her keys traced to her bag, and raced down the stairs, out of the building and down Mott. She very nearly tripped over a Chinese boy on a tricycle as she skimmed the scrawl.

> *Dear U,*                            *1 August*
> *I've been catching bits of the Channel 4 series Manhattan After Dark and thinking of you. I hope it's not too difficult and you're being careful. The flat is so empty without you. Everyone's asking after you. Smoke a fat one for me. Love and luck, P*

Robbed of her momentum, Utopia stood on the corner of Kenmare and Lafayette and bit down on her lip.

Four years together, living together, then the decision to escape to New York and now this. A trickle of postcards. Reminders of what had been abandoned in London, they reaffirmed her decision and yet saddened her. They hadn't spoken in over three weeks. He had stopped leaving messages. She no longer returned them. When she first arrived, he was a constant presence. She had sought his advice about everything she did. They would speak every day, then at weekends, now not at all. There was a time when she would leave messages back from some bar drunk on emotion and bottles of beer. She would whisper amorous confessions.

There was talk of missing him. P, when are you coming to see me?

Not any more. Things had changed. Distance had covered her tracks.

She hadn't opened her laptop in weeks. When she was at *Music Today* and he was at home writing scripts they would send each other e-mails, sometimes five times a day. Things they wanted to do together, do to each other, words and phrases like silly in-jokes. When she decided to leave for New York, she had agreed to log on and type a few words every day. Just the temperature, even, they had joked. But somehow the closeness of dialogue felt wrong.

She didn't want to share it all with him.

So instead, by tacit agreement, they wrote long-hand, cards and letters. Envelopes dropped in the mailbox, as opposed to his silent voice on her computer screen awaiting a response, gave her space. But she had even failed at this and letters started were never finished.

There were photographs of P slotted into her bedroom mirror. P at his desk, P in black rubber with his arm around a surfboard, P asleep. But his serious eyes behind tortoise-shell frames, the snatched grin, had become hidden beneath the New York clutter that framed her reflection. The *Note* party invitations, flyers, magazine clips, postcards, telephone messages, gym timetables, air-mile information, take-out menus, film programmes.

P's correspondence left her with guilt as she lay in bed with Saul harbouring secrets and lies. She was being so selfish. So bloody-minded.

Was any of it fair?

It was her need for distance, she tried to remember. To feel anything at all she had to be apart from him, her family, London's wet pavements. Thinking of P led her straight back to those final months of her mother's illness. It was winter nights black with fear, midnight walks on Hampstead Heath as her sister assumed bedside vigil and P forced her to take a break, to exercise her lungs, to talk. It was the journey back to the hospital across the Thames, the nurses with their cautious words. It was the smell of illness like damp, her father's face and her aunt cursing in the kitchen as she made more soup. It was her mother's parchment skin and her search to understand what it meant to lose your mother so soon.

P was the pain she fought to forget so she had left him in order to move on.

She stumbled off the kerb.

She shoved P's postcard into her bag and wiped her eyes. It would be all right, she calmed herself. She would write and tell him that everything was all right. She was headed for the Spring Street subway. She glanced at her watch. She had less than twenty minutes to get to 53rd street. She was going to be late. It was not an auspicious start to the week.

"You made it. You look hot," said Jean as Utopia poked her head round her door.

She had been befriended by a fashion assistant in the lift. The girl had ushered her in through the maze of corridors and desks while Utopia had struggled to memorise the sequence. Left, right, right, straight, through two sets of swing doors, past the photocopier. It was useless. The white décor with its framed *HQ* covers and inquisitive faces had left her snow-blind. It was as though she had been hauled out of the audience and forced to take a turn on stage. She felt amateurish and now here she was clutching the door for support.

"Come in. There's a lot to do today. Meg should have left you a list. And you know about Xyrite, don't you? That's the computer system here."

Beads of spit nestled in the corners of Jean's orange-painted lips. She was wearing a Pucci shirt choked with swirls of turquoise and rose and a string of cherry beads. It was an aristocratic messiness, thought Utopia, as she entered the office and took a seat.

Jean was eating alternate mouthfuls of pretzel and caramel yoghurt. Crumbs and drips littered the desk. Behind her was a panoramic view of the Hudson river with New Jersey's industrial shoreline, a serration of chimneys and towers, beyond.

"Fantastic view."

"Where is it? Can you see it? It's got the White House logo on the top. A letter . . ." Jean was scrabbling through memos, magazines, newspapers, faxes, menus, invitations, press releases, bills, invoices, photographs and books that threatened to avalanche off her desk at any moment.

"What are you looking for?" Utopia thought she must have missed something.

"A letter from the White House."

"Oh."

Sheets of paper slid on to the floor as Jean continued rummaging.

"Hi Jean. Everything OK?" called a voice at the door.

They both looked up.

"Todd, hi. Trying to find that letter from the First Lady's office. Did you call to check his birthplace? You've got to do it today, Todd. Confirm everything and put the piece through."

"Sure, Jean," he replied, before scuttling off.

"Here it is."

Utopia volunteered a smile.

"This is an emergency. We've got to write another letter

to the White House. We're trying to get the First Lady for an interview."

"I see."

"I need a letter in response to the last rejection from her press secretary, here take this, reiterating our demand and making it clearer what we want. We're on her side. We at *HQ* think she's the best thing America's got going for it right now, etcetera, etcetera. Got it?"

"Yes."

Utopia felt a panic sensation creep across her forehead then clamp her chest and seize her gut. Was she being made personally responsible for determining *HQ*'s success in securing an interview with the First Lady? It sounded like it.

"Meg should have the letter on her computer. Could be under White House. Use that. Push everything. We want her side of the story. We'll do her in fashion. Raphael will do her hair. She can wear Bill Blass, Chanel, whoever the hell she wants. Anything she wants. Right? Great." Jean picked up her telephone and began dialling out.

Utopia froze. Was that it? Was this her brief? She stood up slowly and lingered at the door.

"Come back if there's a problem. The desk's beyond the hall. Meg's left a list of how it all works on her desk . . . Jean Weiner here, is he there?"

Time to go.

Utopia nodded obediently and tip-toed out of the room.

Her desk, or rather Meg's desk, was hidden behind a partition and organised with military precision. Utopia surveyed her weaponry with curiosity. She found headed notepaper, pencils and pens, a well-thumbed Rolodex, files labelled *Costs and Expenses*, ordered back issues of *HQ,* a set of reference books, a file marked *Stories In Progress* and another, *Babes & Dudes*. It was the force of order needed to combat Jean's elbow-deep chaos. The promised list of whats and hows was nowhere to be seen.

"Hi," called a voice over the wall.

It was the boy she had seen minutes earlier at Jean's door.

"Todd."

"Utopia."

A cock amongst the hens, Todd looked pleased with the latest addition to the brood. He had a jowly face and playful hair, which stood upright in clumps. He was chewing gum like a sports coach and a pencil lay above his left ear. "I'm in fact-checking. Twenty-eight. Jean'll probably send you down at some point. Down the hall, turn right and it's third on your left. Extension 225. Let me know if you need any help."

"Well, actually, can you show me how the computer works? I've got to find a letter called White House."

"Back on that, huh?" said Todd, reappearing on her side and switching on her computer. "The ed's real keen to snag her. Have you met Diane? You know she's British too."

Utopia was aware of this. She wondered if it mightn't have something to do with Jean's interest in her. Diane was a member of New York's élite. She was endlessly photographed at galas, premières, fashion shows and openings. She was a face familiar to Utopia from paparazzi shots.

"Here's the letter and you're all set."

"Thanks," said Utopia, and watched him disappear.

Deprived of a view, not a window in a sight, she was sealed in an office that buzzed and sang. There were the air-conditioning vents overhead, the surrounding computer screens, the security-coded door as it flew open, the flick of the switch on the water-cooler followed by a glub-glub of water poured into a cup.

She flicked through an *HQ* magazine lying on the desk and gazed at the models in black and white, at the movie stars in their LA homes, and European royalty having fun in the sun. At the back were the features. There was a story on child-custody wars, an original concept art story involving shoes and garbage, and a think piece on "Nineties Newness". How irony can remodel yesterday's ideas. She tore out the perfume samples and rubbed them on her wrist, the whiff of luxury consumed like a drug.

She came up for air.

Swanning along the corridor came the editors. The fashion editors were identifiable by their skinny figures and wobbly heels. They wore their hair swept behind sunglasses and carried portfolios and coffees in outstretched hands. A few of them glanced over. One smiled. The rest strode past like catwalk dolls. Hips forward, shoulders back. Other editors and assistants appeared. They were less photogenic and had thighs and arses. Some were short, one was male. Their degrees of eye-contact appeared to reflect rank.

"Hey, ya," said a Southern accent in a lavender suit.

Utopia guessed she was an assistant. "Hello," she replied, happy to be noticed.

The corridor emptied.

All went quiet like the dying shrill of a whistle. With nothing left to distract her, Utopia transferred her attention to the letter on the screen. She read it twice. She found that it dwelt exclusively on the First Lady's so-called female interests. The premise was "The First Lady At Home". Decoration of the White House, her designer favourites, rearing her daughter and dietary tips. This made it easy to know what to do. The letter's message was that if the First Lady felt misunderstood, which of course she did, *HQ* was there to put the record straight. It was the emotional trump card. But Meg's letter was clumsy, all flattery and no bite. The First Lady had to be convinced that doing this interview was right now the most important thing she could do.

It was time to explain.

Utopia gathered her thoughts. She began. The white font lit up the cobalt blue in streaks of light. She was away.

*We at HQ feel that the First Lady has been grossly misrepresented in the press of late. We want, in response, to present a balanced portrait of her as wife, mother and role model for American women everywhere.*

*Our aim is to forget politics and address the personal as political. Our focus would be exclusively on the First Lady and not the President. HQ's one million readers would be thrilled to learn of her tips as a homemaker in the White House and as a US ambassador abroad.*

*We also promise a glamorous wardrobe from this season's collections and will be using award-winning photographer and HQ contributor Joseph D'Souza.*

Utopia imagined the First Lady sitting at her desk overlooking the lawn in front of the Oval Office with her press secretary at her elbow as she contemplated the request. Maybe she would read it out to her daughter, back from college, sitting in a corner armchair sucking a diet soda through a straw.

"Do you think I should do it, honey?"

"Hey mom, it'd be cool."

The red light flashed.

"Todd's taking you for lunch. Up any minute. Meg's list, did you find it?" Jean spoke in soundbites.

"Er . . . no. I can't see one."

"Honestly. Impossible. I'll see you after lunch. We'll go over the letter."

Jean hung up. Utopia reread the letter. She paused. She wasn't sure about 'ambassador'. Was there a better word?

"Hey." Todd's face reappeared above the wall. She sensed puppy-dog excitement and a wagging tail. An unlit cigarette was parked in the corner of his mouth. It jiggled as he spoke. "Hungry?"

"Very."

She saved her document, picked up her bag and they headed for the elevator together.

Outside the streets were busy with lunchtime trade.

"Where do you normally go?" she asked.

He gestured and she followed, arriving at an Italian deli on 57th Street where salamis were stacked in pyramid formations in the window. Their server was wearing a badge: *Lose Weight Now, Ask Me How*. Utopia was mesmerised. She watched as he carved tracing paper slices of Emmental cheese. Every inch of his body was fluid with fat. His knuckles had retreated beneath flesh and his forearms were like loaves. Bulges protruded from unimaginable places. He was the largest specimen yet. "Pay at the counter," he said.

They found a table and began unpacking their sandwiches so that they could fit them in their mouths. Layer upon layer of meat, cheese, tomato, lettuce and bread mounded high on their paper plates. Todd repositioned his cigarette behind his ear and cleared his throat. Without prompting, he began to fill her in on office gossip. "The managing editor's fucking the creative director. They do it underneath the layout table after work. If Jean makes you work late, you got to knock. I once caught them at it. Gross out. They were making these animal noises. He's Italian. The managing editor's a total bitch."

Utopia continued eating as he continued talking.

"The fashion director's trying to get the shopping editor fired. She's from Jersey. Oh, yeah, no more expenses. We used to go for pitchers in Jack's Bar on press days. The managing editor's just sent this memo saying drinking's against magazine policy. My arse. Just because she's gone fucking AA."

Utopia speared gherkin rounds with a fork. She was fascinated. That these details were about editors formerly encountered as names in a magazine she used to flick though in her newsagent back home was hard to believe.

"How's London?"

"Oh, fine."

"Did you ever see *Repulsion?*"

"Yes."

"I'm trying to write a novel like that. I want to go to London to do it. Do you think it'd be difficult?"

"No. I mean, I don't see why it should."

Baffled by this sudden revelation, Utopia wondered if it wasn't Todd's way of showing that his tastes sat just as easily with the *Times Literary Review* as they did supermodel profiles. She licked her coffee froth as he looked at his watch.

"Got a million calls to make. I've been trying to get through to this author down in Savannah all week. He hasn't got an ansaphone. Can you believe that? What century is the guy living in? Man, someone ought to tell him," he said.

They made their way slowly back to the office. Todd smoked furiously. Lighting a fresh one from the butt of the last, he administered his afternoon's nicotine fix. "Everyone in fact-checking smokes," he said. "Not in the office because the managing editor's had those alarms put in that piss on you. I figure smoking's a literary thing."

Utopia nodded.

She decided she liked Todd, as she did her job. She was looking forward to her afternoon with Jean.

# Chapter Five

Utopia pushed open the door. As she entered the restaurant she felt the entire room look up from their tables and remark upon her arrival.

She stood six feet tall in her heels. Heels were meant to promote self-confidence but arriving alone always made her uneasy. She would never choose to arrive alone, given the choice. She shoved her bag into her armpit and forced a smile. "I'm meeting a party under the name Jean . . ." she justified herself to the mealy-mouthed brunette who arrived to intercept her.

"Who?"

Deafened by a roar from a nearby table then inspected by a pair of talking heads, she was immobilised by an attack of self-consciousness. She had forgotten who she was meeting. "Jean . . ."

"Weiner? The *HQ* party?"

"Yes."

"Over at the bar. Table's not ready."

Utopia had to tread cautiously in her break-neck shoes. She began to wonder why she had worn them. It was always the same. She made her way to the ocean-liner bar, a curvature of polished rails and coloured bottles. She had been brought here once before by Marina. The faces of TriBeCa artists, their mistresses, wives and critics had been pointed out to her like sights of the city. Utopia glanced up at the slanted mirrors on the wall. Strategically placed to eliminate rubber-necking, they enabled maximum monitoring with minimum effort. She watched the seated row of men in linen suits and elegant women with coiled chignons maintain a semblance of disinterest while they clocked every entrance, every exit, every pairing.

Utopia spied Jean at the far end. She was raised on a stool. She went to join them.

"Utopia. Hi. You made it," said Jean, sounding as surprised as she had this morning.

"Yes."

As she hovered by Jean's side, she tried to remember whose dinner this was. After her first day at *HQ*, she was flattered to have found herself invited. Someone was leaving. Someone from shopping features?

Jean handed her a glass of wine.

"Thanks," she said.

Two gulps and her glass was two-thirds empty. She hoped in vain that the alcohol would convert her silence into flowery chatter. It sank to her stomach like lead. Words eluded her like a foreign language. Glancing down at her black slip dress, a fleamarket purchase, a stain winked at her beneath a spotlight and she realised in horror that she hadn't washed it. For a horrible moment, she thought it might smell. She scratched discreetly at the stain with a fingernail and sniffed the air. All she could smell was garlic and hot bread.

Jean was talking to the managing editor. It was talk of late deadlines, someone downloading porn in the art room and the hiring of a fleet of US Army helicopters for a fashion shoot which had sent the story way over budget.

"Don't tell Diane," said the managing editor.

And yet all Utopia could think about was this woman before her, prostrate beneath the layout table with her skirt hitched up to her waist, her black tights balled around an ankle as she panted beneath the creative director. The managing editor caught her eye and Utopia hurriedly looked away.

She spied instead on the *HQ* girls with honey tans hugging the bar beyond. They were all familiar faces from the office today. They were a tight clique, impregnable behind a wall of gossip, yet for a moment Utopia wondered whether to go and join them. She hadn't the nerve. She imagined her reception of vacant eyes and herself blushing and stumbling over her words in a clumsy getaway.

She disposed of the contents of her glass.

The maître d' came to announce their table.

Jean the Pied Piper in a crimson trouser suit led the way through a sea of cocktail dresses, fashion-campaign faces, illicit cigarettes and champagne suppers. Utopia joined the end of the line. The restaurant crowded before her like the front row view of the cinema screen. It was loud and disorientating and she thought she might trip.

"Utopia, why don't you sit beside me," said Jean.

Utopia now found herself among six females with perfect noses and yards of shiny hair. There was a strawberry blonde, two streaky highlights, two shiny brunettes and one Vampira grey. All had anatomically correct faces like Maybelline girls. Glossy magazines demanded perfection. Her three months in New York had taught her this. Candidates were obliged to pass a beauty test, one she herself had unwittingly passed somewhere along the way. No one plain or flawed need apply, or perhaps they did and failed.

The *HQ* girls appeared severely high-maintenance. No doubt they booked in regularly to be dyed, plucked, shaved, waxed, pummelled, massaged, trimmed, peeled and injected. Given the relative scale of such things, Utopia felt dowdy. She would rank as a low-maintenance girl, she decided. In truth, the rituals of femininity had never inspired much interest.

Her relationship with her features was one of resignation. She had grown to accept them as she had her family, begrudgingly. Appearance while a priority was a perfunctory affair. She had never shaved her legs. Perhaps she was lucky but their smoothness didn't warrant it. She hated hairdressers. She was suspicious of men with scissors and hidden agendas, styles inappropriate to the customer while novel for them. She employed her friend Lou to chop the bottom, usually at the end of an evening when they'd had a few drinks. "For Christ's sake, do it in a straight line," was her only demand.

She had once had a facial. It had been a gift voucher from her sister for her birthday. While the steam machine and herbal wraps had proven pleasant enough, the woman in a white coat applying pressure to her skin had been an unwelcome addition. She had found herself apologising profusely as the gloved fingers pinched her face and she had sworn never again to submit to such humiliation.

Her gaze shifted from table to girl and back again in search of a resting place and some sign of approval. She had made it this far. She was convinced she could fit. Someone, was it Brandy?, reciprocated with a smile. Utopia returned the courtesy. It was going to work, she told herself. She observed the girl to her left hail a waiter for an ashtray. The out-of-work model clenched his muscles.

"Smoking is illegal."

"Oh, please. You think I don't know that?"

The girl lit up and tossed the match on to the floor. Utopia thought it was somehow fitting that smoking had been banned. The restaurant had slat blinds and low lighting and an ambience that was a throwback to a decadent past. It provided the idea that all this was special and not just another Monday night. Across the table, the managing editor was scanning the other tables and sizing up the pecking order in an audible whisper. A frenzy of glances broke out as the girls strained to see who the couple was at the corner table. They began to argue about the identity of the man with the well-known columnist hidden behind the pillar.

"Business or sex?"

"*Quelle différence?*"

And they all looked away.

Utopia had no clue about any of them and yet, as someone fond of staring and who enjoyed public transport for the caravan of characters on offer, she couldn't help but be delighted by such shameless proceedings. There were no misconceptions as to why everyone was here.

"Utopia."

The sound of her name startled her. It came again through the clatter of cutlery and conversation and this time louder. She looked up from the table. She couldn't see anyone. Then she recognised Felix with his velvety sheen of hair and his penny glasses. He was tunnelling his way through the crowded room with his arms outstretched in mock embrace.

"Ladies."

He kissed each in turn but fixed his focus on Utopia. He had kind eyes, which promised forgiveness. She felt as though his arrival signified first prize and that she was the most important person alive. She laughed as he bent to whisper in her ear.

"Want to join me?"

He motioned for her to follow. She was intrigued by his offer of a secret and inched up from her chair. The *HQ* girls pretended not to notice but she could feel their gaze hot on her back and was amused to think that they all knew who he was but not how she knew him.

Utopia followed Felix into the gents'.

Locked in a cubicle with her back against the wall, she watched him remove the lid from a tiny silver box and deposit a mound of cocaine on a pocket mirror. Away from the table, no longer on best behaviour, she was sixteen again and an impressionable schoolgirl. Beyond the door, a stream of piss splashed against a urinal and she wanted to laugh. Felix shook his head and handed her a fifty. She slowly rolled the dollar bill as he chopped the rocks with his Amex. He gestured for her to do a line. She inhaled and then again. He followed. It had been a long time since she remembered this taste and she was excited by the sensation of powdered adrenalin as it drip-dripped down the back of her throat.

Seconds later came the staccato heartbeat. This was serious. She swallowed hard.

"Ready?" he said, wiping his nose.

He unbolted the door and they ventured out. He released it and it jerked shut behind them. Upstairs the restaurant's overture had reached a crescendo. Pulsing with euphoria, Utopia felt weightless as though walking on air. She was flattered by the attentions of her new-found friend. That her instincts had proven true and she was in the right place left her flush with contentment. She felt happy.

"I hope your week at *HQ* works out," he said, as they stopped beside a table stacked with bread baskets and dishes filled with oval butters.

Utopia nodded. All she could hear was her racing heart.

"I'll get your number from Marina. We should go out."

She nodded again, still mute.

"Got to get back. Paul wants to eat."

"Paul?" She found her voice.

"Boyfriend."

She had suspected as much, though felt disappointed, which was silly, so then felt embarrassed.

"See you soon," he said.

She waved.

Back at the table the food had arrived. She couldn't remember ordering anything but there was her plate. No one seemed to notice her late arrival. A boy in an FBI cap had joined their table and was sipping champagne through a straw. He was a fashion assistant and back from a shoot at the zoo in the Bronx. It was an animal-print story and a giraffe had been used as a prop. They had wanted an alligator but the model had refused to get into the tank. The Polaroids were awesome. He passed them around the table and everybody was suitably impressed.

"Not missing London, then?"

Utopia turned her head. Jean was looking at her, a mange-tout swinging from her fork like a flag.

She shook her head "No," she said.

"You prefer New York?"

She cleared her throat. "I'd always wanted to come back to New York." She took a sip of water to wet her mouth. "I was born here you see, and . . ."

Utopia found herself folding her napkin into miniature triangles, smaller and smaller, as her trickle of words became a torrent. Faster and faster they spilled as though sucked from within by Jean's focus. Three months and three thousand miles away and it felt like a lifetime.

"Not hungry?"

She stopped.

Jean was staring at her. She felt sure she was perspiring. She imagined her face as a shiny beacon and her jaw out of synch with her speech. She rubbed a finger across her top lip and found moisture. She examined her food. A slab of plum coloured tuna lay within a fennel garnish and lace of sauce tartare. Marooned within the vast white plate, it looked like a Japanese print. But her mouth had been anaesthetised to a distant place and her appetite squandered in the gents'.

She watched Jean fork a morsel and did the same but the tuna, though tender, was tasteless. She toyed with it with her tongue, took a sip of water and gulped it down.

"It's going to be good working together," said Jean now, unprompted.

At this point Utopia was struck by a nervous spasm, a sort of drug induced twitch in her right eye. She concentrated hard on composing her face. She prayed that it was invisible and a neurological tic exclusive to the brain.

"Let's see what happens this week."

Opening and shutting her mouth like a land-locked fish, Utopia didn't know what to say. This week? She only had one week, didn't she? Could Jean be implying something more?

She forked another sliver of tuna into her mouth and it lay there like slime. She watched Jean take her compact from her pocket-book, snap it open and fluff her hair. She went to stab an olive and missed. It flew from her plate and spun across the table, coming to rest with a plop in giraffe boy's glass. She pretended not to notice.

"I'd like that," she said quickly.

# Chapter Six

Utopia unlocked the door to the apartment. Inside she was greeted by a wall of soupy air and the sight of Johann sitting with an African drum between his knees. He was in the middle of the room, had taken off his shirt and his pigeon chest was out on show. He had a handlebar moustache and a prematurely balding crown. Johann was Swedish. "Joint's by the cooker," he shouted.

Humming with adrenaline, Utopia wandered into the kitchen, found the joint in a saucer and lit it. She sucked until the ember toasted her fingers. The smoke brought calm. She arranged herself on the wicker sofa as his palms beat their music softly around the room. Johann's bongo-playing was the only worthwhile feature of the cover band he played with. She went to their gigs because she had to. It was one of their unspoken agreements. He dealt with the apartment's vermin problem and cooked for her at night, and she clapped loudly at the end of his shows.

It wasn't such a bad deal.

She kicked off her shoes and adjusted the cushion beneath her head. Only now was she able to digest the full impact of the past twenty-four hours. It had happened so fast. First the party, then meeting Jean, her first day at *HQ* and now dinner tonight. Had she found a friend in Jean? It seemed she had. All past employers had been male, she realised, as she ran through her list. There was Keith, her boss at *Music Today*, Pete, the manager of Waterstones, and top and tailing them had been an army of restaurant managers, short, Mediterranean and male.

That Jean had seen in Utopia something that elevated her above the rest made her blood run fast. Fears of failure dissolved like mist. Staring up at the ceiling, it was as though she were floating.

She struggled to decipher the beat of the fan. It had an irregular rotation. The whir of the blades did nothing to dispel the humidity that clung to her like a wet blanket. She could feel rivulets of sweat trickling down her spine to gather in her knicker elastic. They had been waiting for air-conditioning units for over a month. There was no reason for the delay and Johann was meant to be chasing it up. Johann, though, had an AC unit in his bedroom.

When temperatures topped record highs – which they frequently did – Utopia was forced to take refuge in there with him. Strictly as the last resort. Johann was the proud owner of a water-bed, which squelched when he squirmed. As the strange sound effects infiltrated her dreams, sleep became fitful. At the first sign of daybreak, she would drag her futon back to her room and throw open the window, desperate to breathe.

What had happened to the air?

She counted his ribs.

Johann had an unhealthy pallor, like a prisoner of solitary confinement on recent release. By day he was an account planner for an advertising agency and by night a bongo player. They had met in a bar. "From London?" he had asked, as she sat alone.

Her companion, an American, had gone to the john. Utopia's box-fresh Nikes and fair complexion might have given him a clue but Johann had also, no doubt, been eaves-dropping. She admitted she was staying with friends on the Upper West Side.

"I used to live off Carnaby Street," he said. "Here's my number. Let's have coffee sometime."

Why on earth she would want to have coffee with this man, she didn't know. She had gone around wondering about it for weeks. Then she called. She had learned early on that nothing happened if you didn't. And so they met for pancakes, Sunday brunch at Time Café, and she discovered that he lived in Little Italy. What's more, he had a room-mate about to depart at the end of the month and his only criteria for finding a replacement were that she must be female and European. Men were untidy, and as for Americans, well, he had enough of them in the office.

Utopia couldn't believe her luck or the casualness of the arrangement and moved in. There was something about his Scandinavian frankness she trusted. Initially, anyway.

Five days later she had been woken by Johann clamber-ing into her bed. He was very drunk and his breath reeked of methylated spirits. He had snuggled up next to her, gur-gling and pawing her. Utopia had pushed him on to the floor. The next day it had taken a vow of abstinence from him for her to agree to stay put. The ramshackle apartment was too good to give up and she was in love with Little Italy. She had begun to see him as the delinquent younger brother she had never had. "Johann, can't you just grow up?" she would complain.

And he was now a friend of sorts.

He was the person she went home to but rarely saw out. She preferred it that way. Their semi-conscious encounters, the entrance and exit to each day, acted as pillars of support as she battled with the anonymity of life in the city.

She surveyed their apartment.

It was a vision of chaos.

Distinguished by a lack of furniture, the living area was home to a selection of fleamarket chairs scattered for no particular reason, their paint jobs peeling like sunburnt skin. The kitchen table pressed against the wall was blanketed beneath magazines and newspapers. A vase of crumbling cornflowers and pieces of crockery punctuated the overflow, and a collection of books, most of which were in Swedish, was stacked in piles on the floor. Johann had been in New York four years yet his attitude to domesticity was as temporary as Utopia's. Comfort was not a priority, transience was. His sole concession to ownership was a stereo, TV and VCR yet this was definitely home for now.

In the window opposite sat two hunched figures bent over sewing-machines. They were obviously intent on working their way through the night. A naked bulb burned above their backs.

Johann's moustache had begun to droop like the whiskers of a disgraced cat.

Utopia yawned. "Bed," she said, preparing herself for another night with her head beside a fan.

Johann stopped his drumming. "I need that thirty for the electricity."

Their silence was stirred by the syncopation from above.

"Oh." She reached for her bag. She found her wallet and flicked it open. Without warning, the photograph of herself and Liberty with their mother in the park crushed her. It was the same black and white snapshot she glanced at twenty times a day, every time she was called upon to produce cash. But as her day shuddered to a halt, the image was a reminder that things were not as they seemed, that her family was no longer complete, that relations with her mother had never been easy and now there was the issue of her sister to bear.

She blinked back tears and the room gelled into a mirage of colours.

When her mother died, her life had been cancelled. Yet now, here, she was so removed from it all while maternal emotions came seeped in guilt. When cancer was found to have spread, and the doctor's voice wavered as though falling from a great height, Utopia remembered her distress blurred by fury. Not only was there anger at her mother's pain but their miscommunication, fired for so long like missiles, would be left unresolved.

The last few months with her mother hadn't been time enough for anything. There had been so much to say. Utopia had sat beside her day after day, desperate to extract every detail and inherit her life. She had resented her mother for leaving with so little warning, then despised herself for feeling resentful. Why had it always been so difficult, she wanted to know.

"You're both too alike," her father would conclude as together they hunted for clues.

Perhaps he was right.

Her mother's absence haunted her like the trace of a bell that seemed to ring forever in her ears. It was a sound disturbed only by her sister's accusation that she had been an accomplice to her mother's illness.

Remembering it now still shocked her.

When their mother's cancer was first diagnosed, Liberty had flown into a rage of such viciousness that their father had to intervene. Liberty had accused Utopia of causing their mother such long-term anxiety that it had taken its toll. Disease had struck. Curiously, at the time Utopia had found herself able to forgive her sister this attack. Everything became so surreal, emotions so jumbled, that words which sprang from the dark like wolves melted like snow. Consumed as she was by fear for her mother, she found herself immune to her sister's hysteria.

It was only later when the emptiness swallowed them up, when her mother's bed lay bare and all that remained were the bathroom's plastic pots rattling with chemical warfare, the brush snarled with balls of hair, a wardrobe of memories, pairs of empty shoes that Liberty's rage returned to haunt her. How dare she use her as an emotional scapegoat? And a few months later out it poured. It had been a barrage of fear and despair barbed with hatred for her sister's attack. They had fought and screamed like never before. Then Utopia had left. She had packed her suitcase and crossed the ocean just to get away.

Johann's hands appeared to be dancing.

She wondered whether she would ever feel forgiveness for her sister. Would they find peace? It had all started long before this. The real issue for Liberty was that she, Utopia, had always been the wild one. She had usurped her older sister at every turn. She had stayed out all night long before Liberty experienced a double bed, travelled to India while Liberty was driving to France with the parents and had entertained a series of boyfriends of whom Liberty had disapproved.

Rick, a graffiti artist responsible for spraying I LOVE UTOPIA in four-foot-high letters on a District Line train, a train they had sat at Moorgate tube station at six a.m. to watch pulling into the platform, had provoked particular dislike.

He had been Utopia's first love.

Rick was an ex-boxer who could spin on his head. He was six two and suitably brutish. He had a number two skin and a scar above his lip in the shape of an anchor. She had met him on a dance floor in a West End club when he slipped and landed on her feet with a thump. "Fuck," she swore, "that hurt." Laughing, a voracious laugh, he announced he liked posh girls who swore. Like Utopia.

She was sixteen and easily smitten.

She had never known infatuation until she met Rick. A reluctant conversationalist, his discourse was limited to physical assault and defiance. He liked to paint walls and fuck, preferably alfresco, alleyways, bus-stops, parks, garages. Theirs was carnal communication. They were once caught in Soho Square, trousers down, four a.m. by a disgusted guard with a torch. They had jumped the railings. She remembered the bruises lining her inner thighs. Rick was easily provoked. She had seen him lash out on a Saturday night more than once. The smash of fist and the sound of pain as he tore into another man terrified her and she would vow never to see him again as she bolted in search of a taxi home.

But there he would be the next day, his knuckles raw and eyes watery with shame. Begging forgiveness, he would kiss her neck and bury his hand in her knickers. She could never say no. He was a boxer, he would say. It's what his uncle Jimmy taught him. Uncle Jimmy had been a boxer before an adversary put him in intensive care. He later bought a shop on the Old Kent Road selling reclaimed mantelpieces. "That's for me to know and the customers not to mind," he would say when asked where they came from. Afternoons were spent at the back of Jimmy's shop drinking tea and smoking Rothmans, while Bully his pitbull chewed a cut in the corner. There was always a man with a van late for a pick-up.

To say Utopia's mother had been unhappy with the situation would be an understatement. Rick proceeded to graffiti her parents' entire neighbourhood with his signature tag. *Rick 86* appeared on every sign and wall and he was banned from the house. Even so it worked out as a three-year addiction. Weaning herself off wasn't easy when he proceeded to follow her home, sit outside the house and spray graffiti-art declarations of love on neighbours' walls. He grew belligerent. "I'm not goin' till you change your fucking mind," he would shout at the closed door. His persistence scared her, though in the end he found another as she knew he would.

It was a whole year later that P arrived.

She had started at the University of North London and was sharing a flat off the Holloway Road with her friend Lou. Life was calmer now. His name was Piers Lisson, but never Piers. It had been his father's name and grandfather's before him but had been shed early, along with his milk teeth. And so it was P who walked into Waterstone's, where she worked – her supplementary student loan job – one evening with a pint of milk and a packet of spaghetti. It was his height she first noticed. Height was her weakness and there were so few tall men around. P, in common with Rick, was over six feet tall. He wore an expression less of concentration than of boredom as he bent to pick up each book and skim the back. He wore brown-framed glasses, shabby corduroys and a tatty leather jacket, which should have been discarded a long time ago and might have put off a more discerning person.

Utopia was curious.

He began to put in an appearance every time she was

there. At first she thought he might be a shop lifter. From behind the till, she would watch him make his round of the shop, stopping each time at the same tables and shelves in precisely the same order. She then discovered that it was a behavioural trait true of all regular browsers. Starting with *New Fiction* he would proceed to *New Titles* then on to *Waterstone's Recommends* followed by a quick scan of the *Twenty Per Cent Off* table before arriving at the *Screen and Theatre Plays* which is where she later found he had been headed all along. She also learned that he came for the free wine and the smell of books. The funny thing was, she had taken the job for the very same reasons. She thought she had found her ideal man.

They made eye-contact on day one but it wasn't until several weeks later that they spoke. His first question had been to ask her who was speaking upstairs. An Israeli short-story writer. His second, was she new? Yes. Finally, when she thought it would never happen, they went for a drink at the pub down the road then to a film. Two weeks later she had coffee sitting on his kitchen counter top as he jammed a knife into the toaster to extract the toast and electrocuted himself. He dropped the knife to rub his arm and she burst out laughing. "I'm sorry," she choked, biting her lip so hard that she had a hole there the next day. It was one of her flaws, a habit most people manage to outgrow, the tendency to laugh at others' distress. Then he, too, began laughing so she wasn't alone and they went to have breakfast at the greasy spoon down the road.

P was the antithesis of Rick. Erudite, compassionate, a conversationalist and with a full head of hair, he ranked considerably higher up the evolutionary chain. Never before had someone wanted to know everything about her, then try to work it out. With Rick it had always been recriminations.

He would tell her she was stupid and that she didn't understand. "Get a fucking life," he'd say.

The pain he made her feel was part of what they were. Not with P. "You make me laugh," he would say.

"Why?"

"Because you're gorgeous."

She had moved into his flat a year ago at his suggestion. "I think we should see more of each other," was how he had put it.

Her mother had even managed to have misgivings about P. He was eight years her senior and divorced. At the age of twenty-four he had married an American who wanted to work in England. It was typical P. Doing her a favour. His end of the deal had never come through, no green card, no nothing. His wife promptly moved back to the States only to disappear without trace. Utopia's mother, who was never prepared to accept anything without bloody dissection, was suspicious. "Who is he and why's he so old? I hope you're not spending all your time with him when you're meant to be studying. Why can't you find a nice boy your own age? It's important not to lose perspective." Perspective was one of her mother's favourite words.

As for Liberty, she had been slowly getting on with it. She had passed her law exams and acquired a group of friends with mortgages and must-have-you-over kitchen tables. She had enjoyed a steady run at monogamy with university boys for respectable lengths of time. Boys with rugby-playing shoulders and racing-green jumpers. Boys who took her for weekends in Hampshire, served gin and tonic without ice and Twiglets in bowls.

Liberty enjoyed an uncomplicated bond with their mother. They went Saturday curtain-shopping together and swapped recipes torn out of magazines. They talked about hair and flowers and diets. Utopia had always envied Liberty's female rapport with their mother while Liberty's grievance was with Utopia's free-spiritedness.

Why did she always have to spoil everything?

Equally pig-headed, they were forever locked in stalemate. And so they fought just as they always fought.

"You asleep?"

Utopia opened her eyes.

"How was the job?"

"Good," she told him, producing the notes from her wallet and lining them up on the table.

She stood up. Her entire body felt numb. Her head was spinning. "Bed," she mumbled.

But Johann didn't hear. Drumming had resumed and his head was nodding up and down like a yo-yo.

# Chapter Seven

Day two had disappeared and it was already day three. How had that happened? The week was fading like quick-fix nostalgia, was all she could think.

With the straw from her iced coffee lodged like a fuel pipe between closed lips, Utopia was catching up on celebrity news. It was a crucial part of the day. Photocopies of the tabloids' gossip columns were handed out each morning by one of Diane's assistants. Silence descended as everyone in the office caught up on sightings, hearsay and speculation. It was very important to know who was sleeping with whom, who next week's stars on the sitcom of the season were, and whether Hollywood's top-earning female actress would or would not be presenting an award at the third ceremony of the week. What had once constituted killing time, skimming magazines on news-stands, now comprised work.

What could be better?

Utopia felt heady with the implications of where she found herself each morning. It was a thrill in the same way the sight of the young actor ambling down the corridor with his hands in his back pockets was a thrill. Or the invitation from the fashion department to come and claim free shoes.

The biggest thrill of all was the discovery that she could do the job.

There was no reason why she shouldn't but it hadn't stopped her worrying. So far she was pretty sure she had failed at nothing. Her battle to get through to a succession of White House aides had paid off with the promise of an answer to the interview request by next week. Her suggested coverline using the word "Unmasked" was going to make the cover. And she had made sense of Jean's expenses which was no mean feat. Keith at *Music Today* had been a big spender though nothing like this. It had taken an entire morning but she had managed to account for every cent of Jean's $4360.67. Jean had been delighted when the managing editor signed them off, no quibbling.

She had grown fond of her corner. So much so in fact that she had made a few personal revisions, just little things. Her first alteration had been to swap chairs. The straight-backed chair stolen from another cubicle forced her to sit upright, which meant better viewing over the wall. This enabled her to work out who did what and why. She had then reorganised the desk to clear some space. She had pushed Meg's folders to one side, shoved her trinkets to th other and swapped the in-tray for the out-tray.

Meg must be right-handed.

There was also the issue of an eye-level photo a ginger-haired boy with a goofy smile. He had eyes t shadowed her, and although he was only a periph distraction, she could never forget he was there. She came across a fashion spread in last month's *HQ*. It photograph of a girl in a white bikini lying face u swimming pool. The bottom of the pool was th with light. In the distance were mountains. Overhead was a plane.

It was a reminder of something like a lost dream so she tore it out and pinned it on top. No more Mr Ginger.

Jean was late. She flew past Utopia's desk in a sorbet-coloured coat and saucer sunglasses like Big Bird on speed. Utopia's stomach lurched in sympathy. She was instructed to follow through with a copy of the letter to the White House.

She joined Jean in her office.

She felt exhilarated by the thrill of the chase and that they were in this together. Jean was eating. Crumbs from her cappuccino-chip muffin dropped from her lips on to the desk. She didn't seem to care. "Diane's worried we're going to lose the story. We've got to stay on top of this," she said, chomping furiously. "Where's the letter?"

Utopia passed it over and Jean began to read.

As she waited for a response, Utopia watched the beltway of cars stream up and down the West Side highway below. The Hudson's tide crawled sluggishly north. She spied a figure ascending the steps of a prison barge. There was something chilling about floating jails, the way they were out there on public view. They were almost as barbaric as public floggings. She thought that she could see the prisoner's shackles but he then disappeared.

Jean was still reading.

Her eyes darted across the page like flies. Utopia wondered what she would say. She then wondered about Jean's comment made in the restaurant last night about them working together. Had she meant it?

The red light flashed and Jean picked up the phone. She responded with affirmatives and brushed herself down before standing up. "Diane wants to have a look if you want to come."

Utopia needed no persuading. Despite feeling under-dressed, same black trousers, different shirt, she had been awaiting the opportunity to enter the glass doors at the end of the hall and meet the legendary editor-in-chief all week. "Yes please," she said.

She shadowed Jean along the corridor. It was a perfect opportunity to steal a tour of her surroundings, since so far she had been largely confined to her desk. On either side, offices with their doors cracked offered glimpses of girls with aerobicised legs swinging their feet at desks and talking on telephones. She guessed at titles. Fashion-features writers, sittings director, the managing editor's assistant, the shopping editor.

They were approaching Diane's office.

Utopia was aware of the carpet treading thicker and a reverent silence. There was the scent of flowers as opposed to the staleness of refrigerated air. Jean knocked and they ventured in. Utopia held her breath. The glass office was suspended above the city like a bubble. There was an aerial view of skinny Manhattan. The room was decorated with a vase of arum lilies, a squashy white sofa, a row of black and white prints and framed magazine awards. Diane was trying on shoes. "Fab-u-lous." Her overly enthusiastic assistant was clapping her hands.

"Heavenly. Aren't they?" said Diane. "I'll have a pair in every colour."

The pin-thin editor removed the shoes from her feet and they were replaced in the box. Utopia was mesmerised. Diane was the image of forty-something perfection. The length of her skirt was daringly short. She had not a hair out of place and she wasn't a pound overweight. She had movie-star quality. She was quite as slick as any one of her air-brushed covers.

"Diane. Hi," Jean greeted her. "I've got the letter and I want you to meet Utopia. She's filling in for Meg."

Diane was as uninterested in Utopia as in last season's collections. Utopia managed a whispery hello like the autograph hunter in the presence of a star. Diane nodded.

"Right. This damn interview. Have we sent flowers?"

Her manner was clipped and business-like. She had the growl of a smoker or an ex-smoker. It was impossible to tell.

"Rule number one. Flowers."

"Sure. Flowers."

Utopia found herself nodding alongside Jean. She supposed it was important to make a note of whatever came up.

"Have you said how much we adore her and that we think of her as an *HQ* woman?"

"Yes."

Diane moved round behind her empty glass desk and stared through it at the floor.

"We have to do something about her hair," she said, looking up after a moment's deliberation. "This season's about romance. Femininity is very, very strong, and she could look so feminine. It will be a cover but do you think she'll show her upper arms? Does anyone know what her upper arms look like? Too flabby is what I'm afraid of. Who's her trainer? Does anyone know? Oh dear, it would be too darling. Find a photo of her upper arms ASAP. This has to be considered an emergency."

"Right."

"And whatever you do, don't forget flowers. Lots of them. Anyway, must dash. Charity do in London at seven. The car's waiting. Concorde won't." She laughed gaily and Jean handed her the letter.

They left the office.

Utopia was disappointed. She hadn't managed a single

word, Diane had looked straight through her and now Jean appeared distracted. Jean ran a hand through her hair. Her breathing was erratic. It was the flustered response to a reprimand, thought Utopia. From behind, she watched Jean tug the wrinkles out of her skirt. She had a shambling gait and the hands of a man. Her gesture was one of vexation. According to Marina, Jean was a former society girl who had sat for Andy Warhol and been there for the excesses of Studio 54. She had even been known to Truman Capote by name. It was hard to believe and Utopia was keen to know more but Jean was giving nothing away.

"I need you at your desk," she said before retreating behind a closed door. "I'm expecting a call."

"Hey."

It was Todd. "What gives?"

She shrugged.

"You want anything? I'm doing a deli run."

She paused to consider the offer as Todd planted his chin on the divide. His voice dropped to a whisper. "I've got the mother of hangovers. You want to know why? Because of the cutest Russian stripper with the sexiest butt."

"A stripper?"

"Driving me fucking nuts. She dances in this bar over on the West Side right near my apartment. Man, you should see her. She cuts these moves."

Utopia laughed.

"And she speaks American. Went to one of those stripper schools in Moscow but she's real natural. I mean, she doesn't dye her hair or her . . ."

"OK, OK."

He nodded. "Iced tea?"

"Mango," she said, as she watched him tramp down the hallway. He was wearing the black rubber sandals patronised by surfers for their ability to stick to the board, and the seat of his khakis hung like sacking. If his testosterone out-pouring was faintly ridiculous, his candour tickled. He never failed to surprise her.

The red light blinked.

"I still haven't heard."

It was Jean.

"From who?"

"John Travolta's publicist. It's the party tonight and I've been waiting to hear about my invite all day."

"Oh."

"Everyone's going to be there." She sounded edgy.

"Have you called?"

"I've been calling all day. Meg forgot to RSVP. God, it makes me so mad."

As she digested the facts, Utopia's suspicion grew that a move of opportunism could save the day.

"Do you want me to phone a friend to see if she can help?"

"Anything."

Without a moment's delay, Utopia phoned Marina. Marina laughed very loudly.

"A spare ticket for the Travolta party? You're joking, right?"

"No."

Only Marina could effect a result. "All right, darling, sit tight. I'll see what I can do."

Forced to endure nervous anticipation, Utopia wan-dered along to the office kitchen. Expectations now ran as high as her emotions. The kitchen strip-light, about to perish, was strobing erratically. She poured coffee from the pot into her *HQ* cup and her movements flowed awkwardly, dismembered by slow motion. She waved her hand in front of her face like a slowly ticking stop-watch, backwards and forwards. It was strangely hypnotic. A photocopied notice was sellotaped to the cupboard door.

*Looking for a share in Southampton? Five girls who know how to party looking for one more. Call Cola on ext. 256.*

Of the ten rip-off fingers listing Cola's number, only two remained. Utopia took one.

"Hi." It was Julie the other features assistant.

"Oh, hello there."

The strobe fractured Julie's face into segments of displeasure as she caught sight of the piece of paper dangling from Utopia's fingers. As though caught handling incriminating evidence, Utopia crumpled it into a ball and stashed it in her palm. Julie said nothing as she placed a poppyseed bagel in the microwave and retrieved a tub of cream cheese from the fridge. Full-fat garlic. Utopia picked up her cup.

" 'Bye then."

Oh dear.

Jean's door was still shut. Utopia remembered the flowers. She had almost forgotten. She found the number dictated by Jean. "Hi, 1-800-BOUQUET, I'm Carol-May and what can I do for you today?" said the voice at the other end.

Carol-May's enthusiasm was liquid down the line.

"Oh, yes. Hello. I'm looking for something special."

"We're in the business to provide something special. Can I give you today's specials?"

"Er yes."

Utopia found herself treated to the top-ten list of seasonal blooms, recommended combinations and job-specific suggestions. She jotted them down. Carol-May spoke slowly and provided spellings, which was helpful. Utopia's suggestions were to be typed up and passed on to one of Diane's lap-dog assistants who guarded her office. "Thanks for thinking of us here at 1-800-BOUQUET and enjoy your night."

Utopia hung up.

She stared at the telephone. Its button lights were dull, unblinking. Ring, she muttered in an attempt to summon Marina's call under telepathic duress.

Nothing.

She scanned the desk. What was next? There, raised on chrome legs in the corner, was Meg's Rolodex. It was like a diary teeming with secrets. It was impossible to resist. Furtively at first, Utopia began leafing through hand-written inserts and typed inserts. Flick by flick, her eyes flew across the names and numbers. There were private carphone numbers, beach-house numbers, movie-mogul hotline numbers, White House numbers, personal-assistant numbers, photographers' numbers. They smacked of importance and a sense of belonging.

Rolling her pen between idle fingers, Utopia nurtured a growing impulse. Others would do the same, she argued. They were only numbers. Spurred by a guilty rush, she ran her finger back through the pages of the Rolodex. Picking out names of people and companies, she began scribbling them down. Her hand tore across the page of her notebook as each one precipitated the next.

She was startled by the ring of the telephone.

Her pen slipped and flew across the page leaving an untidy black line. Her hand was shaking. She looked at her watch. She hoisted herself up from her chair. The entire floor was empty. Jean's door was closed. It was past seven.

"I'll give her my extra ticket. It was supposed to be for Dorian."

"Are you sure?"

"Utopia, do not ask me if I'm sure."

"Oh thank you, Marina."

"By the way, Dora's doing one of her salons tomorrow night. I think you should come."

"Dorian?"

"Dora. Lit clit."

"Oh. Right. OK," she responded, confused.

There was no time for it now. They hung up and she phoned through to Jean to tell her the good news.

"That's so great, Utopia. I've decided we're going to make this thing work, you and me."

Utopia was aware of a conspiratorial tone to Jean's words, and the thrill of suspense lodged high in her throat. Jean continued talking.

"I inherited Meg with the furniture. I never intended keeping her on."

Keeping her on? Was she to infer from this that Jean was considering letting her go?

Utopia held her breath as Jean's other line went.

"I've got to get that."

"OK."

"See you tomorrow."

They hung up in tandem.

# Chapter Eight

The East Village apartment was dark and cluttered. With its collection of mahogany furniture and dusty rubber plants, it resembled a Victorian drawing room in miniature. White doilies fringed bookshelves. A beaded curtain was strung between the living room with a flocked sofa and a bedroom housing a foldaway bed. Peering over the shoulder of their hostess, Utopia could make out groups of conversationalists. The sincere-looking faces supping claret and nibbling cheese straws turned to inspect the new arrivals. Their curiosity satisfied, they resumed talk of that week's pressing issues in excitable voices.

There was mention of a Khmer Rouge ambush in Cambodia. Utopia picked up on the fact that the writer had survived blindfolds and man-traps and a nearly fatal bout of malaria. The story was now set to be a Pulitzer prizewinner. Then came the implications of Martha's departure from the fact-checking department. An indispensable asset to the magazine for over seven years she was the only person who could work with you-know-who. Martha would visit him personally in his Upper East Side apartment to iron out the finer points of his Middle Eastern stories. Who on earth could replace her? they agonised.

Utopia was intrigued.

This was a seam of New York previously unexplored. It was the closest she had come yet to a London drinks party, in as much as it was a gathering at home with wine and not a model or paparazzi magnet in sight, at any rate.

"Marina, how wonderful to see you and how divine that you've brought a friend. A writer, I hope."

"Dora, this is Utopia."

"Oh, how I swoon with envy. How I would adore such a name. Such grandiloquence. And how long have you been in New York?"

"Three months."

"And why, oh why, have you left that most glorious of cities, London?"

Utopia laughed. "I was born in New York."

"Well, there are more Brits here than we know what to do with. I mean, really, it would only be fair if they let me go over there for a time, wouldn't it?"

"You're quite welcome to it, darling," remarked Marina who, as Utopia knew only too well, wouldn't move back if you paid her.

"Anyway, you two, drinks are over there. Do help yourself. I've got to run and talk to Mikhail. He's just over from Moscow for a week. Writing a book on economic espionage and looks perfectly lost, wouldn't you agree?" Dora nodded towards the back of the room where a man in a trench coat was seen to be sitting in a window-seat, his head swathed in cigarette smoke.

"He looks about to deliver an urgent message," said Marina.

"Quite," said Dora and marched off to receive this message, her heaped cleavage wobbling in anticipation.

On the way over in the cab, Marina had filled Utopia in

on what to expect. She had done a good job. Dora's sexual orientation was anyone's guess, said Marina. She loved men, she loved women, she had once been married and lived with three cats, neutered toms, Zeus, Apollo and Poseidon. She was a free spirit. This Utopia could see.

Dora was a small, voluptuous creature pressed into a velvet *décolleté* dress in royal blue. She couldn't have been five feet tall. Her hair was thin and dark and she had surprised-looking eyes, as though permanently excited. Utopia felt sure that she was. Marina had described her as a latterday Dorothy Parker. She worked at the *New Yorker* and had done so for years. She was the survivor of an era when the tyranny of popular culture was ignored and writers were given free rein to write about whatever they pleased. Dora believed in the value of pooling intellectual resources. Her monthly gatherings of journalists, editors, writers and poets were an attempt to elevate this collective brainpower to something beyond media savvy. Publicists, or enemies of integrity as they were vilified, were banned. So were mobile telephones.

They made their way to the kitchen past a table covered with plates of crudités, blinis and damp quiche squares. They passed a trio of girls in scoop-necked black, discussing a Mexican author in rapturous tones. They found the fridge. Marina got on her hands and knees to try to get a bottle of white from the back of the shelf. She was accosted by a man in a bowtie. "Marina. Good to see you." He had a gruff voice that belied his age. He could have been sixty-five though clearly he wasn't.

"Bob. Hi. How are you?"

He nodded. "Can't complain."

Any minute now, Utopia expected him to put a pipe to his lips and tuck both thumbs into the V of his waistcoat. Dressed in a striped blazer, he appeared as the perfect young fogey. He introduced himself as a Bostonian and his accent came across as Anglo-upper-class with a cold. Marina continued wrestling with retrieving the bottle minus the rest of the fridge.

"How about yourself? Been out to the Hamptons much?"

"As often as I can. I want you to meet Utopia. She hasn't been to one of Dora's salons before."

"How exciting. An *ingénue*. And where do you work?" asked Bob, radiating good-humoured interest.

"I've just moved over from London."

"Ah, so. And how's the general rate of success?"

"Well . . ." started Utopia, unsure about mentioning *HQ* but continuing nonetheless. After all, it was only the last call, future meeting or current commission that validated one's claim to an identity. "I'm working for someone called Jean Weiner up at *HQ*. She says it could turn into something more permanent."

Then, just as the heavy-handed and she now realised presumptuous mention of permanent rolled off her tongue, Utopia noticed that Bob was a redhead. He was also in the process of using his outstretched arm to usher a fourth member into their group.

"I don't think you've met my partner. Meg, Utopia."

Utopia felt weak. She took Meg's hand of introduction and the sensation of being hit from behind by a moving object felt physically real. Prickly heat scorched her cheeks and she forced a smile. So this was Meg, the girl whose Rolodex she had plundered, whose desk she had tampered with. She felt her heart pound. How could she have been so stupid and indiscreet here of all places? she berated herself.

"Are you the one working up at *HQ*?" said Meg.

Meg was agreeably pretty with brown hair pulled back

in a bunch. Her eyebrows met in a stripe when she frowned and she was wearing a long-sleeved white shirt. It was, thought Utopia, a waitress look. "Yes," she said, as cheerfully as she could while hesitant to continue. What she wanted to do was slink back down Dora's hallway, through her metal front door and disappear into the East Village.

"How's it been?"

Utopia nodded. She was unsure of Meg's tone. It was unclear whether Meg had overheard her or not. Yet she found herself fascinated to meet the girl whose identity she had assumed for a week. At the same time she begrudged Meg's existence as she did, say, P's ex-girlfriend. This was the girl who had had first innings. It was an odd feeling and not one with which she felt entirely comfortable. Utopia noticed that Meg was wearing a pair of shoes like some she had left behind in London. They looked a little like brogues.

"Good. How's your week been?"

"Good. I was meant to be going away but had things to do in the city."

Marina had disappeared.

"I see."

"How's Jean?"

"Fine."

"But you might be staying on, you say," interrupted Bob, with immaculate timing.

Utopia stopped short.

Meg frowned. Her expression shut like a trap. "Really?"

"Well, I mean, you know, well, that's what I'd . . . I'd like," Utopia stammered, her tinge blossoming.

"I don't know where."

"No," confirmed Utopia, aware of digging the hole deeper every time she opened her mouth. "It was just something Jean said. That's all."

"Jean?"

There was a strangulated silence. Utopia watched as, without another word, Meg left for the kitchen. Bob followed.

Cringing, Utopia peered into her glass.

She wanted to dive in and drown face down in her measly inch of alcohol. Instead she went in search of Marina. She found her propping up a bookshelf. She was in conversation with a tall female wearing a ruby silk jacket. With her hair piled on her head, the woman had the haughty air of a Republican wife. Her name was Lewis. Lewis covered social affairs for the *New York Observer*. The two women were outraged by the mediocrity of August's calendar. It had been an unforgivably dull month. Jigging from foot to foot like a small child, too distracted to decipher whatever it was they were talking about, Utopia agonised over what to do. A minute later she bolted for the bathroom and shut the door.

She stood in front of the mirror and turned on the taps. She opened wide her eyes and pursed her lips. She wasn't one of life's natural pouters, she hadn't the lips, but that didn't stop her trying when no one else could see. She felt heady not with wine but risk. She didn't know what to think. That Jean had created a political triangle struck her as cruel yet her cheeks burned brighter at the thought. Did she really know something of Meg's future that Meg did not? It seemed far-fetched. It could so easily prove to have been an indiscretion prompted by Jean's over-enthusiasm at the party invitation.

Utopia studied her reflection.

There was the strawberry vein on her left cheek, the dry skin above her eyes and the makeup clotting her lashes. What was new was the ambition that had lodged in her chest like indigestion. She wanted to stay on at *HQ* more than anything else. For a moment the person looking back at her, a person free of doubt, was a stranger.

She dabbed at her face with cold water and turned off the taps. She took a final uneasy glance at herself, then dried her hands on a towel. Rubbing them, she remembered Meg's face. There had been a flicker of horror that this girl before her, Utopia, posed a threat. Meg's eyes had searched her face for an understanding that had failed to come.

Stabbed by a twinge of remorse, Utopia wondered if she shouldn't find Meg to try and fudge an explanation. She hated leaving it like this but what was there to say? She couldn't properly clarify matters when she herself knew nothing and probably had it all wrong.

She unlocked the door.

She ran straight into Dora, who was transporting a plate of stuffed cabbage leaves.

"There you are. Come and meet Larry. He used to be an editor on *Newsweek*. Now he writes books on political thought," she said. "And he speaks Swahili."

Utopia followed Dora into the kitchen. The absence of the bathroom door unnerved her. Perhaps Meg had been telling people about their conversation. Perhaps she would find herself being asked to leave for making trouble and upsetting the guests. She was introduced to Larry.

Larry had a blotchy face like a baked potato. He was waving a breadstick. He was talking about the plight of the Tamils in Sri Lanka, having recently returned from a posting in Colombo as Sri Lankan correspondent. He glanced at Utopia with disdain as Dora introduced her, "She does arts things," and continued his conversation with an Asian girl pinned against the door. Utopia lingered, an unwelcome straggler, and her eyes travelled the room.

Everyone she looked at resembled Meg so she stopped looking.

Then her mind wandered and she found herself with Saul. He had left a message to say that he was cooking dinner. There would be a few of them over. Why didn't she come join them?

She mulled it over. There was no reason why not.

All of a sudden she had to escape this literary love-in with its damask curtains and wilting celery sticks. She couldn't face bumping into Meg. She had nothing to say. She felt trapped. Looking around, she ruled the men too small and the women fierce and all with such earnest faces. She had to get out.

She made her way to the door. Dora was pressed against a rakish male, long in the tooth with a receding hair line. She was smoking cigarettes from a mother-of-pearl cigarette holder and chuckling deliciously. Butting in, Utopia went to thank her. Dora planted air kisses, three of them, just beyond reach. Her eyes were animated while inexpressive and she smelt carelessly of gin or was it vodka. Marina was ensconced nearby with the Russian. They were smoking his filterless cigarettes, which burned with the aroma of bonfire leaves.

"I'm off."

"Really? Well, I'm going to stay a little longer, darling," said Marina.

"I'm going to Saul's."

"OK. *Ciao, bella.*"

Marina turned to her new friend "Now, how far exactly is your dacha from Moscow? I absolutely must visit Russia sometime soon. I feel so dreadfully out of touch."

# Chapter Nine

Dora's street was busy with police manoeuvres. The local station was on her block and the NYPD ocean of blue had spilt out of the doors and on to the tarmac. Cars were pulling up, officers clambering out, ambulance chasers loitering while suspects were being dragged into the building. Utopia caught a couple of wolf whistles as she wound her way through the mayhem.

On the corner of Avenue A she hailed a cab.

It didn't take long.

Drawing up outside Saul's studio, she saw the disco ball in motion. Globules of light were whirling across the room. She pounded on the steel mesh, then peered in between the metal rods through the frosted glass. Saul's head appeared from behind a shelf. He walked over to the door and unlocked it. He kissed her. "We've just started."

"Eating?"

"Cooking. Vivienne's here."

Vivienne was the new assistant. The one with the laugh. Utopia felt herself bristle.

"Hi," a voice called.

Just as she had imagined Vivienne was blonde. She also

had a pierced nose and gamine crop. She was dressed in a T-shirt labelled *Johnson's Baddy Powder* and a denim skirt made out of an old pair of jeans.

"What do you want to drink?" asked Saul.

"Vodka. With cranberry."

Vivienne was tearing at the romaine lettuce. She was wearing two plastic rings, which clicked when they met. Utopia stirred her Sea Breeze with a teaspoon which clinked noisily. Her irritation at finding Vivienne here was unfair. Saul's assistants always hung out after work. But she couldn't help herself. She took a sip of vodka and its fiery breath roared through her.

Saul joined her at the table and the stranglehold of her day began to let go. His tangle of curls was pushed up from his face by the goggles he wore on top of his head. She watched his lashes stroke the hollows beneath his eyes. They were ringed with smoky shadows, which tormented her with thoughts of lust. She was sometimes forced to look away.

"I want to take your clothes off," he would whisper beneath his breath.

She wanted to kiss him but grabbed a slab of forearm instead. "Who's coming?"

"Kurt. Anna. I called Felix after you said you'd seen him. It's been a while. He had to go to some opening at the Whitney. Might cruise by later."

The metal mesh crashed against the glass. Kurt's voice was heard through the door. "Hello."

Saul leaped up to turn down the flame. The pan of water was boiling over. Utopia went to get the door.

"Hi," said Anna, Kurt's girlfriend, as she greeted her with an embrace. Her eyes were wet with enthusiasm. "Great to see you."

Anna was waifishly thin, berry brown and immaculately

dressed. This evening it was a silk dress and silver sandals. Utopia led them to the kitchen, where Kurt deposited a six-pack on the table. The light reflected off his sheen of sweat in mirror image of the disco ball.

"Yo, what's up dude?" called Saul, who always indulged his Bart Simpson banter with his German neighbour. It was a form of male bonding, which stopped just short of a quick wrestle.

"Ja. Most excellent, dude."

Utopia laughed as Anna winced. Her tiny shoulders rose and fell in a shrug. Anna hated the Americanisms encouraged by Saul. Her preferred image of Kurt was as a sophisticated Berliner. She liked all the hard edges implicit in his heavy accent. Utopia had noticed her to use European where others used cool. To be European was the highest commendation available. Anna worked for a German-owned gallery.

"Can I get a vodka on the rocks, Saul?" Anna interrupted.

"So, man, I've got the contacts back from the night shoot and they're great," said Kurt. "The wide-angle lens brings it all out, man. It looks surreal with your white skin and the flashing lights. Ja, it's really wild."

Saul poured Absolut into a row of tumblers on the counter and grinned. Vivienne sat down at the table and reached for a cigarette. "I'm Vivienne," she introduced herself.

"Vivienne's working for me. Getting this order finished," said Saul, turning round.

"Do you do sculpture?" asked Anna.

"Paint, but I got to pay the rent. And it's great to learn how to use a blow-torch," she added, with a sidelong glance at Saul.

There was a pause.

"Yeah. So, how's the gallery?" he asked.

"Great," said Anna. "We've got an exhibition by this female artist from New Mexico. She uses rock. We've had to have the floor redone. Seriously, guys, one of her pieces fell right through it."

"How long's it on for?"

"And you would love her, Saul. She's this ex-New Yorker who's totally out there. She lives in an adobe house, drives a Chevvy with, like, no brakes, takes peyote with, like, the Hopis and she's a total dynamite freak."

"Hey. Sounds like my kind of woman."

Saul's other hobby besides welding was blowing things up. It was Kurt's job to film the spectacle on the roof of their building. He had recently showed a video art piece at a mixed group show in which one of his sculptures was blasted to the skies. After the explosion the camera lingered on the smoking remains of the crumpled metal while a German choral arrangement played in the background. The art critic from *New York* magazine hated it. She described it as fascistic. Saul accused her of missing the point and failing to see the sense of humour in the work. He had then gone on to say that he had laughed all the way through *Reservoir Dogs*, which did nothing to win her favour. She criticised his fascination with bombs as violent dementia. This he loved.

"You can meet her," Anna promised. "She'll be in town next week."

As Saul chopped onions, Kurt topped up the drinks. At the end of the table, Utopia began to feel invisible. She watched Vivienne talking and laughing and found herself beset by doubts, which descended like night. It was as though she were watching the scene from afar. She was no longer sure why she was here.

She watched Saul pour a bag of pasta into the pot. The pockets of his trousers were fat with wads of paper, a drill head, charcoal pencils, a steel ruler and a dentist's torch. She wanted him to care but he wasn't looking. Kurt had his arm around him and they were talking shop. The second time she slept with Saul he had made an announcement.

"Right now, I don't do relationships."

Utopia had smiled. Well, surprise, surprise.

"Me neither," she heard herself say.

"OK. So, who are you honest with?" he asked.

"Me? What's it got to do with me?"

"I want to know."

"I don't know. It depends. Some days you're honest, other days it's all a lie. I'm honest with different people in different ways, I suppose. Everybody is."

"Right. That's why I've got Gerta."

"Who?"

"My shrink."

So there was no point saying Utopia hadn't been told. Saul was self-sufficient and needed no one but Gerta. Ironically it was probably this I'm-so-complex-nobody-understands-me statement that had attracted her in the first place. She had been offered a challenge and accepted it. Stupidly.

Overhead the disco ball was leisurely twisting the night away. The beams from the lamps hit the sphere's mirrored surfaces like lasers. Balls of light spun round the studio. They glided across the abstract triptych on the wall. They slithered over the shelves stacked with tools, past the fluorescent yellow generator and the glass-fronted apothecary cabinet found on the street and lit up the exhaust pipe that snaked its way along the length of the room. The fan was on in an attempt to extricate some of the heat. Its fuzz whirred alongside the stereo jazz.

"Yo. We're eating," said Saul.

He passed plates of pasta along the table. Kurt wolfed while Anna picked. Sitting opposite Saul, Utopia toyed with hers. All of a sudden too tired to eat, she thought of Jean and her crayola makeup and machine-gun laugh, her technicolour dress sense and rivers of paper. She couldn't stop speculating on what Jean's declarations would turn out to mean.

"You know, Saul, the next bomb we build should be out in the desert, man. Let's go to Death Valley and make the biggest fucking bang," said Kurt, ripping a piece of bread off the loaf.

"Jesus, are you trying to kill yourself?" said Anna, slowly winding her fork. She wasn't the sort of girl to be seen with pasta dangling from her mouth, thought Utopia.

"Relax. Saul knows what he's doing."

Saul said nothing but continued sucking strings of tagliatelle into his mouth with a smirk. Utopia knew that expression. She wanted to feel his mouth beneath hers. But she finished what she could and went and put her plate in the sink. "I'm going," she said.

"No," he said, seizing her wrist as she stood by his side. "I bought pastries for dessert. I bought them for you. Stay."

"Can't."

She wanted to ensure a place in his bed but she didn't want to share him. It was that simple. She bent to kiss him. He refused to let go. "Stay."

"Can't."

"You mean won't."

She looked at him hard, with feelings too vague for words.

"OK, OK."

He followed her to the door. She was tempted to reverse her decision but it was better this way.

" 'Bye," she said.

# Chapter Ten

"Utopia, a table at Marco's for one at the back. Number will be in Meg's Rolodex," said Jean, ringing through.

Utopia was opening the mail. She was sorting it into piles. Invitations worth considering, *Vanity Fair's* Hollywood Issue Party, made the A-list pile. Others such as Newark Library's Thirtieth Anniversary Poetry and Music Night, were flipped on to the to-think-about pile. To her left mounted a stack of press releases, cassettes and CDs, magazines and readers letters. She had been told to put Meg's mail in a metal basket. It didn't take a genius to work out which of these envelopes contained prizes, the concert tickets, backstage passes, première invitations and VIP accreditations. She was now on the hunt.

"Pink envelope. Sort of transparent. Servin & Lilyman at the top," Marina had said.

It was an invitation to *the* party of next week she was looking for. It was the publication of a screenplay by a Hollywood screenwriter and was taking place in an Ivy League club. Utopia had been taken to lunch at the very same club by an ex-colleague of her father. It was Gothic and gloomy. She had been struck by the number of old men curled up in armchairs like bats.

Anyway, here she was desperately rooting through the mail for a condom-coloured envelope as though it was her dream ticket. She understood the need to get out, she had met Jean at a party after all, but this was more about Marina's ability to instill a sense of having to be there which bordered on panic. Life would not be worth living if she didn't make it to this party.

"It's all a lottery," Marina had said. "And this could be your lucky number."

She supposed.

Jean was occupied with calls.

The red buttons on Utopia's telephone were flashing up and down like power-surging traffic-lights. The level of anxiety generated by the White House story was marked by closed doors, rounds of meetings and a trail of empty cups and cans left in offices and conference rooms. Another two faxes had been fired off this morning and another Fed-Ex had been sent. Diane had breezed past Utopia's desk and into Jean's office first thing this morning with her dark glasses on. Jean had still been involved with her muffin.

The secrecy shrouding the event and the talk of espionage enlisted to secure it made for paranoia. There had even been mention of bugging. Utopia had overheard Goldie, the celebrity booker, being ordered to deploy her columnist spies to discover just how close New York's other top glossy was to securing the interview of the year. The First Lady was only prepared to talk to one of America's two leading magazines and they were running neck and neck. Todd had suggested they start taking bets.

Utopia couldn't concentrate.

Anxiety over lunch with Jean and what would or would

not be said far surpassed fears regarding the First Lady's decision. And yet Utopia felt she had done OK this week. She had found Jean an invitation to *the* party of this week and everyone had been there, according to Marina who had got lucky with a South African model. She had also suggested three features ideas, and Jean had seemed pretty keen on the one about the next generation of astronaut wives.

As for Meg, the memory of their awkward silence continued to stir feelings of guilt, and she could hardly escape Meg's existence when she was sitting at her desk surrounded by her possessions. There was the potted Saguaro cactus from Santa Fé, the Graceland calendar and the multi-coloured Barbados sand in a jar. But somehow she had managed to divorce her hopes from her conscience. She wanted something belonging to someone else and she wasn't going to deny it.

Perhaps it was being in New York that had toughened her up.

"Hey."

"Why do you always have to do that?"

"Because I can."

It was Todd. He was wearing a green tie crawling with serpents.

"What are they?"

"The serpents of lust."

"Right."

"I'm going to need that music story you've been editing. I'll need to start checking it before you go."

The finality of his words sent deflation coursing through her. "Of course."

"Lunch?"

"I'm going out with Jean."

"Another time then, huh?"

She nodded.

With a shrug of his shoulders, he left her. She watched his bobbing head disappear round the corner. She wrestled with goodbye. She had to face facts. Obediently shoving the mail to one side, she found the music story. It was a profile of three bands from Texas with devil in their name. Todd was right. It was her last day. She had better finish up.

"Your usual table, Ms Weiner," said the restaurateur.

He was wearing a mustard sweater thrown over his shoulders and tied in a knot. He looked like a boy scout, thought Utopia as she waited for him to do the salute.

"Marco, you're a god," said Jean as she kissed him.

The restaurant was walking distance from the office. Only now that they had arrived did Utopia realise that her personal running commentary had encompassed every trivial – and not so trivial – thought to have flitted through her mind. This had gone so far as to mention Jean's ex-husband, the one subject she knew from Todd to be strictly off limits.

According to Todd, Jean's father was a millionaire who had made his fortune in cardboard boxes. Jean was involved in a legal suit with her ex-husband who was trying to sue her for alimony. And while Jean was infertile – an STD problem, said Todd, who clearly knew more than he ought – her husband's twenty-one-year-old assistant was expecting his baby. Knowing all this, Utopia had managed to ask if he lived in New York. Jesus Christ, what was she trying to do? Beg Jean to call it a day. The palms of her hands were filmy with sweat. She was anxious and it showed.

"Thank you," said Jean, as Marco showed them up to the mezzanine.

The restaurant was crowded with midtown business. Tables of suits were grazing on roasted vegetables, a Mexican boy was operating a pepper-pot and someone was making a goodbye speech. Utopia took the seat at the table and tried to ignore the man's parting words. On either side the walls were hung with cheery abstract paintings. The result was garish. Utopia took the menu and read it to conceal her angst.

Marco was going nowhere. Chit-chat tinkled from his lips. He was talking either about the price of his new car or a new bar. Utopia reread the menu but she couldn't see a thing. What she craved was a large glass of white wine but no one drank at lunch in New York, well, no one except Marina who would order a bottle, then another, to get – as she said – the show on the road.

Jean ordered and Utopia went for the same.

A salmon Caesar salad, dressing on the side, and a Pellegrino water with lime, no ice. Marco took his cue.

Jean began breaking off pieces of bread, dipping them into the plate of olive oil and putting them into her mouth all at once. She had a horsey mouth and a scrum of teeth. "So, how do you feel this week's gone?" she asked.

Utopia paused. This was multiple choice and she had to get it right. Jean chewed as she waited for an answer and her rainy eyes rippled as she blinked.

"Great. Very great. I mean, very good. Yes."

Jean didn't seem perturbed by her failure of a response. "Right. Well, I think it's been good. I like the way you work. You get on with the others and you're connected."

Connected?

Utopia was far from sure about this final remark, although since she did have Marina as well as a few stolen numbers from Meg's Rolodex, perhaps it was true.

She surveyed Jean's face. Her skin was pulled tight over big bones and her copper lipstick had bled into the creases around her mouth like varicose veins.

"And I've just got to get rid of that girl."

Utopia held her breath. She couldn't believe it. She began rolling a piece of bread into a greasy ball, harder and harder, until finally it collapsed beneath the strain. She could feel herself blush.

"Meg's done her time. She's been hanging on, hoping something else would come up but no one *told* her to wait around."

Utopia nodded. Jean was telling her story. "So what does she do? Tells Diane that she isn't happy with the way the department's being run. Says she wants more responsibility and that we're being scooped on all the features. Not a clever move, coming from a girl who's got a master's in journalism from Yale, is it?"

Jean took a long drink of water as Utopia digested what was being said. Unprepared for this confession, she couldn't help but enjoy the offer of preferential treatment.

"So," said Jean as she poured the remainder of the water bottle into her glass, "I'm going to tell her Monday."

Monday sounded very soon. It was two days away, Utopia realised.

"Better for both of us if she moves on. In the meantime, you've got to keep this to yourself. Meg's been on the magazine a couple of years and people can have feelings about this kind of thing."

Utopia was stunned into silence. "Yes, no. Of course."

A waiter had begun sweeping the crumbs from their table with a miniature dustpan and brush. Its swishing couched their pause in a whisper. Jean had devoured her salad and her plate lay bare. Utopia's remained untouched, its stack of leaves congealed into a soggy mass. The waiter hesitated. "Finished. Thanks," she told him.

"It's going to work out, you and me. Yes, you're really going make a difference. I can see that," said Jean as she waved for the bill.

It arrived pronto and Utopia watched Jean sign her name. It was a quick-fire signature, grandiose and indecipherable, rather like Jean. With her scalp tingling in disbelief, Utopia was tempted to squeeze Jean's gold ringed hands spread before her. Instead she twisted her napkin into a knot.

They stood up to leave.

The restaurant door swung shut behind them.

Outside all was white, distant and atomised. Waiting for the street to re-emerge Utopia was reminded by something, perhaps the light's brilliance, like a studio back-drop, of her mother's modelling here in New York. It had only lasted a year, if that. The opportunity had fallen into her lap. A man at a party had fallen in love with her face and said that, with her long hair and skinny hips, she was an archetypal London girl. He said he wanted to shoot her. Her mother had two small children yet saw no reason why not so she did it.

Utopia had always been intrigued by the black and white photographs in her parents' hallway. The pictures of her mother, with kohl-striped eyes and flying hair, a loose limb shooting ahead as she stared into the camera, had represented all that was cavalier, glamorous even, about her parents' past. When her mother had stifled her with her pettiness, she had looked to these images for another truth. Her mother as a free spirit. And, as she fumbled through those messy teenage years, she had wondered how, if ever, she could replicate her mother's perfection. With Liberty it was different. Comparisons were redundant. She was big and blonde, and the differences were what they were.

Utopia paused.

It was odd but, thinking back to it now, it wasn't impossible that her mother had been photographed for *HQ*.

Jean had donned a pair of white Chanel sunglasses like two mini life rings and they entered the sea of shoulders pouring down Madison Avenue. The ground beneath Utopia's feet rattled. Looking down, she found herself stranded on a grating beneath which the city's bowels disappeared into darkness. The ground shuddered. Piles of litter blew like autumn leaves as a train rumbled past. Momentarily paralysed, she leaped back on to the sidewalk in fear for her life. The crowds seemed to part as she caught up with Jean. "Thought I'd lost you," said Jean.

Utopia imagined her mother's response to the news. She would have been impressed to see her daughter embraced by New York's glossy establishment, she thought. It was a happy sentiment.

# Chapter Eleven

Every day was garbage day where Little Italy met Chinatown. By six a.m. the bleeping trucks were annihilating the
peace as they cleared the streets of bin-bags, boxes and
restaurant remains. Utopia glanced at her clock and fell
back on her pillow with a sigh. The noise pollution never
died in the city that never slept.

She drifted back to sleep. She found herself in her
grandmother's house, a strawberry bungalow minutes from
the sea. A water pipe was leaking in the broom cupboard
underneath the stairs. Utopia and Liberty were showing it
to the plumber, who was wielding various lethal-looking
tools. Her grandmother and mother were arguing.

"You let them run wild, those girls. It's not right." Her
grandmother was shaking her frosty curls.

Crammed into the cupboard, Utopia struggled with
claustrophobia. It was the same sense of entrapment associated with her grandmother's larder. In the middle of cake-
baking, it was customary for Utopia to have to find the
bottle of vanilla essence on the second shelf. The fear of
entering that long strip pantry, with its dim light and neg-
lected mouse traps, was suffocating. The odour of rotting

mice, like the mysteries of death, terrified. Utopia would insist on keeping the door ajar. Light now came streaming in.

"Yoo-hoo."

It was Johann.

She kicked to the surface. She sometimes wrote down her dreams in the hope of finding clues. Dreams were by definition the better place to be. For months following her mother's death, there had been a recurrent one in which both were sitting side by side at the piano. Her mother was playing and Utopia was turning the pages of music, sheet by sheet. Nothing happened and neither spoke but it was the sense of togetherness she cherished. For a time it was the most vivid image she had of her mother before the cancer took hold.

She rolled over and closed her eyes.

England was still a place of death.

When she thought of home, it was the shiny black cars snaking their way up to the crematorium in a dreary north London suburb she remembered. It was her sister's comment that her skirt was too short, did she have to wear stockings, and P's head-shake and strong hand. It was the church service and her struggle to locate her mother as they stood to sing hymns familiar from school. Her nervousness at leaving the pew to climb the pulpit, put down her book and clutch the sides of the lectern as she cleared her throat. "Blackberrying" by Sylvia Plath. The poem was a favourite of hers and her mother's. Her mother had read it to her as a child. There was a line about a blackberry alley going down to the sea, which they liked to imagine was the one at the back of her grandmother's house.

She had watched her father cry.

Later, when the sun came out, she and her sister carried

the bunches of lilies used to decorate the church back to the house. It was a short distance and the only time that the two of them were alone together. The flowers shimmered in the afternoon light, and as they walked in silence, both tipped their heads at precisely the same moment to bury their noses in the petals. Why had this moment remained with her? For the simple reason it was shared with her sister.

"A hundred."

"What?"

"Fahrenheit."

"Oh, Jesus."

Still standing at her door, Johann was knotting his tie, a strip of tangerine rind. It meant that today was Monday. Disorientated, Utopia rubbed her eyes as England shrank from view and movement from the fan fluttered across her face.

Where had the weekend gone?

She waited as, step by step, it came flooding back.

Saul had been holed up in his studio and refused to see her. He was on deadline, he said. So she had gone with Johann to a party on a roof in Brooklyn. There was a recollection of him dancing on a table and a fish tank bleeding crimson as someone unkindly tipped in a bottle of wine. They had emerged home yesterday at sometime around midday. Neither had had enough for the cab fare across the river so they had been forced to ride the subway with cheery Sunday families on their way to Prospect Park.

"Postcard." Johann dropped it on the bed and left for work.

Utopia examined it.

It was a Union Jack defaced with safety pins. She flipped it over and held it close to avoid the fingers of sunlight clawing her face. She heard his voice pronouncing each word in turn.

> *Dear U*                                     *10 August*
>     *Went to see the Edward Hopper retrospective at the Tate and thought of you sitting in New York diners, planning your next move. Julian has moved in while he has his roof done. He can't get rid of the builders. I can't get rid of him. Finished the first draft. Working title "Walking in Circles". What do you think? How's work? Be careful. Love and luck, P*

Arrested in print and the sentiment of distance, she missed him. It was his shiny, soaped face and wet hair, the nicotined fingers and roaring breath, the sound of his keyboard tapping and the hungry call of his voice as she lay in bed. "Oi, U."

But regret confused things in the same way that thoughts of P in the company of Saul left her scrambled with panic, her loyalties shot. Emotions refused to remain where they ought. She no longer knew what was right or what was wrong.

And where did that leave her?

Alone in New York she guessed.

She read the card again and waited for the tremor to pass. She quickly filed it between the pages of a book.

In her grey T-shirt, which curtained her knickers, she dragged herself out of bed and went to make coffee. She felt dizzy with emotion, hung-over from the weekend, and worryingly disconnected from the floor beneath her feet. The sun was climbing. Soon it would be positioned right above the building and her body temperature would follow its ascent. She gazed out of the open windows at the skyline. The water towers that stalked the horizon appeared somehow content and she wished she could join them.

But she was restless. She needed to talk so she picked up the telephone and dialled his number.

"Studio."

"Vivienne?"

She looked at her watch. It was nine fifteen. It was too early for Vivienne's Monday shift and Saul refused to pay out for assistants at the weekend. Anyway, he said he was going to be working alone because he needed the space.

"Is Saul there?"

"In the shower."

"Oh."

No other words came.

She hung up.

Haunted by Vivienne's face and her overnight hair, Utopia wandered distractedly around the apartment. What was there to doubt? Vivienne had spent the night in the studio with Saul. She felt humiliated. Despite predicting exactly this, despite what she knew him to be, she had hoped he would extend his feelings beyond the bedroom and respect her absence. But no.

What a useless fuck.

In the building opposite a blind flew up to reveal a naked man. He opened the window and yawned. There was movement in the bed behind and a developed flank of thigh shot out from beneath a sheet. It was a familiar scene. She tried to calculate how long it had been, her affair with Saul.

She had telephoned him a few weeks after arriving, had discovered that he lived round the corner and been in and out of his bed ever since. The casual and somehow reckless nature of the affair wasn't something she had experienced before. It had nothing to do with P and their relationship back home, well, not in real terms. How she could be attracted to one when she was attached to another, she didn't know and didn't want to know.

She was beyond explaining.

Saul was a friend of a friend of a friend.

Their affair was an extension of her affair with the city. He possessed the same magnetic energy and the same frantic pace. Saul had no time for hesitancy since what was there to doubt? And she never had to endure the stage of saying things she didn't want to say because Saul had invited her in without demanding anything in return. She was attracted to his sense of belonging and the way he found something to say to every person who lived on the block, Puerto Rican, Korean, Cuban, Chinese. There was always the exchange of a handshake or a couple of words.

Hey man, *que pasa?*

She felt secure with the fluid, one-handed way he reversed his truck into a space with one hand on the wheel and the other round her, as cans of fuel, tools and empties rolled around in the boot. Saul had a different way of doing things. He would solder the handle back on a pan instead of throwing it away. He listened to hip-hop and baked his own bread. She was curious about his ways and wanted to have a look round.

She was a tourist here, after all.

Their first date had been at a show in the corridor of a Russian Orthodox church on the Bowery. It was an exhibition of paraphernalia from the former Soviet Union, military documents, newspaper cuttings, ticket stubs and slices of map. She had wandered along the hallway, oblivious to the anonymous faces until she spotted him beside an ice barrel full of beers. He was wearing orange overalls and his fireman's coat. He was shorter than she had imagined but he had charisma.

You couldn't miss him.

"I'm Utopia," she introduced herself.

"Hey, I was wondering what happened to you," he enthused, and forgot his companion. "Have you checked out the work?"

"Yes."

"I've got an idea. How about we go to the KGB bar for vodka? D'you know it or do you want to stay?" He spoke fast gripping her arm.

"Yes. No. I don't know. The where?"

"The KGB bar. It's the old Ukrainian Communist head-quarters. Not far."

KGB's was virtually empty. They settled in a dim corner and their discussion had grown heated over glasses of Stoli. Frozen. Saul talked Russia, his studio and Bonnie his ex. Utopia in turn tried to summarise her reasons for coming to New York but out it all came in a torrent as though she had been mute for a month.

She paused.

Though passionate it had never been much of a romance. Saul was by nature selfish and her intention had been to spend time alone, to simplify her life and think for one, not for two. There had always been a strict set of rules. Saul had been adamant that their time together could never take priority but had to be spontaneous and by implication free. Yet somehow this was fine by her. Meanwhile everything else came fastidiously ordered. Work schedules, assistants' tasks, timetables, phone costs and lunch expenses were all itemised, typed out on recycled paper and displayed around the studio. Above all, Saul was a control freak.

Utopia picked up the phone.

The temptation to ring his number again was excruciating although she knew it was pointless. She would hang up as soon as he answered. She couldn't explain the logic of it because there wasn't any. It was like digging your fingernails into your palms until they grazed or chewing your lip until pulpy shreds came away like boiled tomato skin.

She hung up.

She could hear a Chinese neighbour listening to his messages. The whir of the tape's rewind motion was followed by a burst of choppy Cantonese. She could smell spicy noodles from the restaurant next door. It was a reminder of the mass of life that supported her fifth floor existence. The sewing-machinists were there on the third floor opposite and the naked man, one floor below, was crouching in front of his fridge and scratching like a monkey.

She felt her top lip glisten.

She impulsively yanked her T-shirt up and over her face. It bunched behind her head and left her breasts defiantly on show. The blades rotating above applauded with a waft of air. It tickled and felt devilishly good. But Monkey Man had spotted her. He waved. She blushed, embarrassed, what was she thinking?, and hastily rearranged her T-shirt.

Hey, check out the crazy chick opposite – she's exposing herself again.

Through the haze now came the memory of Jean and her promised call. Disillusioned and angry with Saul, Utopia couldn't face the prospect of yet more disappointment. It threatened like a slow puncture.

What if Jean didn't call?

What if no one ever called?

She couldn't just sit here and wait to be let down. She had to get out. She would take the N or the R uptown and have other thoughts, happy thoughts, in the pool, she decided. She stood up and went to find her goggles.

Monkey Man's mate had disappeared and he was making the bed.

# Chapter Twelve

Slicing through the water led to thoughts of sex. Conscious of every muscle in her body, she used all the strength of her legs to power her. Lap after lap she swam. She was alone in the pool and the water felt clean and invigorating. She fantasised about doing it right here, right now, and her body ached in anticipation. She opened her eyes. The sun cast streaks of light across the water, and as she swam through these, she felt goaded into swimming longer and further. Gliding faster and faster, she lost all sense of time and place to the throb of her breathing and the pattern of her strokes. The words Fuck You Saul formed an easy beat as her arms hit the water.

Harder and harder.

Fuck you, fuck you, fuck you.

Until finally there was nothing but blue.

As her pounding eased, Utopia ruled this hotel pool to be her own swimmer's paradise. It was both glamorous and tawdry. It was her fantasy while she was here that she was just passing through, had someone waiting for her upstairs in a carpeted room and was having a dip before meeting him downstairs in the bar. She loved the luxury of towelling robes, breaking open seals on soaps and shampoos and having a Spanish woman ask if you wanted massage.

All for twelve bucks.

The hotel fell into the midtown zone where the city's tourist attractions, Broadway musicals and stereo shops overlapped with a once-thriving red light district. She looked out at the blinking neon of Times Square and a vertical *Girls Girls Girls* sign through the plate-glass window. The giant logos and thirty-foot models reaffirmed why she was in this city. Communing with Times Square was about communing with America. It was greedy and she liked it.

Her serenity died.

Two flabby men began swimming butterfly stroke and waves began hitting the tiles. Butterfly stroke was so antisocial. She dipped down underwater and spied on their bloated bodies magnified under water like hippos travelling upstream. Mesmerised, she was tempted to stay and watch a little longer but her pit of anxiety wasn't going away. She needed an answer from Jean. She needed to know.

She went to get changed.

She stood in the shower and worried. Then she focused on the water bruising her face and forced her mind blank. She got out. She put on her skirt, clipped on her bra, tugged on her vest and smudged moisturiser into her skin, pink like a baby. The indentation of the goggles left her eyes rimmed purple so she hid the battering behind sunglasses.

Outside, she barged her way on to the human conveyor belt and headed down Seventh Avenue. She felt restored by the sensation of sun on her skin. She passed an amputee on a skateboard begging outside a crowded deli. "Man, I ain't got nothing not even my legs," he said, catching her eye.

She gave him a handful of change, a quarter, two dimes, a nickel and a spray of copper. She found a telephone on the corner of 49th. She dialled her number. The man in the adjacent booth was smoking a reefer. She could smell its sweetness like summer. "You have two messages," announced the automated voice on her machine."

"Yes, it's April here, friend of Marina's. We met down Nylon a couple of weeks ago. I'm doing my Wednesday night club. I was wondering if you could do the door. A hundred bucks. Giz a ring, babe. I gotta sort it out. Cheers."

Click, click, click.

"Utopia, it's Jean. She's taken it OK. I'm giving her two days to finish up. I'll need you Thursday. Call me."

"Fuck," she shrieked, hurled the receiver at the cradle and missed.

The impact caused the phone booth to rock in its foundations.

Jean had done it. Meg was out and she was in. The implications flashed before her like a sheet of light. The bike courier in the next-door booth was wearing spectral mirror shades and grinned appreciatively. "Go, girl!" he said, and offered her a toke.

"Not before lunch. But thanks anyway."

She dawdled, watching the traffic-lights, the *Walk, Don't Walk*, flash one to the next, backwards and forwards. She watched the tide of people mass and depart each time.

The traffic blazed a trail through Times Square.

The wash of voices and honking horns engulfed her in a tunnel of sound. Then she heard her stomach. She had forgotten to eat.

She thumbed another quarter into the slot and dialled Marina's number. She craved the sound of Marina's voice like maternal praise. Perhaps they could get lunch together. She fancied sushi. There was something about the neatness of individual balls of rice, the fine slivers of fish, which appealed at times of heightened emotion. They were easily gulped down with excess oxygen and thimbles of saki.

"Hello?"

"Marina. I did it. Jean did it. I've got the job."

"Lunch?"

"Please."

Yippee.

# Chapter Thirteen

It was Wednesday, the air was as thick as a rug and there was a message.

"Utopia. Where are you? Call me."

She was kneeling on the chair and smoking the end of Johann's joint. She stared at the telephone. She was naked in a bra and towel. It was a white towel embossed with the logo of the hotel pool and it sagged at her waist and flapped at her knees like a slice of soggy bread.

Nothing dried in this humidity.

It was nine o'clock.

She was expected at April's club on the Lower East Side in an hour's time. Though more important than tonight, even, was tomorrow. Tomorrow was her first official day at *HQ*. She had called Jean from Marina's office when she went to meet her for lunch.

"She's clearing her desk," said Jean. "It's quick but quick is good. With the White House story still going nuts, I'll need you Thursday."

So Thursday it was.

As for Meg, it was as though she had never existed at all. Utopia opened and closed the towel and wrapped it tighter. She was going to be late. Johann used tweezers when he smoked the butt ends of joints. Utopia burnt her fingers as she stole a final drag. She was trying to decide whether to ring Saul or not.

"Call him," shouted Johann from his room. He had had enough of her twenty minute repeat play of the same message. Even Utopia was bored.

"No," she shouted back.

"What's your problem?"

"He slept with his assistant. Jesus."

"Isn't that what they're for?"

"You don't even like him."

"Don't be so pathetic."

"Why am I pathetic?"

"Oh, for Christ's sake," he said, before swearing in Swedish. Now he was angry.

She hesitated before picking up the telephone and dialling his number. "You've reached the warehouse of Siseman Salvage Inc. Please leave a message or send a fax after the beep."

She hung up.

A pall of anti-climax descended. They had enjoyed a casual fling and it was over, she told herself. There was never to be any investment made. She knew the rules. It was as temporary as her proposed stay in New York. But it was the thought of being replaced by Vivienne that depressed her. She reminded herself of his anal retentiveness and his vanity. The life-size photograph of himself that hung in the bedroom with the message CAN I HAVE MY FUCKING FORESKIN BACK? in silver letters along the bottom gave her the creeps. He was probably getting high with Vivienne. Vivienne was bound to indulge now and again.

Utopia opened a pot of black varnish and began painting her nails with daubs of teenage rebellion.

"Where's the club?" shouted Johann.

"Houston and First. You going to come down?"

"Thought I might. I need to get laid."

Utopia laughed "When was the last time? The Finnish au pair?"

"Dutch translator," he called back, "who was sick on the bed."

Utopia tried to decide what to wear.

She was standing inside her walk-in closet. It was like a supermarket supply room: it was stacked with empty cardboard boxes. She intended getting rid of them but something stopped her. It was in case she decided to go tomorrow and needed to pack. Although she pretended it was because she would rather not carry them all the way down five flights of stairs. Not that anyone else knew of their existence.

Garments hung from the rail in staggered lengths.

She had two trouser suits, a selection of skirts, flea-market shirts in garish prints, a leopardskin coat, which was moulting, and four dresses. These were her mother's dresses. She had more of them in London. Liberty was a shapely size fourteen and didn't fit them. They strained across her breasts and cut into her armpits. But Utopia shared her mother's size ten and could fit into them all. With her she had brought a black crêpe, a miniature check, a floral print and another in faded denim. She leaned forward and brushed against the fabric in search of a scent, a hint of something. Nothing. They smelt of crumbling cardboard.

She sneezed and slid shut the door.

Yanking open her chest of drawers, she found a pair of jeans and a shirt that was as transparent as négligé and quite as cool. It was an East Village venue. There was no point overdoing it. Cross-legged on her bed, she propped up her mirror and applied colour. She had a collection of her mother's lipsticks and eyeshadows, cracked Yardleys and Mary Quants, in chalky pinks and blues. Their fragrances and shades evoked memories. She often looked at them but never wore them. They were her mother's colours not hers.

Instead she painted her mouth plum then sprinkled her eyelids with almond sparkle to highlight her freckles. Her heels were added as an afterthought. Height, if nothing else, would validate her role as nightclub hostess. Combing her hair flat behind her ears, she flicked the ends.

The reflection peering back at her smiled.


The windows outside the theatre were boarded over. The walls had been blitzed with graffiti and the charred remains of a tree stood with only a plastic bag for foliage. April was waiting for her. She waved excitedly as the cab pulled up. "Come meet Terry," she said.

Terry the bouncer was a moon-faced man with inflated biceps straining against a T-shirt that read *Crunch*. He said, "Hi," in a lazy drawl and bounced his weight from foot to foot as he cracked his knuckles. April filled her in on door policy. "It's very simple. No freebies. Ten bucks from every-one and come and get me if there's any trouble. I'll be in and out all night and Terry's a big sweetheart."

April was a coil of nervous energy. She had a rail-thin body, wore her hair in bunches and spoke a curious blend of mock-Cockney and transatlantic jive. She wore her ciga-rettes clamped down her cleavage and a bindi, which had slipped down her forehead to the top of her nose. "It's like

Nylon's blowing up," she said. "Got a mention on last week's Page Six."

Utopia looked blank

"Gossip page in the *New York Post*. Wicked place to be."

April disappeared inside and Utopia was left on a stool with a ripped leather seat. She climbed on to it and found that it wobbled. But she could see for miles and felt on top of the world. She had passed another of New York's intangible tests and was now some kind of member. First had come news of the *HQ* job and now this. If only P could see her, she thought, before remembering that he hadn't been invited.

The streets were crawling with tribes. She could see hippies, preppies in khakis, home boys, club kids, panhandlers and street men with shabby For Sale items laid out on the sidewalk in front. It was like a street fair. She watched a boy smash his fists on the bonnet of a police car. "Motherfuckers," he shouted, as he threw back his head.

Two policemen snapped cuffs on his wrists and stuffed him into the back of the car. The pulsing lights sped away.

"Motherfuckers," echoed Terry, shaking his head.

A small group had started to gather beside the door. Utopia began taking money. A figure approached with a bag of mikes trailing their leads. He was wearing a white stetson, no shirt. Fur coat, no knickers. It was Miles.

"Hey, you." He flashed a grin then took off his hat and fanned his face. "Where's April?"

"Inside."

"I need to get round the back with the truck."

"Oh. Do you want me to see if I can find her?" Utopia was keen to have a look.

"You honey."

Terry gave her permission and she left her post and wandered into the hall. Cloaked in darkness, it was illuminated with swirling psychedelia. The DJ booth was up on stage and behind it a photograph of a topless woman in a tiara had been projected on to a screen. It was a photograph of April. Pockets of people lurked in the corners, drinking and talking. Utopia climbed on stage. She cupped her hand over her eyes and peered into the gloom.

"Utopia."

She froze.

Silhouetted at the back of the room was Saul. He appeared small and insignificant but her heart began instantly to thump as she began to catalogue her thoughts of the past few days. Only hours ago she had craved his company yet now here he was and she felt annoyed.

"What are you doing?" he asked, standing at the foot of the stage.

"I'm trying to find April. Someone's looking for her."

"Is she wearing a lace dress?"

"Yes."

"She was walking out the door."

"Oh."

"Cool place," he said.

They stared up at the ceiling, at the skeletal remains of a burnt-out chandelier and peeling gilt flecks.

"Johann told me you were here."

"I've got to get back."

"Want a drink?"

"Vodka and cranberry."

She made her way back to the entrance. April was outside with Miles. He was deconstructing his latest song. "It's about that guy who tracks UFOs in Arizona. That's what I mean when I sing 'Blood in the sand but who pulled the trigger?'"

"God, how fucking beautiful," said April.

Saul arrived and gave her her drink. He climbed on her stool.

He laughed. "Damn, this thing's out of control," he said, rocking from side to side so that the stool began to sway like a fair ride.

"Hey, is this Nylon?" interrupted a boy with a nose-ring.

"Ten bucks," said Utopia.

The boy turned to confer with his friend. Saul reached for Utopia's shoulder to steady himself. She turned round. "Vivienne answered the phone on Monday."

"Oh yeah?"

"Yes. Monday first thing." Utopia took the boys' dollar bills and stood back to let them pass.

"And?" He took a swig.

"And that's what I'm asking. And what?"

"Did she stay the night in the studio? Yeah. I had Marcus on my back all fucking weekend because they want fucking everything this week. I called Vivienne and we were up all night. And, yeah, she crashed. On the spare futon."

Utopia's stony stare failed to move him. Saul exuded a confident calm.

"I don't believe you, Saul," she said, shaking her head, wanting for the sake of peace, for the sake of tonight, to forget the whole thing.

Jealousy she associated with teenage angst, with Rick. Rick had flirted for years with a rival for his affections. Her name was Des'ree, she wore white Lycra dresses with holes at the side and announced that she wanted his babies. In the end he gave her one.

"Hey," he said, encircling her waist, "she's working for me. I don't know why you've got such a problem with that."

As he held her, Utopia surrendered to a sense of relief. It was a yearning for his hold to give way to an embrace. Meanwhile, the truth slipped quietly out of the frame.

The door was busy. Throngs of girls emerged from the dirty night with their pierced navels out on show.

"Ten each," said Utopia like a pro.

A car load of New Jersey boys with scrubbing-brush haircuts and beery breath lurched to the door.

"This is a private party," Terry told them.

"'Man. We've come all the way from Elizabeth."

"We don't want any trouble here, OK? The Tunnel ain't far."

The out-of-towners knocked back cans of Bud and checked out the girls. Another brood of boys tried to blast their way in.

"Yo, ten each," said Terry.

This provoked heckles from the New Jersey crew. "You're bullshitting us. This ain't no private party. How come they're getting in?"

"They might but you ain't."

The rap posse handed over their money, skipped past Utopia, calling out shame, as they high-fived each other. Miles was on stage. Utopia could hear his voice above the traffic.

"What time do you get out of this place?" asked Saul.

"Why?"

"I thought we could go back to mine."

She narrowed her eyes. "We'll have to see about that."

A stretch limo pulled up. "Where's April?" demanded an English voice. A Manchester United football shirt and mop of greasy hair fell out of the door. Three others followed as April flew through the doors.

"Hello, darlings," she lavished them, throwing her arms

around the tallest, the leader, his eyes concealed behind Lennonesque shades. "How was the gig?"

Utopia looked on curiously, then over at Saul leaning against the wall. There was no mistaking their identities. Saul in oil-splattered fatigues and workboots was conspicuously American. He was an artistic nerd with rugged edges. Brit boys were, by comparison, self-consciously smooth. Yet tonight she felt happy to be with an American and feel part of the city.

April and the band disappeared inside. Saul pulled her towards him. "You're crazy, Utopia, just like your name. You know that, don't you?"

"Me?" She laughed. "Look who's talking."

# Chapter Fourteen

It was an easy stroll back to his studio. The streets were deserted but for pale-faced revellers and sidewalk vagrants. Fleets of cabs coasted down Houston's dual-carriageway. A jeep with its sound system booming roared up from behind and hooted. The horn made them jump.

"Fuck you," Saul called after the driver, and took Utopia's hand.

They stopped to buy cigarettes and beers at the Korean deli on the corner of Mulberry. Trays of meat and noodles lay congealing like swamp matter beneath hot lights.

Back outside Utopia was greeted by a serenading beggar. "Beautiful and tall. The girl's got it all," he sang, through a lopsided grin.

She gave him a dollar.

They began drifting down through Little Italy, drinking out of mandatory brown-paper bags. Boys in string vests and webbed tattoos were sitting on stoops as pomaded girls heavy with gold sat opposite. It was too hot to be indoors. Utopia began wondering about the dynamics of foreplay. The sexes were obviously going to spend all night on separate sides of the street exchanging salacious wind-ups then go home for a fuck at the end of it all.

Not so dissimilar from herself and Saul, she reflected.

They took a right on Grand.

Saul threw his empty into a passing bin and the glass smashed, shattering into the paper bag like a controlled explosion. The studio grille was locked. He unbolted the door. The air inside smelt of cat and Saul went to switch on the fan. Max was mewing for food with the television playing MTV in the background as a companion for him.

Utopia threw herself down on the springy leather sofa and realised that she had missed his studio this week. She kicked off her sandals and squirmed for comfort. The sofa had a tendency to expel comfort seekers like peas from a pod. The art of positioning took practice. Scenes of drive-by shootings executed by hoodlums in hoods flickered by softly on the TV.

"You hungry?" asked Saul, from behind the fridge door. Utopia shook her head. "Not for me."

She lay transfixed by the close-ups of the snarling rapper and his girls wiggling their arses as they dangled off a fire escape. Saul joined her at the end of the sofa with a sand-wich in his mouth. He tugged her feet on to his lap and tickled her soles.

"Don't." He refused to let go.

"Saul. I'm ticklish."

"Isn't that the point?"

She tried kicking. It was no good. Throwing the remains of his sandwich to Max, Saul moved his hands from her feet to her stomach to the place beneath her arms. Still laugh-ing, Utopia pulled him to her and embraced the hard pres-sure of his chest. His breath tasted salty. Meaty. Parma ham and mayonnaise.

They scrambled to readjust themselves as their legs intertwined. Saul was an intelligent kisser never sloppy. Nor was he one of those lizard kissers with a darting tongue like others she had tried. His stubble felt scratchy on her skin. He fumbled for her zip. He sat back and tugged off her jeans. The leather felt cold and clinical like the shiver of a gynaecologist's couch. He seized her thighs and she slid across the sofa and on to his lap. Their mouths locked as their fingers attacked his American Eagle buckle. The panting grew heavier as it resisted their efforts.

"Let me do it," he insisted.

She repositioned herself on his lap. She gasped and drew her legs tight around his waist. Bouncing with the sofa's suspension, they struggled not to hit the floor.

Staring at Saul, she suddenly lost sight of who she was with.

His curled lashes and hungry mouth appeared abstract. Foreign. Afraid to look, she gripped the back of the sofa as images of P spun through her mind. She felt P's breath on her neck, his fingers across her back. She saw his green eyes staring longingly. "Are you brother and sister?" people would ask.

Not now, she forced herself. Saul moved, pushing deeper inside. Heat rose higher and higher until their bodies met in a tide of shudders, snaking from one to the other and back again. She hugged him closer and looked cautiously.

"Wham, bam, thank you, ma'am," he said, tracing her lips with a finger.

Utopia laughed and bit his hand.

"Christ. What the hell's that?" he said.

It was the sound of the metal shop front reverberating against the glass.

Turning to look, they were in time to see a row of ogling

faces pressed up against the window. Caught in the act, they fell away to disappear into the night.

"Fuck," shouted Saul.

They scrambled to the end of the sofa and hit the floor.

"Those fuckers," he swore, running to the door.

But the three boys had taken off down the street.

"Yo, she gave it to you good, man." Utopia could hear them whistling as Saul stood outside on the sidewalk. "She gave it to you real good, man."

Lying on the floor, Utopia laughed. "How long were they there, do you think?" she called, as he slammed the door and switched off the overhead lights.

"I know who they are. They work in the recording studio next door."

"That's what happens when you live in a glass box," she teased, reaching for his hand.

Shaking his head, he lay back down beside her. She studied his bobbing Adam's apple and the outline of his jaw through half-closed eyes. "Have you ever watched a couple having sex?" she heard herself ask.

A flicker of recognition passed across his face. "What? A sex show?"

"I don't know. Any kind of sex."

"I've seen two girls at it down at some girlie club on Varick. Why?"

"Don't know, really. Just wondering."

She imagined he must have tried most things. He rarely said no.

"We can go if you want." He laughed, reaching over to kiss her. "I'd like to see your face. "

She caught his lips between hers and was happy to stay there but Saul was never good at afterwards. Refreshed and ready to go, he would jump up and take off. Otherwise, exhausted, he would turn over and fall asleep. It was for Utopia to stare at the crumpled space or into the darkness monitoring his breathing. Talk to me, she wanted to say. But somehow it wasn't part of their deal. Theirs was passion without tenderness. Saul looked at his watch then leaped up to go and perform his ablutions. Time to mouthwash and floss.

Unbuttoned on the floor, spellbound by the disco ball as it caught the fly-by glare of passing lights, Utopia considered his offer. She had seen more than one strip show. In a Bethnal Green pub one Sunday afternoon, she had once watched a sixteen-year-old Thai girl, a girl then the same age as herself, slice a cucumber with a razor blade inside her. Rick had taken her there to score an ounce of hash. He sorted the deal in the gents' while she was left to watch the show. She had left feeling soiled and dirty. She had hated Rick for taking her there.

"Why do you have to go there to buy it?"

"She's all right," he told her. "Makes more money than she does at home."

Utopia had said nothing. It was always the same. Refusing to concede an alternative point of view, he would swear if she put up a fight.

"Come on, then. What the fuck do you know about it?"

Two weeks ago Marina had taken her to a strip-joint on Sixth. They were meeting Dorian for drinks. It was a bar where inflated breasts remained inert while fit bodies slid vigorously up and down a pole. It was a Hollywood hang-out. They had spotted a trio of male movie stars seated at the back with girls in feathers across their laps. But Utopia had felt uncomfortable. She failed to see how one woman's enjoyment of another's sexual provocations was empowering or liberating. She got the feeling that the stripper, with her petulant mouth and whirring nipple tassels, would rather she had been of the opposite sex. Marina had forced her to give the girl twenty bucks. "You can't sit here and not tip. They make their living in tips. Go stuff it down the side of her G-string."

Utopia couldn't. She had passed the dollar bill into the girl's hand. She had then tried to leave.

"Another Cosmopolitan for the road," Marina had insisted, and Utopia's excuses fell on deaf ears. She had found herself watching Dorian caress Marina's leg instead.

Staring up at the studio's railroad beams, its steel chain like a hangman's noose, Utopia remembered Vivienne. Had Vivienne assumed this very position on Sunday night? she wondered. The whoring sculptor. She didn't want to think about it. Not now. Launching herself upright, she went to get into Saul's bed and bathe in frozen air. She wanted to forget everything.

Tomorrow was Thursday.

# Chapter Fifteen

Another day, another postcard. It was of a balaclava-clad terrorist with a sawn-off shot gun framed across his chest.

*Dear U*                             *17 August*
*More meetings with the producer about the London romance. I'll have grown a beard before I get my money. London is sweltering. The road has melted. Have been barbecuing in the back with everyone round. Off to Julian's house in Spain for a week. What's up with you? Running the show yet? Thinking of you daily, nightly. Love and luck, P*

The subway car smelt of bodies, suited, polyester-sealed, poured into stone-washed jeans and leaking out of pastel shorts. Even in an air-conditioned carriage, the proximity of skin first thing was painful. Cocooned in fatigue, Utopia remembered P's postcard, abandoned in a pool on the bathroom tiles. She had raced home for a shower while Saul was asleep. There had been no time for it this morning.

She tried to focus on her *Times*.

She craved an antidote to the trivia that swamped her brain. Keeping track of world affairs demanded focus. She had learned early on that it was much easier to pick up the *Post*, turn to Page Six and catch up on who was where last night. Her appetite for gossip seemed to have grown in direct proportion to the length of time spent in New York. Besides, she was on her way to *HQ*, a world of moisturised women who discussed their moisturisers. It was talk of calibrated parties at the Hamptons, which place on 54th did better salmon rolls and who was already wearing *next* season's shoes, which set the agenda. Then came the serious issues, shopaholicism, plastic-surgery abuse, editor's attempts to climb Mount Everest with cosmetics bags and satellite phones, the stories she — a junior features editor — would now be researching and editing.

The prospect of it made her feel grown-up. Well, almost.

The train entered the 49th street platform.

She recognised her stop. Flurries of nausea rose and fell. The doors slid open and a wall of spray flooded the car. She joined the commuters streaming off the train into the concrete inferno. She began to perspire.

Stay cool, stay calm, she ordered herself.

This was it.


"I need to find a file labelled Divorce Stories. It's out there somewhere. Check Meg's files," Jean phoned through.

Jean's door had been shut ever since Utopia had arrived half an hour ago to an empty desk and a feeling of displacement. All this was hers and yet nothing was clear. She stared at the blank noticeboard ahead, the spot where Meg's snapshot should have been, and tried to figure out her next move. What would Meg be doing? she wondered.

Her fill-in week had in theory provided a dry run but this – the real thing – was different. This time round she was assumed to know what was what. She wondered if there was a specialised knowledge she lacked. She had begun devising lists and flow-charts with arrows outlining tasks ahead or, at best, her idea of what they might be. Then there were the people and companies she thought she might call and inform of her arrival. She wasn't sure who they might be.

She was trying to itemise the daily routine with numbered tasks from one to ten. She was stuck on four. She looked up from her desk and scanned the corridor. Where was he? She was looking for the mailman, Eddy, an equal-opportunities employee with an S-shaped limp. She had ordered a New York Film Festival programme for Jean to be sent in her name. "Utopia Holmes, HQ, Features Department, 29th floor, 1188 Broadway, New York 10019." This she couldn't wait to see. Maybe then it would seem real.

Eddy was late.

The features department arrived.

There was Brooke, the senior features editor, who wore buttoned-up shirts and had sturdy legs, Ron, the executive articles editor who reminded Utopia of a vole with his starey eyes and pointy jaw, and Julie, their shared assistant, who was bouncy with copper curls. They greeted her as they passed with brown-paper bags and papers. But their hellos had a hollow ring.

Sensitive to this, Utopia began arranging her pens in a row as she fought to organise her thoughts. She had expected them to feel odd about her arrival and Meg's dismissal. But Jean must have filled them in on the change. For a moment, she wondered whether it wasn't all a terrible mistake but it was too late for that.

She wondered how easy it would be to compete with Meg's ghost and work around personal loyalties. Would they all become friends? Drinks after work? Laughs in the hallway? The normal stuff. She hoped so. She had noticed that as a department they were hardly a team. Aside from their features meetings, they didn't appear to communicate at all. If they did, it was via e-mail. Only Goldie, the rock chick editor, had popped her head over the partition to say hi like she meant it. Utopia remembered Jean's file. She stood up from her desk. She didn't want to keep Jean waiting.

Her desk was hemmed in with a wall of cold metal. She dragged open the top drawer of the filing cabinet to find it crammed with yellowing paper folders like the gills of a fish. A pile of old *HQ*s was squashed at the back. The remaining three drawers were empty. She ran a finger across the bottom of them and felt excited by the idea that these represented her future and would fill up accordingly. She put a clip board in each and returned to the top.

She ploughed her way through. The files and envelopes were packed so close together that it was hard to see anything. At last she found it. The Divorce file had been shunted to the Cs. It was buried between Celebrity Shoots and Christmas Movies She removed it and closed it with a pat.

Jean's office was awash with light.

Sunshine poured in through the very clean windows. Jean was wearing a navy skirt suit collared with a string of pearls. She appeared smarter than usual, like a business executive, but her expression was pinched. Her lips' signature colour was absent and she looked older than before. Utopia took a seat.

"There was a mistake in the letter sent to the First Lady's office," Jean said without looking up.

Utopia felt sick. "A mistake?"

"The name of the press secretary was spelt incorrectly. The White House were concerned. It did not give the impression that, right now, *HQ* gravely needs." Her words were thin and grey like bullets. Impossible to dodge.

"The press secretary's name?"

Neill Ash. N-e-i-l-l. Not N-e-a-l."

Utopia remained dumbfounded. What was there to say? She wanted this to be a nightmare the night before day one. But this was day one. She was living it.

"Too late now," continued Jean, looking up from her storm of paper and fixing her with an unpleasant stare. "You had better go talk to the managing editor about contracts. Right away."

"Oh, OK. Right. Thanks."

Jean tugged the lid from her pen with her teeth and resumed making notes. Utopia stood up and headed gingerly in the direction of the managing editor's office. She felt shell-shocked and studied her shoes as they slip-slided across the camel carpet. A misspelling on a letter to the White House? She was mortifed. Both Jean and Diane had proof-read the letter for possible inaccuracies but that link in the chain was forgotten now that an error had managed to slip through.

The managing editor was on the telephone.

She gestured for Utopia to come in and take a seat. She was a pixie-like woman with steely eyes and a helmet of jet hair. Her sleeveless dress was cut to reveal a pair of chiselled arms. Her office was as severe as her demeanour. There were black Bauhaus chairs, which were impossible to get out of, and her desk, which was bare except for a framed photograph of a chihuahua, and a corporate toy made out of wires and pins. A pair of weights sat crossed on the floor beside her feet. She opened a desk drawer, produced a stack of paper and began passing the sheets over. "If you want to sign there, there and there," she said.

There was no time to read the print as the documents flew across the desk. Utopia paused with her pen poised above the first dotted line.

"There's a three-month trial period. We pay directly into your bank account. I need your social security number. Jean has explained the requirements of the job to you. We expect all our staff to be here at nine sharp, all expense sheets have to be signed by me – for cabs and lunches – and we'll organise for you to meet Diane officially sometime next week. No smoking anywhere."

"Thanks," said Utopia, signing her name along one, two, three, four blank lines.

She stared at *Utopia Holmes* crowned with the *HQ* logo. The managing editor took a call and Utopia allowed herself a smile. Now it was official.

Back at the desk, and it was her desk, she began arranging her stationery into strategic groups and patterns. She had notepads, letter paper, envelopes, post-its, cards and Rolodex leaves. She swept the last remaining traces of Meg into the bin, a couple of crumbling rubbers, a half-eaten jar of marshmallow spread, an invitation to a black-tie opening at the Museum of Modern Art, a theatre programme, bent paper clips, a Barney's calendar, and a layer of dust. They could have been anyone's.

"Hi."

It was Julie the features assistant.

"Oh, hi there."

Finding Utopia in the act of disposing of Meg, a frown passed across Julie's face like a shadow. Utopia caught it but refused to admit wrongdoing. She had been brought in by Jean and signed up by the managing editor. Even Diane must have approved the move.

POP.

A pistachio bubble punctured against Julie's teeth. It was an angry sound. Leaning her head over the partition, aniseed twists of hair falling on either side, Julie informed her that there was a features meeting at twelve. "And you've got to have your ideas typed up and ready for presentation," she said. This news was presented as a challenge.

With a nod, her stomach knotted like rope, Utopia smiled. "Jean told me," she lied.


They had gathered in the conference room.

Before them towered a mountain of bagels, speckled, raisined and blanched. At the foot of the mountain sat tubs of cream cheese. Beside the tubs was a ring of iced coffees helmed with straws. Utopia had noticed that all meetings came accompanied by enough food to feed an army. It was the American work ethic — feed at all times. The features meeting was in progress.

"Addiction on the job," said Jean. "Ron?"

Utopia watched Jean slide her index finger up and down her band of pearls in the gesture of captor to hangman. Off with his head.

When Jean had finally re-emerged from her office, her mouth had been dipped scarlet like red alert. She had told Utopia that it would be her job to take notes. Utopia gripped her pen between white-knuckled fingers. The responsibility far outweighed the task.

Ron took a slurp of coffee. He burped silently with his mouth closed. "Fine. The writer says he can get it in by next Wednesday. He's speaking to one more addict this week. Some actress who shoots up on set."

"Good. 'At Home', Goldie?"

Her tone of enquiry was harsh, reflected Utopia, observing as Jean picked them off at random. Her insides performed somersaults at the prospect of her turn.

"He's screening his calls but I spoke to his publicist. We've got an exclusive."

Goldie had a voice like butter and she appeared unperturbed by Jean. Her answers were delivered leisurely as she twisted her namesake mane into a braid. She wore black leather, her lips were glossed like glacé cherries and her lashes were quite possibly false. Utopia had overheard her on the telephone. Her after-hours life took place backstage.

"How was the meeting with the band?"

"Cool. Shooting them at the Chateau."

Utopia scribbled down COOL in capital letters followed by Chateau, whatever that meant. Jean was shuffling her papers. Utopia held her breath.

"Julie. Art stories for the new year?"

Julie began reeling off names and dates of forthcoming shows. There was a retrospective at the Met, a MOMA season of Eastern European photographers. A series of coffee-table books were coming out with the shows.

Utopia's hand tore across the page in an attempt to keep up.

"Utopia. Anything from you?"

There was a difficult pause as she tried to clear her throat. She was dazzled by the glare of five expectant sets of eyes. Her cheeks scorched and her mind went blank. She needed one detail to jog her memory, just one. She had found the idea in a paper . . . "*Globe*," she said, as the name of the paper shot from her mouth. She had skimmed it at the stand at the subway.

Ron scratched his head.

"My favourite bar," said Goldie.

But Jean wasn't listening. She was pulling chunks of dough off a cinnamon-raisin bagel and squashing them into her mouth. Ron coughed.

"I – er – found a story about a fire-fighter, a woman, in San Francisco," Utopia started up again. "She's about to have a sex change."

The room went deathly silent. Someone was filling the kettle in the kitchen next door. She could hear soft humming. It was a two-word repetition.

"She is about to have an operation to become a man and . . ." She was deaf to the sound of her own voice. Could anybody hear? . . . "I thought perhaps *HQ* could organise for him, I mean her, to keep a diary of the operation then the follow-up when he returns to work as a man. It could be interesting." She stopped. Her words were taking an extraordinarily long time to land.

They probably considered the idea too trashy but that was the point. She saw it as a sensationalist story to be tastefully done. She saw it designed in *HQ*'s minimalist chic. She saw a before-and-after in stark black and white, a double page portrait of the fireman by his truck, a mackerel-sky and a No Way Out sign by his side.

"I think it's interesting," said Ron, and nodded his crinkly cap of curls.

Utopia was surprised.

Jean, too, began nodding. It was movement designed to induce a decision. "Yes. OK. Find a contact and that's yours to look after. But do it now. We'll need an exclusive."

Utopia found herself scrawling FIND TRANNIE!!!!!!!!!!! across the bottom of the page. The exclamation marks ran off the edge of the paper and she stubbed her nib on the table top. Her script was scratchy.

"Anything from you, Brooke?" said Jean, demolishing her bagel.

Brooke was po-faced. She came across as serious and sensible, and was responsible amongst other things for the books pages. "Only to ask about the First Lady."

Jean groaned. It was the bellow of a barnyard animal. "She's being taken care of. That's all you need know." She reared up from the table. "No further questions? We're done. Utopia, I'll need these notes typed up from the meeting immediately."

Jean strode out of the room.

Utopia caught Goldie's eye as she closed her notebook. Goldie smiled. "Hey girl, you did good."

# Chapter Sixteen

She flipped on her Aviators and smoothed together her lips. The streets were in flux. It was pedestrian rush-hour. She walked fast, surfing the crowds, riding the tide before turning against it. She took a right on 44th Street. Returning to her desk, there had been a message on her voicemail. "Celebration drinks at seven o'clock. Don't even think about saying no." It was Marina. How could she?

She was headed for the Royalton with a sense of success. After her first official day at *HQ* the plan to meet at this New York hotel seemed appropriate. It was a New York temple. It provided a feeling of VIP status without the red rope. It was Marina's regular after-work meeting place. Grand Central Station without the trains, she called it.

Utopia entered the lobby and there she was.

Marina was sitting against the far wall in a dress that spouted dollops of cleavage. Marina, a salon-enhanced brunette, was noticeable in the same way as a metallic blonde could be. She made it her business to be so. Everything she wore was strikingly figure-hugging and she favoured front and back cleavage. "I'm not getting any younger," she argued, which was true.

Marina projected her persona like the scent of fame. On the street Utopia had seen people do a double-take, thinking they knew her. But from where? Her TV punditry, perhaps, but probably not. It was her chesty strut with everything held high that did it. Her body was as much her weapon as her wit. She caught every glance and lapped it up.

She waved at Utopia. Utopia waved back and tripped as she went down the steps to join her.

"Survived your first day, then?"

Utopia took a seat. "Yes."

"Go on. Ask me how I am?"

Utopia frowned. "How are you?"

"I, darling, have just had my first colonic."

"That's disgusting."

"With another session booked for next week. The beauty director has been bullying me to go forever and now I understand why. Really, darling, did somebody switch on the lights?"

Utopia shook her head.

"Yes. Reborn. Can you think of a better way to lose five pounds? Feel my stomach. Flat. Well, almost."

Utopia had her hand held against Marina's almost flat stomach.

They were interrupted by a boy in black with his hair slicked back who appeared with a bottle in a bucket. He popped the cork. They sat and watched as he filled each glass with artful exactness. He handed each a glass.

"To us. To *HQ*. To New York," sang Marina, scrabbling in her bag for cigarettes.

Utopia laughed. "To New York."

Stoked with bubbles and twinned with Marina, Utopia began to unwind. She had had a good day, despite the White House blunder. Her only complaint was with Saul.

She had wanted to see him and celebrate together so had called the studio.

"Coolin' in the house. What's up?" It was Kurt trying to be an American.

"It's me. Is he there?"

"He's out the door with Don."

Don was the scrap dealer.

"Can you tell him it's me."

When Saul made it to the phone, he sounded faraway.

"Are you stoned?"

"Yeah. Just been to Tompkins to score some pot."

She imagined his hooded eyes and Kurt behind him, pulling faces.

"What's going on?" he said.

"What are you doing later?"

"I'm going over to Long Island City to check out Andrew's iron. Kurt's doing a night shoot for some German magazine."

Utopia was disappointed. She knew it was pointless to ask him to alter his plans. She couldn't compete with Kurt or Andrew. "I see."

"You want to come round later? Like after one?"

"I'm working tomorrow."

There was silence.

"You OK?"

"Fine."

She sounded catty. She couldn't help herself.

"Hang in there," he said, before putting down the phone.

Hang in there?

What was that meant to mean?

But she knew what it meant. It was the same as take care, be brave or be good. I'll call you when I call you, see you when I see you. Saul and Kurt fed off each other's competitive enthusiasm. Kurt used Saul's installations to hang his work at his shows. Saul appeared in the pictures. It was a mutual-appreciation club from which Utopia was excluded.

She poked her tongue into her glass. The bubbles burst like goldfish kisses. It was a hang-over from childhood and the stolen glass at Christmas from her father. Marina had launched into an account of the Christmas fashion shoot she was working on. It was going to be a who's who of next year's faces. She wanted to find a derelict theatre and shoot them on stage in Savile Row suits.

"Anyway, how was today? You haven't told me."

"Fine," said Utopia, still caught up with Saul.

"Dora called. Meg is furious."

It took a moment for Utopia to absorb what was being said. "Oh. Oh dear."

She began running her finger round and round the top of her glass and it hummed. She didn't know what to think. She had adversely affected someone else's life and she wasn't proud of it. But wasn't it all part of the grand shuffle? Jean had pulled her in and Meg had moved on.

"I wouldn't worry about it, darling. It happens all the time. Dora's a good friend of hers, that's all."

She wondered how long Jean's campaign against Meg had been going on. Weeks, months, longer even? It had started before she had met Jean, that much she knew. Everything in life was about timing, and there was no doubt about it, her timing had been impeccable. The right person at the right place at the right time.

"Here's to office politics," said Marina, lighting up. "Otherwise you'd be out of a job."

Utopia raised her glass as the waiter reappeared.

"Everything OK?"

"Gorgeous," said Marina, and ordered another bottle of champagne and a dozen oysters all on expenses. If Marina could have charged her rent to the magazine she would have. She already charged her phone bill, dry-cleaning bills, grocery bills and beauty treatments. "If Cheshire wants me in touch and looking good, he can damn well pay for it," was what she said. Put like this it made perfect sense but then Marina could sound convincing about most things.

"How's the D-man?"

"Did the dinner-sex thing last night."

"Really?" This was news.

"A fuck a month does not a relationship make, but anyway . . . He's just got back from Brazil and showed me his pictures of the tribes. Incredible faces. I mean, to do them in fashion would be a showstopper."

"Fashion?"

"You know, darling, with models like that Masai story *Vogue* do every year. Dorian wants to do a kind of disappearing world series. Well, even Sting can't save them."

For some reason, Utopia found herself laughing. It was Marina's deadpan delivery and the ludicrousness of it all. It was the cartoon emphasis of her plucked eyebrows and ruby lips, and the bored outrage of what she had to say. Utopia continued to laugh and huge flurries of breath and sound poured from her mouth like the sound of a horse. She became hysterical and gasped for breath. Marina passed her a napkin as she managed to snort a bit of oyster up her nose. Tears streamed from her eyes. "We'll probably be asked to leave," she spluttered, catching a flinty stare from a couple nearby.

"It wouldn't be the first time."

"No. When?"

"I had a huge fight with Dorian about a year ago. I can't

remember what it was about. We were very, very drunk, and I ended up throwing an ashtray at him. Missed the bastard, hit this woman's glass and covered her with red wine. We were both asked to leave. Lucky we weren't sued, I suppose."

A resurgence of laughter threatened to topple Utopia to the floor. She rocked on her chair with her head collapsed in her lap as champagne dribbled from her mouth and her nose. Every emotion suppressed by the day found its way out. She was no longer sure if she was laughing or crying. Her sobbing was blind. She wondered how ever to stop. She felt exhausted and begged for mercy. "Marina, please."

"Darling, enjoy it. Our market editor had to go to a laughter workshop in New Hampshire last weekend. She's forgotten how to laugh since her divorce came through. Can you imagine?"

Utopia shook her head.

She couldn't. And yet there had been a time when she did lose the freedom of mirth. She couldn't remember the last time she had been seized by hysteria. She sank back into her chair blissfully weary. Ahead, hotel traffic cruised the central walkway like figures on ice.

# Chapter Seventeen

Goldie was on the phone. From her desk, Utopia could hear giggling and the repeated mention of a name like a moan. Goldie's voice was trailed by a sense of exclusion. It was the merriment of a party as heard from outside. Utopia tried hard to block out the flirtation. Not only did she have a stack of letters to type but she had last night chiselling at her brain.

All of this was incidental.

Looping through her vision like a news flash came last night's news of P. It was impossible to focus on anything else. Nothing else mattered.

She had arrived back at the apartment to find a message on her machine "U, it's me. Lou. You don't phone, you don't write. What the hell's going on over there? Better be good. Anyway [pause] . . . I don't want to talk about this on your machine. It's P. I think he's [voice dropped] seeing someone. Apparently they were together at Julian's party. Liz told me. No. Fuck this. I'm not going to say . . . just call me. [Pause] OK? . . ."

Utopia made it to the bathroom just in time to stick her head down the bowl.

She sat and stared at her vomit flecked with pink luminescence until Johann said that he was desperate to piss and she had to stand up. She hated herself for the joint shared with Marina on the way home. She could taste the grass even now and wanted to die.

Then she phoned Lou but no one was there. "Where the hell are you?" she had screamed into the void.

Lou was her oldest schoolfriend. Aged thirteen, they had shared their first cigarette on the park bench. Aged fourteen, each had ordered half a cider, a packet of salt and vinegar crisps and the same again, please, for the two boys with them, who looked too young to approach the bar – unlike themselves. Aged sixteen, they had lost their virginity side by side on job-specific mattresses. It was a Cinzano Bianco party in a parental house where the parental bedroom, lights out, had witnessed fumbling lead to a bony jab and much giggling. She couldn't remember his name. Sisterhood, the benign kind, was synonymous with affection for Lou.

So where was she?

Beyond caring about the time difference and about waking them up, Utopia called every number she had. She needed an explanation. She couldn't leave it like this. What the hell did she mean, seeing someone? Eventually getting nowhere, which was hardly surprising when England was asleep, she gave up. This morning, first thing, she had managed to get through to Lou's office and was told to leave a message. Lou, a theatrical agent, would be in meetings all afternoon.

In a surge of panic, she telephoned P just to hear his voice but he too was out and she wasn't going to leave a message. What was she going to say? Are you fucking someone else? Her mind swirled with conspiracy theories as she imagined a plot under way to freeze her out. No one was telling her what was going on.

Distracted and queasy, she reread the tasks for the day.

1. Find number for SF trannie.
2. Find contact for Times writer in Havana – will Castro agree to talk?
3. Check release dates of Fall chick flicks.
4. Phone attorney 324-6678 – ask to send affidavit by messenger.
5. Book table for 2 at Four Seasons, Fri. 15th.

They aroused zero interest. She stretched her legs and tried to find the motivation to pick up the phone. Instead she kicked her bag. Alerted to the one thing capable of taking her mind off P, her mood lifted. Her last call of the night had been to Marina. She had been tired and distraught.

"No one's answering. I don't know what to do."

"Beach tomorrow with Felix."

"What?"

"Gloria's invited me, I absolutely cannot go because I've got someone coming to town so I'm sending you instead. My little envoy."

"You can't do that."

"She'll love you."

"Who?"

"Gloria. I'm calling Felix now. Take your things with you to the office. He likes to get away early."

And so it was that her overnight bag, toothbrush, bikini and sun cream intact, was ready to go, stowed beneath her desk.

"Any news on the transsexual?"

Utopia looked up from her desk. Towering above her with an expression of displeasure twisting her face, was Jean. Utopia winced. "I – er – left two messages with the fire department yesterday."

"You have to act on these things," she snapped. "Now

we need to send another fax to the White House. In my office."

Picking up her pad, she followed Jean in.


It was one o'clock. There was still no message from Lou and her hangover had evolved into hunger. She phoned Todd. "Are you busy?"

"No. Let's hit the park. Come get me."

She went to clear it with Jean but Jean's door was closed. Murmurings like bubbling lava were heard from inside. Utopia went to knock but her fist froze an inch from the door and her arm dropped to her side. She couldn't do it. Instead she went to find Todd unauthorised.

Stuck in the elevator with a dozen jarring voices, Utopia shook her head in dismay as Todd stuck out his tongue behind the managing editor's back. She was responsible for challenging staff expenses and had just this morning banned him from subscribing to his fifteen different literary magazines and reviews. He mouthed, "Fucking philistine," and Utopia nodded.

Outside she squinted in the glare and Todd lit up.

It was hard to believe that, along with everything else, she now had Jean to worry about. She was unidentifiable as the person who had offered Utopia the job and the person-ality change was bewildering. Where once she had been so enthusiastic about Utopia's future role, now all she did was complain. Everything was Utopia's fault, copy coming in late, the photocopier not working, the sushi boy failing to deliver wasabi, the search for a health magazine last seen in one of her slush piles.

Utopia wondered whether Todd had noticed anything strange.

He hadn't mentioned anything.

They stopped at a deli on 57th Street.

Todd ordered a foot-long, everything-to-go sandwich while Utopia pick 'n' mixed at the salad bar. She loaded her transparent box with chicken mayonnaise, potato salad, a hard-boiled egg, curly pasta and a slice of challah bread. A dish of mandarin slices in orange jelly wobbled at her and her nausea returned. She bought a litre of cold water and tore off the seal.

They crossed 59th Street and entered the park. Packs of roller-bladers whistled past them. A crew of street kids was break-dancing in front of a boogie box. Squirrels scampered over the dusty ground, scavenging amongst the litter for pretzels and crusts. *Do Not Feed the Rats*, read the sign in the flowerless flower-bed.

"I once saw a rat dragging a pizza down the path here," announced Todd, as they found a bench overlooking a pool of water. It glistened like an oil slick. "Thought it was a fucking dog."

He attacked his sandwich. Mayonnaise oozed from the corners of his mouth and shreds of ham flew in the direction of Utopia's face. She moved along the bench and reflected on the reality of working life. Here she was with Todd, a frat boy who denied any ongoing allegiance to Sigma Gamma Beta. A preppy who never wore loafers. At any rate, an American boy who overate and manifested a sister complex. It was the gender/job thing. She worked as a producer for CBS news while he toiled on a women's magazine. "Hey, dude, should-n't it be the other way round?" she had overheard someone ribbing him in the elevator.

Todd's look featured shapeless T-shirts bearing pointless logos. Today's was *San Diego Catamaran Heats 1987*. He said he picked them up along the way and didn't even notice their slogans. They were part of America's disposable culture. He wore them until they hung in tatters. Utopia liked Todd. He was never short of things to say and had become her magazine ally. He was even making headway with the stripper and was notably less crazed. He no longer ranted every morning with ardent frustration. Misha, that was her name, was talking to him. He said he might have her over for dinner in which case Utopia should come. They sat in silence as he continued to chew.

"Do you think something's wrong with Jean?" she finally asked.

"Ha." He snorted, as though she had only just got the joke. "There's always something wrong with Jean."

"In what way?"

"Every way."

"What do you mean?"

"She's wacked out."

"Wacked out?"

"Crackerjacked. You never seen the way she looks at you with those bulging eyes?"

"Oh. Great."

Their conversation was going nowhere. All Todd was doing was fanning her anxiety. Jean's foul mood was caused by stress, she consoled herself. It had to be.

She sucked on a piece of cantaloupe and juice trickled down her chin. She watched a man in a sleeping-bag slither out from behind a rock. He looked a little disorientated then found a cigarette above an ear and lit it. There was no escaping the masses, even in the park she reflected. There had to be hundreds of thousands of people for every blade of grass.

"Better get back," said Todd, scrunching his brown-paper bag into a ball. He tossed it at the bin and missed.

On their way back to the office, Utopia beat off her

misgivings like pesky mosquitoes. Things would pan out. They always did, she lied.

There was a note from Jean on her desk. *Diane wants* exclusive *on SF transsexual!!!* Utopia was thrilled that her idea now had the support of the editor-in-chief. She found the number and dialled through to the West Coast.

"Yes?"

"Hello, I'm trying to get through to a Lesley Cranley. I'm phoning from *HQ* in New York."

"Speaking."

"Oh. Right, well, I don't know quite how to phrase this but we're interested in . . . er . . . "

"My transitioning?"

"Trans-what?"

"Transference from female to male status on the job."

"Right."

"Did you speak to my publicist?"

"No."

"There's a bidding war on. You want an exclusive? Call Bluey."

"Right." Utopia took the number and hung up. Was she the only person who didn't have a publicist? Now what? Then she remembered Goldie.

Utopia left her desk and wandered along the corridor past a row of closed doors until she reached the one with the gold star. She knocked.

"Aha?"

Utopia poked her head round the door. Goldie was on the telephone. The entire wall behind her desk was papered with shots of pouting waifs and tough guys posing. It was a celebrity shrine.

"I've got a question."

"Take a seat, babe."

Sinking into the tan leather sofa, Utopia stared at Goldie. She was wearing a low-cut shirt, which revealed a big slash of bosom. Utopia was mesmerised by her perfectly formed breasts. Were they real? If not, did they gurgle, bounce like jelly or perhaps they had the firmness of dough?

"So?" said Goldie, hanging up.

Utopia removed her gaze. "So, yes. I'm trying to get this fire-fighter to do a diary of her sex change."

"Aha." Goldie offered Utopia a stick of gum. Her breasts nudged as she leaned forward.

"Thanks. Well, I spoke to him, I mean her and she's got a publicist."

"Sure."

"So, well, what should I say? I mean, what if—"

"Who is he?"

"The publicist? He's called Bluey."

"I know him. Looked after my ex's band in LA. Tell me what you want, I'll get it." She chewed as she spoke. "Put a call through by the end of the day."

"Gosh. Thanks." But Goldie was already back on the phone.

Back at her desk, Utopia found another note from Jean. It depressed her. She wondered if this was how they were to communicate from now on.

*Where are you? Did you send that fax to WH?*

Utopia resented having her competence undermined. Yes, she wanted to shout through Jean's door. She had witnessed it slide through the fax machine not once but twice, several hours ago. What was wrong with Jean, for God's sake?

She looked at her watch. It was five o'clock. Felix was coming to pick her up in an hour. For once she couldn't wait to get away.

# Chapter Eighteen

It was six thirty and the traffic was at a standstill. Cars were crawling their way along the Long Island expressway out of Manhattan and off to the Hamptons. It was the weekend exodus to the beach and an escape from Manhattan's humidity. They were listening to Frank Sinatra's "Later Years" on CD and Felix knew all the words. He had seen him sing at Caesar's Palace in Las Vegas twice. That was dedication. Utopia was impressed.

She was also relieved to be leaving the city, so relieved, in fact, that Marina's absence had gone unremarked. Until Felix brought it up. "Who is he?"

"Who?"

"Marina's mystery man."

"I don't know. Maybe he's a movie star."

"Maybe he's the President?"

"She's had him already."

Felix laughed and Utopia returned to the September issue of *HQ* open on her lap. It was as fat as a phone directory and filled with photographs of a young British starlet in various stages of undress. "Oh, listen to this." She laughed. It was her first laugh all day. " 'This fall sees a return of the elegant pant suit with the jacket which doesn't quite cloak the behind. This means there's no escaping the underwear challenge. The crucial detail is the thong. In order to avoid the VPL (visible panty line), it's essential to find a perfect fit, and to thong-shop successfully you must take time out to try plenty on.' "

Felix put his foot down as the traffic eased.

"That's hilarious. I mean, who actually goes thong-shopping?"

"Women in the big cities, the state capitals, LA. There are a lot of people out there and they don't all buy their clothes at K-Mart."

"No," said Utopia, and turned to look out at Brooklyn's brownstones, the scuffed basketball courts, at the Virginia Slim hoardings with mouthy girls in skinny jeans smiling at the carriageways of cars. *You've Come A Long Way, Baby*, they told her.

"So, tell me. How was it?"

Utopia looked at Felix.

He was dressed all in black and, with his velvety voice and hint of a smile, there was something almost priestly about him. The glasses with lilac lenses possibly gave it away. But he had an ease about him and a generous laugh that made you want to tell him things. What things exactly she wasn't sure, though everything would be her guess. She had known this man only weeks but it felt so much longer. There seemed nothing remarkable about travelling together like this, sharing the week's news, on their way to an unknown destination. She had discovered life in a foreign place to have a way of prompting instant friendships but this – being here – was different. This was about Felix, and by association, Marina. She was in very good hands.

"Fine."

"Just fine?"

"Still adjusting I suppose."

"To Jean?"

"Yes." She nodded, afraid of sounding disloyal.

She wondered if doubt wasn't part of the deal.

With the honeymoon over, the reality was bound to drag a little. Or was it her capacity to be content that was flawed? She had always had a tendency to seek out the next move before completing the last. It was the same way that she always considered herself a year older than she was. It was a sense of herself in a place not her own. Forever chasing something though she never knew what.

She stared out of the window at the promise of escape.

Beyond the freeway, suburban Queens had given way to a verdant horizon. With it came the sensation of being released from a cupboard and the joy of seeing light. Felix's Jeep gave them a clear advantage for spying on the fleets of German cars that raced by with strapped-in children and miniature dogs.

"Gloria's house is right by the sea," he said.

"Can't wait." She smiled and rested her feet upon the dashboard.

Almost every Sunday, since the heat had exploded, she had made the forty-five-minute train ride from Penn Station to Long Beach. It was New York's release valve. She had originally been taken by Saul, but she sometimes went alone. It was popular with Manhattanites and their Sunday papers, Brooklynites with babies and Spanish-speaking clans from Queens. It was a far cry from what she had seen of the Hamptons where she had been just the once with Marina. It had all the typical beachside attractions, a boardwalk with hot-dog men and ice-cream vendors. Girls with perms playing volleyball, men glazed in coconut oil and women in leopard-print swimsuits and glasses hanging from crinkly necks. Then there were the seagulls that patrolled the beach. Gorged on pretzels, they were the size of storks. They blocked out the sun when they flew overhead. They were frightening.

"You've never been to Southampton?"

"No. Well, maybe when I was young."

"Vacation?"

"I was born here. I lived here until I was four." She somehow assumed he knew these things.

"What were your parents doing in New York?"

"My father was at Columbia University. He's a professor now in London."

"And your mom?"

"She died in January." Her voice wavered as she studied the view.

"I'm sorry."

He paused. "Brothers? Sisters?"

"Sister. Liberty. Twenty-eight going on forty." She laughed. "She's a barrister and frighteningly grown-up. She thinks I'm the most irresponsible person in the world."

"So you're the brat?"

Utopia looked at him "Yes, though I'd never thought of it like that."

Felix overtook the jitney, the Manhattan to Hamptons coach, and they dragged the conversation back to the present. "Gloria's one of my clients," he told her. "She's probably my best client. Two seasons ago, she bought my entire collection just like that. And that's kind of how we met."

"She likes jewellery."

"Big-time. She's turned all her friends on to me and, boy, does she know how to party. She gets her blow from Peru, her tequila from Mexico and her rum from Cuba. She's in her mid-thirties, looks nineteen and she hasn't had surgery. Well, I believe her. Others might not"

"Who else is going to be there?"

"Isabella, her daughter. She's fifteen. She's a model. Brute, Gloria's best friend, is a permanent guest. He was voted *Town & Country* bachelor of the year in about 1982 and doesn't realise that over a decade has passed since then."

Utopia laughed.

"There's Eliza. I can't remember how they met. She used to be an author but she's had writer's block for ever. She was shortlisted for the National Book Award a long time ago. It's set in the South, Mississippi somewhere. It's about an incestuous relationship, brother and sister. I don't know why but I've always kind of figured it might be autobiographical . . . Shit. Here's our exit."

They left the freeway and veered into Southampton. It was a fairytale land of white mansions hidden behind tall brick walls, security gates and foliage trained as protection from prying eyes. The streets were deserted until they passed a row of boutiques and saw people skipping out of Ralph Lauren with bags in both hands.

It reminded Utopia of Connecticut.

She had once spent a weekend with Saul at Regine's house while Regine was away in Palm Beach. It had been a blissful two days. They had got drunk on raspberry martinis, cooked more lobsters than they could eat and downed a handful of Quaaludes from his mother's bedside drawer. It was the only time she had spent with Saul away from his studio and might even have been construed as romantic if Kurt hadn't shown up on Saturday night. It had been a full moon and they were naked in the pool. She could still feel the touch of slippery skin as their bodies melted into blackness. It was quiet but for the rustle of the trees. Then out of nowhere they had been interrupted with a dive-bomb.

"Hey man, I didn't think you'd make it." Saul had laughed, swimming over to duck his friend's head underwater.

Bloody Kurt.

"What a nightmare being in the studio all weekend," she said, thinking out loud.

"Saul?"

"Yes. When he's blasting flames, it's like a furnace in there."

"You should be careful," said Felix, turning left at a set of lights. "You've got it bad."

"What?"

"Saul."

"It's nothing serious."

They locked eyes in the overhead mirror.

"OK, I'm going to say one thing here because I've known him longer than you have . . ."

She nodded.

"The only thing Saul's in love with is his work. Sure he loves girls, I'm sure he loves you, but he loves his work more."

She was interested to hear Felix confirm what she had known all along. Still, it left an emptiness. What was the point in being with someone who wasn't with you?

"I know that," she said. "Anyway, there's P . . ."

She stopped as Felix turned right up a gravel drive. She would do no more back-pedalling. She refused to dwell on P, Saul, Jean, on any of it. She had left New York behind and, with it, her emotional baggage. This was supposed to be a weekend away. "How do you know Saul anyway?"

"I've known him for years. When I used to go clubbing in the eighties, I'd always see him out at the Palladium and Area. He was really young and thought he was a Beastie Boy. Have you met Regine? She buys my jewellery. I've been to stay up at their house in Connecticut a couple of times. She makes this chicken tarragon and I don't know what her secret is . . ."

He braked.

". . . this is it."

Out of the darkness emerged a large wooden beach-house.

The flicker of garden flares threw leafy shadows across the slats. Wicker furniture sat on the porch. The sound of samba could be heard from within. It was so secluded, it was magical.

"Darlings," a girlish voice called from the verandah, "I am so glad you're here."

A face then a figure appeared from behind the mosquito door. It was Gloria. She looked golden, her teeth smiling white against the night. She had a polished face and almond eyes. With her hands on her hips, wrapped in a sarong, she appeared beside the car and embraced Utopia like a long-lost friend.

"Uteepee. Felix has told me all about you."

# Chapter Nineteen

Utopia followed Gloria's gold sandals into a conservatory trellised with grape-vines and bougainvillaea. Then came the living room. The mantelpiece was studded with shells, conches were scattered on window-ledges and a pair of arm-chairs and a sofa dominated the room. On the floor lay a pair of leather riding boots and a whip. They were Brute's apparently. Utopia blinked at the multifarious nothingness. Everything was white.

They proceeded upstairs.

"You're in here," said Gloria.

Utopia was shown into a bedroom with a raised wooden bed covered by a mosquito net, which fell from a beam. She dropped her bag on the floor.

"You like?"

"It's wonderful."

"Brute, he's next door."

Felix's room was on the floor above and had a blue theme. It had an indigo bedspread and two ceramic vases overflowing with cornflowers. Utopia watched him unpack. Piles of grey and white T-shirts emerged from his leather bag like a display at Gap. She bounced up and down on the bed. She was six years old again and staying with her grandmother while her parents disappeared for a weekend away. She began to laugh. Felix joined her. It was contagious.

"What's wrong with you?" he asked.

"Weekend delirium I think. We're not meant to change, are we?"

"Not unless you're thinking of seducing Brute."

Utopia hit him. "Where is this Brute, anyway?"

"He should be back for nine o'clock cocktails, so any minute now, I guess."

She left Felix and wandered downstairs and through the back doors on to the terrace. It was fashioned from rows of logs and trimmed with a wooden bench. The garden was hidden behind a veil of pitch and resonant with humming cicadas. The air was silky smooth and Gloria was prostrate with a glass of Scotch in her hand. Beside her was a willowy woman in a butter-coloured dress.

"Uteepee," sang Gloria, without getting up. "This is Eliza and you must have a drink."

"I'd love one."

"Over there, darling. Help yourself." Gloria waved in the direction of a drinks trolley.

Utopia stood in front of the jumble of spirit bottles, gin, Scotch, vodka, tequila, and wondered what to do. Crash, the glass door slammed against the wall. A man burst on to the terrace panting like a hound. Seeing Utopia, he smiled. A rose flopped from a buttonhole and as he unexpectedly kissed her she could smell his breath. She could almost taste his whisky, the smell was so strong.

"Hello," she said, but he ignored her.

He poured himself a drink, then fell into Gloria's outstretched arms and buried his face in her cleavage.

"Brute, baby," she said, stroking his hair. "What a big baby you are."

"Perhaps you'd prefer wine?" suggested Eliza, standing up.

"Yes. Thanks," said Utopia.

In the kitchen a Filipino maid was stirring tiger prawns into a very large risotto. She lowered her gaze and wiped moisture from her brow. Utopia joined Eliza in front of the fridge. She was hit by the odour of sweat and had to prevent herself from reeling. It was very stale and very unexpected. "Felix tells me you're a writer," she said, moving a little away, as together they retrieved bottles of Chilean white.

"Oh, is that what I am?" laughed Eliza, revealing two rows of nicotine-stained teeth. "I thought I was mother to my girls." She coughed a tar-racked cough.

"Have you met them? Franklin and Eleanor."

Utopia shook her head. "I've just moved here," she told her, but Eliza wasn't listening.

Ice cubes rattled from the ice-dispenser into the hand-held bowl. The fridge door made a sucking sound as it was closed. They returned to the table.

Felix was chatting to Gloria while Brute prowled nearby. The smell of his cigar drifted across the terrace. Eliza lit a cigarette and disappeared into the garden to look for the dogs, her girls. "Here, Frankie, Ellie baby."

Utopia drank her wine. Squinting in the darkness, she detected a tree hung with a hammock. It was just possible to make out the shape of a body swinging gently.

"Who's that?" she asked.

"Isabella," said Felix. "She's a teenager. It's her job to be bored."

Utopia watched her rock.

She had become aware of Brute's undressing eyes. She

felt him peel away her T-shirt then trace the contour of her legs beneath her skirt. His attention was like a wolf-whistle, it provoked dirty flattery. She looked over and, from the corner of her eye, she watched a ribbon of smoke curl out of his mouth. Then he winked. She had been caught and an embarrassed smile spread across her lips. She looked away quickly and pretended he wasn't there. She thought she heard him laugh. From behind a row of pines came the vast churning of the ocean. The samba music played on inside and she felt herself relax.

Peace at last.

"Look," said Felix.

Two giraffe legs were dangling over the edge of the hammock. Isabella had decided to join them. She was slender with tumbling hair. Her languid approach was marked by an attempt to conceal an extra inch of thigh. She tugged hopelessly at her skimpy dress. Laughing, Gloria held out her arms and rocked her daughter in a embrace. "My beautiful daughter," she introduced her.

Utopia smiled.

She was entranced by Gloria. Here in the Hamptons she had crowned herself queen. Sit back, enjoy, she seemed to insist.

The maid appeared to set the table and Brute went inside. "I think he likes you," Gloria hissed.

Utopia let forth a difficult laugh and blushed.

"And he is my very best friend."

"I'm sure he's very nice," she responded, feeling typecast as the corseted female from the cold-blooded country.

"And you know? He is very, very heterosexual," she growled her Rs.

At this point Felix offered a hearty laugh. "Now that is

funny," he said. Gloria looked at him. "What? You think is wrong I say that?"

Utopia shook her head and shrugged and laughed all at the same time. Brute emerged with a bottle of champagne and didn't seem to notice. He was dressed in the uniform of a playboy, a navy double-breasted jacket, polo shirt, Gucci loafers, and he had a rich abundance of hair. He wasn't unattractive, thought Utopia, but difficult to look at all the same.

"Risotto. My favourite," said Felix, squeezing Utopia's hand as they moved to the table.

Gloria proceeded to spoon out the rice, and Isabella sucked her thumb like a sullen Lolita. She twisted a strand of hair around a finger and began listing the rock concerts she had attended this summer. She dropped names shamelessly. As an exotic Brazilian babe with an American education, she had the perfect credentials for attracting rock stars, thought Utopia. She tried to recall appearing as sexually confident aged fifteen. She couldn't. She remembered the bottles of antiseptic face-wash lining her basin like armaments. The agenda had been war not seduction. War against her pores, parents, and personal malaise. It had been anger that charted many of those years.

Round the table everyone chattered but nothing was said. Utopia caught tail-ends of conversation like the patter of rain. Satisfied with two dainty mouthfuls, Gloria had begun chopping up lines of cocaine on a mirror beside her. Brute poured more champagne and smiled as though the entire scene had been orchestrated for his selfish pleasure. "What is your name?" he now asked Utopia, with a waft of his arm.

She stared. Was he serious?

"Heaven," said Gloria, chop-chopping away.

Utopia continued eating. Heaven. She liked it. There was no point confusing the poor man.

Pushing aside her plate with a sigh, goddess Isabella adjusted her Walkman over her ears and retreated to the garden.

"Mmm, Heaven," repeated Brute, his eyelids hovering like tired moths. "A beautiful name for a beautiful girl."

Gloria snorted a line. "Never too much," she murmured. "Always a little, a little."

Brute followed and wiped his nose on his cuff. His eyelids came alive.

Gloria passed the mirror to Utopia and stood up.

"We dance."

She strutted on to the terrace like a prima ballerina and shook her hips to reveal a pancake-flat stomach. Brute stamped his foot with the passion of a flamenco dancer as she snaked in and out of his grasp. He flattered her, moving from foot to foot. Utopia was impressed.

"Yes, a wonderful dancer," said Eliza. "She used to win all the competitions when she was a girl in São Paolo. She was sixteen when she met her husband. They met on the dance floor. Both of them were with different partners. So romantic, don't you think?"

'Does she have a boyfriend now?" asked Utopia.

"A German apparently," said Felix. "Probably much younger. They normally are. The last one, an Argentinian film-maker, was only twenty-four."

"I see," said Utopia, who saw nothing but a hot summer night.

# Chapter Twenty

Lying beneath the net, Utopia listened to the roar of the ocean. Free from distractions she reflected on P. There was no escaping him. His laughing eyes, the crestfallen look of dejection trapped in his brow and the lines around his mouth as she announced her decision to leave. "It'll make life easier for both of us if I go away for a while," she had said. "I'll regret it if I don't."

Since the death of her mother, nothing had been the same. She couldn't focus on work, the future or their relationship. She had watched herself become a ball of fury and blame him for things that had only to do with herself. Yet still she had needed his approval to travel all this way and he had given it to her, unconditionally, as she knew he would.

But news of his liaison weighed as heavy as grief.

When she had finally got through to Lou before leaving the office, the sound of her voice had reduced Utopia to tears.

"It's probably bullshit," Lou had whispered down the phone. "You know what Liz is like. She's a fucking trouble-maker."

"But what did she say?"

"P was at Julian's party with some woman, that's all. They were together all evening and then all of a sudden they weren't there any more."

"And?" she demanded, forcing Lou to make the connection because she wasn't about to make it herself.

"She just thought, and you know what she's like, that they might have left together. But, honestly, U, I mean, really? What does it mean?"

What it meant was that Lou had telephoned to leave a message on her machine in the middle of the night. What it meant was that she now had the sensation of being swallowed alive.

She had not thought it possible but of course it was. P was just as capable of infidelity as she was. So confident was she of her place in his life, that he would wait for ever, his ego intact, as she flitted closer and closer to the flame, promising soon to return. Who was she kidding? They had never discussed affairs and she had never mentioned Saul. Trust had been given. Perhaps he had sensed her duplicity.

Remembering the conversation sent her head rocketing skywards. Her eyes, though tired, refused to close as the cocktail of stimulants coursed through her body. Her hands travelled down to her stomach. She poked the soft inch of padding gathered at her waist, her New York fat. She pinched it before moving to the warmth between her legs. Comforting and secretive, it enveloped her hands, palms together, knees folded up to her chest.

P's face then flickered into view.

It was the breath of rainy sex beneath Brighton pier. It was their conspicuous efforts to remain invisible thwarted by a flat-capped man who emerged out of the mist with a metal detector. Both of them were wrapped in P's mac, with Utopia thrust against a pole.

"Afternoon," he had grunted, his sniffing collie running circles around them, yapping excitedly.

With her hand between her legs, Utopia felt the strain of P's broad shoulders, his body pressed against hers. Her legs opened and her body tautened with longing. Alone with P.

Then, seconds later, as if on cue, a rival set of breathing patterns stole the silence. Utopia lay motionless as the outline of a figure approached. She recognised Brute. "What are you doing?" She raised her voice.

"What are you doing?" he asked, ambling towards the bed.

He sat down beside her, his eyes glinting and his breathing damp and laboured. Utopia pulled the sheet up to her chin, staring at him, her responses inert.

"It's crazy," he whispered, "you lonely in here and me lonely over there. Eh? What you say?"

She remained silent. Her breathing accelerated as his insinuation turned sour in her mouth.

"I don't know what you're doing in here."

"I came to see you," he said, as he raised the net.

Still frozen, Utopia saw her cocooned world vanish. A liquid stillness captured her limbs as she anticipated what was to happen.

"Come," he murmured.

Utopia tasted fear yield an unsolicited thrill.

"Heaven." He smiled, running his hand up her arm. He eased the sheet from her clutch. She lay quiet, her heart pounding as he pulled it back. His hand journeyed down her body very slowly. What are you doing? she asked herself, daring herself to surrender, second by second.

Gripped by curious detachment, she returned to P as, drenched with rain, they caught the wind beneath the coat.

His hand had nestled between her legs. She closed her eyes. He moved closer and the fumes of wine and smoke tickled her nostrils. Fumbling against her, he rolled on to the bed and she blindly gauged his movements, the unbuckling of the belt, the rip of the zip and the trousers hastily yanked off.

As she gave in to Brute's body in motion, she could hear P's voice being blown out to sea. Barely able to hear each other speak, they pursed their lips to each other's ears. "I think we should stay here for ever," he shouted into the wind.

With their hair plastered flat to their scalps, their faces streaming with water, they clung to each other amid the fog. She felt P's mouth planting kisses on her lips, across her cheeks, eyelids and forehead. She tipped her head back in contentment.

Brute wrenched himself off her. Utopia watched him through half-closed eyes. She turned on her side and he lay next to her in the darkness. His breath was calm as the shuddering ceased. Just go now, she urged silently. We've done it. It's over. Please go.

"Heaven," he whispered, tapping her arm.

She feigned sleep.

Swinging his feet to the floor, he eased himself out from under the net and left the room. Utopia opened her eyes and studied the gloom. Harsh tears stung her eyes. She begged for sleep and dreams of familiar places.

# Chapter Twenty-one

"Uteepee," called Gloria, as she stepped on to the terrace the next morning. It was all clear at the breakfast table with the sky stretched like sari silk overhead. "Good sleep?"

"Yes, thanks."

"You like the room?"

"Yes."

"The bed?"

"Very comfy," she said, rubbing her eyes.

Gloria's leopardskin bikini top matched her hot-pants. She was sipping coffee and her blonde mane was yanked in a knot. Eliza was in yesterday's dress and was reading *Pride and Prejudice*. She wore a serene smile and was lost to a world of fine bone china and drawing-room pleasantries. She had a dog under each arm like a cushion.

Utopia had woken to a raging headache and an overwhelming sense of disorientation. Then she remembered Brute. She had pulled her sheet over her head to commune with regret. It was a shabby feeling and she didn't want to share it. Her immersion beneath the shower for ten minutes had done nothing to restore her. She was grouchy and loath to speak. She took a seat on the bench.

The maid appeared with a basket of croissants as Felix and Isabella emerged through the gate. "Fantastic," he said, rubbing his hair with a wedge of towel.

"Too cold," pouted Isabella, as she moved in to nestle beside her mother. Her expanse of body was decorated with a microscopic bikini.

"How are you? You look half asleep." He turned to Utopia, his tufts of hair glistening with water. "And where's Brute?"

Utopia stared out at the garden. She had done her best to push his face to the back of her mind. Unprotected sex. How could she? She cringed and poured a cup of coffee. Adding milk, she watched black yield to brown like mud. She stared out at the tree with its empty hammock. The sun, already high in the sky, was pelting them with its thirsty heat. The flowers looked unnaturally bright, electric yellows, reds and oranges. From the lawn came the steady psst-psst-psst of the concealed sprinklers. An expensive Eden.

Felix was wearing navy swimming trunks. His body had a schoolboy youthfulness about it. Utopia smiled as he crossed his legs. His limbs were painfully thin.

"Are you laughing at me?" he asked, catching her.

"No. Well, yes. You just look so, I don't know, boyish." She laughed, properly this time.

Dipping her croissant into her coffee and sucking it, Utopia tuned in to snippets of Gloria's chat. Brute had gone to Easthampton for a friend's daughter's wedding, she gathered. Friends and family had jetted in from all over Brazil, Argentina and the States, but Gloria wanted nothing to do with it. They were her husband's friends, she complained. She ran her fingers through her hair and her nails scraped against her scalp. "They all want to know about my new life so they can hurt me." She sighed. "And I have my friend at four."

Utopia finished her coffee.

She felt uncomfortable with Gloria's insinuations. She was convinced Gloria had winked at her. Twice. She had a horrible suspicion that Brute had bragged of his conquest and that she had put him up to it. It was all becoming too like the plot from *Dangerous Liaisons*. It made her feel as though she was losing control.

Unable to sit there any longer, she ran upstairs to collect a towel for the beach.

She entered the bedroom and the rumpled sheets filled her with loathing. She saw herself as a lifeless form feeling nothing but his weight on top.

Frightened by herself, she fled to the bathroom.

In front of the mirror, she adjusted her red bikini. It was her mother's bikini, bought years ago in France. There was a time when she would turn up the music and dance in front of the mirror in the living room at home. She would turn it up another notch each time and her arms would flail higher and her legs move faster until the neighbour would bang or P would enter the room. "What the hell are you doing?" He would laugh. That was a long time ago now. Instead she saw P and the faceless girl in their bed. She saw the window cracked on to the garden and a warm breeze condoning their pleasure. She felt angry.

Stricken with despair, she raced to get out of the room, the house. She felt sick with herself, with Brute, with P.

"I'm off."

"Wait for me," said Felix.

"I'll meet you there."

"Oh. OK." He nodded. "Just follow the path."

She tugged open the gate and exited on to the track. It

was flanked by two steep banks of hawthorn. The sun on her face pummelled like a fist. Happy with her solitude and lured on by the booming of the ocean, she walked fast and quickly reached the dunes. She took off her shoes and ground her feet into the sand. The grains seeped between her toes and the clumps of marram grass pricked her soles. Beyond the shore a veil of spit crowned the waves as they crashed and came rolling in.

She sprinted across the wet sand, took off her shorts, threw down her towel and ran into the sea. Jumping the waves, she dived under and swam vigorously. The heads of a couple were visible like two floating buoys. She rolled over to lie on her back at the mercy of the currents and stared up at the sky. She closed her eyes in search of the space governed by breathing and the sensation of floating. With her arms outstretched like a star, she listened to the thunder of the sea as it echoed her heartbeat.

She imagined the mass of sea life below, a traffic of scales and gills moving in schools. Sensing her intrusion, they would change tack and weave away. She turned on to her front and swam a fast crawl. When her mother died, swimming had been a source of peace. The Highbury pool had been her sanctuary. Lap after lap she would swim, her goggles blind with tears, her limbs frantic with despair. It was all so simple when viewed from underwater. Just as the beach made you beautiful, so water made you strong.

A wave washed over her face and rinsed out her mouth.

"Have a nice day," said a man, as he swam past and waved.

"I'm trying," she told him.

She dipped down underwater.

She reappeared a few yards on, her lungs bursting for air. Ducking down again and again, she emerged each time to sunlight on her face until, like a shooting pain Brute burst into memory. She gagged on a wave. The thought of him repulsed her. As she continued to swim, she thought about what to do. It would be madness to go on when she was this far from home. To spend another night at Gloria's would be reckless. She couldn't do it. She would catch the train back to Manhattan this afternoon, she decided.

As though heralding the event, her name came to find her. Turning to swim back to shore, she spied Felix on the beach, his arms waving like streamers above his head. "Thought you'd swum home," he said, as her feet touched the shallow.

She laughed. "I feel human again."

They sat on the sand with their legs in the water and contemplated the glittering ocean and cloudless sky. Nearby a boat-house jutted out from the dunes with its stars and stripes attempting abortive flaps in the heat. Families from the pages of a J. Crew catalogue were setting up camp. Fathers in baseball caps were erecting striped beach umbrellas while mothers smothered children with cream.

"I'm going back," she announced, cupping handfuls of water to splash on her legs.

"To London?" He looked confused.

"Manhattan. I want to catch the train."

"But we just got here."

She stalled for a moment. "I just need to." It was more instinct than reason.

"But we're having a big barbecue tonight."

She paused. It was useless. She had to leave. "I'm just feeling a bit overwhelmed by everything. It's hard to explain." She was going round in circles. She sighed and hugged her legs to her chest.

"Hey, whatever you have to do is fine by me," he said,

and smiled. "It's just a shame, that's all."

Utopia nodded. She couldn't explain. She hadn't exactly fought him off.

She would have liked to make light of it, to laugh at it like a silly one-night stand, just one of those things.

For some reason she couldn't.

They stood up to shake off the sand and Utopia drew her towel round her waist. They began trudging back through the dunes. A kite fringed with tendrils took a nose-dive and disappeared behind a beard of grass. The wail of a child pierced the silence. Filled with affection for Felix, she linked an arm with his. You are the centre of the benign universe, she would tell him if this was a movie. She gripped his arm tighter. They walked back in silence. The child's crying faded with the sea. Sticky with salt and caked with sand, her skin tingled.

Back at the house, a shiny white Neon Dodge was parked outside. It was a rental car.

"Why, that'll be the gentleman caller," drawled Felix. "Come to see the lady at home, I do suppose."

Utopia went to pack, hastily flinging her clothing into a rucksack before racing downstairs and on to the terrace. "Gloria, I'm off. Oh. Oh, my God."

There, cradling Gloria's head in his lap, was none other than Kurt.

"Uteepee, Felix says you are going. No. I don't understand," Gloria whinnied, without getting up.

"Yes, I have to get out," fumbled Utopia.

Kurt's surprise had triggered a guilty flush. He coughed. "Utopia."

Gloria lifted her head to look at him, then at Utopia. "You are friends?" she asked, sensing the mood change in his limbs. "How you know each other?"

"Through Saul."

Looking on in bemusement, Felix said nothing.

"I'm leaving. Have to catch a train," said Utopia.

"Right, *ja*. I see."

"So, thanks," she said, as she threw her bag over her shoulder. "It's been lovely. Really. Thanks so much, Gloria."

"Come on. You don't want to miss the four o'clock," said Felix.

With a wave, Utopia followed.

They drove to the station accompanied by country-and-western songs of disappointed love. Utopia felt dirty. It was all so incestuous.

"I didn't know Gloria knows Saul."

"Me neither," he said, turning into the station car-park.

They parked and went to buy a ticket, then wandered along the empty platform. The rough surface of the tarmac pricked the soles of her flip-flops. The air was balmy. Nothing stirred. They found a bench.

"Brute came to find you, did he?" said Felix, finding a bent cigarette in a soft pack. He began smoothing it out between finger and thumb.

She nodded.

"He's kind of clever like that."

On the platform opposite two boys were playing frisbee.

"Can you play?" he asked.

"Yes. Actually I'm quite good."

"You should have said. I've got one in the car. It glows in the dark. Next time we'll have a game."

"Yes." She smiled. "I'd like that."

# Chapter Twenty-two

"Don't you realise who I am? I am the features director of *HQ!* I have every right to insist you give us an answer on the story. I know the First Lady has a tight schedule *BUT SO DO I!*"

Utopia looked up from her desk in time to catch Diane's expression of horror as she glided past Jean's office. Diane was the mistress of stealth. She had a knack of appearing from nowhere. It instilled a sense of caution. Hands masked receivers and exchanges were conducted in hallways. But Jean's door was ajar and her voice was raised. Her voice was on the verge of cracking like that of a vengeful soprano. With a frown, Diane moved swiftly on. The satin lining of her pencil skirt rustled as she went.

Jean had arrived an hour ago sibilant with wrath. Her coffee was cold and her pumpkin muffin was stale. Utopia had been sent for replacements. The music story Utopia was editing had been detained in fact-checking because Todd had lost the proofs in the park. He had taken them with him at lunch and left them on a bench. But it was Utopia who had been summoned into Jean's office. "I gave you this job for a reason, to get the job done. Now what's going on? Is there something you want to tell me?" she had shrieked.

Utopia had sat frozen to her chair unable to move or to speak.

Jean's words stung. The air inside her office had smelt stale, funky, as though someone had spent the night here. Perhaps she had. Jean looked haggard. Her eyes were couched in bruises and her white linen shirt was splattered with breakfast fall-out.

Utopia had fled to the bathroom to gather herself and blow her nose. She wondered how the others in the features department, Ron and Brooke, managed to ignore Jean's mood swings. Perhaps it was resistance built up over time. Perhaps she too would grow immune. They were polite enough when Utopia knocked on one of their doors about a proof, a reference book or telephone number, but she had never once been invited in for a chat.

Perhaps they would never forgive her for replacing Meg.

Perhaps they considered her part of the enemy camp as Jean's co-conspirator. She was meant to be having a drink tonight with Jean. It was a date fixed up last week. She wasn't looking forward to it. In fact, she prayed that in Jean's madness, she had forgotten.

She was waiting for a fax.

The office airlessness had begun to encroach on her sanity. Above her was an endless track of strip-lighting. She felt entombed in bad air and bad light. It was that same sensation of being trapped in an airplane — no way out.

She felt almost nostalgic about her job at *Music Today*, something she swore she would never let happen. But it was nostalgia for Keith's bad jokes, the blaring music, her frantic role compiling trend reports and sifting through advance cassettes in search of "New Band of the Week". She even felt sentimental about Saturdays spent in photographic studios with whichever blonde was flavour of the month. *Music Today* liked their cover girls in the same pose everytime. Hipster trousers, midriff bared and hands cupped over naked breasts. It was Utopia's job to keep every one happy by providing whatever was wanted.

There was a wistfulness associated with the magazine's organised rowdiness. She missed the brain-storming sessions in the pub after work, the birthday parties, press parties, leaving parties, sales-figures parties. Life in the office was never dull. Bike couriers with drop-offs would hang out for a smoke. There were impromptu football games and an endless stream of visitors. It did at least function with a level of communication, unlike this place. This place was like a morgue, she decided, as she waited for a pin to drop.

"Hey."

Todd's head reared up from behind the partition like a ventriloquist's doll. The evil puppet who murders his master. Utopia looked at her watch. It was twenty past one and Jean's door was closed. She had been on the telephone for over forty-five minutes, Utopia calculated.

"Still in therapy?" Todd asked.

"What?"

"Her therapist lives in LA."

"No?"

"I can't believe you didn't know."

Utopia shook her head.

"Her therapist moved to Bel Air. Jean does it every lunchtime. It's the therapist who holds her shit together."

How could she have missed this? "Can you really do it over the phone?" she whispered.

"Sure. Every one does," replied Todd.

Then, just as they broke into laughter, Jean stormed out of her office. Utopia cringed and Todd bolted. Jean looked a fright. Trails of mascara eclipsed her eyes which were puffy and bloodshot. Her lipstick was smeared and her foundation bleached with tears. She blinked wide-eyed like an ostrich and then took off down the hall. Not a word was said.

Unsure of what next to do or whether or not she was authorised to leave, Utopia studied her desk for something to occupy her. It was more than likely that Jean would arrive back any minute with a task for which she must be found waiting.

She pulled over a pile of old *HQ*s from the shelf beside her. They were from the seventies. She turned one over. It was dated June 1974. Its paper had a dense, porous quality. There were advertisments for wedge shoes, a Madison Avenue hair salon and bikinis at Saks Fifth Avenue. There was an essay by Tom Wolfe and a series of black and white photographs of New York street life; a woman in a fur walking a dog, a cop in a leather jacket bending to talk to a small child, the Guggenheim Museum casting spaceship shadows across Fifth Avenue. The references were dated but the mood seemed modern and the style free.

Working from back to front, Utopia arrived at a con-tributors' page. Her eyes skimmed what she thought to be a snapshot. For a split second, it looked like her parents. She scrutinised the picture. It was of two heads side by side, those of a man and a woman. They were smiling. He was in a polo-neck shirt and had a thicket of curls and dark eyes. He was holding a camera. Wispy strands of hair framed the female's face. She had cheekbones like weaponry and a pouting mouth. She was standing behind him with her shoulders bared and her head balanced on his shoulder.

*Model Sandra Holmes with photographer Robert Shanks* read the caption.

The model was her mother.

Utopia raced to the back of the magazine. She knew what she was looking for. Pages 118–24. There they were, the pictures she had grown up with, the photographs set against the navy wall in the hallway on the way to the kitchen. It was her mother in a floral A-line skirt and a cloche. She had exaggerated eyes and her hands butterflied her face like a geisha girl's. There was another shot of her mother from the back in flared white trousers and spotted halter-neck. She had coat-hanger shoulder-blades.

Utopia returned to the contributors' page.

The double portrait shocked her, although she wasn't sure why. Meeting her mother like this provoked a mixed reception. She felt pride and disdain indistinguishably mingled. The past to which she was excluded cast her mother as a stranger. It challenged her version of events. She stared until the photograph dissolved to grey. She rolled up the magazine and hid it in her bag.

Her telephone went. "What are you doing later? We're going to the concert in the park. Come."

It was Marina.

"Where?"

"Central Park."

"Oh."

"Swing by the office."

"When?"

"I'm on deadline. Say, eight."

"Tonight?"

"Are you OK?"

"Yes, fine," she mumbled. "Are you sure it's not a date? I don't want to play gooseberry."

"Oh, yes, hot date with Dorian and his assistant. See you here at eight." Marina hung up.

"Utopia, there's a fax for you in the tray."

It was Jean. "And don't forget our drink."

SLAM. The door shut behind her.

Punished by Jean's silence, Utopia had become a prisoner of Jean's caprice. It was a role she was beginning to resent. She returned to the photograph of her mother. She looked so happy. Whatever happened to Robert Shanks?

They were sitting in the coffee shop on the ground floor of *HQ*'s building. World music chanted from invisible speakers. Gliding between tables came waiters with sandwiches decked with Cellophane flags. Utopia fancied a martini. Make that two olives, as Marina would say. But, no, right now a café latte was what she had in front of her.

She was sitting opposite her boss. Jean had repaired her mandarin lips and brushed her hair. Utopia tried to relax. It wasn't easy. She would much rather be with Marina or, better still, alone with her thoughts and understand what it was that she had found in the June 1974 copy of *HQ*. But here she was with Jean's jittery smile and a plateful of cookies.

"Almond biscotte. My favourite," said Jean, dunking it into a mug of coffee. Jean's mood had altered dramatically since leaving the office and ordering biscuits. She had a serious sweet tooth. Earlier today Utopia had stepped on a Hershey's Kiss lying on Jean's floor. The chocolate had oozed from its foil and soiled the carpet but she hadn't dared mention it.

She felt bereft of small talk. Here they were sat like two old friends when only this morning Jean's words had prompted her to mutter, "Bitch, bitch, bitch," as she took refuge in the ladies.

"I just wanted to say today was hell," said Jean. "It's been one of those days and sometimes it's hard."

Utopia smiled. So, they were having their drink for Jean to reveal her human side again.

"I like you and I think you're smart." And now came the boss part. "You've just got to stay on top of things. This First Lady story is a big deal." And now the reprimand. "I know you can do this job. It's just that, well, I've got a lot on my mind at the moment."

Utopia watched Jean's eyes start to well. They were beginning to darken. She sniffed. "Michael's trying to cheat me out of Daddy's money. I've got the court case in two weeks and I don't even know if I can trust my lawyer. He was best man at our wedding and now he's in on Michael's plot to steal the Picassos."

If Michael was Jean's ex-husband, where were the Picassos? she wondered. She didn't dare ask. "I see."

"Christ, they're having a baby." Jean retched, expelling her horror along with the news.

Utopia watched Jean's bottom lip curl. Glassy tears popped from the corners of her eyes. Her shelf of bosom rose and fell. To her horror, Jean had begun to cry.

"Have you told Diane about this?" she asked, at a loss as to what else to say.

"Diane?"

"I'm sure she'd understand."

Jean wiped her eyes. Tracks of black clawed their way down her face. "Yes," she agreed. "You're probably right." She sounded weary.

Someone adjusted the stereo. The didgeridoo grew louder, and outside the street had turned indigo. Utopia looked at her watch. It was a quarter to eight. She was meeting Marina in fifteen minutes' time. Jean was staring at her own reflection set against the darkening glass.

"The transsexual story looks like it's going to happen," said Utopia, her enthusiasm a hopeful ticket out.

Jean said nothing. Utopia started again. "The transsexual—"

"You probably want to go. You must have things to do," Jean interrupted her, rubbing her eyes in a blind attempt to repair the damage. "I ought to go finish up in the office."

"Yes. If you're OK."

"Sure. Fine. Really."

Her eyes were distant. Perhaps she already felt she had said too much. She was nodding. Utopia stood up. "Yes. So, I'll see you tomorrow, then."

"Yes."

"Thanks for the coffee."

Utopia pushed her chair beneath the table and fled. She didn't know whether to laugh or cry. On Seventh Avenue she hailed a cab.

# Chapter Twenty-three

"I'm here to meet Marina Lansdowne," she told the security guard at reception.

He was reading a hair-trade magazine. *Truly, Madly, Blondy,* read the headline from upside down. He rang through. "Marina? Ethiopia for you."

Utopia rolled her eyes. It wasn't the first time. He authorised her entrance into the sprawl of white cubicles spread across the open-plan floor. The cathedral-sized room was illuminated by two floor-to-ceiling windows and disturbed only by the tapping of keyboards and murmurings of conversation. Utopia could see Marina's head above her station. She heard her barking laugh like feeding time in the seal pool.

"Hello," she whispered, arriving at Marina's desk.

"Darling. I'm on the phone," Marina mouthed. She pointed for Utopia to sit down.

Utopia studied Marina's pinboard. It was covered with celebrity ephemera, with photographs of Marina being manhandled by a man in a tuxedo, shaking hands with Liz Taylor, giggling with a pretty girl. There was an invitation to Swifty Lazar's Oscar-night party, a note from someone thanking her for the "swell interview" and a Chinese fortune-cookie slip which read, 'Serendipity is tomorrow's dawn'.

But in truth she saw only her mother. It was her mother as a photographer's muse, semi-naked, lithe-limbed. It was her coy contentment to nuzzle close to the man not her husband. Utopia was jealous of this man. She felt protective of her father. She had no right to be suspicious of her mother yet it wouldn't go away.

Marina finished. She hung up. "Jesus fucking oh-my-God-Christ, I love him, I love him." She squeezed Utopia's knee hard.

Utopia jumped. "What?"

"OK," she said, her eyes all pupils and her face flushed. "Right. Well, you know I couldn't come to the beach because someone was coming to town?"

"Yes."

"That was him. Donald. He had to fly back to LA first thing Sunday morning and I've been waiting for him to call ever since."

"You never told me about this."

"Complicated, darling. I've known him for ten years but also the ex-wife. Anyway, Friday night we went for dinner. Gorgeous, lovely, but that was that. Saturday night, I went to meet him at his hotel for cocktails. We never left. Sex like I haven't had in years. I mean, bang against the wall—"

"Hey, I'm still here you know," a voice piped up from the other side of the wall. It was the voice of a man castrated by a lifelong devotion to fashion.

"Charlie, don't be such a prude." She winked and switched off her computer. "Better go. Said we'd meet Dorian at eight thirty."

"Have you told him?"

"No. We never fuck. Well, hardly."

"Please," Charlie begged, "can't it wait?"

"OK. No more revelations until tomorrow. Promise. 'Bye."

" 'Bye," he replied gruffly.

Standing in the lift, watching the illuminated numbers drop from 26 to L, Utopia laughed. "Poor Charlie. He must hear everything."

"Hardly. I'm a pro when it comes to phone etiquette. Besides, Charlie's a celibate old queen. It makes his juices run."

"Ugh."

They were sniggering like teenagers as the rotating door tossed them on to the street. The evening was sticky and lifeless.

"Please let there be some air in the park," said Marina, as they flew up Madison Avenue in a cab.

They cut through to Fifth and Utopia felt humbled by the genteel respectability this side of the park. To their left Central Park's lushness enhanced the spectacle of wealth. In New York only the very rich could afford to live amongst trees. Winding down the window, she inhaled the oxygenated air and the scent of foliage like a rare and expensive commodity.

Enjoy it while you can.

They arrived at 72nd Street, paid the cab and joined the strollers on the path leading over to Summer Stage.

"You still haven't told me about your weekend," said Marina, as they waited for Dorian by a row of Portacabins. "Who was there?"

"Gloria. Isabella . . ." She tailed off. "It's all a bit of a blur."

"What can you mean?"

"We got very drunk very quickly and . . ."

"Why are you looking so guilty? What happened? Come on."

"I had a, em, drunken night with a man who was there. He had the room next door. A friend of Gloria's."

The words spun as they fell to earth. She wanted to grind them underfoot and destroy all trace.

Marina began to laugh. "Tell me it wasn't Brute. It was, wasn't it? Darling, you have been on the rampage."

Utopia twisted her ring round her index finger. It was a Celtic cross, a gift from Felix.

"It wasn't really like that."

"How do you mean?"

"He just appeared in my bedroom. He pulled down my sheet and—" She stopped. "I escaped the next day so I didn't have to see him."

"Christ, he didn't force you, did he?"

"No. No, he didn't."

"Phew." she plucked her cigarette from her mouth. "You had me worried. Fun?"

"Maybe for a moment."

"A stupid one-night stand, then."

"Yes. I suppose."

Utopia waited for her regret to pass. The memory left her reeling. It was like stumbling drunkenly in the dark. She hated herself for sleeping with Brute. She hated herself for lying to P. She hated P for lying to her. All such a fuck-up. Communing with Central Park was an effective antidote to the loneliness of remorse, at least. She was in the right place.

"All right, gels?' And here was Dorian.

Waving as he heckled them, he swaggered over. It was a sexual swagger, thought Utopia, as she watched him, like a self-conscious approach to a bed. He worked out at the gym every day and wore very tight T-shirts.

"Utopia," he said, embracing her roughly. "Did anyone ever tell you you've got the stupidest bloody name?"

"Never."

"That's all right, then. I want you to meet Paulo, my assistant." He introduced a slim-shouldered boy in a red vest with 99 on the front.

An assistant was *the* accessory for nineties living, thought Utopia. She smiled at him and he smiled back.

"Did you bring drinks?" asked Marina. "We forgot."

"Do you two ever stop gossiping? I can't think what you ever did before Utopia moved to New York."

"Spent more time with you?" she said, and slid her glasses over her eyes.

"Yeah, right. So are we going to find somewhere to sit or what?"

"Yes, but we don't want to wade through thousands of people."

"Marina, we're going to have do that anyway."

He was right. The lawn in front of the Summer Stage was hidden beneath a sea of New Yorkers. Students were sitting with brown-paper bags between their legs. Afro-American families in rainbow robes were unpacking baskets. Suited young professionals were loosening their ties as they shared their day with partners in headbands and flesh-coloured stockings and hustlers peddled cold drinks. Beneath the trees well-fed cops chewed gum and thumbed loaded belts.

Dorian led the way. They played stepping-stones between camps, negotiating for patches of grass between buckets of potato salad and sleeping heads. Every inch of ground had been stolen. Beyond was a ring of trees and

New York's skyline, the Dakota Building and red rock, Central Park West, further on. The first flickerings of twilight offered no relief from the humidity, which was going to crawl through the night. The evening was as airless as a nightclub with the night stars the ceiling fresco.

"Stop," said Marina, as they found a square of bald turf.

They arranged themselves as best they could.

Cross-legged on the ground, Utopia strained to see who was on stage. It might as well have been a mile away as the sound of drums resonated across the park. But a trio of women were just visible dancing at the front. They were leaping and sailing and their voices unleashed a haunting cry. Then a huge cheer ripped through the crowd, there were whistles and applause. The singer had arrived. She could just make him out. He was a slight Senegalese man draped in magenta robes.

"On nights like this, you know why we live in New York," said Dorian, passing Utopia a beer as Broadway's sirens joined the musical score.

Utopia nodded. Dorian was right. She was transfixed by the music and heat. It was all so much bigger than she was. She felt her grievances perspire in steady drips.

Marina was fanning herself with a magazine. She had kicked off her sandals and tugged her sequined skirt up to her crotch. Her legs were stretched out in front. The seam of her knickers was visible. Utopia looked again. "You're not wearing knickers." The words flew from her mouth.

"Should I be?"

"It might get you into trouble, that's all."

"No thong, no VPL, darling."

Utopia nodded and watched trickles of sweat smudge the creases in Marina's neck. The lines in a woman's neck, like the rings in a tree, were the true determinant of age, she reflected, as she tried to recall having spent a day in an office knickerless. She couldn't. It was funny how Marina could make her feel prudish. Perhaps it was the difference in their age. She felt quite sure that Marina was growing more bawdy with the years.

Dorian was chatting to Paulo in Spanish. Their return trip to Brazil was planned for the following week. Dorian was a bore about work. He wasn't interested in anything he didn't think was worth photographing. Life itself existed for the sole purpose of being blown up and sold in the Krauthoffer-Flinne Gallery on Broome. Utopia had been to his last opening. Venus Rising, it had been called. It had been a series of blown-up photographs of models shot underwater in ballgowns billowing around their heads like passengers off the *Titanic*.

Dorian said it was an attempt to explode the myth. Which myth exactly, Utopia wasn't sure.

"Nor's he," was Marina's comment. "But it sounds pretentious enough to go in the catalogue, that's the main thing."

"*Tenemos que estar preparados*," Utopia heard Dorian say, as Paulo rolled a joint.

Prepared for what? wondered Utopia.

Her few words of Spanish she had learned from P. And then a whisper of air traced its way through the trees and licked her face like a cat. What a treat.

# Chapter Twenty-four

The concert ended with cheering, which swept across the park like a wave. Arms dipped and swayed for as far as the eye could see. Even now Utopia had the sound of ringing in her ears. The four of them were sharing a cab downtown. Staring out of the window at the blur of Times Square, she remembered the magazine hidden in her bag. The cab stopped at a red light for the pedestrians at 42nd Street to cross. A rotund family wobbled across the windscreen.

"What do they feed them out west?" laughed Dorian, smoothing his hand across his bald head. "Quarter-pounders for breakfast?"

Utopia noticed that hair grew on his knuckles.

Squashed between Marina and Paulo in the back, she found herself in her father's car on the drive down to Kent. It had been her mother's wishes that they scatter her ashes in the sea. Liberty was in the passenger seat and she was behind. It was a journey taut with emotion, though little was said. By the time they arrived, it was late afternoon and the sun had left them a soft opal light.

They parked and went to fetch her grandmother, who put on her coat and tied her headscarf beneath her chin. They walked in single file along the back lane to the beach, with her grandmother's terrier George yapping in front. They were alone in the bay, buffeted by gusts that filled their mouths and nostrils with the taste of cold. The seagulls whirred and an oyster-catcher screeched. They stopped beside a washed-up snake of rope.

"Here?" said their father.

"Further along," said her sister.

Twenty yards on, they stopped again.

"But you can't see the point."

"Well, you can see the sea," said their grandmother, which was true.

Her father tore the seal on the bag. He threw the ashes in an arc but the wind had dropped. They fell into the wet sand and dissolved underfoot. No one knew what to say. Liberty was next. She shook the bag so hard that for a moment Utopia thought there would be nothing left. Then she took a palmful. She held out her hand, uncurled her fingers and in a flash the wind had sucked them up and into her eyes so that she couldn't see.

"I've got them in my eyes," she cried.

"Oh, don't be so stupid," said Liberty.

"There she goes," whispered her grandmother, but there was nothing to see.

In the distance there was only sea and sky. So they huddled together and watched the sun drop like a yolk behind the horizon. Only the fact that this was a view her mother had loved made any sense.

Shivering, Utopia hugged her bag and forced her focus outside on the street. Memory was cruel, she reflected. No regard for time or place.

"Pull over," Dorian was shouting at the cab driver.

They were half way down Broadway. The cab braked.

"I'm picking up my Brazil rolls," said Dorian, as he scrambled out.

"Sold any stories?" asked Marina.

"Breakfast at the *Times* tomorrow. Should be able to flog them something."

He poked his head through the window of the back seat. "What do you know about the Save the Rainforest fund-raiser at Radio City Hall?"

"It's set for the first week of October."

"Aha. Thought maybe that's the peg."

"Why not?"

Paulo got out of the front seat and the cab drove off.

"I've actually been asked to join their select committee," said Marina.

"Oh," said Utopia. "That sounds grand."

The cab turned left then right. Utopia's stop.

"Crazy day tomorrow. I'll call you late. *Ciao.*"

Utopia slammed the door and watched the cab speed off.

She tugged open her front door. It was unlocked and freshly plastered with posters promoting a gig at Irving Plaza. Marina never said goodbye without scheduling when they would speak next. Marina was the only person who knew of her day-to-day whereabouts, she realised. She supposed it was important that someone did.

She unlocked the apartment door. The answering-machine on the table was flashing. She hit PLAY and leant her head over the box. "Hello. It's Utopia Holmes' father here ringing to say hello and see how you're faring. I've been asked to come over and deliver a lecture at Columbia. Oh, yes, I went to see the Edward Hopper retrospective and bumped into P. Asked after you. Anyway. Do ring soon. Yes, all right, bye, then . . ."

She listened to her father's wireless enunciation and emotions flowed as inevitably as rain. She felt sad. She worried about him swallowed up in London's leafy darkness. He was alone in a house enshrined to her mother. When her mother was alive the house had been alive with amaryllis, narcissi, lilies, African violets, gladioli, peonies, agapanthus. She had been passionate about flowers. Now the house was empty. Did Liberty go to see him enough? Did he resent her absence? So many questions. Nothing would make her happier than to see him. She must ring.

She had, in fact, been meaning to do so for days, weeks even, but something resisted as he must have guessed. Twinned with a sense of pride was the transatlantic divide. It was a mutually exclusive arrangement. Distance sanctioned silence. She didn't want to explain because she didn't want interference. Avoidance had always been one of her strengths. She could hold a grudge for weeks. It used to drive P mad. "I need sub-titles to understand what's going on in your head," he would complain.

Why she couldn't tell him that his ex-girlfriend coming to stay for two weeks was too long when she treated the flat like a hotel and Utopia like the lodger, she didn't know. Perhaps that was why it was so easy with Saul. There was no pressure to talk, no pressure to care. Perhaps that was why she couldn't telephone P to find out the truth.

She switched on the fan and opened the windows.

The night air was as black as treacle. She swung open the fridge door, leaned her body towards the cool air and left it there. The electric hum was soothing. She stared into the fridge and wondered what to eat. There was a giant mayonnaise jar with a turquoise lid, a withered frisée lettuce, a whole shelf of halfeaten jams and jellies, mustards and pickles, and a wad of shrivelled bacon rashers. There was nothing to eat. She grabbed the gallon container of chilled water, poured herself a glass and moved to the table.

Clearing a space, she began sorting through the stack of postcards that lived at one end. They were cards bought in museums, galleries, news kiosks, drugstores, bookshops. They were freebies picked up in restaurants, diners, coffee shops and bars. She knew what she was looking for. It was something bright and greedy. There it was, a hot-dog slathered in mustard. She flipped it over and sucked the end of her pen as she deliberated over what to say.

*Dear P*                           *20 August*
    *New York is a blast.* HQ *is going well. I'm on the hotline to the White House and chasing a transsexual. Just back from a w/e at the Hamptons, staying at a beach-house by the surf. Have been to a couple of concerts at Summer Stage in Central Park. Little Italy is a riot. I love it. Love U*

She stared at the 'Love U' and paused, but the tone pleased her. Her life read as fast-track and loads of fun.

Was it? This was New York so she supposed it was. She studied her words. Did they read as guarded or free and easy, a spontaneous scrawl? She was being ridiculous, she couldn't tell. She needed him to know she was thinking of him, that's all.

She looked up. Johann was unbuttoning his shirt. He levered the top off a beer. She watched him wipe foam from his moustache and unwrap a greased-paper package of sausages. He laid them out in a frying-pan and stabbed them with a fork.

"My dad's coming to New York."

"Better clean up."

She looked over at the magazines spread across the floor, the row of empty bottles on the top shelf like a shooting gallery, the mismatched shoes by the door, and realised he was right. "Any luck with the Norwegian girl?"

Johann shrugged.

"What about American girls?"

"They're not sexy," he said, jerking the sausages so that the fat began to spit.

"But I thought they were meant to be so sexually liberated."

She was thinking of a British banker friend of Marina's. He had discovered that buying a pitcher of daiquiris for a female colleague bought him a night of passion. He had spoken of nothing else, kinky stuff, he said, the one time they met. Utopia had been less shocked by the revelation than his assumption that she wanted to know.

"All I want is a Swedish girl who lives in New York," he said. "You eating?"

He joined her at the table and passed her a plate. They ate in silence, spearing lumps of meat and slices of balsamic tomato. She thought of P sitting at his desk reading her postcard. She imagined his vicarious thrill at the mention of the White House. She then wondered who else was there and banished both from her mind.

Johann had turned to the personal columns at the back of the *New York Press*, the free weekly listings rag.

"Here's one. '*Twenty something, East Village W.F. seeks companion with possibility of making a love connection. Must be Georgie Fame fan, HIV neg, non-smoker.*'"

"Not."

The telephone rang. Johann answered and passed it to her.

"Utopia, hi." It was Anna.

This was the moment Utopia had been dreading all week. She said thanks to Anna's invitation to a gallery opening the following week but offered nothing in return. She hated the fact that Kurt's secret was hers. She refused to accept that it was her responsibility to alert Anna to the fact that Kurt was a rat. The way Saul explained it, Anna and Kurt were an on-off item, always had been. Perhaps this was the acceptable face of dating. She made it brief and hung up.

"Something wrong?" said Johann, who never missed a trick.

"You don't want to know," said Utopia, and sliced her sausage in half.


It was late.

Johann had a presentation to deliver at eight the next morning so slunk off to bed. Utopia watched Monkey Man prepare for a night on the town. Each arm was held aloft and deodorant sprayed. He was ironing a white T-shirt and rocking his upper body. He tensed his pectorals from one to the other then both at the same time. It was a skilled performance.

Utopia watched as she fiddled with her pen, gathered more postcards and put together a list of family and friends. Months had passed and she had managed to avoid the act of getting in touch. But it was suddenly important that they knew. Her message back varied little. It was the bang-them-out formula of thank-you letters but they weren't to know that. "Thinking of you," she wrote and she was. Finally.

She licked stamps and placed the postcards ready to be sent. Offerings on TV were dull. She flicked up to ninety-five and back down again. There was a made-for-TV movie about child abuse, *Sounds of the Eighties* on VH1, a Rita Hayworth film on Turner Classics, a documentary on gulags on PBS, *I Love Lucy* in black and white, and a feast of ads on the channels in between.

She went to have a bath. It was a meagre tub but the trick was to fill it to the brim and slide down low. She found a box of matches and lit three candles. This was Johann's touch. He said it was to remind him of his Swedish summer-house. She wanted to believe him. She got in and submerged herself to chin level.

The window was open and the current of incoming air was warm. She listened to the sirens ricocheting down Houston as the flames sent shadows chasing each other across the ceiling's freckled mould. She watched them dance and her thoughts spooled from her mother to P to her father and back again. She wondered at her distance from them and the reasons why. She wondered at her parents' love affair here in New York, at their long-ago departure, at Robert Shanks.

Lacking answers, she slid underwater and held her breath. She began counting in Spanish. *Uno, dos, tres, cuatro, cinco.* She had begun watching the Spanish channel last thing late at night. The line-up was beauty pageants, cookery shows, soap operas and rape-fire-murder news but the familiarity of the foreign tongue pleased her.

"*Ahora las noticias con Maria Malconado,*" said the woman on the news.

It reminded her of P and the teach-yourself-Spanish tape he listened to in the car. The instructor on the tape was called Maria. It was their joke. Maria was the other woman in his life. Utopia stopped.

Why did she always come back to this same place?

She had to get some sleep.

To cope with Jean, she had to be punctual. Her plan was to hit the subway, pick up a coffee at the 53rd Street deli and be at her desk by eight forty-five. Hoisting herself upright, she reached for a towel.

# Chapter Twenty-five

As she walked into the building's marble foyer, Utopia felt dwarfed. She had overslept. It was nine forty and with every footstep came a reduced sense of worth. This entrance was designed to instill in the worker a belief in their purpose, a grandness of purpose. Yet for that to happen it was necessary to start out with more than zero. This morning she had had no head start.

She flashed her ID at Moses the security man. He waved his cup at her and she rode the elevator alone. She studied her reflection in the brass control panel. She should have applied colour. She had been used as a punch-bag by last night's lack of sleep. Morning had been creeping into the room by the time sleep arrived. She then missed her alarm, couldn't find her keys and overshot her subway stop. Her eyes were little slits and creases from the bedclothes ran down her face. She looked exhausted.

The doors slid open on the twenty-ninth floor.

"*HQ*, good morning. Can you hold? *HQ*, good morning. Can you hold?"

The receptionist, Louetta, was an ex-Las Vegas croupier with a hang-dog face. "Roll the dice", she would say as a way of making conversation. It was the gambler's equivalent of "Have a nice day." She ignored Utopia as she punched in the door's security code. It took three attempts to use the four-digit number, which never seemed to work. Utopia entered the main drag. She forced herself to look assertive. She forced her gaze upwards. Be tall, be brave, look awake, she told herself.

She spotted Brooke trailed by Julie heading for Diane's office. The beauty department, five girls in white shirts, were staggering bottles of perfume according to size on a desk. They were taking it in turns to smell each fragrance and take notes. Utopia smiled and said hi.

She arrived at her desk. The morning's stack of mail, newspapers and magazines was late, later than she was, which did something to make her feel better. She stuffed her bag underneath her desk and prepared to make her excuses. Smoothing down her skirt, she scooted round the wall.

Jean's door was open. She entered. The office was bare, like the smooth hollow of an eggshell. Nothing but white. Freshly painted white. The fumes attacked her nostrils and her eyes smarted.

"Oh, no," she said.

"She had it coming to her for a long time," said Todd, with a nod, and passed Utopia his box of Kleenex. She was sitting in his office on the twenty-eighth floor, which was strewn with cuttings, encyclopedias, CDs, *HQ*s, sweaty T-shirts and towels, a jock-strap and a bicycle wheel.

Her face was hot with tears.

She had stood hugging Jean's door unsure of what to do for what felt like an eternity. She couldn't tell if it was real or whether she was still inhabiting one of last night's dreams. Then Goldie wandered by. She was so nonchalant that Utopia found it hard to believe she knew of what had happened. She had emerged from her office smiling.

"Honey, you missed it. Take it from me, you're happy you weren't here. Not a happy sight."

"What happened?"

"Don't ask, honey."

And off she sashayed.

Her next stop, at Julie's instructions, had been to see the managing editor. Her lips were pursed like a beak and she wore her arms wrapped tightly across her chest. She did nothing to soften the blow. She was so officious, she hardly appeared to be human at all. Confused, Utopia had scanned her face for a flicker of emotion but the black eyes had only reflected her own anguish. Her glassy exterior was modelled on *HQ*'s mirrored exterior.

Utopia had watched the managing editor's lips form words without expression and realised that she would be forgotten by lunchtime. She had already been clocked out. "Now that Jean's gone, there's not an appropriate place for you here at *HQ*," she said.

Unable to find the words to express a reaction, Utopia had inhaled. "I see."

Then exhaled.

"But why?"

"Jean lost the story," explained Todd, handing her a butter-rum Lifesaver. A tiny ring of preserving sugar. "Jean blew it big time."

*HQ* had lost the First Lady to the other magazine was what had happened.

"It was the final straw," explained Todd, piercing the foil with his thumb before unwrapping the tube to feed her another.

It was the sugar-at-times-of-crisis remedy, a favourite of her grandmother's with her cups of sweet tea. Jean's neuroses, her hours spent in therapy and her failing editorial judgement had given Diane food for complaint for sometime apparently. And now this. Not only had they lost their Christmas-issue cover story but there was *HQ*'s reputation to consider. The First Lady was so incensed at the manner in which her press secretary had been treated that she had penned a personal letter of complaint to Diane which arrived by US Government Special Delivery last night.

As she listened and sucked, poking the tip of her tongue through the hole and feeling the Lifesaver's size diminish, Utopia retreated to a safe distance. She was being entertained with farce. It was the way Todd told it, if only she could laugh. She bit down on the sweet and the crunch echoed in her ears. She picked the splinters from her teeth then sucked her finger.

She had seen Diane's displeasure.

Barking at the White House was never going to win Jean any favours. Anyone could have told her that. Utopia was tempted to feel sorry for her, if only she had any sympathy left to give. She felt all used up.

Outside it had begun to rain.

Rising steam wrapped itself around the buildings, which jostled for space like subway commuters. A neon bird of prey, a beer promotion erected high on a skyscraper, was flapping its wings. Utopia squinted and watched it fly.

"Fuck them," said Todd. He was composing an e-mail. His brother was a coffee broker based in Mexico City. "Crazy bitches, the lot of them. You're better going someplace else."

"So why are you still here?"

"I'm on twenty-eight. If I had to be up there with them? Man, I'd jump off the fucking roof."

Utopia laughed. She knew what they would say. Easy come, easy go. She was Jean's employee and it made no sense for her to stay on without Jean. Brooke didn't want her and she didn't want Brooke, but the transience troubled her. Perhaps she was jinxed. Why was everything cut short? she needed to know. She paused, but it was too late.

Her fear of loss produced an image she had long fought to ban. It was an image associated with her mother's death. It was a photograph she had discovered in a gynaecology book. When her mother was diagnosed with ovarian cancer in its tertiary stage, Utopia had looked it up in a book. Flicking through page after page, she had stumbled across a picture that was so malignant it had seized her imagination. It was an ovarian cyst with teeth and hair. It had grown to haunt her. It was how she envisaged her mother's death, eaten from within by a growth so advanced it manifested long black whiskers and chomping molars. There was an arrogance to its evolution. How dare such a mutation exist?

It wasn't much later that she had become convinced that she, too, had been invaded by these offensive tumours, Liberty also. The nightmares grew worse.

Gripping the back of the sofa, she saw it again but she wasn't going to give in. Gazing out at the traces of rain sketched across the sky, she stared unblinking until finally there was nothing but water falling all at once from above.

"You want to get something to eat?" said Todd.

She noticed that he was wearing a biscuit coloured T-shirt with a faded stencil of *The A-Team* on it.

"Or a drink?"

"What about my desk? My stuff?"

"I'll get it messengered. Unless you want to go back up."

She didn't.

"I'll send this e-m to my bro then we'll go."

The neon eagle winged its way through the mist and her time at *HQ* took flight. She couldn't believe it was over.

# Chapter Twenty-six

The rain had stopped. The temperature had dropped. Marching along West Broadway with the World Trade Center soaring above, Utopia concentrated on the stretch of her limbs. She had got off the subway at Canal Street because she needed to walk.

Troubled by a wet emptiness, she inhaled the smell of the city. The wind whipping in off the nearby Hudson river was oily with diesel fumes. TriBeCa's vacant streets offered relief. There was just the voices of people falling out of restaurants and into bars and the whoosh of cabs as they hurtled past her and into the city.

Her heels clip-clopped as she increased her pace. The wind blinded her eyes with pools of tears and she turned right on Warren Street. She crossed over and rang Marina's buzzer. Opposite, the neighbourhood crackhead was pacing the car-park and ranting as he swung an A & P plastic bag.

"Come on, Marina. Open the door."

The boy was always there and he always scared her.

"Hello."

"It's me."

The door mechanism activated and Utopia flew inside.

She slammed it behind her. The apartment was a five-floor walk up. She hiked up her skirt and took the creaking wooden staircase two at a time. The door was open. Wet footprints led back to the bathroom.

"I'm in the bath. Get yourself a drink."

Utopia caught her breath.

The apartment was a large L-shaped studio with a separate bedroom and bathroom. It was blissfully cool. It was sparsely furnished with a few selectively chosen pieces including an asymmetrical red sofa and a glass table shaped like a puddle. The facing wall was hung with a floor-to-ceiling piece of conceptual art. It had been a present from Dorian a few years back and was an expanse of mounted greenish-grey carpet that sloped down to a plug. It was mottled with patches of sticky residue like dirty water draining out. There was something appealing about its mildewed surface and the ridiculousness of hanging a scummy bath on your wall, Utopia thought.

"What are you doing?" shouted Marina.

Utopia poured herself a glass of water and proceeded to the bathroom.

"That boy in the car-park scares me," she said, sitting on the wicker chair buried beneath damp towels and dirty underwear.

The air was thick with peppermint oil.

"Me too."

With her naked skin and slicked-back hair, she was unrecognisable as Marina the editor. She could have been a pretty matador.

"One day when he's really high, he's going to jump me. But let's not talk about him. How are you, darling? It's all too awful. Though, to be honest, Jean did sound barking.

They say Diane had been looking for an excuse to get rid of her for months."

"And I'm the last one to know," said Utopia, feeling calmer now that she was in familiar territory.

The proposed drink with Todd had led to an afternoon of Guinness-drinking in an Irish tavern somewhere just off 53rd. It was Todd's midtown local. He knew the barman, even a few of the figures hunched over their pints. The Guinness had proven an effective sponge in soaking up her distress. Todd had ended up telling her about his grandmother's battle with Parkinson's disease. It had made her feel quite soppy about him until, in the middle of his story, he uttered the loudest burp she had ever heard. She realised then that it was probably a mistake to feel too sentimental about Todd.

Marina was smoking.

Her feet were pressed flat against the wall at the end of the bath. She had been a cross-country runner as a girl and her muscular definition hadn't faded. She had a generous bust and her breasts bounced like two buffalo mozzarellas as she readjusted her position. There was silence as she turned on the hot tap with her toes. Utopia's melancholia rose like steam. She watched Marina turn off the tap then poke her girth. "Not long before lipo beckons, I reckon."

Utopia stared.

Perhaps Marina was right. Perhaps it was the mundanities of life she needed right now, trivia like pills. Marina continued pinching as Utopia looked on. Shorter than Utopia, Marina was a fierce critic of New York's fitness culture. She refused to give up her daily diet of cigarettes and alcohol. As far as Utopia could determine, it was the only aspect of her adopted culture she hadn't embraced. She was committedly high maintenance in every regard. She did therapy on Park Avenue and went for manicures, pedicures, eyebrow waxings at Bergdorf's, twice-weekly hair appointments, and facials at Bliss. These included having the inside of her nose waxed. Hair looked unclean, she said.

It was that American thing about hygiene again.

Then had come the news of her botox injections. Every six months Marina had a neuromuscular blocking agent injected into her brow to rid her forehead of wrinkles. There was a risk that it could drip down and paralyse the entire face. But it was worth the risk.

"You're a slave to your wrinkles."

"Just you wait," said Marina.

Marina sat up to soap beneath her arms.

"I'm going on a fast. Miso soup and grapefruit for ten days. Always works."

Utopia couldn't help but feel a certain solidarity in this talk of extra baggage. There was no denying America made you fat. The promise of low-fat was a conspiracy to lure you into the ranks of the obese. The extra pounds spread like an insidious force. Despite her fast metabolism, she felt heavier. She felt full. Though this was only half the story.

She had lost her appetite in the winter months.

Then she arrived in New York and it had returned and how. It had inspired a love affair. Toasted bagels with cream cheese and lox, corn chips and guacamole, quesadillas with pinto beans, tortillas in sour cream, chocolate milk and frosted donuts, banana muffins, corn bread, chicken salads dripping in sesame dressing, stacked pancakes with blueberries and maple syrup, buttery waffles, Thai spring rolls with peanut sauce, Vietnamese noodles, crispy fries, hamburgers, cheeseburgers. She had even once sampled a moose burger.

Taste had spawned greed and she had caught sight of

her stomach rippling like water. She was going to have to cut back before it spilled down her hips and her legs. She was a stranger to fat and the metamorphosis shocked her. Her mother had always been slim and so by genetic inheritance had she. It was Liberty who had thighs and wore her femininity as flesh. It was Liberty who fitted the description womanly and to whom one kind boyfriend declared, "The more of you there is, the more there is to love." Not Utopia. Utopia had always been boyish or willowy. She liked being willowy.

She could so easily imagine her mother's response.

"Darling, you've become fat. It doesn't suit you."

"Do you think New York is good to women?" she asked, thinking out loud.

"What, darling? Yes, of course. I mean, look at Tina Brown. New York raises the glass ceiling up and up and up." Marina drowned her cigarette in the bath and hurled the stub into the bin.

"Do you think it makes for a happy life?"

"Well, I hardly know who's happy these days unless you're talking millions. Once I've sold my movie script and moved to LA then I'll be happy."

Utopia nodded.

She had heard all this before. Ultimately it was a question of degree, a matter of interpretation rather than fact. Yet the toughness of New York women was daunting. This was a city where working women put their eggs on ice as opposed to getting pregnant, *HQ*'s managing editor for one. Where taking a break entailed a long weekend once a year. In Marina's book anyway.

Was this the worthwhile exchange for success or was it the passage of time that left you jaded wherever you were?

Their thoughts were lulled by the sound of the bathwater slapping against Marina's legs. Marina lit another cigarette as the weatherbeaten voice of Marianne Faithfull turned over in the tape machine. "Did I tell you I'm having my tits done?"

Utopia blinked. "Done?"

"Lifted."

"Why?"

"There's nothing perky about them any more. The beauty editor knows a great surgeon and my life needs some serious perking up right now."

Utopia peered for a closer look. She remembered an advert for Constructive Surgery spotted in the subway train.

*The most important decision I ever made was choosing my spouse. The second, my plastic surgeon.*

Marina didn't have a spouse so perhaps now was the time to establish ties with the man who could boost your morale by boosting your tits. On the train she had thought it a depressing prospect, although now she wasn't so sure. Perhaps she, too, was jaded yet if that's all it took then why not?

Marina went underwater. "I'd better get out," she said, coming up. "The opening's at eight."

"What opening?" There was no point being surprised.

"I can't remember. It's on the invitation. Some new Chelsea gallery. Everyone going's to be there. Why don't you come, darling? It'll do you good."

"Oh, no. I couldn't." Utopia shook her head. Marina wasn't about to cancel her evening. It was work like everything. But it was more than that. Marina's busy schedule served now to compound her solitude. Where previously there had at least been Jean, her benefactor, there was now only herself. Marina was the sun around which she orbited and their planetary order would never change.

Utopia watched her get out of the bath and stand before the mirror. Water sluiced across the tiles and splashed Utopia's toes. With her nose pressed against the glass, Marina began examining her face. Despite all her protestations to the contrary, Marina was more than content with her lot, realised Utopia. In need of no one, married to her job and wedded to the city, she was oblivious to what went on beyond. She hadn't visited England in over five years.

Life's too short, she said. There's no point going all the way there when you know exactly what you're going to find and you've got St Bart's on your doorstep.

"I look geriatric."

Marina was thirty-five.

"Well, don't yank your skin like that. You're making it worse."

"I look like shit," she said, applying moisturiser like margarine around her eyes.

When her mother was thirty-five, she had been eleven, Utopia realised, as Marina began searching for her neck cream. The doors to the cabinet were spread wide. Visible along its glass shelves were rows and rows of bottles and jars, toners, conditioners, cleansers, purifiers, exfoliants and oils. She wondered whether Marina would ever have children. She doubted it somehow. Her maternal instinct had been buried beneath years of New York conditioning. Vulnerability, even childish vulnerability, was a sign of weakness not growth.

Marina had switched on the hair-dryer. She was hanging upside down and blow-drying her hair. Utopia was granted a bull's-eye view of her bikini mark. It was a triangle of sunless skin like half a sandwich. The noise filled the windowless bathroom, forcing her out.

In the kitchen she leaned against the sink and stared out of the window at the financial district's skyscrapers illuminated with thousands of strip-lights left on in vacant offices and echoing corridors. They appeared as flat as backdrops and had a ghostly quality. She was rootless in New York, she reflected, as Marina turned up the hair-dryer and the noise began to scream.

What now?

# Chapter Twenty-seven

Johann was toasting Portuguese muffins and making espresso. She could smell it. The radio in the kitchen was blaring. She could hear it. The DJ was already cracking jokes about the President's legendary endowment.

"Turn it down," Utopia yelled, pulling her sheet over her ears. She had never understood the desire to be heckled before fully gaining consciousness. But the show's humour appealed to Johann's secret weakness for smutty jokes. It was his way of getting going in the morning.

Her futon was second hand and corrugated through over use. She slid over to find a soft spot and stared up at the ceiling. Lethargy sucked the wind from her limbs. The noise outside on the street was obtrusive. She wasn't part of it today. The bedside fan sent ripples through her hair and a loose strand jabbed her eye then stuck to her mouth. At the end of the bed sat a grey box marked with her name and address. *Utopia Holmes, 118 Mott Street, apt. D, New York, 10013*. Todd had had it sent over yesterday afternoon. It had a hopelessness about it. It resembled a tombstone, she thought. Still staring, she suddenly remembered the picture of her mother. She leaned out of bed and began scrabbling through a nearby pile of papers. Her bed was girded by an apron of useful things. It was her life within arm's reach in case her prone position was to become a permanent thing.

She found the magazine and turned to page fourteen and that same heaviness winged through her heart. She couldn't get rid of a sense of exclusion. It was those curls and their two heads touching. But she had an idea. Crawling to the end of her bed, shedding the sheet like a skin, she reached for the box and from it her Rolodex. She flicked to the back. Under P, Meg had compiled a catalogue of photographers' names. She had copied them into her own Rolodex and there they all were. She hadn't thought before to look. P, Q, R, S, Sands, Sebrith, Shanks, R.

There he was. His existence rattled her. He had found his way into her apartment and her life. It was eerie. There were two contact numbers, one for his studio and one for home. She fell back on the mattress, her mind racing, as she wondered what to do. His name went round and round her mind. It was now so familiar that its intimacy disturbed her. She watched a cockroach trace the cornice and disappear through a crack. She was afraid it might fall and squirm against her skin so she pulled up her sheet and held it as though she were in purdah beneath her eyes.

"Can you call the AC guy?" shouted Johann, as the door slammed.

The abrasive radio show was over and it was soft-rock hour.

With the sheet wrapped around her like a toga, Utopia forced herself out of bed. In the kitchen she watched pigeons take flight from the roof opposite and wondered what happened when they died. Did they drop from the sky or roll from the roof? Did anyone know?

She made coffee.

Saul was away. He would be back at the weekend, he said. He had driven down to Jersey with Vivienne to go and visit dealers in search of scrap. He was looking for airplane parts, heavy-duty fuselage and the front of a truck, if he could find one. His sculptures were getting bigger. Right now, Utopia felt too truncated to miss him or even to question Vivienne's role. Opposite, Monkey Man's blinds were pulled tight. He had probably just retired to bed.

As she drank her coffee, she found herself staring at the leaf from the Rolodex stuck to her palm. Shanks, R. She toyed with it as it goaded her into action. She knew what she had to do. She picked up the telephone. Her eyes followed her fingers as she dialled the number.

"Robert Shanks's studio," said a voice at the other end.

She pronounced studio 'stoodio' and Utopia squirmed, the sheet slipping to her waist. She draped it back across her shoulder. "Is he there please?"

"He's shooting. Can I say who's calling?"

"My name's Utopia Holmes. If you . . . er . . . just tell him that it's Sandra Holmes's daughter."

"Aha. Well, I'm going to put you on hold."

Utopia was left with a wall of silence. She caught herself grinding her teeth. She was tapping her toe.

"Hi. Can I help?"

"Oh," she exclaimed, surprised. "Er, yes. My name is Utopia Holmes. You knew my mother."

"Your mother?"

"Sandra Holmes."

"You sure?"

"You photographed her for *HQ*. In nineteen seventy-four."

"Seventy-four? Hey, now that's going back a ways."

Perhaps she had it all wrong.

"Yes. Woah. And you're who?"

"Utopia."

"Wasn't there another daughter?"

"Liberty." So he did remember.

"Sandra. How could I forget? How's she doing? It's been a while."

Utopia paused. For some reason, she hadn't anticipated breaking the news of her mother's death to this man, this stranger. She was no longer sure why she had phoned.

"She died. In January."

"Oh. I'm real sorry to hear that."

"Yes." She hesitated. But she wanted to tell him. She heard her emotions rushing ahead of her thoughts. "Your photographs are hanging in my parents' house back in London. I've been living in New York for a few months now and I was curious . . ."

"How about we meet? You want to meet for coffee? I've got to finish up with this beauty story then I'm done. I've got to meet someone round the corner at Starbucks. Where did you say you are?"

"Mott."

"I'm on Church. How about you come find me at the Starbucks on the corner of Broadway and White? I'll be there at three."

"OK."

"Do you look like your mother?"

"Sort of."

"Yeah? OK. Great. See you at three."

# Chapter Twenty-eight

She was unsure of her decision to meet Robert Shanks. Nevertheless, at two thirty she brushed her teeth, sprayed her neck and wrists, picked up her rucksack and locked the door. She stopped at the tobacco store on the corner of Mott. The air inside was fragrant with cigar smoke and the rhythms of Cuban *guajiras*. A queue of women were waiting to buy lottery tickets. A dollar and a dream and perennial disappointment. Their faces were maps of resignation.

Utopia skirted past them and moved to the magazine shelves. She flicked through the week's paparazzi shots. She devoured the pretty pictures greedily until she couldn't take any more. She stared at the rack of *HQ*s and stomached a wave of regret. She purchased her *Times* and left.

Taking her time, she ambled along Broadway past the bootleggers hawking Chanel bags, Rolex watches, Hermès scarves and Gucci belts, their chants as she approached like the aviary at dawn. She tried to organise her thoughts. The purpose of their rendezvous was vague. It smacked of betrayal. She didn't like it. At the corner of Canal, she stopped. She allowed the lights to change four times before crossing. On the south side of the street there was an incline, which slowed her pace further. A wind was blowing. She let it blow her until her feet hardly moved. Then she spotted the sign.

She quickly crossed the street.

She needed to see him before he saw her.

Shielded behind sunglasses, she walked past the coffee shop and looked in. There was no missing him. He was seated in the window. A black polo-neck rose to meet thinning curls. He was smoking. Beside him was a girl. She was very tall. She appeared to be showing him a book. He was turning each page slowly and methodically, leaning forward for a sharper view before reaching up to plant a kiss on her cheek. Utopia watched as the girl ran her fingers through his hair. He craned to whisper in her ear and kissed her once more, this time burying his face in her neck.

Utopia was paralysed with apprehension but she forced her foot into the kerb. She was counting on her instincts to decide her mind. The street was clear. It was an invitation to cross. She darted to the other side and pushed open the door. The boy behind the counter was adjusting the fastenings on his dungarees. He looked up and smiled as a man in shorts enquired about the salt content of the zucchini bread. A woman with a dog was reading a book in the corner and the Weather Channel was showing on the ceiling TV.

Utopia had hoped Robert might see her.

But his arm had lassoed the girl's waist and her head was on his shoulder.

"Robert?"

Turning he squinted then broke into a smile. "I know exactly who you are but I can't remember your name."

"Utopia," she said, extending her hand. He took it. His palm was warm and he held it for longer than was required.

His companion, a schoolgirl, looked on with teenage contempt.

"You look just like her," he said.

His hair lay against his head in wavy strands, greying at the temples.

Utopia smiled then nodded. It was partially true.

"Well, so, do you want to head back to the studio? I had to meet Susie here to give her copies of the tests we shot last week. They worked out great, didn't they?" He raised an eyebrow at Susie.

Susie lifted one foot off the ground and held it behind her like a flamingo. She was wearing tiny black shorts, her thighs were no thicker than her calves and she had a daisy chain tattooed around an ankle.

"Shall I get a coffee first?" said Utopia, as though she, too, were an aspiring model and needed his consent.

'Sure."

Standing at the counter, her eyes ran blindly up and down the coffee menu board. She was distracted by Robert and Susie behind. She tried to concentrate on making a decision. When finally the iced skinny latte was planted in front of her, Susie had left and Robert was stationed beside her.

"Done?"

"Sure," she replied, just like an American.

They cut back to Church Street past industrial workfronts and strip-joints. The Baby Doll Lounge. The Blue Angel. A couple of backs were seen scuttling inside.

Robert was excited about Susie. "We're going to cut her hair short. I can tell when a girl's got it and Susie's got it. I found her on the Staten Island ferry and she's not even done with high school. I got her signed up with Elite. I'm up for the Nordstrom's campaign. Swimwear. If I get it, I'll use

Susie. She's fit. Not too skinny. But everything's in the right place."

Utopia wondered why he was telling her this. He was making her nervous and she couldn't see where her mother fitted in. Though handsome, with a Marlboro man squint and complexion he appeared as the perennial party-goer pursuing a lifestyle others quit decades ago. He was slightly bow-legged with a vigorous stride. His leather flight jacket was crumpled with age, and she imagined he must be sweating underneath his black polo-neck shirt.

"Home sweet home."

They had arrived at a metal door littered with fist-sized dents.

"How long have you been here?"

He delved deep in his pocket to find his keys. "Mmmm. Going on twenty-five years."

Utopia experienced a wave of *déjà vu*. This was the exact same place to which her mother had come before her while her daughters were left with the upstairs neighbour. Shan't be long, darlings, be good. The repetition of history was disconcerting. It was a decision not of her making but an impulse and she could do nothing to alter its course.

She waited as Robert unlocked the door. His hand twisted round and round as the metal tongues were released with a clunk. Following him in, she mounted the cold stone steps. They reached a landing and to their left was another door. He pushed it open. They were met by a girl at a desk twiddling her hair. "Gina at the agency is sending a girl tomorrow at ten for the lingerie catalogue. The lab called. The contacts are ready," she said.

He led Utopia past a wall of mirrors, a counter dotted with make-up, an empty clothes rail strung with empty hangers and a music centre piled high with CDs. They stopped in front of a black leather sofa. A coffee table was accessorised with glossy magazines displayed in user-friendly fans. A glass ashtray was clogged with lipstick-stained butts and chewed wads of gum.

"Take a seat. I've a couple of calls to make. You want a beer?"

"OK. Thanks," she said, discarding her coffee.

Robert disappeared behind a screen and Utopia sank into the seat. She crossed her legs. Her skirt rode up and she tugged it down. She was struck by the same sense she had experienced in the coffee shop of being here to audition. She felt very young, vulnerable even. She stared up at the skylight then ahead at a roll of paper, which fell to cover the floor, and black scaffolding rigged with lights. She had spent countless afternoons and evenings in photographic studios overseeing shoots for *Music Today* but this was different. This time she felt as though she were the subject. She was aware of the spell of seduction. Ten feet away stood a camera on a tripod, Its power of persuasion was that of a wink, sly and provocative. The inclination to bare all for the man with the camera wasn't so far-fetched.

"Did you get that beer?" asked Robert.

He had removed his jacket and had one hand up his shirt to caress his chest.

"No."

"I'll get it."

He wandered off again, was talking to the girl in Reception and Utopia listened to the sound of his voice. It echoed around the room. It bounced off the walls and hugged the floor. This was his world. Here he was God. For some reason it made her feel important to be part of it.

"So, here. Cheerio," said Robert, back again, handing her

a beer, clinking her bottle with his own. He took a swig. "Sandy's daughter. My god. What a surprise."

He took a seat beside her. "Cigarette?"

"No, thanks."

He lit his with a Zippo, which he flicked just the once. She could feel his presence. He had eyes which looked too hard.

"Sandy was special. You know, I can still remember her laugh."

Utopia nodded.

"I'm glad you looked me up. I often wondered—" He broke off and his gaze travelled round the room as though he had lost something. "How's New York been treating you? Going to lots of parties?"

"Yes. Quite a few."

"I took Sandy to a couple of parties."

"Really."

"You know what we should really do? Take a picture. Would you like that? We could have some fun. Ever had your picture taken? Professionally, I mean?"

With the top of the bottle flat against her lips, Utopia felt numb. She suddenly realised how easy it would be, whatever it was. Perhaps he saw her sent in her mother's place as a reminder of his past when he was the young hotshot *HQ* photographer everyone wanted to be with.

He fielded memories as he toyed with his Zippo. "A natural your mother. She loved the camera. She was a real performer. Did she ever tell you that? She had those long arms like a bird and I never had to tell her what to do. Every shot a different pose. We did some good work together." He looked up. "And now here's Sandy's daughter. You've got her height, her legs. The same elegant neck." He suddenly leaned forward to trace the softness beneath her chin then drew his hand away. She wasn't sure he knew who he was touching.

But he was nodding, far away, and his smoky voice caressed the words as he recalled her mother's afternoons here. Utopia saw winter luminescence through the skylight. She heard Sly and the Family Stone from the speakers.

As children they would sing along to 'It's a Family Affair' on drives down to the coast. For some reason she felt sure that it was here that her mother first heard it. Her father's musical tastes went about as far as Elvis Presley, no further.

She saw Robert fiddling with rolls of film and her mother drinking from a bottle of beer. She saw her mother slipping into the designated outfits, laughing. She saw her mother smouldering for the camera, her self-consciousness forsaken, as she was cajoled by Robert with his words of courage. She saw them brush against each other as he came to lend advice. She saw Robert in action and her mother succumb.

As she surveyed the studio, suddenly so vivid, Utopia was struck by a stab of certainty. She hated it. There was no need to hear any more. She couldn't bear to see any more. Enough. Leaning forward to put her beer on the table, she scrambled to her feet. "I've got to go," she told him, bumping into his lazily stretched legs.

"Hey. What's wrong?" His face rumpled.

But she was already away, past the girl at the desk, out through the door, down the stairs and on to the street. She clamped her sunglasses over her face and began running towards Canal. The downhill gradient accelerated her speed and she broke into a sprint. She looked over her shoulder and saw his face but he wasn't there.

She was met by a vendor on the corner. The hotplate

greeted her with a wall of fat. Breathless, she stopped to buy a pretzel and squirted it with so much honey mustard that the proprietor grew impatient. "Hey, miss, are you done yet?"

She replaced the bottle. A sea of rock salt covered her chest and the dough congealed in her mouth. She chewed in search of saliva, afraid she might choke. She ate to comfort herself and mask the taste of disgust with a paste of bread.

She remembered she was wearing her mother's dress. It was a relic from her mother's seventies incarnation. It was dotted with pinhead lilac blossoms and stirred from the body like puffed air. Utopia felt ashamed of herself and her mother. She felt cheap. She hated herself for contacting this man. She hated her mother for knowing him. Resentment blazed. Whatever act her mother had committed with him was part of her inheritance yet no one had told her.

She tossed the pretzel into a bin.

She stepped into the gridlocked traffic and felt her hostility swept up in a tide of road rage. As she jaywalked through the cars and cabs, she could hear nothing but the sound of their horns. The city's wrath stoked her anger and demanded resolution. She would confront her father and demand an answer. She began softly to cry.

# Chapter Twenty-nine

It was Saturday afternoon and the flea market was awash with beautiful people milling about in lemony light. Marina was wearing a floaty dress by an LA designer. It was her weekend attempt at dressing down, she said. Utopia was in jeans and a new pair of Nike Airs with a rose bubble in the heel. They were a pick-me-up to provide extra bounce. When her natural bounce was waning, a trip to Nike Town worked wonders every time.

They walked slowly, hidden behind dark glasses.

The whites of their eyes were flushed incriminating pink.

Integral to the spirit of the weekend was the one-skin joint they shared with midday coffee. Their stoned gaze tracked an *Alice In Wonderland* porcelain set, a Pop Art coffee table, an ivory inlaid Chinese screen. On either side of them very tall women in tiny T-shirts were looking for vintage to decorate their lofts. Gay men in couples were flicking through old vinyl in search of original Barbra Streisands in the one-dollar racks. Antique lace, fashionable polyester and cracked animal skins hung next to tables creaking beneath the weight of clocks, coins, table lamps and chocolate box art. No one was stuck for choice.

Marina was looking for a table for her bedroom, something to double as a desk and a surface for the TV. Utopia had come along for the ride. Absorbed by proceedings with the sun on her face, she savoured the sensation of drifting. No need to think. At the end of a week she wouldn't wish to relive, and still fearful of what was to come, she had woken this morning thankful to have reached the other side.

"How about this one?" said Marina, fingering an oak table with a drawer.

"How much?"

"Three. Two fifty if I'm good."

They circled the table. They ran their hands over its surface and slid the drawer in and out until it escaped the grooves. Marina caught it before it hit the ground. Another interested buyer began circling. Marina pulled a rude face and he changed his mind. He disappeared. Satisfied, Marina looked up and caught Utopia's eye. Their focus locked curiously on two figures beyond. A couple had their fingers intertwined and their heads bowed together, the peaks of their caps locked like horns. Marina frowned as Utopia winced.

"Marina!"

"Dorian!"

"Er . . .What are you doing here?"

"Shopping. How about you?"

"Just looking."

"Looks like you're doing more than that to me."

"Yeah, em, Paulo and I've just been for breakfast. At Aggie's. On Houston."

"I know where it is. Jesus. And I'm in the middle of a transaction."

Marina left to discuss prices with the dealer. Utopia

offered Dorian a hesitant smile before joining her amongst the tables, chairs and wardrobes. But he followed.

"Babe," he pleaded, throwing an arm round Marina's shoulder. "It's not what you think."

She shook him off. "Oh? And just what the fuck do I think?"

"That . . . you know."

"Dorian, forget it. OK? I really don't give a fuck."

"Marina, listen—"

"No, you listen. I don't want to hear any more of your crap. Now just fuck off and leave me alone," she ordered him, in a low, angry hiss.

He stared at her and his blood rose as his eyes bulged, toad-like. He raised his hands to argue his case but words failed him and Marina turned her back. "For Christ's sake," he said, before vanishing into the crowd.

Paulo scampered behind with his skateboard tied to his back. Utopia looked on in horror.

"You OK, lady?" said the stall-owner.

"Perfect," Marina told him and produced a pen from her bag. She calmly purchased the table for the negotiated sum of two seventy-five and scribbled down her address for it to be delivered that evening. She grabbed Utopia's wrist and they left the market and charged down Sixth Avenue as though they were being chased. They stopped to catch their breath. They took refuge in the doorway of an office building. Sitting on a step, out of the sun, Marina lit up.

"They're fucking. Jesus Christ. They're actually fucking."

"Not necessarily."

"Come on. They were holding hands."

"It could be a flirtation. He's very pretty."

"Prettier than me?"

"Don't. When was the last time you spoke to Dorian?"

Marina shook her head.

"And saw him?"

She shrugged.

"It's over. You know he sees other women."

"Not bum-fluff boys."

"Perhaps this is something new and he was going to tell you later."

"Later? God, how could I be so fucking stupid? Him and his assistant? I should have guessed."

"How could you have guessed?"

"Because all the fucking men in this city are gay."

Utopia groaned. It was farcical. The end of a relationship had been brought about by an affair with a skateboard kid. She had never trusted Dorian; neither, she suspected, had Marina. In fact, she had begun to feel that there was a definite problem with men in this city. She understood the effect of the disproportionate gender ratio, that men were spoilt for choice, that there was always another and no guarantees. But whatever remained was a loveless greed.

Marina had finished her cigarette. She applied warpaint, a slug of cherry across her lips and rouge across each cheek. But her battering was hard to disguise. The ends of her mouth sloped in a pucker and the pallor of her face was bloodless and stunned.

"What happened to Donald?"

"Don't ask. A slut, according to my brother, and he was right. Not a word."

Utopia was disappointed though hardly surprised. "That's too bad."

"Darling. Enough."

They went to buy Energy Shakes, large, please, at the health-food store on 13th street. A boy in an apron was spraying the organic produce fresh from Vermont with mist.

A Buddhist chant was heard from the kitchen and there was a special on low-cal guarana bars. Four for a dollar. Marina took eight from the barrel then put five jars of homeopathic remedies on her business charge card. An American Express Gold. "It's that damn office which makes me sick," she complained.

They went outside. The bench in the shade of a magnolia tree was free so they took it. A man arranged in a lotus position with his shoes off was eating veggies and rice on the sidewalk.

"It's over," said Marina. "The only person interested in me is Harold. Sometimes he stays and I fix him a drink when he brings up my groceries."

Utopia choked on a lump of protein powder.

"You cannot have an affair with your super."

"Anyway, when's your father coming? I'm dying to meet him."

"Tomorrow," Utopia told her. "Late afternoon."

# Chapter Thirty

Her father looked older than she remembered. He had a firm jaw and an angular face and cheekbones on which as a child she would try to balance pennies. But the skin beneath his eyes hung in creases like the folds of a lizard's belly. Too many sleepless nights. It was only her mother's threats that had stopped him working all night, every night. "I'll divorce you if you keep on any longer. I'm not hanging around to see you give yourself a bloody heart-attack," she would say.

He didn't, and now she was gone. His capacity for exhaustion went unchecked. His hair was as fine as a dandelion clock and in disarray as he ran his hand through it, again and again. He examined the drinks menu through half-moon glasses. They were glasses she hadn't seen before. They made him look distinguished but older.

"What are you having? Thought I might have a beer." He looked up.

"You know how pissy American beers are, Dad. Have something stronger. Have a cocktail."

He frowned and returned to the fourteen-page list of alcoholic beverages.

She couldn't believe he was here. It was Sunday. They were sitting in the gold bar next door to the art-deco Rainbow Room on the sixty-fifth floor of the Rockefeller Center. The piano player in the dining room was playing bossa nova tunes. Beside them, Middle Eastern women were grouped round tray-sized tables while Japanese tourists wielded cameras behind. It was her father's choice of location. Something over the top and special to New York had been the requirements, and to be fair, the bird's-eye view of the island was spectacular. She ordered a margarita. He had a martini.

"How's Libby?"

"Good. Yes. She's got a new boyfriend. Nice chap. Cambridge. I think they're off to the Caribbean together some time next month."

"Really? Well, they're not coming to see me. She hasn't been in touch or anything."

"Come on, you know what these package holidays are like. They fly you straight to your hotel."

Utopia shrugged. He was probably right but that wasn't the point. She wasn't convinced it would be a good idea to see her sister but the snub hurt. It was typical of her that she should venture this far yet not go the extra distance to see her. To want to see her. Utopia had escaped to New York. One – nil. Liberty doesn't visit. One all. There was always this seesaw of vying emotions as each entered a new phase of her respective life.

She couldn't remember the last time Liberty had phoned to say hello, and the few times she had phoned no reference was made to Liberty's vitriolic outburst. It lurked at the fringes of their chat like a vagrant, dependent on the goodwill of others only to be disappointed.

"I want to hear all about what's been going on with you.

We've hardly heard a peep out of you. You have been keeping yourself busy."

She nodded. She had told him about the job or the lack of such in the cab over here but of course there was more. Much more. She hardly knew where to begin.

"Yes," she said.

The waiter brought over their drinks and all she could think about was Robert Shanks. She had come to feel that her father's honour was at stake and it was her wretched fault. Yet looking at him across the table, she couldn't ask now. To invite Robert Shanks to join them was obscene.

"I told you I bumped into P, didn't I?"

She nodded. "How was he?"

"Looked jolly well, actually. Just back from Spain."

It pained her to think of him looking so well without her. She said nothing. Since the events of last week and with Saul away she had thought about calling him every single day. Something had stopped her. P was friendly with her father. Both were optimists and they enjoyed talking books. P had once accused her of manifesting an Electra complex. "I won't bloody well write your dissertation. I'm not your bloody father. You're just spoilt," he said.

She sometimes thought he might not be wrong. She and her father shared traits close to her heart. Where they would both, without explanation, set off the security alarms at airports, her mother and Liberty never had. Both needed coffee in the morning, her mother milky tea. Both were left-handed, had a tendency to be late and shared a taste for French toast on Sunday mornings. It was her father's treat. Her mother didn't eat until lunchtime. It was one of her rules. Others included watering the garden after dark, never throwing away shoes and using a separate spoon for the sugar.

Utopia had never doubted her affinity with her father the way she had with her mother. Then again, it was her mother who had the tougher job of standing firm as the voice of authority. All joint parental decisions were handed down by her mother. But her mother chose to be difficult, she had always felt.

Her father had been the first to accept P. Four years they had been together yet still her mother had refused to accept him. She envisaged Utopia with a doctor, barrister, broker, banker. There was no fathoming why. Given everything Utopia was and had always been, why would she make such a choice? Even in the end, she had encouraged dissent. "Darling, promise me you'll think long and hard before marrying him," she had said.

Nodding, Utopia had stroked her hand. She had to respect her mother's tenacity since otherwise there would be nothing left. Even so, her mother's insistence had left her distressed. In the past she had told Utopia to stop talking nonsense if ever the L-word was mentioned.

Love? Utopia, you don't know the meaning of the word. You still have so much growing up to do. You're not married, you're not divorced so you're single."

"Now who's talking crap? You were married at twenty-one."

"And I was much too young."

It was a no-win situation.

It was her father who had stood by her decision to stay in London and study at the University of North London, originally because it meant being with Rick. It was an institution that, as her mother pointed out, looked like a car-park. She wanted to know why Utopia couldn't go to a proper university like her sister. By proper university she meant Oxbridge. It appealed to her snobbery and her own unfulfilled aspirations. Yet though Liberty had studied at Cambridge, Utopia didn't want to go further than N1. Her campus was strewn all the way down a polluted, traffic-bound artery of North London. Perfect.

"You didn't even go to university," Utopia had argued with her.

But that too was the point.

Then, to her her mother's profound irritation, she switched from English Literature to Media and Communications Studies. Her final dissertation was titled "The Relocation and Exploitation of Humour in Soap Opera Spin-offs". She loved her course. She saw its ephemerality as a plus not a minus. It offered practical training for what she knew to be next, magazine journalism. She found herself skilled at netting trends to create a story – the more obvious the better. Her first feature at *Music Today* had been "Rock Locks". It was her idea. Rock-stars and their hair cuts. The semiotics of tresses and their definitions of musical genres. It was worthy of a five-thousand-word modular thesis.

Her mother had not been happy. "What is that? Telly studies? Oh, honestly, Utopia, you don't help yourself. You have a good brain but you insist on wasting it. What sort of a perspective is that going to give you on life?"

They had been sitting at the post-prandial kitchen table. It was a familiar combination, coffee and maternal critique. Utopia could see the chicken carcass on the counter behind her mother's head with a lemon peering out of its arse. Perspective. That word again. How she hated it, she remembered thinking. Whose perspective were they discussing, anyway?

Utopia took a gulp of margarita. It was a hopeless attempt to dilute the guilt felt on cross-questioning her mother but what alternative was there? Her mother ought to be sitting there beside her father and all these points would then come up in the natural course of things. She so needed to believe that their last year together had marked a turning point. That their relationship had begun to reveal truths of which she wasn't afraid. Instead here she was with her home-spun psychoanalysis and too many holes.

For an independent sixties creature who had thumbed her way across the States, her mother's role as mother and home-maker left too many gaps. That was the point. She should have done something for herself. Instead she nurtured a garden, chaired local pressure groups, cooked dinner parties for twenty-five and championed her daughters' extra-curricular activities. It was this obsessive focus that Utopia then had fought.

"Why can't you just leave me alone?" she would demand.

But she couldn't. Her mother had lived vicariously through her daughters' successes and failures, in particular failures. Utopia had long felt she couldn't live up to her mother's definition of success She was never good enough. Too many failed exams and shocking report cards. *Could do better if we saw more of her.* She had flirted with truancy as she did with the local boys. Ultimately, avoidance of maternal strife came to mean avoidance of her mother.

"You still haven't told me about what happened with your job," said her father.

"Haven't I?"

"No."

"It's not very interesting."

"You keep saying that but I'd like to know."

She stared into her glass with its turquoise stirrer indented with a dolphin and the torn paper parasol. The hunk of lime floated round and round. The problem was there had been a time when she thought her job at *HQ* would prove the answer. She now knew otherwise. There had been a time when she thought New York would sink the emptiness. But still the questions spewed as furiously as doubt.

Someone was taking photographs of the view with a flash. Splintered light bounced off the windows and all she could see were dancing dots. In the distance, the sky was painted an explosion of pinks and coppers, vivid and enraged. High in the sky with her cocktail and anguish, Utopia felt reassured by the presence of her father. A confirmation of herself and her place in the world, it was a sense of belonging she hadn't had since jacking it all in and escaping here. How she had craved the anonymity of this city. Yet now, on seeing him, everything shifted as the memory of her family, her former life, engaged her.

"Are you going to be able to find another job?" he asked, his face knotted with concern.

Did she have to talk about it?

"Marina has found me some waitressing work. Until I find something else."

"Well, that's a start, I suppose."

She shrugged. She sometimes wondered what her father imagined she was doing with her life. "We should talk about your career," he occasionally liked to say.

"No we shouldn't," she would answer.

And then he would sigh and that would be that.

It wasn't necessarily easy convincing someone in academia that her devotion to glossy magazines had any value. Admittedly her father's texts were American not Chaucerian, twentieth-century heroes, but it was the fact that her work had no hidden subtext that puzzled him. "It's entertainment," she had told him more than once. It was famous people packaged as real people then flogged on the appeal of their celebrity status. He didn't look convinced.

She knew her father understood why she was here, though still he worried. I'm doing New York, was what she was trying to say. Just as you did, just as Mum did. She paused. She fought the temptation to admit that she, too, had doubts.

"Are you hungry? You look tired."

He was yawning.

"Do you know somewhere nice?"

"We'll find somewhere over near Seventh. There's a Japanese place. What time do you have to get up?"

"My lecture's at nine. I've still got to write it."

"Oh, honestly Dad."

He yawned again. Her protestations, echoing her mother's, went unheard. She waved at the waitress to bring the bill.

On the corner of 53rd an Elvis with sideburns and angel wings was busking, karaoke-style, to a tape. He looked Puerto Rican. He was singing "Love Me Tender" against the traffic. They stopped for her father to give him a dollar.

"Not bad," he remarked.

"*Muchas gracias*," said Elvis.

She took his arm. She felt protective of him out on the street. This was her city now and the role reversal was significant. She found herself wondering what would have been if her mother had borne a third child as planned. Unable to conceive again, she had embarked upon a course of fertility drugs, which were thought later to have triggered her cancer. What if there had been a younger brother? she reflected. How different it would be. Instead it had been for Utopia to accompany her father to five-a-side football matches, organised by a family of four brothers who lived down the street, on Sunday mornings at the local park.

Utopia had been adopted as an honorary member until her hormones revolted.

She turned thirteen and lost interest in kicking a ball and her father lost his football partner. Two daughters and no son. He had lost out, she thought, as the lights changed and they quickened their pace to reach the other side.

# Chapter Thirty-one

"Hello, luv," screeched Trudi, as Utopia pushed open the door with its lace curtain and bumper sticker, NO AMERICANS ALLOWED – NOT. It was a slogan that encapsulated Trudi's sense of humour.

Welcome to Home Comforts.

Trudi was a long-standing friend of Marina. Both residents of ten years, they were ex-pat sisters bonded through loyalty to their adopted home. Trudi had secured amnesty under Reagan's presidency when illegal residents of five years were instructed to come forward and claim a green card, as if on a game show. Utopia had been shown her certificate from Immigration, which hung behind greasy glass in the kitchen.

Trudi was the teashop madame. She was also the self-appointed queen of New York's ex-pat community. Utopia had realised this the last time she visited, the only time she had visited. All resident and visiting Brits were expected to call. It was protocol, the same as visiting the Empire State Building or buying bulk loads of thirty-buck 501s and Calvin Klein briefs.

Utopia's lack of interest was likely deemed unpatriotic.

She had visited just the once and had enjoyed her Welsh rarebit with Brown Sauce and Earl Grey tea. But in truth English teatime fare, news of the royals and first-division updates were not things she had missed since moving to New York. In fact, they depressed her. There were other things, things she didn't want to dwell on right now, which she missed.

"You're late. Oi, Maggie, get down."

With her hands on her hips and a Medusan tangle of curls on her head, Trudi cut a formidable figure. She was not someone you would choose to antagonise, thought Utopia, as she stared down at a bulldog, skeins of dribble hanging from its speckled gums, which was trying unsuccessfully to mount her leg. Wanting to kick it off, she patted the top of its head and made an encouraging there-good-doggy noise. It was what was expected. The only dogs she was good with were her grandmother's terriers but it was never a natural instinct to want to stroke them. Free to choose, she would rather beat them off every time.

"Don't put your fingers in her mouth."

"Oh."

"Now, go get a kidney from the kitchen," Trudi ordered the dog, who scampered off, her stomach trailing on the floor. "Want a coffee?"

Utopia nodded as Trudi poured coffee for the two of them. She was wearing a black T-shirt with a white teacup logo and her hands were shaking. She was smoking and her fingernails were painted black. She was an adrenaline junkie, thought Utopia. She survived on caffeine and nicotine, a fact to which her under-eye bruising and smoke lines bore testimony.

"How's Marina? Any shagging?"

"She's fine," confirmed Utopia, wanting to feel grateful

for Trudi's offer of work when it was resentment she felt. Resentment that she was going to be cooped up in here all day.

She drank coffee from her Home Comforts mug, and struggled to acclimatise to her doll's-house surroundings. Every inch of ceiling, floor and wall was covered with bric-à-brac and memorabilia. Framed photographs of the royal family immortalised in the fifties hung next to tin advertisements for Oxo cubes. Rows of chipped teacups sat on top of crooked shelves supported with leatherbound copies of *Peter Pan* and *Winnie the Pooh*. A grandfather clock that doubled as a pinboard and was missing a hand stood in the corner. On the television in the corner a video of last week's England versus Chile game was on.

"Ooh. Penalty kick," shouted Trudi, waving her fist. "Guess who I had in here last night?"

Utopia had noticed Trudi to have a particular way of speaking. It was either of the knock-knock-who's-there variety or it was a tendency to bang home platitudes until the next piece of invaluable information was seized upon.

"Who?"

"The Dalai Lama. Guess who he was with?"

"Who?"

"Head of the UN. What's 'is name, that nice man?"

"I know the one."

"Guess what they had?"

"Steak and kidney pudding?"

"Fish pie, extra mash, mushy peas, summer pudding and a pot of Lapsang Souchong."

Trudi was a firm believer in fame by association. Her list of celebrity guests was endless as she was only too happy to report.

"That Dalai does like his food," she clucked, approvingly. "I don't think he gets enough to eat where he comes from. Took a doggy-bag with him, an' all."

Utopia was conscious of the rising temperature.

The trapped air was like marshmallow, swollen and sweet, which the air-conditioning unit perched above the door did little to combat. She felt her scalp prickle.

"First of all, take a little look at this, luv," said Trudi, finding a press-cuttings book from amongst a row of ragged cookbooks. "Then you know what to tell the tourists."

Utopia began a randomly chosen article. *Home Comforts, the home of shepherd's pie and bangers and mash, is a home from home for increasing numbers of English professionals who've made New York their home . . .* Right. *The lady of the manor, Trudi Baggage, has proven with unqualified success that English cooking has finally said goodbye to its sorry image of soggy fish and chips and has engineered a gastronomic return . . .*

There was no need to read on. Utopia knew where she was. A Union Jack beside a fan was flapping above her head, for God's sake.

"All right, luv. Kick-off time. Apron on . . . Ooh, get it in, Dawson, you cunt," she screamed at the TV.

Briefed on what was expected, it didn't take long and she wasn't a virgin to the finer points of waitressing, take-order-to-kitchen-wait-for-chef-to-shout-abuse-return-to-table-with-order, Utopia toured the fifteen-by-fifteen-foot room. She was reminded of her grandmother and the cream teas served by septuagenarians with bandaged ankles beneath brown stockings in her grandmother's local rose garden. She had always been fascinated by her grandmother: by the pouch of skin which sagged behind each elbow, her bosomy smell of talcum powder and the string of pearls that Utopia would rub against her teeth to vouch for authenticity.

Her grandmother was a gambler. She played poker three times a week, though never on Fridays because on Fridays she and her cronies took the bus to go to the market and have their hair done. Utopia loved their gossip and their gallows humour. She loved that they referred to themselves as 'girls' like disco dollies. Disco doilies, her father called them. Where her mother said darling, her grandmother used dear, but her grandmother had outlived both husband and daughter. Utopia had visited her grandmother the weekend before she left. She had looked as frail as her dying mother. "It's not right," she had despaired, crumpled beneath a blanket in the thin April sun. "It wasn't meant to be like this."

Utopia hated herself for leaving it so long. She should call her grandmother. These recent months had been so selfish.

"Skiver. Table two," bellowed Trudi though the kitchen hatch.

Utopia was startled into action. She hadn't noticed the Long Island grandmothers, each one larger than the next, who were waving their menus at her. "Yoo-hoooo," they called.

She went to take their orders.

"We're real curious about spotted dick," they told her, mascaraed eyes swimming behind thick-lensed glasses.

"Right, well, spotted dick is a suet pudding . . ."

"Is that like trifle?"

"No, it's like . . ."

"Ya know what, honey? We're gonna try it. Whatever the goddam hell it is. It's English, right? It's got to be good. Give us five of those with custard and a big pot of breakfast tea."

The Long Islanders were visibly excited. It was clear that they were enjoying the novelty of foreign food as though it was foreign travel. They rattled their Mall gold and picked up the cups in search of names they might know. Utopia went to hand the order to Eduardo the Mexican chef. "You be must be quick now," he chastised her, shaking a porky finger.

The door flew open. Utopia looked round to see a boy in an Adidas shirt with slicked-back hair stomp his feet and remove a pair of sunglasses.

"Tel, darling. What you having, gorgeous? Your regular?"

Trudi summoned Utopia, her mouth flickering. Sexual tension filled the room. The kettle boiled. Steam cushioned the ceiling. Utopia wiped her brow on the back of her hand. "Tel works for a record company," Trudi told her, explaining the need of special treatment. "He'll have eggs, bacon, mushrooms, white toast and a big pot of strong tea. Put both mustards on his table, luv. I know just how he likes it, don't I?"

"Don't you just." He winked, grabbing a pile of the English tabloids before claiming a seat. "Yeah, and I'll have my tea now, luv."

Looking up from the counter, Utopia was just in time to see Terence seize his throat in both hands before looking down at his watch. The implications were clear. Do I have to wait longer than it takes to read a *Sun* headline before I get my tea? Utopia swallowed her rage. Who the hell did he think he was? Carrying the pot full to the brim, she swung it down on to the table. Water strewn with tea leaves gushed out of the spout and into his lap. "For fuck's sake, woman!" he yelled, jumping up from his seat. The chair flew back with an ear-splitting screech of wood against the stone floor.

"Sorry. No third-degree burns, I hope."

No one laughed.

"I'll go and fetch a cloth."

Back in the kitchen Eduardo was vibrating with bottled mirth as he concentrated on smashing a pile of walnuts. "Very good," he told her.

Utopia acknowledged the note of solidarity.

"Where's that cloth?" yelled Trudi.

Utopia emerged to re-apologise. "Sorry."

"You get the other tables and mind Maggie, she's napping."

Maggie was lying sprawled in the middle of the floor with her tongue out. She was snoring.

"Goal. Fucking luv-er-ly."


They had reached the pre-dinner lull.

A few stragglers were grazing on refills, *Pub Songs Volume III* was warbling in the background, an English sports quiz was being screened on TV and there were no tables left to serve. Utopia watched Trudi light a cigarette from the glowing end of Terence's while it was still in his mouth before retreating to the kitchen.

The kitchen was damp with the moisture of human skin and freshly baked cakes. Cakes on racks covered every surface. Eduardo flashed a grin. He had a tooth-pick in the corner of his mouth and a gold cross at his neck. His plump cheeks glistened like dim sum. Utopia was impressed by his composure in the face of Trudi's chaos. While she screamed blue murder, he silently got on with turning out ginger-breads, chocolate cakes, fruit cakes, scones, flapjacks, short-bread biscuits, tarts, apple crumbles, summer puddings, bread and butter puddings, jam rolls and treacle puddings, worthy of the plummiest church fête. Trudi had trained him well. Utopia found him taking a break. He was reading a porn magazine slotted beneath his chopping board. "Big tits." He grinned.

She took a look. *Big Jugs.* Distended flesh, nipples and lace curtained a double page. She pulled a face.

"You no like?"

"Udders," she said.

She lowered herself on to an upturned milk crate and surrendered to aching feet. The day dripped from her forehead as all of a sudden the desire to bawl out loud ripped through her. What the hell was she doing here? It was cultural purgatory. It was everything she had avoided at home. It was so far from her point of departure she wondered how she would ever get back.

With her head in her hands, she slowly counted to ten. Anxiety welled like rising dough. Self-pity soaked like sweat. It was as though her ill-fated encounter with Jean and the hopelessness of her predicament hit her now for the first time. She had no job, no income, no prospects. It was over. She didn't want to be a waitress. She couldn't do this any more. She felt discarded. All washed up.

"Oi. Tart." Trudi poked her head through the hatch. "What you doing in there? Reading Ed's wank mags? Blower."

"For me?"

"No, Princess fucking Diana."

Utopia stood up and her apron fell to her knees. She left the kitchen. The butter-fingered telephone was buried beneath a mountain of English heritage. She counted *Beano* albums, tabloids, Home Comforts stationery, Virgin Atlantic giveaways, *EastEnders* fanzines, BBC notepaper, a *Radio Times*, a *Time Out Guide to London*, British Rail timetables, a Green Line Bus calendar, an *All-Bran Cookery Book*. She picked up.

"Hello?"

"How are you?"

It was her father.

"I'm fine," she lied. "How was your day?"

"Everyone generally in good shape. The lecture went well. Do you fancy getting some supper together?"

"Why don't you come and meet me at the apartment? We can go round the corner."

"OK. What time?"

"Any time after seven."

"Marvellous."

She returned to the kitchen. Eduardo was cementing sponge cakes with a layer of strawberry jam. He was spreading it on with a rubber trowel. "What do you do when you're not working?" she asked, as she snapped the corner off a shortbread square and placed it on her tongue. It melted like a lick of butter.

"Drink beer, watch the game and I like to screw."

Utopia nodded, well, she had asked, then went to clear table four. Trudi was playing footsies with Terence and they were sharing a treacle pudding sitting in a lake of custard. Calorific love.

"Hot date?"

"My father."

"And I had you as one of them who shags granddads. Anyway, luv, do us a refill. And can you chop up some liver for Maggie before you go? I don't like Ed touching it when he's doing the cakes."

Utopia went to collect their teapot and nearly broke her neck falling over the dog. "Your dog's too fat."

"Fat and happy, luv. Like me."

"Ha," said Terence, turning the page.

✳

It was much later.

She was sitting next to her father on the sofa and staring at her feet. The humming of sewing-machines washed in through the windows. Aware that every minute spent together was a minute closer to her father's departure, she felt the knot tightening at her throat. They had ended up going for Italian at a place with sidewalk tables over on Mulberry Street. A man in a white shirt had serenaded them on the violin. His son in a black waistcoat had forced them to buy a wilted rose in a Cellophane wrap. "But I'm his daughter," she said.

"You could be my future wife," he said, which was nice so she had to buy a rose.

She felt bleary with wine and heavy with ricotta tortellini, gnocchi, garlic bread, olives and tiramisu. Her feet were resting on top of her father's leather briefcase and its contents had spilled on to the floor. He was writing dates in his diary with a fountain pen. Utopia's proposed Christmas visit was ushered in with a black U and a chorus of question marks. She watched him write. His nib scratched the paper and spewed globs of ink.

"You can't be more specific?"

"No."

"You don't have to be here. You know that, don't you?" He slid the lid over the pen. "You don't have to prove yourself to me or your mother."

"I'm not. Anyway, I haven't been away that long."

"I just don't want you being sad."

"I'm not sad," she fired back, afraid she might cry.

"All right."

"I'm happy here." She reneged. "Sort of."

Her father nodded and leaned back against the sofa. Monkey Man was entertaining at home. Bronzed men with big arms in skinny vests were standing in the kitchen.

Bright lights and music poured out of the windows.

"I went to meet Robert Shanks."

The words tumbled from her lips and fell to the floor. There was quiet. Utopia braced herself for his response. From the corner of her eye, she watched his brow furrow, his crow's feet jerk, his duck blue eyes grow cloudy. They had crossed into forbidden territory and she didn't like what was happening but there was no turning back.

"I went to his studio."

He began rubbing his face with his hands. His reading glasses were hanging from a string around his neck. There was only the flutter of the fan. He looked up. "I see."

"I found a photo of him and Mum in an old copy of *HQ*."

"Yes."

"So I rang him. He invited me to come and see him." She drew breath. "Did something happen?" She winced.

He nodded. "Yes. An affair."

The unthinkable had become thinkable.

Severed from her surroundings, she felt suffused with emotion. The weight of confession was a responsibility and there could be no childish recriminations, no wild-eyed histrionics. She had to accept it. She waited for him to speak. When it came, it came from a long way away.

"It didn't last long. We were both very young. We were your age. I think she felt frustrated not having a career of her own. She had just lost her third child with her miscarriage. She felt hopeless. Then she fell into modelling and felt extraordinarily liberated by it. That man Shanks was responsible, you see, and she was weak. He played on that weakness."

"Fucking creep." She felt angry. With all of them.

"Well, yes. I suppose so."

"Suppose so? Christ, Dad, he made my skin crawl." She felt her heart pound.

Her father nodded. "You mustn't be angry with her. She always said it meant nothing and it didn't."

"I just needed to know, that's all." She shook her head. "You're not angry I found out, are you?"

"No." He smiled. "You always were more intuitive than your sister." He placed his arm around her shoulders. "Just like your mother."

Johann appeared, wearing her lemon sarong. Why did he always have to wear her lemon sarong? "Todd left a message on the machine. He says it's about work. You should call him."

"Todd?"

"Yes."

"Thanks."

"OK. Goodnight."

Utopia stood up to fetch a glass of water.

"Well, there you go," said her father. "Work."

She shrugged.

A siren howled.

She drank her water standing at the sink. Her father began shovelling papers back into his briefcase. She didn't want him to leave. She wanted to talk about it.

"Did you talk about it?"

"Of course." He sounded tired. He removed his glasses from around his neck and put them in his pocket.

"Was it why we left New York?"

"Well, that and my job. It all happened at the same time, really."

"Did it make a difference? To you, I mean."

"Oh, no." He shook his head. "I never loved her any less for it. It was a crisis thing. We pulled through."

"And the pictures in the hallway?"

"They were about your mother. Not him. Things fade with time."

Utopia returned to the sofa and put her arm around him. She had always admired his uxoriousness. Her parents' marriage was a champion amid the graveyard of divorces through which they passed. And now this. She wasn't sure what to do with it. There was a stiffness in her father's hunch as she maintained her grip round his breadth. She absorbed the rhythm of his breathing. He was wearing a white shirt underneath a beige jacket. One of the collar tips had broken free and been left upturned. He sighed and leaned forward to tug at the buckle of the briefcase. It was leaking papers. The buckle's strap hung from the leather flap and threatened to break free. The leather was cracked and peeling.

"You need a new briefcase."

"But I like this old one. I bought it when you were still in nappies." He successfully propelled the pin through the hole as Monkey Man turned up the volume. "What a racket," he said.

"Do you want a quick cup of tea before you go?" she offered, looking at her watch. It was almost one.

"Why not?"

She felt alert with fatigue.

It was the end of the party when the lights come on. The truth stung but she felt no pain. This was her mother and these were the facts. She wondered at her father's resilience. She marvelled at her parents' love despite the affair. Nothing was absolute yet endurance had endured. That the two were not mutually exclusive was something new. It was the unfamiliarity of once familiar places but she wasn't afraid. She felt different. She wasn't sure yet how.

# Chapter Thirty-two

"You honestly didn't know Kurt was seeing Gloria?"

Utopia was sitting in a supermarket trolley recycled as a chair. The front of the grille had been removed and her legs were poking out in front.

"No. Well, not exactly." He was scrabbling through a drawer of nails. She couldn't see his face.

"How do you know her anyway?"

"I met her upstairs."

"At Kurt's?"

"Yeah."

"She comes round a lot?"

"No. I don't know. Look, the guy Kurt buys from was going over to his place and asked Gloria to meet him there," he said, turning round.

"So they met through their dealer?"

"Yeah. I guess."

They were drinking lemonade at the front end of the studio with the glass doors open on to the street. Tuesday was salvage day and the scrap king was late. Saul was waiting for his yodel from the street as he drove by in his truck in the hope he might have some parts worth bartering for. He usually did. Above the police building the evening sky was doing tricks with a kaleidoscope of fire.

"You're not giving much away, are you?"

Utopia hadn't seen Saul in over a week. It felt much longer with everything that had happened and here they were rowing. She couldn't help herself. His reticence provoked her. She felt determined to ram her way through the barricades of male solidarity. "You never mentioned Kurt when I said I was going to Gloria's."

"I didn't know he was going," he said, and tugged the mask over his eyes.

End of conversation. Bring on the flame-thrower. Utopia watched him weld. Her voice was drowned in the growl of the generator. The blow-torch hissed and breathed chemical fire. Saul's T-shirt was smeared with oil and wet half-moons were visible beneath his arms. His curls were coiled like wood shavings. She looked over at Max, the marmalade mound by the door. He displayed no desire to go out.

"How's Vivienne?" she shouted over the din.

"Come on, like you care," said Saul, taking a break between bursts of heat.

"Did you find what you were looking for in Jersey?" She had noticed a propeller leaning against a far wall and what looked to be the bumper of a truck.

"Yeah." He nodded, deflecting the bigger question. "We did."

"Where did you go?"

"All over. Big yard down near Elizabeth."

"And she's become Miss Welder?"

"Give me a break."

"Saul. I'm just trying to catch up."

She was actually testing her reactions and his. She was

aware of feeling oddly removed from him, their relationship and, by implication, Vivienne. The emotions stirred up on leaving *HQ* and by her father's visit meant that she had moved on in some way. There was still a side to her that wanted to feel engaged in Saul's studio politics but her infatuation had dwindled since their last night together. It was as though someone had yanked out the plug and her fascination had sloped off down the pipe like scurfy bath water.

His talk of a desert trip out west to explode bombs, of running into Bonnie, that he had bought some dope and they were going to make a night of it washed over her. Suspicions of an affair with Vivienne seemed as obvious as recognising that Saul wasn't faithful to anyone. The realisation was as stark as the fact that Saul refused to discuss his mother. And, what was more, Utopia no longer cared.

Perhaps in retrospect it was her encounter with Regine three weeks ago that had done it. She had arrived at the studio and found the door open. Inside she had found Saul massaging his mother's feet. Her soles were nestled in his lap. She had been issuing words of encouragement. "Mmm, honey. No not there. There. Yes."

"Mom's just been shopping," said Saul, without looking up.

It was this absent gesture that said more than anything he could have voiced. At the time she had buried the incident. She now considered his mother-love the truth by which all else was measured. Marina's theory was that males skilled in technique had been likely seduced by older women as boys. Utopia felt hesitant about applying this theory to Saul.

She watched him propel the flame and thought about her father. He had left for London this morning and was now mid-way across the Atlantic, Bordeaux splashing out of a plastic glass as he tried to write a paper, watch the film, prise himself from the confessional clutches of an American neighbour. She missed him already.

"Got plans for dinner?" asked Saul, switching off his generator and prising off his mask. "How about King Doi's for noodles?"

"Then a couple of tequila shots and the obligatory fuck?"

Saul stared at her. "What is with you today? Why are you being so confrontational?"

"Am I?" She sighed. "I don't know."

"You don't know what? Why you're being such an argumentative fuck or whether you want to go eat?"

"I don't know what I'm doing in New York half the time. Yes, and, actually, Saul, I don't know what we had between us."

"What are you talking about?" He frowned, wiping his hands on a rag. "We've had some fun times."

"Fun times, eh?" she murmured, jolting the chair so that it slithered across the floor on skittish wheels.

"Sure. Hey, is this still about Vivienne? Because it's kind of nuts this thing you have about her."

"No, it's not about her, Saul. It's about everything. I don't even care what you do with Vivienne. It's just, I don't know, the way you treat people."

She stopped.

She was ranting but as her voice grew louder, she felt frustration pour from the vacuum left by her night in Southampton, by her disappointment with Saul and her disenchantment with herself. She had made some pretty poor choices. Lust was lust but with Saul there was meant to be more. Maybe not much but a little.

"I don't know what to say," he said, walking over to the

table to find his wallet. "I see who I want when I want."

"Yeah. Like Kurt."

Now they were getting somewhere. Where previously she and Saul never discussed anything tangible because conversation was limited to chit-chat and daily events, his life, that time was over.

"That's why telling me nothing happened with you and Vivienne is bollocks when she answers the phone before you're even up."

Saul began to laugh. It was a laugh shared with Kurt. It was a bullying laugh designed to shut out the rest. He was pushing her away. "Man," he said, sliding his wallet into his backpocket, "you're really going off on this shit, aren't you?"

Utopia felt her cheeks flush and her breathing lodge, indignant, in her throat. "You don't give a fuck about anyone, do you Saul?"

There was silence. Saul went to pick up his keys from the workbench. He jangled them between his fingers. Utopia squeezed herself from out of the trolley chair and followed him on to the street. She stood motionless as he locked up.

"My opening's Tuesday. Invite's in the mail."

They parted ways and headed for opposite ends of the street, his conciliatory footnote, if that was what it was, ringing in her ears. Her stomach flip-flopped. Accusations of dishonesty were a joke, she reflected. She wondered who was being honest around here. Yet it was strange how the challenge to possess Saul had evaporated like tropical rain. She felt deliriously calm. Side-stepping the bags of stinking refuse mounded on the sidewalk, she reached her door and pushed it open.

Why did no one ever lock it?

# Chapter Thirty-three

She was stranded in limbo between sleep and consciousness. Washes of memory triggered sudden alertness. Opening her eyes, she remembered Todd. She was supposed to have called him. Rolling over, she reached out of bed and scrabbled around for something to write with. She wrote down his name. She would call him tomorrow.

"Utopia." Johann was banging on the door.

"What? Christ, I'm trying to sleep."

"It's Kurt."

She looked at her watch. It was two a.m.

"What does he want?"

"I don't know. I think you should talk to him." Johann pushed open the door to pass her the phone.

"I don't believe this. Hello?"

"Fuck, man. It's Saul. I don't know what to do." Kurt's voice was breathy with panic.

Utopia's stomach curdled as she absorbed his distress. "What's he done? What's happened?"

"We had some dope, *ja*, and—"

"What's happened?"

"He's just fucking passed out, man. I don't know what the fuck to do."

"What do you mean passed out?"

"Cold. *Ja*. On the fucking floor. Jesus."

"Have you called the ambulance?"

"*Ja, ja*. I will. Oh, fuck. Look, man, I've got dope here. I've got to get rid of it. Oh, man, can you come?"

"OK, OK."

Throwing on her clothes, she ran in to find Johann. He was curled up beneath his sheet. His water bed belched as she prodded him. "Johann. Something's happened."

He reluctantly opened his eyes. "Who?"

"Something's happened."

"What's the time?"

"Please, Johann."

"What?"

"Come with me," she shrieked, the situation suddenly intolerable.

He shook his head, swung his legs out of bed and pulled on his jeans. She led the way. They flew down the stairs, two at a time, pounding the hollow steps. The street was deserted. They left Mott, headed down Center Street then took a right onto Grand. Kurt's elevator entrance opened on to the street. It was waiting for them. Stepping inside the gaping steel mouth, Utopia shivered. She steadied her gaze on Johann. He looked exhausted but wasn't complaining. The lift rattled and squeaked as it rose.

Emerging on the third floor, they were met by Kurt. He had a piece of foil balled in his palm. He was wittering. He seemed slightly mad.

"Here. Thank Gott you're here. Jesus fucking Christ. What the fuck are we going to do?"

"Where's Saul?"

They followed him into the bedroom. Saul was splayed out on the floor, shirtless. His face was ashen. His lips were lilac.

"Oh, no," said Utopia, as she fell by his side. She took his glassy wrist.

She was seized by the image of her mother's face when she looked like a bird. When her cheeks were concave. She couldn't bear it. "For fuck's sake, Kurt," she said angrily, "what were you doing?"

"I don't know. We were snorting lines."

"Of coke?"

"Of dope."

"Heroin?"

"His stuff. He got pains in his chest and down his arms and then . . . Jesus, man, it wasn't my dope." He thrust out his hand. "What are we going to do with it?"

Johann took it. "I'll get rid of it." He disappeared.

Utopia sat with Saul, unable to let go, as Kurt paced backwards and forwards. The memory of her mother joined her again in the room. Refusing the nurse's morphine, her mother had wanted to be there with them lucid. Utopia had looked into her mother's eyes more deeply then than ever before. She had been afraid to blink. It was her mother's calm that had alleviated their despair. Utopia's Spanish numbers filtered through the stillness as she recited them over and over again, never reaching ten.

*Uno, dos, tres, cuatro* . . .

She tried to count the curled black hairs on Saul's chest. She tried to calculate the number of tea-strainer freckles he had shadowing his eyes, the lace holes in his boots, the books towering by the door. Kurt was on the phone. She heard him barking at the emergency services in a rage. "Are you just going to let him fucking die?"

She felt nothing but skin. Papery smooth. At last the elevator doors opened. A pair of paramedics in saviour white and institution green rushed in. They were accompanied by two cops as broad as they were squat. They swaggered like cowboys. She baulked, afraid, as they entered the room. Pressed against a wall, she watched their judicious focus sweep across the floor, over the mattress to take in the bedside table. It was bare except for a pool of wax. When last Utopia had looked, it had been littered with matchboxes, a roll of foil, cigarette papers and a can of lighter fuel.

"Ninth Precinct," said one of the cops, by way of an introduction.

"What happened?" demanded a paramedic, bent over Saul and rolling back his eyelids. Utopia could see his pupils. They were pin points. Fixed.

"He got pains down his arms. Across his chest."

"Drugs?" She watched Kurt shake his head. "No," she heard him say.

She bit her lip, guilty, watching as the paramedics unfurled a resuscitation kit chequered with syringes and tubes. A needle was hastily inserted into Saul's arm. A syringe fitted to the end of the line. Whoosh. He pumped the arm of the syringe. They examined his face. No response.

"Bag him," said the other, placing a mask over Saul's mouth.

While one ventilated a bag attached with a tube to the mask, the other, his hands on Saul's chest, began manually to pump his heart. He was counting. One, two, three. One, two, three. Utopia's clammy palms were clasped over her mouth. She looked on in horror. Please, she willed his heart. She wanted Saul's eyes to open and him to move his lips, cough, struggle, laugh at this desperate scene. She wanted this to be another of his charades set up for the camera.

"Come on," she said.

"Who lives here?" barked cop one, with an expressionless face. He had a broad Queens accent and jelly donut jowls.

Utopia felt his question pin her accusingly against the wall. She felt her hands drop to her side. "He does," came her response, as she swallowed then nodded in the direction of Kurt. It was his fault. His apartment. His sordid entertainment.

"Who's coming to the hospital?" the other demanded, his belt shifting in synch with his weight.

Utopia's worried eyes rotated around his waist. His .38 service revolver sat in a holster to his right. Saul had a government issue .38 just like it. It had been purchased on the street for some future project. She had once handled it at Saul's persuasion. Saul had taken a Polaroid of her aiming it at him. Freeze, motherfucker – put your hands where I can see them! She had been transfixed by its menace as an extension of herself. For a Hollywood moment.

She hated guns.

Against the cop's left leg swung his billy club. A leather pouch of cartridges and a can of mace sandwiched its handle. As he turned, she caught sight of his handcuffs dangling at his coccyx. She noticed that he was missing a button and that his undershirt was no longer white. He was wearing a wedding ring. Kurt wiped his brow. "I do."

"And who are you?" said cop one, returning to Utopia.

"Me? Em, a friend."

"Name?"

"Utopia Holmes," she told him, as the idea of giving a fake spun through her mind. Too late.

"D'you live in New York City?"

"Yes."

"Legal?"

"Yes."

"You got papers?"

"A passport."

"And you?"

"An H-1," said Kurt.

"What's that?"

"A work visa. I'm a photographer."

"Oh."

Cop two was writing something down in a spiralled notepad. His tongue lolled from his mouth as he scribbled. It was a concentration tic. Looking over his shoulder, she saw slabs of jelly, pink like smoked salmon, being slapped across Saul's chest. "Stand clear. Shock," she heard one of the paramedics order, as paddles leading back to a small black box via a frenzy of wires were banged on Saul's chest. His body jerked violently as the voltage was applied.

She whimpered and bit down on fingers caught between her teeth. Unable to see the monitor screen, she studied their faces in search of relief. It failed to come.

"Push another adrenaline."

Another needle was jabbed into the milky smooth of his forearm. Another syringe. Cop two was on the radio. "We've got someone suspended."

With a paramedic at each end, they lifted Saul up and flung him on to a low framed trolley. His arm slipped and was left dangling. The glass face of his diving watch banged against the trolley leg. Its lugubrious rattle sent shivers down her spine. She wanted to save it and restore it to his side but there was no time. He was gone. The paramedics steered the trolley back out of the room and disappeared inside the lift flanked by the cops. Cop one had Kurt's elbow cupped in his hand.

Left behind, Utopia sat on the bed.

She collapsed on her back. Stretching her arms towards the ceiling in an imaginary embrace, she studied her hands. They looked older than she remembered. The scaly texture around the knuckles had developed webbed creases and the skin was coarser. They were her mother's hands with their twiggy fingers and bony wrists. Why hadn't she accompanied them to the hospital? she now needed to know. Kurt didn't want her there, that's why. He was going to call Regine from St Vincent's. "Let's keep it simple," he said.

Simple? Jesus Christ. When was life ever simple?

Introspection capitulated to fear and her world darkened.

Lurching forward, she sat bolt upright. On her feet in a second, she made for the emergency exit. She didn't want to be alone. She counted the stairs as she descended, her flip-flops slapping against their stony surface. She never went in elevators by herself if she could help it. The racing fear of entrapment spooked her. Claustrophobia was something she had acquired with age. It was the horror of standing in packed subway cars, battling fears of mass suffocation, wondering whether to share these anxieties with her neighbour's bulk. "Excuse me but I'm about to freak out. D'you think you could catch me when I fall?"

She pushed open the vault-like door on to the street and was enveloped by a gust of wind. It left her dizzy. Gasping for air, she waited to regain her balance. Rap echoed through the walls of the recording studio next door. A buttery moon was shining.

A white stretch limo was pulling up outside the police building. Look at me, it begged, arching its back and shaking its tail. A woman in black with sunglasses wrapped around her pale face emerged to mount the steps. Deprived of the paparazzi with only Utopia to acknowledge her moment of arrival, she appeared self-conscious and alone. Almost as alone as Utopia felt.

She ought to get back and sit by the telephone. Wait for news.

"You OK?" said Johann, as she entered the apartment.

He was sitting at the table drinking a beer. The smell of meat and garlic lingered in the air like yesterday's diary insert. Nostalgia for the past.

"Any message from the hospital?"

"Not yet."

"I should have gone."

"It's probably OK."

"Fucking Kurt. It's all his fault. God, what a fucking mess," cried Utopia as, letting go, her words cut through her numbness and anger, and tears spilled forth like vomit. Uncontrollable and acid, they burned her throat and stung her eyes bringing instant relief. Johann brought her a cup of tea dotted with white flecks that spun like stardust around and around. A galaxy of sour milk.

"I'm not supposed to drink this, am I?" She laughed, a snail path of snot glistening beneath her nose.

He pulled a face and poured it down the sink.

They sat in silence and listened to the tinkly wail of a bootlegged Chinese film playing in one of the nearby apartments. It was a background tune of peasants and warriors, unrequited love and avenging death. The ten-dollar fan mowed the air with fragrant sighs while Johann rolled a joint. Utopia phoned Kurt. No answer. She phoned Anna. Nothing. She telephoned the hospital but got lost in the telephone-answering system. Trying to fathom her way through the maze of question and answers, she was directed up to the X-ray department before being put on hold.

Johann poured her a whisky and they looked despairingly at each other as the horror of not knowing went on. Was no news good news? No news could mean anything. She inhaled and felt the smoke fill her mouth and her lungs and the space behind her eyes. It moved to the jellied crevices of her brain before travelling along her veins to the tips of her limbs. With her fingers tingling, she imagined the grip of Saul's hands around her.

She opened her eyes and the darkness confused her. The ring of the phone seemed to carry from a long way off. It cut through the silence like the end of the world. Her hand thump-thumped against the floor as she searched for the receiver. She wanted it to stop.

"Saul . . ." She was groggy with whisky.

"It's Felix. I'm here with Regine. The party's over."

"Over?"

"He blew it."

Utopia held her breath. She couldn't breathe. She heard Felix inhale on the other end, like an old man's wheeze. He spoke slowly. "The fucker blew it. Big time."

She bit her lip as his voice cracked. She waited, afraid, as he regained his composure. He released a mournful sound, which went straight through her. She felt very cold.

"I just wanted to let you know. I know you tried to help."

"Help?"

"I'll call you tomorrow. Try and get some sleep."

With the telephone cradled in her arms, Utopia lay wide awake. She saw Saul in the coffin in the hole in the street.

She saw him welding and his face illuminated in flame. Outside the twenty-four-hour deli on the corner a couple were rowing. Someone kicked over a trash can and it fell to the street and rolled along the gutter.

Frightened, she started on her numbers as the pearly light of dawn crept through the curtains.

# Chapter Thirty-four

"We were on a bus full of people on our way through the desert. I was with Saul but I recognised it. It was the journey I did with P our first summer together when we had our car stolen with the insurance papers inside and had to get the bus to LA. Anyway, the bus stopped at a crossroads on a highway, it parked and we all got out. Saul wanted to walk to the supermarket along the road. I said there wasn't time so he went by himself. When I got back on the bus, he wasn't there. His seat was empty. The driver was revving the engine as everyone reboarded. It made me nervous but I was sure he'd get back any minute. Then the doors closed and the driver began driving away.

'Stop. He's not here,' I shouted, and charged down the aisle.

'Sorry, lady,' the driver told me. 'I can't afford to mess up the schedule.'

'It's not worth my job,' he told me.

"So there I was trapped on this bus without Saul, screaming at the driver who was ignoring me. I was filled with panic. Then we pulled out on to the highway and I saw him. He was spreadeagled on a police car with his hands behind his head. He was being arrested. I was banging my fist against the glass so that he would see me but he didn't. I shouted to the driver to stop but he wouldn't. It was awful. I felt so helpless, so guilty. I knew that I should have gone with him to the shop. I knew something horrible was going to happen. And I could not get off the bus."

Tears dirtied with mascara slid down Utopia's cheeks. She felt watery with despair.

"You poor darling," said Marina, leaning across the wooden table to attempt an embrace. "What a terrible dream."

They were sitting in Mott Street's local bar, the Glory Lounge, in a corner booth drowning Utopia's grief in tall vodka-cranberries. A taxidermal mongoose with its teeth bared was mounted on the wall behind in a glass cabinet. The light was dreary and their privacy complete. The entire day had been held hostage by a feeling of detachment. She had been woken by her dream as though being dragged, involuntarily, away from the place she wanted to go.

The truth did nothing to alleviate the pain.

She had waited for her panic to pass.

It was not a foreign sensation. Since her mother's death, she had found herself visited without warning by spasms that tore across her chest and trailed her arms. The first time it happened she had made P drive her to Casualty. "I'm having a heart-attack," she had sobbed, as he tore up the Holloway Road to the Whittington Hospital with one hand on the steering-wheel and the other on hers. "I'm dying."

"You're not. Just relax," he told her, shooting a red.

This was the first of what were diagnosed as panic attacks, a complaint formerly unheard of. She had never known panic attacks, just as she had never known fear. Trapped-in-a-box-with-the-lid-pulled-shut type fear.

"Put your head between your knees and take deep breaths," the doctor ordered her, as she sat in a cubicle with P. "You'll be fine."

And she was.

This morning she had lain in bed for hours, unable to stir, as the finality of Saul's death stole the oxygen from the room. Later roaming the apartment like a stranger picking things up, putting them down, flicking through books, staring out of the window, she found herself reliving their last evening. Already his face was a blur. Their last encounter had been an emotional blaze and now this. Denied the storm's soothing aftermath she had been cast adrift.

"I see who I want when I want," he had told her.

"Go fuck yourself," she had wanted to say.

But he had beaten her to it. The final fling. The big bang. And then nothingness.

She hated him for it as she hated his absence and his submission to stereotype. His validation of the maxim "Those who burn brighter burn out" wasn't brave. It was stupid and weak. But Saul was the type who had always been lucky. He thought he was charmed and that he could get away with it every time. Not this time. Not his mother, his therapist or his hubris could save him this time.

"More drinks?" said Marina, wiggling past her and making for the bar.

Utopia looked up. "OK, Doctor."

Her sobriety was improving the more she drank. Right now her mind felt razor sharp and it was her responses that were dull. She imagined that this was how it was to be comatose. To be trapped in a body with the brain active but nobody listening. She was no stranger to the intimacy of death. Not a day went by when she didn't feel its shadow. She had been there for her mother's final whisper. She had sat with her father and Liberty and they had listened to her mother' breathing grow shallower and shallower. Willing it to end while despising its arrest, they had witnessed its peace as it stole her away. She loathed its company as cunning as a stalker. It had taken her mother six months to die. Leave me alone, she wanted to cry.

Powerless to forget, she peered into her glass for clues.

Someone put a song on the jukebox. Two bearded men were doing shots at the bar and slamming the empty glasses down on the counter. The bar was a refuge for occupational drinkers. With its worn oak pews and saloon privacy, it was her favourite New York corner. She occasionally came with Johann for a whisky or to shoot a game of pool. He had taught her how to beat him. She had once brought Saul. They were on their way to a movie and had stopped in for a beer. He had put a song on the jukebox. She couldn't remember whose, though it might have been Lou Reed.

"Another round, please, Jim," ordered one of the beards.

Marina returned. "This should keep us going," she said passing along a pink glass.

Utopia drank thirstily.

The vodka washed down like punch. It muffled her emotions but conjured up a time and a place. She was with Saul at his kitchen table. The disco ball was spinning overhead and modernist plink-plonk jazz was tinkling from the stereo. Saul was on the telephone flirting with Marcus and fondling the cat. She was laughing as she rolled on his sofa and tried not to fall off. Then he was lying sprawled on Kurt's floor and his face was blue like ice.

Marina had unsnapped her powder compact and was smoothing her complexion. Observing her, Utopia wanted to slide to the end of the bench, bring both knees to her chest and bury her face in her lap. She felt defeated by this destruction of precious things. She felt devoid of hope. Solitude pressed upon her without compassion.

Why had it happened?

"I need to speak to P."

"Am I being useless?" said Marina, looking up.

"No."

"Meaning yes."

Utopia tried to laugh.

"I'm sorry, darling. My head is all over the place. I wish I didn't have to leave you but Cheshire's expecting me. Everyone's going to be there. Are you sure you'll be all right? Why don't we call Felix and see if you can go there for the night?"

"I'll be fine. I need to talk to P. That's all."

"Are you sure?"

"Yes. Really."

It was one of Marina's stock phrases, 'Everyone's going to be there,' but Utopia couldn't have been less impressed had Marina been on her way to meet the President. She imagined all those proffered cheeks and pressing palms and felt ill. Time to go.

They finished their drinks and split.


Back in the apartment Utopia counted the rings as the telephone crossed the Atlantic. She felt relatively sane, it was all right to be alone, now that she had seen Marina. She imagined P in the kitchen, cooking pasta, pouring a beer as the local pirate station played big-shout-going-out requests and lame Blackie nuzzled against his leg. "I've already fed you this evening, now fuck off."

Blackie had come in through the back door last summer

and never left. P had never liked cats and Blackie never reciprocated P's hospitality with the vaguest hint of affection. Their rapport was built on suspicion yet seemed to endure. Their feigned indifference was a male thing, Utopia had decided.

She looked at her watch.

It was eight o'clock her time, one a.m. his time.

Where was he? He could be anywhere. Still counting the rings, she watched his faceless female friend emerge to stand at the sink. She was holding a glass of wine. Utopia watched her bend her leg to hoist herself on to the sideboard as she would have done. She saw her position her back against the wall and move her head to avoid the shelf of glasses and collection of ashtrays.

She saw the woman cross her legs and P slicing red and yellow peppers to arrange beneath the grill. Grilled peppers were a favourite, guaranteed to be tastier properly marinated the next day. She watched him toss them in a plastic bag to cool and the vacuum full with condensation. She saw the crispy skins part from the flesh as he peeled them off. She saw their strips of colour laid out in a bowl, slick with olive oil and dotted with capers. His betrayal pained her. Their shared routine was not a casual affair with which he could solicit others. Didn't he know that?

"Hello . . ."

Finally. There was the sound of long-winded panting.

"P? It's U."

"U, my love. How are you?"

His cheeriness choked her. "Good. Yes. Did I wake you?"

"I've just got in. I've been in town. A meeting. We went drinking. How's the Big Apple?"

"Good. Yes, it's good."

"So, what have you been doing? How's work?"

"Fine."

She hesitated, her voice faltering as she struggled to retain her composure.

"Are you all right?"

He wasn't a fool. He could detect these things.

"No," she heard herself say, as she promised she wouldn't but knew she would. It was, after all, why she had phoned.

"What's happened?"

"Someone died."

"Died? You're joking. Who died?" His voice sounded strong, crisp, English. Concerned.

"A friend. An accident. He was snorting lines of heroin."

"Jesus."

"He had a heart attack."

"That's terrible. When did it happen?"

"Last night. It was awful."

"I'm sorry."

Silent tears began to roll and it made her feel better.

"How did you know him?"

Utopia paused. "I'd only known him a few months."

"I see."

"So, what have you been doing?" she asked, her voice thin, not her own.

"Watching my fingers turn grey like my computer. Two of the scripts look like they're finally going ahead, though I'm not holding my breath. Not yet. We're waiting for lottery money like the rest of the world."

"How's Julian?"

"Back in his flat. My hall is still filled with his crap. He's a lazy cunt."

She laughed, then wondered who else had been spending time in the flat and her throat dried up. She wanted to hear him tell her something he thought she didn't know. She wanted to hear his steady, familiar intonation reassure her that it was a lie. That nothing about the world as she knew it had been corrupted.

"I wish I was there."

At last he had said it.

"Why aren't you?"

There was a transatlantic delay or so it seemed.

"You know why."

She couldn't help herself. "Do I?" She was shaking her head.

"U, I'm sorry I haven't phoned. This fucking romantic comedy. I hate it. It's not funny and it's not romantic."

"No."

"I wish I was with you in New York. I want to know what your apartment looks like."

She heard him light a cigarette. She didn't want to talk. She wanted to listen to his breathing. She wanted to remember the smell of his skin, her face pressed against his neck as his warmth enveloped her, late at night, early morning, finding him there.

"You still there?"

"Yes."

She imagined his lip brushing against the telephone. "Where are you? Which room?"

"The study."

"What are you wearing?"

Her inner thighs were sticky with perspiration. She pressed her palm between her legs as she heard P laugh.

"Jeans and a T-shirt. Oh, yeah. My Discount

Productions T-shirt. Hang on, that's better, I've taken it off."
His voice dropped. "What are you wearing?"

"A towel I stole from the hotel I swim at. I've just had a
shower. My fourth today."

"I like that. A hotel towel. Is it hot?"

"Baking."

"It's warm here. I've just opened the skylight. No stars."
He paused. "Are the lights on?"

"Off."

She heard his breathing falter. It was the quiver of suspense.

"'It's cooler in the dark. There are too many lights on in
the other buildings for it to be dark-dark but I like it like
this. I can see my neighbours but they can't see me."

"Any action?"

She laughed. "This is New York. There's always action."

"OK. Tell us what you've got."

"Well, the gay bloke opposite is out. I reckon he's a rent-
boy. He's out all night and sleeps all day. Every morning he
says goodbye to a different bloke. Oh, but I can see his fat
cat squashed up against the window. All the cats in New
York are fat. They never go out. I can see a woman on the
next floor up, she's got the exterminator in and they're both
wearing masks. Now they're crouching on the floor like
cockroaches. Weird. And the bloke on the top floor has his
decks in front of an open window and he's playing something though I can't hear it. He's wearing earphones."

"You win. All I can see are the lights of a plane going
over. Going, going, gone."

He smoked. "God, I miss you."

She felt her jaw tighten. Incipient regret. Nails pressed
into her skin leaving marks. It hurt. "I've missed you."

"Have you?"

"I've got to go." She couldn't bear it. "I've had a long day," she said, wanting his voice to comfort her while afraid of the consequences. What if she surrendered? Come and take me away.

"Are you by yourself?"

"Yes."

"Where's your flatmate?"

"I'll be fine. I just need to sleep."

He coughed. "I'll phone tomorrow."

" 'Bye."

She hung up and collapsed on the floor. She lay there and wanted to dissolve into darkness and be nowhere at all. She wanted him so much that she ached. She stared out at the roofs of Chinatown and wondered what she was doing in this godforsaken city. This rotten apple.

# Chapter Thirty-five

Despite all that had happened, she felt rejuvenated by the new day. She crossed the street and entered Washington Square Park. It was too early for the skateboarders to have gathered by the fountain and too soon for the homeless sleepers on the benches to have been moved on. NYU students in sweats came jogging past her. A street-cleaning truck was edging its way down Washington Square West and its revolving brush stirred up clouds of dust.

An old woman in curlers was tossing crusts at the pigeons and cooing like a hairdryer at them. They weren't afraid. Utopia thought of Henry James and how much the square had changed. He knew lawn and flowers, not these scuffed tracts of dirt given over to dogs and their walkers, these trees without bark and cracked tarmac. Had he known Triumphal Arch under which she now passed? She wasn't sure.

"Smoke, smoke," said a voice behind her, but she didn't bother looking back. All she could think of was seeing Felix and food.

"Come for breakfast," he had said, when she phoned hoping he was up. And he was. Sleep didn't take precedence in Felix's world. He was one of those four-hours-a-night people.

She took a left on to 8th Street and realised something else. It wasn't just the early hour, not yet nine, which provided a sense of renewal. It was September, waiting in the wings about to make its entrance. The humidity had been beaten into remission and the air felt feathery and light. Every season the weather changed and every season felt like the first time. She felt happy to be alive as she crossed Greenwich Avenue.

She spotted Felix from outside the diner. His head was capped by the orange S in Sunshine Diner and he was reading the paper. Sensing her approach, he looked up and waved. She pushed open the door and went to join him in the booth. She leant to kiss him, then eased herself in behind the Formica table. Their feet met as Billy, their name-tagged waitress, arrived with a pot of coffee. Utopia ordered scrambled eggs on wholegrain toast and a side of bacon.

The shelf of black-cherry cheesecakes behind the lunch counter was humming noisily. It was the moment before take-off at the back of a plane. The chef was flipping hash browns, which hissed as they landed, and Billy poured coffee. She left to administer refills elsewhere and the white bow of her apron bounced like a rabbit tail against her black-skirted rear.

They sat in silence. Utopia began twisting her cup round and round on the saucer until the grating china screamed. Felix was smoking a cigarette and fondled it between drags. He took off his glasses and rubbed his eyes. "Funeral's Monday."

"In Connecticut?"

"Yes."

"How's Regine?"

"Sedated."

She reached for his pack of Winstons. "Can I have one?"

"Be my guest. I thought you'd quit."

"Yes, well. Almost four months. One won't kill me."

If this meant failing New York then so be it. New York had failed her. Besides, smoking would give her something else to think about. The filter tasted spongy between her lips. The pull of tobacco felt smooth and noxious. The nicotine sent her brain spinning and her pulse racing. She loved and hated it for corrupting her so effortlessly. Elation like poison flowed through her veins.

"How have you been?" asked Felix, slicing a waffle with the side of his fork.

"I had a dream about him."

"Happy or sad?"

"Guilty, I think."

"Don't feel guilty."

"And how's everyone else? Coping, I mean."

"Kurt's gone to rehab in Arizona. Saul's dad cleared things with the police. He's a lawyer. He plays golf with the district attorney. So he's taken care of all that."

"I see."

"Regine asked me to make a few calls. To let people know. His friends." He smeared a blob of butter into his other waffle. "Vivienne's finishing off in the studio. The store still want the installations as a tribute, which is nice. They're talking about giving him a whole window. Now, he would have really dug that." He paused. "And Gloria's called."

"About Kurt?"

"Sure but also . . ."

"Saul?"

Felix's look of dismay betrayed whatever he knew. Utopia stared at him and shook her head. He couldn't have. He didn't. He did, didn't he?

"How well did they know each other?"

"Well enough."

"What do you mean?"

"Yes, I do mean. Kurt told me. But, let's be honest here, both of us knew Saul."

Utopia said nothing. She found a crack in the Formica filled with grains of crystalline sugar and began dislodging them, one by one.

"Do you want to know?"

She shrugged. Of course she did.

"They met through Dimitrios, their dealer. Russian. Big guy. Big dog. You've probably seen him around."

Utopia nodded.

"So there was this one weekend when he was away . . ."

"Who?"

"Kurt."

"Which weekend?"

"Not that long ago. He was shooting down in the Keys or somewhere. Gloria wanted some for the weekend so Dimitrios told her to meet him at Saul's."

Utopia suddenly knew exactly which weekend it was. She had been taken by Marina to a spa in Jamaica's Blue Mountains. It had been a freebie courtesy of Marina's magazine. They had had to come up with five hundred words each for the beauty page. They had been treated to massages, glycolic peels, hydrotherapy, seaweed wraps, a Himalayan body treatment and the strongest weed she had ever smoked. She had started hallucinating and had had to go to bed. Marina had spent the night with the barman, who knew how to read palms and had soulful eyes. His name was Holiday.

"I suppose they did blow all night and you can imagine the rest."

"Yes," she said, watching her ash crumble on the table.

"I just found out he had a bad heart. He was born with a hole in it, a congenital thing. I've known Saul ten years but I never knew that. And it never stopped him doing drugs."

There was a tone of resignation to this delivery of fact. It was an admission of inevitability which she had tried so hard to avoid. She took a bite of toast and poked at her eggs with her fork. They bounced. Had she ever known him at all?

"Hi, guys." It was Billy. "More coffee?"

"Thanks."

Utopia watched the brown water splash down the sides of her cup and collect in a puddle in her saucer. She lit another cigarette to compensate for the disappointments and misfortunes. Sinfulness always felt electric. It was life affirming, she decided, as outside the light turned green and a fleet of cabs took off like a rally race.

"You look like you're really enjoying that cigarette."

"God, am I that transparent?"

"Human, that's all," he said, and squeezed her arm.

She wondered at Saul and Kurt. They had shared downtime, high time, and even Gloria, she now found out. It was this last revelation that cheapened everything shared with Saul. Saul the boy who liked to have a good time. Work all night then go to bed with a Brazilian bunny hanging out in the studio. Lines chopped out on the mirror, the bottle of Cuervo steadily emptying, Gloria's talons running through his hair.

It came as no surprise but that didn't prevent her feeling excluded. Privately she had thought that what they shared was special, different from the rest. How naive. Saul was

Saul and the women flocked. He had never sought to hide the fact, why should he, and who was she to feel resentful of another's exploits?

"What happened to your boyfriend? The one in London?" asked Felix, tracking her thoughts with predictable precision.

She looked at him, surprised.

"You never talk about him."

"Don't I? No, I suppose I don't. Well, I just spoke to him."

"Why did you leave him?"

"We both agreed, well, I decided I needed to get away. I told you, after my mother died."

"So you left him temporarily. To see what life was like without him?"

She nodded and remembered P's words. On the single occasion that he had contested her decision, when she had been lachrymose in the kitchen and he had his head in his hands, he had remarked that to piss your life away in the hope of finding the answer wasn't impossible. Perhaps he was right. The problem was, there were no eternal truths. Priorities had a clever way of redefining themselves like undulating sand dunes. Just when you thought you had it all worked out, your set of values shifted again. Ultimately it was just a gamble.

"I'm sort of half-way in and half-way out."

"In what?"

"I don't know."

In truth, she was aware of missing him more each day. She had started seeing him everywhere she went. The sight of a tall man in glasses, any tall man at all, was enough for her to quicken her pace, the flush of recognition playing tricks with her head. It was never him. Someone else's P. In the last few weeks, she had taken to sleeping with a pillow between her arms. She couldn't sleep without it, so much did she want him.

Where previously emotions for P had been eclipsed by wretched January nights, a feeling of isolation and then a desperation to leave, she had returned to the person she would choose above anyone else. P was the person she told everything to because he legitimised what she had to say and her place in the world. He was the only person who took photographs of her she liked. With him she was free. He got that.

It was P who had taught her to drive in his highly prized turquoise Ford Capri then flown her to Rome as a consolation prize for failing her driving test three times due to criminally bad reverse parking. "Sounds like carnage," he said, when she described the scene. Hub-caps grating the side of the kerb, smoking rubber, the rear bumper pranged. P could reverse with one hand on the wheel and the other round her shoulders like someone else she had known. It was the only trait he shared with Saul that she was prepared to admit.

It was the day-to-day she missed. Being in the flat together on the sofa as he worked his way through a stack of newspapers skimming for stories and tit-bits while she ate biscuits. He had a particular way of wearing his glasses after he had worn them for too long. To relieve the pressure from the bridge of his nose he would rest them low so that the arms framed his face without sitting on his ears. He looked about ten. He was the boy who sat at the back of the class because he was scared of the others.

Right now they were on the sofa and he was telling her about a treatment for a screenplay submitted that morning. Only under duress. "I don't want to talk about it. It mightn't come off."

"Oh, don't be so bloody cynical." She was prodding him with her foot. "All you ever do is work. If you can't enjoy it even for a minute, you might as well give up."

And he smiled then shook his head because he knew she was right.

"What's his name."

"Piers."

"Maybe you should visit."

"Yes. Maybe you're right."

"Check." He waved at Billy then looked at his watch. "I've got appointments all afternoon."

They paid and left the diner, grabbing a handful of mints from the bowl by the cash till. A delivery boy on a bicycle flew round the corner and swerved to miss them. He skidded as he braked and swore as he tore off. They burst out laughing. Utopia was shaking. "That was close."

They stood for a moment before embracing with a fervour that touched her.

"Check out train times to Riverside from Grand Central. I'll come pick you up," he said, waving his newspaper with what she knew to be false cheer.

# Chapter Thirty-six

"How was it?"

She was sitting on a bench with Marina, looking out over the river, at the Colgate clock and New Jersey shore beyond.

"I'm glad I went."

"Was it churchy?"

"They're Jewish."

"So what happened?"

"It was a memorial service in their garden. People spoke and then we had drinks. I spent most of my time with Felix. It was sad."

The funeral had taken place yesterday. Utopia had taken the 11.05 train from Grand Central Station to Riverside, Connecticut, by herself. The train took a scenic route past rows of firs and vistas of water and she couldn't remember ever having been so happy to see greenery or an empty sky. Felix had met her at the station in a black suit with a sober face. "What do you think Saul would make of the great day?" he asked, as she got into the car, but Utopia could think of nothing to say.

Instead she found herself reminiscing about times spent together. Their late-night walks through Chinatown as he shot Polaroids of faces engorged in neon, the discovery of a piece of furniture on the street to be dragged back to the studio where immediate decisions would have to be made on what exactly it was good for. Out would come the power drill and the saw.

"He would want us to have a good time," said Felix, as he reversed into Regine's garage.

He missed the brake and accelerated. He sent a set of skis and a bag of golf clubs flying. A toboggan fell off the wall and Utopia caught sight of Max curled up in a basket on the washing-machine before he bolted for cover.

She adjusted her sandal strap and got out of the car. "I'm going to try," she said.

They found Regine in a veil and kabuki make-up. She looked very dramatic. She had faraway eyes and appeared oblivious to her stiletto heels stabbing the lawn and impairing her step as she zigzagged across the garden. She was swaying dangerously and Utopia had to rescue a tray of glasses and hand it to a waiter before she dropped them on the ground. "I've cancelled the firecrackers," she said.

No one mentioned Kurt.

Saul's boss Marcus gave an address full of fiery imagery and talk of a spirit who burned too bright. She recognised the Saul she knew, and his words moved her. Yet seated at the back, beside assorted cousins in patent-leather shoes with their hands clasped in neat laps, Utopia felt increasingly angry. It was everything she knew to be true but the cliché was sickening. He knew what he was doing, she couldn't help but think. Fuck him.

While her mother was so suffused with pain that the morphine pills, pumps and injections couldn't dull it, Saul had decided to gorge himself to death. It had been left for others to wonder why. She began to cry and soon couldn't stop. She had to leave the marquee. Her sobs had become audible and her chest heaved.

The immaculate lawn sloped down to a lake. A game of croquet would not have lasted long. As with the ocean, it was impossible to see the other side. She sat down at the edge of the jetty and, with her legs swinging, she watched yachts with tall sails glide by in the distance. Willows trailed their branches in the water. The lapping water soothed and the view distracted and she felt her sorrow recede and her breathing slacken. Someone nearby was mowing a lawn. It was a sound like domesticity, which provided a healing calm. She heard murmurs of conversation as everyone spilled out of the tent and Felix came to find her. "You OK?"

She nodded then shook her head. Without another word, Felix drew her into his arms and rubbed her back.

He led her back to the party only to be ambushed by Regine. Utopia watched him go. Entering the throng, avoiding Vivienne with an involuntary stiffening of her shoulders, she circulated aimlessly and eavesdropped on Regine's neighbours as they enquired after Saul's art. When would it be on sale, they all wanted to know. The commodification of death so soon after the event struck her as insensitive but Saul would have loved it. His army of assistants had all turned up in denim and leather jackets, loops of chain hanging from pockets and buckles. Saul would have approved of their informality too, she thought, and felt pleased by this verdict and its offer of consolation.

She rejoined Felix at the bar. He was talking to an expensive-looking man who was smoking an unlit cigar.

"Have you met Mr Siseman?"

She hadn't. "Utopia," she introduced herself.

He extended a hand and smiled, his eyes sparkling like jewels. "Trying to quit."

"Yes. I can see."

Saul had always been reticent on the subject of his father. He was the antithesis of his son but she could see the connection. With a slippery crown of jet, unashamedly dyed, and a face as unlined as a baby's, he was Mr Corporate. She spotted his peeping Rolex and hairy wrists.

"My son had good taste," he said.

She smiled, he was flirting with her now, and she was glad. She saw Saul in later life having become just as greedy.

"He was a connoisseur."

"To the end."

"Yes."

She looked down at her feet. "I'm so sorry . . ." she began.

He nodded and she couldn't think what else to say. It was all about sorry but it didn't change a thing.

"I always told him it's the company you keep." He took a long drink from his glass and the tinkle of ice-cubes decorated their silence. "You take good care of yourself," he said suddenly, tasting his cigar. "Life's too short for quitters."

He left her.

"You'll miss that train if we don't go now." It was Felix. He was giving her a ride to the station. They went to find Regine.

Regine's cheek froze like marble against her own when Utopia embraced her. How many Valiums had she washed down with syrupy vermouth? Utopia wondered. Regine was anaesthetised beyond reach.

They made the train with a second to spare. The electronic doors were wheezing as she flew on to the platform and into her seat. From behind the coolness of glass, she watched Felix become a stick man before she was saved by sleep.

Marina nodded.

"I always thought that's what I was going to have to go through with my brother," she said. "Thank God he became a Buddhist."

The evening was drifting in and the park appeared submerged in clear honey. There was a breeze. Hudson River Park was home to fathers jogging with ergonomic pushchairs and roller-bladers doing backwards laps. Dow Jones traders with jackets swung over shoulders were descending from the city in the sky like caped crusaders. It was a stomping ground for successful urbanites, thought Utopia, as she watched a woman limbering up on the grass with an arm stretching up and over her head. No wasters, liggers or bums allowed.

Marina was eyeing the men as they sauntered past. She was wearing her new white Yves Saint Laurent suit, which had been a gift from a PR to thank her for a write-up in the September issue. She looked like royalty, thought Utopia, who had learned early on that when Marina was down she dressed up.

Marina opened her leather bag with a click. "I'm on Prozac."

"What?"

"I went to see my therapist and demanded a prescription. I'm a basket case. I've been breaking down and crying at work. Everyone's been worried. Dorian and that Brazilian gigolo were the final straw. He's been leaving messages on my machine. Give me one good reason why I should call him."

Utopia couldn't. "No news from Donald?"

"Screwing some girl from the Hills apparently. Men are like cats, as my mother used to say. They go where they feel safe. So predictable."

"Yes."

"And I so wanted to meet your father. I had this vision of a dashing older man with lots of wild stories and mad-professor hair. I wish you hadn't kept him from me."

"Oh. I'm sorry."

"Damned if I ever had a relationship with my father."

Utopia was surprised by this final remark and the note of seriousness to have crept into their conversation. The level at which she and Marina discussed emotions went usually as far as sex and men but little further.

"My father never gave a fuck." Her smoking had become angry. "Haven't I ever told you how he left us when I was five?"

Utopia shook her head.

"Ran off with his secretary. I mean, how fucking unoriginal, even her name, Betty. One Saturday every month he'd come and get me and we'd go for lunch at his horrible club off Sloane Square. My brother was at boarding school so didn't have to come. I'd have to eat veal and mashed swede and drink glasses of watered down wine while he'd get pissed and tell me what a cow my mother was. Well, I'd just sit there and would then go and stick my fingers down my throat. Afterwards we'd go to Hamley's and he'd tell me to be quick so I'd panic and choose something I didn't want or, worse still, something I already had. By the time he dropped me off, I'd always be in tears and then my mother would bawl him out and tell him what an oaf he was and that he couldn't see me. Until the next Saturday when he'd

turn up and off I'd have to go again." She lit another cigarette. "So you can see why I decided I'd never talk to him as
soon as I got my inheritance."

"Yes."

"But then I spent it, got into debt and had to bloody
well give him the house. Bastard."

"Where's he now?"

"In a home in Hampshire, rotting. Alzheimer's."

"I'm sorry."

"Well, I'm not. Anyway, I suppose we'd better go if we're
going."

They got up from the bench. Marina's eyes were sad and
Utopia took her arm. They were closer than perhaps she
had realised. She stroked the fabric of Marina's new suit.
Whatever it was, it felt creamy.


Felix's studio was on the third floor of a nineteenth-century
warehouse. It had once been a dairy. It was on Greenwich
Street and two blocks in from the water. Inside was an
expanse of white, which was lined with windows overlooking the TriBeCa Grill. A series of collectable prints lined the
walls. There was a Horst, an early Mapplethorpe, a shot of a
girl on a fire hydrant dressed in a leather skirt and a pair of
silver studs. The earrings were impossible to detect without
a caption but if you knew Felix, as all who visited the studio
did, you knew that the model was wearing his silver studs.

They were late.

The room was heaving with fashion editors, accessories
editors, shopping editors, fashion buyers, Japanese boys and
girls, stylists, models, gallery-owners and TriBeCa people.
They were on familiar turf and all appeared to know each
other. The gathering had an intimate feel: it was Felix At

Home. Yesterday Felix had expressed doubts over whether to host his sale the day after Saul's funeral, a bi-annual event he was reluctant to cancel, but now that they were here Utopia knew it would have made no difference to Saul. If anything, he was with them. "Looks like a party," she could hear him saying.

A table of drinks and rainbow selections of sushi were visible at the end of the room. Prompted by Marina, they steered their way through the mob. Felix's workbench was awash with silver. There were chains, rings, earrings, cuffs, chokers and bangles being snatched up by his devoted fans. Utopia spied the top of Felix's head like travelling peach fuzz. He spotted them and waved before coming to greet them. He looked drawn and had dark circles around his eyes but he was playing the keen host all the same.

"Hey, you," he said.

Utopia squeezed his hand.

"See if there's anything you like. There are pieces out from the last two seasons."

"Goodie," said Marina. "I want one of those drip pendants that sits between your clavicles."

Then through the din came the call Utopia had been dreading. It was the voice she had half expected to hear yesterday only she knew she hadn't been invited. It was the voice played back to herself time and time again as she fought to disentangle memories of Saul from her grasp.

"Uteepee."

Slinking over to them, glass in hand, came Gloria. If she was an animal, what animal would she be? wondered Utopia. Snake? Cat? Wolf? Gloria delivered air kisses with shiny sincerity. She wore her cunning with such grace and such charm.

"Darling, you look tired. How was the funeral? I am

sorry. Too young." she offered her breathy condolences. "And I want you to meet Frederico."

From behind emerged an early model of Brute. He was dressed in a pink V-neck sweater and tortoiseshell shades. Here was her dumb-fuck escort, thought Utopia at a glance.

"Only twenty-three. His father owns half of Belize," whispered Felix into her ear.

She would have expected nothing less.

"How are you, Gloria?" asked Marina.

"Oh, darling, good. Always good." She laughed, tossing her mane in affirmation that she was answerable to no one. "But, Uteepee, I have not seen you again since the Hamptons. What have you been doing?"

As she looked into Gloria's pools of hazel, Utopia shuddered. A sense of futility bled through her like a chill. It was her encounter with Brute, the rift with P, the vacuum left by Saul and his deserted studio. What had she been doing, she wondered. Reflecting on the holes that kept tearing at her life, perhaps. Her mother had died, and while still living in the shadow of that as though it were yesterday, another life had fallen through the net. Neither were in any way connected yet both contributed to where she was today and why.

"Working," she finally said.

Gloria nodded and fiddled with her diamonds like water.

Utopia observed Gloria like a stranger. She saw Gloria as the illusory sparkle of life in New York. She was the glitter swept away at the end of the night. The difference was that Utopia no longer needed to be seduced by everyone she met. She was learning how to be discerning again, judgemental even, character traits she had left behind with P at Heathrow's Terminal 3 when she fled to the other side, game for anything and anybody. Just to forget.

"Uteepee, now, you want come to the bathroom?"

But she didn't.

She knew what she wanted here in New York and, for the first time, what she didn't. She watched Gloria sidle out of the door in her gold-lamé dress to powder her nose and realised, too, that her time with Saul was her own. Gloria, like Vivienne, had been part of the music. Nothing more. She was going to miss Saul, she realised. She had lost a friend.

People began leaving.

Glasses smeared with lipstick lined the window-sills, and corpulent cigarette butts floated in pale liquid. The waiter was clearing the table. He began slotting empty bottles into the compartmentalised cardboard box from left to right, right to left and back again. Utopia gazed out at the quiet streets. She pieced together her day and yesterday and her thoughts journeyed from Saul to her mother then on to her sister.

She wandered back to the bench and decided to buy something for Liberty. It would be a goodwill gesture and an attempt to override their stand-off. She began sifting through what was left in search of a pair of ear-rings that matched.

Felix and Marina were sitting on the only piece of furniture available to the room, a black leather sofa pierced with silver studs. Utopia could hear them talking. Marina wanted to accessorise her New Faces shoot with men's jewellery. The look was Gangster Chic, she said. She wanted cufflinks, knuckle-dusters and big heavy silver bracelets. Felix went off to fetch samples. Finding a pair of earrings she liked, that Liberty too might approve of, Utopia went to join them.

"Any plans for tomorrow?" asked Marina, as she moved in beside her.

"I've got to call an editor at *Mille*. Todd, my fact-checker friend from *HQ*, has put me in touch with her. Callie Chang?"

"Never heard of her, darling, but sounds sweet."

"Right, so, gangster chic, then," interrupted Felix, returning with a black leather briefcase. He thumbed down the locks and the lid sprang open like a booby-trap.

"Sexy spivs. Two double pages," said Marina.

Leaning into the sofa, Utopia tried to remember when last she had spoken to her sister. She realised that she couldn't.

# Chapter Thirty-seven

The subway car's plastic bench was cold and slippery beneath her skin. It felt rude and obtrusive like the hands of a groper. Utopia tugged her skirt to cover her thighs then smiled at the woman next to her, who had turned to see who had nudged her. The woman was Hispanic with flame dyed hair. She was knitting. Utopia watched the needles knit and purl. Their click-clicking was dulcifying, like a nursery rhyme.

It was the sound of her grandmother.

With needles flying, her grandmother used her waxy hands to knit though she needed never look. She could knit as she talked, knit as she drank whisky and soda, knit as she ate coffee cake and got on and off the bus. She had been ordered by the doctor to quit smoking due to a bout of emphysema and had taken it up aged sixty. She became twitchy away from her needles for too long. Beginning with shawls she had proceeded to booties and triumphantly reached cardigans. Utopia had three colour-blind combinations. She occasionally wore them to bed when the central heating failed.

"Off," P would order. "You are not getting in here wearing that scratchy bloody thing."

Her neighbour's staccato merged with the train as it decelerated and the doors buzzed open at 34th Street. Nearly there, she felt nervous. It was one of those days.

When she left her apartment, her anxiety had engendered hostility on the street. She had cowered at the fury of the traffic and the homeless man who yelled, "Bitch," as she ignored his outstretched hand. Then there was the woman shoving in front of her in the token queue before screaming abuse at the man behind the glass because he couldn't change a fifty.

As she waited for the train, the heat had become asphyxiating.

When would it end?

The man opposite her had been eating a burger and the smell of hot meat had turned her stomach. She thought she might retch and wondered if she shouldn't turn back. But she was nearly there now.

Her appointment at *Mille* magazine was thanks to Todd. Callie Chang was Todd's sister's roommate and an editor at *Mille*. *Mille* was a late-teens-early-twenties mag. Callie was putting together a *Mille* Special Issue and she was looking for staff. Utopia had been suspicious. "Are you sure this isn't one of your crazy schemes?" she asked Todd. But she forced herself to ring.

To her surprise, she had been put through without a hitch. What's more, Callie had been friendly and enthusiastic. Todd had been right. She was putting together a February special issue. It was a romance issue. It was going to cover romance on the beach, romance in the office, romance in the subway, romance abroad, romance at home, romance on the Net, romance in the air. "You know the Mile High Club has a website, right?"

Utopia didn't, though clearly she ought.

"And I know what you Brits are like with your sex stories." Callie had laughed, her intonation riding the end of every sentence. "We get complaints if things are too literal here. It's got to be romantic. Don't forget it's a Feb issue. It's Valentines. What do you think?"

"It sounds great."

And it did. She could do romance.

"So, how about you come up this morning? You can get a better picture of what we're doing, we can meet you."

"Love to."

"I'm trying to figure it out but there should be a couple of jobs going." Utopia's heart skipped a beat.

The Sixth Avenue building which was home to *Mille* and its sister magazines, was reassuringly modest. It lacked *HQ's* architectural grandeur and Utopia felt her anxiety levels drop. Grey carpeting and porridge walls as opposed to marble lowered the stakes. The *Mille* receptionist was reading a copy of *People*. Her nails had charms hanging off them, like Christmas decorations. She didn't look up.

"Aha?"

"I'm here to meet Callie Chang."

"Aha."

Utopia moved to the sofa beside the reception desk and sat down. Her nervousness seeped from her gut to her limbs. It was the return to a workplace that triggered it. She had pins and needles everywhere. Her fingers and toes were live with electricity. A forest of stockinged thighs travelled past her eye level trailed by chatter and musk. She flicked through a couple of *Mille's* then stared at her loafers. They had seen better days. They were unpolished and in need of reheeling. They were no longer burgundy but a sort of ugly brown. She examined her hands. Her nails were chewed and her cuticles frayed. One thumb nail was painted black, why just the one she couldn't remember, two were nicotine-stained and the others were bare.

"Hi, I'm Callie."

"Oh."

Utopia looked up. She was greeted by a rather plump female with a flapper bob. She had a contented face and merry eyes. Utopia had been expecting the arrival of an uber-babe. It made the world of difference.

"Shall we go talk in my office?"

Callie was wearing a Tiffany's rock on her engagement finger. Her doughy hands clasped before her on the desk were trimmed with purple nails like baked damsons. She offered Utopia a seat then sent her assistant out for coffees. She insisted Utopia try a goat's milk latte. "They're awesome," she said.

More than happy to oblige, Utopia warmed to Callie's manner. She came across as everyone's best friend. Utopia surveyed her office. A Planet Hollywood calendar was pinned to the wall with "7.30 Ball game – A's place" neatly circled. A pile of self-help books and romance guides was tiered on her desk. A Big Gulp container with attachable bendy straw sat next to her computer.

Callie was the type to organise girly sleepovers at her apartment, decided Utopia, with buckets of popcorn, pay-per-view movies and quizzes on dating. How many days to wait before returning his call? Should I have dinner with my boss even though he's married? What does it mean when he says that work prevents him loving? The thing was, Utopia felt quite happy to have make this realisation. She wasn't averse to the idea of joining Callie's gang.

"So, you're a friend of Todd's."

"Yes."

"He's so cute and he makes me laugh with all those

accents he does. He told me what happened at *HQ*. That was real bad luck."

Utopia was taken aback. She was interested to hear another take on what had happened. Perhaps Callie was right. Perhaps it wasn't her own poor judgement that was exclusively to blame.

"Here are our coffees."

As she sipped her drink through the beaker lid, trying hard not to think about bleating goats with beards and bells, Utopia listened as Callie presented the facts. "This issue's really about celebrity romance," she said. "On set and off set. Romance has got to be now. It's real important to keep up on celebrity dating, watch E! and find out about forthcoming movies. There might be a good tie-in with a Feb film. Something beachy or European would be hot."

"Right."

"We're going to need studmuffins and the hottest bands."

Studmuffins?

"Oh, yeah, and another thing. We're trying to figure out doing an episode for a new TV soap on ABC about a romance in the Hamptons. It's going to be co-written by the editors here and the script writers in LA." Callie took a sip before starting up again. "There's also going to be interviews, maybe a couple of set visits and profiles. Also a few 'real' people to get a balance. How do you like real people?"

"Oh, very much."

"Great. So you're going to love my yesterday," she said, shining her rock with a finger tip. "I met two women, this New Yorker who married the Cuban cigar-seller she met in her Havana hotel lobby. I mean, how cool is that? although she's got to fight Immigration to get him in. Then there's this other woman from Queens who found a husband in one of those Alaskan mail order catalogues." She laughed. "And you know what we really love about these women? They're *Mille* women. Neat, huh?"

Utopia felt goose-pimples prickle her skin. "Brilliant."

And it was.

She now saw herself hanging out on film sets catching actors between takes for quick Q and As. She imagined herself chasing publicists, sourcing interviewees, liaising with Arts. The offer appeared straightforward just as Callie appeared straightforward. She pictured herself here in the *Mille* office devising heads and decks, pulling quotes and running off captions, being on the hotline to LA before hurtling through Times Square in a cab at the end of the day.

Callie was scraping foam from her cup with a stirrer. She licked it off. "Todd told me about your transsexual story and I thought that was a really neat idea. That's what I'm looking for. Someone with neat ideas."

Utopia grinned. She had severed ties with *HQ* so absolutely that the transsexual story had been erased from her mind, along with the paint fumes in Jean's office and the managing editor's black eyes on that miserable, rainy day.

They had finished their coffees.

"We wouldn't need you until next week, I guess, but the best thing right now is for you to meet the Romance editor. You'll be working with her not me."

Utopia couldn't believe what was happening. Summoned for a meeting, it now actually looked as though she was being offered a job. She hardly dared blink for fear of losing the moment and finding it gone.

They proceeded along a corridor. A sharp turn greeted them every few yards and was signalled by the appearance of a water-cooler. Perhaps their provision was enforced by law.

They passed the fashion department where dainty boys with clipboards were seen ticking off shoes while pretty girls with matching faces were counting swimsuits on a rail. They passed the art department and editors huddled over layouts while projected *Mille* covers, next month's issue, were wall papered behind, like a kiosk. They passed desks of girls breathing into telephones and banging keyboards, a row of fax machines and photocopiers, shelves of books and a kitchen before reaching a door at the end.

With every step, Utopia's conviction grew that this was where she wanted to be, back on board a magazine, part of a team.

"Gee, I forgot to mention, she used to work at *HQ*," said Callie, as she pushed open the door. "Maybe you know each other. Utopia, Meg, Meg, Utopia."

Utopia felt her stomach rise and fall. A hot flush rippled at the base of her neck. With her pointy features, her hair scraped back in that familiar bunch and wearing a white shirt, there sat Meg. She looked up and stared. She looked like a woman in charge. Utopia's waitress slur wouldn't stick for a minute.

"Hello," said Utopia.

"Great, you two know each other, huh? That makes things kind of easy," said Callie. "If you two want to go over stuff, we'll meet up in twenty."

"OK."

What could she say? No, get me out of here. It's all a terrible mistake. This is never going to work. It was too late for that. She took a seat and arranged her legs in firmly crossed, defence position.

Meg said nothing. Shuffling her papers, she spat out her gum and gave a cursory nod. "Aha. Sure."

# Chapter Thirty-eight

There was a message: "U. I got the starfish earrings. They're lovely but I'm having them made into cufflinks for Charles who you haven't met because I've let my holes close up. They went septic. I thought you knew. Dad said you had a lovely time. I'll ring again soon. 'Byeeeee . . ."

It was so typical of her sister. Thanks for the thought but I'm having them altered, won't be wearing them, am giving them away and am not about to hide the fact. There was no mention of her forthcoming trip to the Caribbean. Nothing about whether she would or would not be stopping by to see Utopia. There was no hoping that Utopia was well and no enquiring about how she was getting on.

And Utopia had Federal-Expressed them especially.

God, Liberty was a pain in the arse.

Johann arrived home during Utopia's repeat PLAY of Liberty's bossy refrain. It was a habit so entrenched that she was deaf to it. It was Johann who pointed it out. "Trying to break the machine?" he said, sailing through the door, dropping his bag on the floor and heading for the fridge.

"It's broken already," she pointed out, removing the tape to rewind it manually with with a pencil.

Utopia was unapologetic. She saw it as emotional editing. She listened to messages twice on the off-chance that she had missed something first time round. It was to reassess the significance of each stumble, repetition and breathy pause, to glean an unintentional admission of fringe information. It was to savour the voices that grounded her as her London life was allowed in for thirty-second snatches.

"How was the interview?"

He cracked open a beer. It was a German brew and very malty. She could smell it from where she was. She hit STOP. "Don't ask."

"That bad? I thought we had bread."

"We do." She pointed at a brown-paper bag.

"So?"

"Disaster."

"How so?"

Utopia sighed. She had been busted by the Karma Police, though to say as much was to confess her complicity and admit that she deserved it. She felt horribly trapped.

Johann joined her at the table with his sandwich and beer. He loosened his tie. It was a luminescent strip. No one but an advertising account planner would wear such a tie, thought Utopia.

"The girl who was fired from *HQ*, the one who I replaced?"

He nodded.

"I'd be working for her." Her mouth went dry. Voiced from here, her chances of success appeared very slim indeed.

Johann frowned and sucked an olive. "That's very bad."

"Thanks."

He slugged his beer. "But people do get fired."

"That doesn't mean she wants to be my friend."

"True."

Left behind in Meg's office, Utopia had found herself back at her desk at *HQ*. There they all were, the jar of marshmallow spread with its spoon like an oar, the snapshot of Meg's boyfriend, the potted Saguaro cactus, the Niagara Falls snow scene, the Graceland calendar. It was as though Utopia was playing Kim's Game and had been forced to memorise these objects for a later date.

The skin beneath her suit grew clammy and her under-arms pooled with sweat. She wanted to make small-talk and do something to initiate a reconciliation. Yet their shared past, the fact of Jean, remained where it was – kicked under-foot with her bag. She knew that it was her responsibility to offer apologies but the words never came. She was English, too uptight. She hated herself for it later.

Instead she had said how impressed she was with *Mille*, and with Callie. And Meg had proven cordial enough. Between taking calls, "Can I call you later, I'm kind of tied up", she had answered Utopia's questions with an air of efficiency. Yet all the while Utopia's silent fears had descended upon Meg until Meg vanished beneath them. Utopia could hear nothing but accusations growing loud in her ear. She imagined a vein of hostility bubbling beneath Meg's surface. She anticipated it surging forth any minute.

But Meg was giving nothing away. It was torturous.

In the end Callie had returned and walked her to the lift.

"I'll call you Monday," she said with a smile.

An eternity away.


Johann had a date.

She was a Swedish girl who worked at the Swedish embassy and they had met over the telephone. Johann had a problem with his visa and had been trying to enlist the serv-ices of his embassy. He needed them to talk to Immigration and arrange an extension. Midway through last week's two-hour-long discussion, the operator of line nine had accepted his offer of a date. They were going to see a movie, a documentary about a Czech circus for a limited-run-only at Film Forum. He appeared in the kitchen, shiny and scrubbed, with his moustache like a conductor's wave. He smiled.

Utopia frowned. "Can I say one thing?"

He fixed her with a stare. "No."

"Wash off some of your aftershave."

He smelt like a department store. She thought she was going to sneeze. Johann gave her the finger and slammed the door. Utopia laughed. Good luck. Who knows? He might even lure her back for a watery romp.

She needed to talk.

Desperate for a sounding board, she rang Marina but Marina was out. How could she forget? Marina had gone to an Obsessive-Compulsive-Dependency meeting in a church hall on Christopher Street. She had signed up with a twelve-step programme to get rid of feelings for Dorian. She wanted closure. Of course, the ulterior motive was slightly different as Utopia found out. It was all about dating possibilities. Through the same group, the beauty editor at Marina's magazine had met a six-foot-four sculptor who rode a seventies Harley. They were now living together.

When the subject first came up, Utopia had laughed. "I'm not laughing at you," she had pleaded. "I'm just laughing at the idea of it. I don't know. All that weeping and wailing."

"Utopia. A little respect for my problem, please."

"But what is your problem?"

"Dorian still poses a considerable problem to the future of my love life."

If America could be considered a religion, Marina was a convert. She was even beginning to sound like an American, Utopia sometimes thought. All this talk of closure and respect. Was it the too much or the not enough that had induced her to want to open up to a room full of strangers? Marina had struggled to keep a straight face. "OK, I just thought I'd give it a go. You'll be dying to hear all the gory details afterwards," she rightly concluded.

Monkey Man arrived home.

His lights came on. He wasn't alone. The two of them padded into the kitchen, removed their shirts and embraced. Their golden torsos fused like toffee. There was nothing Utopia couldn't see. Struck by her solitary predicament, the voyeur, she felt suddenly homesick. It was parental assurance she sought. Like a rogue pain, the realisation that she wanted to dial home and hear her mother's rousing voice at the other end of the line surprised her. Knowing now what she did, that it was her mother she sought, suggested that reconciliation was long overdue.

She was alone with her parent's past and no one to turn to. She moved to her bedroom, curled up on her bed and dialled London.

"Libby."

"Utopia. What's happened? Has something happened?" Her sister sounded close.

"No, nothing's happened. I just suddenly wanted to talk."

"Oh."

"Are you sleeping?"

"Well, yes. We had a dinner party."

"With Charles?"

"Yes."

"Oh."

'What are you doing? Dad was so vague."

"I've been working on magazines. Different ones."

"Lots of free lipsticks?"

"Free shoes."

"Gosh."

They both started up simultaneously.

"I was just thinking about Mum . . ."

"It's very late . . ."

"What?"

"What?"

"I said that I was just thinking about Mum. It's sad that she doesn't know about any of this. Me being in New York. I found our old apartment."

"We all miss her. "

Utopia took a very deep breath. "But all that stuff you said about me going away not to think about her wasn't fair."

Her sister mumbled something at the other end and Utopia could hear someone, a man, asking who she was speaking to.

"I needed to be here to think about her."

"Yes."

"Our Montessori's been turned into a deli."

"A what?"

"And I found this picture . . ."

"I really have to go . . ."

"Oh."

"Charles has to get up to catch a train at six thirty and I've got this murder trial on in Colchester."

"I just wanted to . . ."

"I'll phone you at the weekend and we can have a proper chat. I can't think straight right now."

"All right."

"Night-night."

" 'Bye."

They hung up.

It was typical Liberty to exert senior status, rush the cut-off point and avoid emotional honesty. But Utopia had said her piece. She had vented her feelings and without recourse to a row. This was significant. As for the picture, Robert Shanks, all that could wait. Liberty wasn't curious in the same way that she was. Perhaps it was better she didn't know of the past. Utopia paused, running an eye along the ceiling in search of activity.

No, to inherit her mother's secret as her own would be wrong. It was not hers to hoard but was to be shared with her sister. This fact of natural division, that it would enforce mutual understanding, made her happy. Sisters together was all she had ever wanted. Was it really so hard? The crack inched to the left.

There was her cockroach.

# Chapter Thirty-nine

It was the weekend again. Trudi had offered her two shifts at Home Comforts – Thursday breakfast and Friday night. She took both. She told herself that it wasn't for ever, that she needed the cash and not to take it personally when Trudi called her a silly cunt in front of a room full of strangers. Then she put on her apron and tied back her hair.

The evening shift had provided her with a hundred and fifty bucks. City boys bloated with Yorkshire pudding and jingoism were generous tippers, she discovered. It was Trudi who perched on laps, fluffed quiffs and uncorked bottles of Pinot Noir while she passed across plates and tried not to spill peas. Afterwards Eduardo the chef took her to a salsa club in Queens and they danced. He was so short that his head nestled happily against her chest. "You have good udders," he told her in the car on the way home, and she took it as a compliment.

Friday afternoon had been spent in Central Park's Sheep's Meadow where offers of massage from men waving joss sticks were declined and roller-bladers stuck band-aids to blistered feet. Then she swam laps in the dusk light and thought about Monday and how much she wanted to work at *Mille*. But she knew it was bad luck to wish too hard so she swam a choppy crawl and tried not to think.

She had called Todd for advice. "You know Meg's working there?"

"You're kidding me."

"I wish I was. Would you want to work with somebody who'd pinched your job?"

"Hey, if you hadn't got Meg's job, someone else would. Those bitches used to scream at each other so bad, the managing editor sent them on an anger-management programme. Callie thinks you're cool."

"Really?"

"She told me."

So maybe there was hope.

Saturday morning first thing Johann appeared in her room with the phone.

"Why do they call so early?"

"Why do you pick up?"

She picked up. "Hello?"

"Sleeping Beauty, it's me."

It was Felix. She looked at her watch. It wasn't even ten.

"How's tricks?"

"Tired."

"Party tonight in Harlem, I'm going with Paul, if you want to come."

"Harlem?"

"Lennox Avenue."

Silence.

"Hello?"

"I'm here. I'm listening," she told him. "I'm just worried about Monday, that's all."

"There's nothing you can do about Monday."

"I know. I don't know. It's still so soon after Saul."

"Hey, you don't think it's important to do something besides feeling depressed? You think Saul would want us depressed? No. Am I right or am I right?"

She was unconvinced. She had visions of being stranded far from home, helpless to get back. "OK."

"Pick you up at ten."

He was probably right. It was good to get out. She liked the way he took charge and it was hard to refuse a man with a plan. Buffeted by the sounds from the street below, she closed her eyes. The cursing of a cab driver, Chinese chatter and the convoy of cars rolling in over the Williamsburg Bridge breezed in through the window like old friends.

Utopia stood in the bathroom brushing her teeth. She listened to the sound of crashing footsteps followed by the echo of another's. She recognised his laugh. She gazed at herself in the mirror and thought she looked better than she had in weeks. Her features appeared relaxed, softened in the wake of a frown, her eyes were bright and her expression sunny. Her skin was sieved with dusty freckles. To see her was to surmise that the worst was over.

She searched for lines.

Her mother always said that emotion, good and bad, left lines on the face but she could see nothing new. There was only the burst capillary on the cheek growing rosier and her top lip getting thinner. She was wearing a red halter-neck dress that had been a present from P. It was one of her favourites. On her feet were a pair of snakeskin sandals found in a box at the flea-market on Grand. She ran the cold tap, gargled and spat in the sink.

"Anyone home?" called Felix, barging through the

unlocked door. "Why aren't any of your doors locked? It's not safe living like this in New York."

"I always lock the downstairs door," she said, skating across the parqueted floor to meet them.

Felix smiled and she was immediately happy to see him. He offered reassurance without even trying. He didn't have to say anything. His smell was familiar, lemony, and his face was uncluttered. She was surprised by his naked eyes. He was wearing contact lenses and a suede shirt.

"This is Paul. I can't remember if you've met?"

They hadn't. Paul, his boyfriend, was of a similar build. His hair was salt and peppered, cut short, and he was wearing trousers that rustled. He had on a pair of Nikes exclusive to Japan, the type so futuristic they resembled airplane socks. Velcro and nylon. Paul worked for a designer, she couldn't remember which, but if he wasn't in New York he was in Tokyo.

"Great space."

"Thanks."

"Want a line?"

Utopia looked at Felix, was on the verge of saying yes, since when did she ever refuse? then shook her head. She didn't want the sensation of a palpitating heart to remind her of another's.

"Mind if we do?"

"Course not."

Watching Felix chop out lines, she thought of Saul and wondered if they were doing the right thing. But there was no turning back.

Paul was wandering round the apartment and inspecting Johann's ad campaigns. Johann was proud of his work. There was a photograph of a truck cruising through clouds, a beer can shooting through the surface of a Caribbean sea, an Eskimo modelling a pair of jeans in a diner. "Someone works in advertising?"

"He also drums."

"Where's he now?"

"On a date."

It was the girl from the embassy again. It had been a home-run success. She had been seduced by the water-bed. According to Johann, it reminded her of home. Exactly why, Utopia wasn't sure though perhaps it was the sensation of boating on fjords. Or perhaps she was missing something.

From the corner of the eye, Utopia saw a ball of fluff dart out from behind the sofa and run the length of the room.

"A mouse!"

"Where?"

But they had missed it.

"There."

Making a bold re-entrance, the mouse merrily traced the skirting board back to its nest.

Felix threw a shoe in the general direction and missed. "You're infested."

Infestation was Johann's department. The first Tuesday of every month brought the exterminator with his cylinder of poison armed to make a dent in New York's cockroach population but the mice problem fell to Johann. His solution was glue traps, little plastic trays of liquid adhesive into which they would wander and squeak themselves to death. It was methodology that wasn't working.

"Come on," said Utopia. "Let them have the run of the place."

For the first time in months, the midnight air felt chilly on her skin.

She should have brought a jacket.

She shivered and drew her arms across her chest. They tried to hail a cab. It wasn't easy finding one prepared to go up to Harlem. Three cabbies shook their heads, fiddled with key-rings then accelerated up the street, afraid of being conscripted. When finally they found one, they discovered that their driver was a disciple of the Nation of Islam. The subject came up within minutes of departure. "Why do you wanna go up to 125th Street, anyway? Trying to get yourselves killed?" he said.

In the back, hunched in the corner, Utopia sank lower and lower into the seat. Felix asked the driver if he could find a dance station on the radio. He pointed to the space below his dashboard. Where there should have been a radio was a disused hole stuffed with candy-bar wrappers, a well-thumbed copy of the Koran and a pack of Newport Lites. "Kids stole it last week," he said.

Through the open window, Utopia watched the secure privilege of the Upper East Side disappear and the tip of Park Avenue make way for the projects: islanded towers of concrete sat amid automobile graveyards. The hand of the speedometer jiggered between fifty and seventy m.p.h. as their driver applied pressure to the pedal.

Utopia felt the rumblings of paranoia. She began to doubt the wisdom of her decision. She should have stayed at home, made pasta and watched the Saturday night movie on HBO as desired all along. Home turf had long since vanished and been replaced by the streets of Harlem. She looked out at people sitting on stoops. Tall trees swayed. The street lighting vanished intermittently leaving only their headlights scanning the road like a cruiseship on high seas. They passed underneath a bridge as a subway car rattled above. The cab turned left, took a right and then came back on itself.

"It's not exactly 125th. Just off it. Near a basketball court," Felix said, unhelpfully.

"Are we lost?" asked Utopia.

"Are you armed?" asked Paul.

"What do you think?" The driver flipped open the glove compartment to reveal his handy-sized piece.

Utopia shivered. She felt horribly sober.

The streets were mostly deserted. A woman in a house-coat was standing with a supermarket trolley beside a wall. Boys were exchanging handshakes in front of a bar, their gleaming cars parked alongside. *Budweiser. The Taste of America,* read the red, white and blue poster in the window. Circling the block for the third time, the cab took a right, another right, and suddenly before them loomed the basket-ball court emblazoned with light. A crowded game was in motion. Boys, friends and neighbours were sprinting across the tarmac as onlookers heckled and cheered. Next door a row of sooty four-storey brownstones lined the street.

"This is it," said Felix, handing the driver a twenty.

At last.

Out of the cab, they filed up the steps and into the house. The front hall was a crush of heat and bodies. Unprepared for this, Utopia's reaction was a desire to turn round and leave immediately. It was impossible. It's only a party, she told herself, and you've just arrived. But she felt awkward and the all male embraces blocking her way heightened her estrangement.

Felix grabbed her hand. They peered into the room on their left and saw that the living room was host to a ceiling-high set of speakers. The floorboards were shaking. A strobe light fragmented the dark and limbs were spinning out of control. A man in a catsuit dotted with holes was tugging at his nipple rings. A fat woman with an arse like a peach was shimmying in front of a speaker. In the corners, little faces looked on like the eyes of a forest. No stranger to the bizarre, this was something special, decided Utopia.

"Let's find the bathroom," said Paul.

Pushing their way downstairs, they discovered a dining-room table set for a feast. There was a mountain of fruit, the bulk of a pig with jellied eyes, sesame-topped loaves of bread and a cake with Happy Birthday written on it in silver balls. It was as incongruous as if they had stumbled upon Miss Haversham's wedding meal. Utopia stared. Two kittens were drinking milk out of a saucer and someone was playing Broadway songs on a baby grand. Couples were sitting on chairs along the wall. Paul bumped into someone he knew, and they said hi and kissed cheeks. They found the bathroom.

"You don't have to go in there to do it," tittered a boy in leg-warmers, as they trooped into the room.

They locked the door. Utopia sat on the edge of the bath and smoked a cigarette. She didn't need drugs to feel wired. Everything glittered, edges were sharp. She watched Felix divide lines on the toilet seat. She wanted to say Saul's name and remind themselves of what used to be but no sound came. She chased him to the back of her mind. Where were they, anyway? No one would know where to find her, she reflected, quite content to stay cocooned within the bathroom's minty walls all night.

Paul was scrutinising bottles of pills from the medicine cabinet. He read their labels and shook their contents. Someone threw a series of violent punches against the door. "Get the fuck out of there," said the angry voice.

Utopia pulled a face.

Felix laughed. "You'll be OK."

They unlocked the door, returned upstairs and pushed their way into the sweat-sopped room.

The music was booming and they began to dance. Flanks of skin shone in the light dripping like sex. All around them Ecstasy-fuelled faces glimmered like death masks. A pierced tongue flew out of the dark and she jumped back thinking it was alive. She closed her eyes. When she opened them she found that Felix and Paul had disappeared. They were gone. Left alone she forced herself to dance. All she had to do was channel herself into the music and block out the rest.

Someone passed her a phial.

It was small and brown.

Without thinking, she put it to her nose and inhaled. Amyl nitrate stung her nostrils and a muffled thickness filled her head. The room began spinning faster and faster. She couldn't see. Her head was thumping. She began to laugh. She couldn't stop dancing, her feet were speeding out of control. I'm having a good time, she wanted to shout. But there was no one out there. Only the death masks contorting horribly. She must keep dancing, she forced herself.

But it was impossible.

All of a sudden, her body felt heavy as her bid for oblivion was interrupted by P. He came to remind her of her distance from everything that had once made sense. The psychedelic room began to assault her. She had to find peace. She left the dance floor and went in search of sanctuary. Jostled by shoulders, she pushed her way through. "Excuse me, excuse me," she said.

Her face felt flushed, her heart combustible. She needed air. Winding her way down to the basement, she found a church pew. It was empty and she sat down. One of the kittens arrived to nest in her lap. Its shrimp tongue scratched at her skin. She felt toxic and thought of Saul and his erupted heart. Then the kitten began to mew so she stroked it.

"Smoke?" A man in a black polo-neck shirt had sat down beside her.

She hesitated. Never trust a man who wears polo-necks, she remembered being told. Who was it who had told her this? She racked her brain. Marina it had to be but, no, it was her mother, she realised in dismay. It had been a throw-away line, something silly to entertain the girls. She hesitated to continue but the name quickly followed.

Robert Shanks.

The realisation was sickening. She didn't want to believe it but there was no escaping the truth. Stunned, she wondered at her mother's guilt. She sensed it as a driving force. This revelation of human frailty, her mother's adultery, did more to explain her mother's inconsistencies than anything prior. It was as though her mother's need to instruct and dominate had been to compensate for her own misdemeanour. To make up for what she once risked losing.

Utopia tasted salt.

They were tears of pity for herself, for her mother, for her father, for her sister even. So liberally had she cried this past year, she had thought they might run dry. Then again she had feared losing the memory of her mother healthy and that all that would be left to her was her mother when she was so thin that the rings on her fingers fell to the ground. Her mother had lost her engagement ring. It was a moonstone set in Russian gold bought in Greenwich Village years ago. She had been distraught. "It was for my girls," she had wept.

And yet with her own life defined by the passage of time since her mother's death, these last few months had unleashed images more brilliantly than ever.

Sitting downstairs in the basement, a feeling of relief

pressed upon Utopia. It was as though there had been a change of weather.

She saw her mother in the garden. It was her favourite place. She was kneeling in the earth and had a pair of seca-teurs in a gloved hand. She was wearing shorts, a tie-dyed T-shirt and black wellington boots. Her silver hair had escaped its fastening to flop forward and hide her face. She was shouting for Utopia to come and sit on the grass and relate her news. Taking two cups of tea, Utopia fought a path through the overgrown flora. The leaves tickled her bare legs as she walked and tried to avoid crunching snails underfoot.

"How's P?" asked her mother, turning to smile and squinting in the sun as Utopia assumed a crosslegged posi-tion beside her.

"Fine."

It was a routine question. Her mother was always candid for better or for worse.

"Now, be a darling and pass me that trowel. This bloody bramble's strangling my camellias."

Utopia did as told and handed her the trowel. She watched her mother at work, her limbs bloody with scratches, her chafed elbows and digging motion, her hips pressing forward as she leaned to uproot the bramble, the back of her hand swiping the hair from her face.

"Are you coming to France?"

"I'm going to Cornwall. I told you."

"We all change our minds." This was her mother making trouble, a not uncommon event. "What have you been doing? We haven't seen you in weeks."

"Working."

"How's the magazine?"

"Busy."

"Been having fun?"

"Lots."

Her mother always said this as though it needed to be said.

"Good. I've got theatre tickets for us to see that new play. Now go and turn on the tap. I disappear for three days to see Granny, come back to find that your father has allowed my entire garden to perish."

Utopia stood up, brushed the lawn off her denim and went to find the tap hidden behind the hydrangeas. Inside the house she heard her father put on a record.

There had been a time when the vastness of her mother's death so consumed her that she hadn't recognised her mother or herself. But with so much left behind, her mother was close. Sorrow embraced her with strong arms and she felt herself guided to a place where she could remember the happy times.

Utopia took a Marlboro. "Thanks."

"I'm a poet," said Polo-neck. "Do you write?"

"Sometimes," she said. "Not often enough."

She smiled and exhaled smoke through her nostrils like cresting waves. She was exhausted. It was time to go. It was time to leave this house which like a paying customer, she had journeyed to see. She wanted to take her memories elsewhere. She turned to her neighbour. "You couldn't help me find a cab? I've lost my friends."

He smiled. "Sure. I'll walk you over to Lexington. Should find one there."

She had no choice. She was going to have to trust him.

The dance floor upstairs was impenetrable. They passed by and out through the carved wooden door.

Outside was quiet.

They marched briskly along the desolate street. The

bag lag was pushing her supermarket trolley along the demarcating white lines. Squeaking and rumbling, it lurched on bent wheels. Shadows skulked and parched leaves rustled. Utopia could hear the blood in her ears rushing like water. She felt scared so she grabbed Polo-neck's arm.

"It's OK," he told her.

They walked together.

They arrived at Lexington Avenue and found that it was barren. Struck by fears of ambush, Utopia peered up the road. "Come on, come on, " she murmured.

At last a lone cab cruised into view.

"Thanks for rescuing me," she said.

"Hey, it's what it's all about." Polo-neck smiled and crossed the street. Just when she thought he had gone, he turned and waved. She waved back.

On the slippery seat, Utopia greeted their approach into familiar terrain with contentment. Fifth Avenue's apartment blocks skimmed the window as the events of the past six hours assumed a dream-like mantle. Been there, done that. No need to go back.

# Chapter Forty

"Can I steal your arts section?" asked the man at the next-door table.

"Be my guest," said Marina.

He picked up the slab of newsprint on the chair beside her and began rifling through it.

"It's the piece about the Hanoi dance troupe I want," he said.

"Darling, it's yours."

It was midday Sunday.

The door was wide open and the café was crowded with brunchers, their hands clasped round bowls of café au lait. Utopia took a drink of orange juice and studied the room through her glass sluiced with pulp. She spotted Miles, the singer from the band Mouthwash. He was sharing an omelette with someone familiar, a girl with a froth of blonde pushed up on her head.

Utopia strained for a better look. It was Goldie from *HQ*. Utopia had heard that Miles's band had been signed so Goldie was probably looking to feature them in the magazine. One thing usually led to the next, and their dynamic had clearly progressed beyond the tan leather sofa in

Goldie's office. They looked very cosy together. Their heads were leaning over the untouched plate of food, their wisps of hair just nudged and a wall of smoke sanctioned their privacy.

Utopia was curious. Was this the morning after the first night before?

Marina was skimming the style section. She was groaning out loud and shaking her head as she read an article on fall fashion predictions. "Oh, Jesus. As if we're seriously going to wear those ugly flats. Christ, who wrote this crap?"

She was wearing her Jackie O's and warbling like a blackbird. In between disputing the verdicts in the paper, she was cooing over Donald. Donald had reappeared from LA. He had flown out this morning, having skipped through town for a meeting with Miramax. It was a possible film project. He had optioned a thriller set in New York based on the true story of the murder of a drag queen and an NYPD cover-up. The meeting had gone well. So well, in fact, that Donald had taken Marina to dinner at a rose-marbled restaurant on the Upper East Side. "We had truffled lobster, pink champagne. And I wore my blonde wig. I can't remember the last time. We skipped coffee and . . . Christ, that man is heaven with a libido," she said, with a smile.

Utopia nodded as she tried to read her menu.

"Ready?" asked the waitress, a pretty Japanese girl with a pierced lip like punishment.

"Yes," said Marina and ordered a feast of eggs, French toast and fries.

Utopia had the same. Both needed coffee refills.

"I'm jealous," said Utopia as the waitress left.

"Do be, darling."

Marina's story was the same old story. Thanks to the offer of sex, Donald's unaccountability, his weeks of silence, were free to go unchallenged. But what was there not to understand? Utopia's own relationship with Saul had been based on the exact same premise. It was all about arousal. Deprived of sex, the libido slunk off and the body cooled down. During those winter months in London and on arrival in New York, sex could not have been further from her mind. Then she met Saul. As soon as sex was back on the agenda, the body woke up to a fever of lust. Marina had been twitchy ever since spending the weekend with Donald. This time next week and she would be complaining once again of his inconsiderateness but that was part of the cycle. It was aggravation that fed the desire.

"And the Prozac's kicked in. Well, my therapist did put me on thrilling doses."

Marina was wearing a pale blue shirt, which captured her eyes like flecks of sky. She looked beautiful, thought Utopia, noticing that her face was make-up free or was it natural-look make-up?

"How can you tell?"

"Tell? Couldn't miss it. The earthquake's stopped. I can wake up in the morning and have a rough idea of how I'll be feeling. Cheshire is so relieved."

"I'm not surprised."

"And what's yours?"

"Mine?"

"News?"

"Tomorrows Monday. *Mille.*"

"How exciting."

"I hope so."

Utopia drank her coffee, nursed her hangover and felt stoically vacant. Today was the trailer before tomorrow's feature. Her recollection of last night was more visceral than real. It had been about clogged air, paranoia and a bid for escape. She could hardly recall the event but it had, in some strange way, provided confirmation that it could only get better.

If Meg would allow it.

She was worried about Meg. But she had a strange hunch that, given the chance, they would actually get on. Any antipathy she felt towards her was jealousy in disguise, she knew that. Their paths had overlapped three times. There was common ground. She was impressed by Meg and she was prepared to admit it, at last.

She listened to the drone of café activity, the door clanging as it ushered in new arrivals, the cappuccino machine hissing, the chime of a glass lid being removed, a French singer rasping from the speakers.

The more she thought about it, the more convinced she was that she was in the right place. She was still blown away by the view of the city from the Queensboro Bridge, she still had to learn the rules of basketball in time for the Knicks game Johann had tickets for, and she had agreed to go Thai boxing with Todd on Tuesday night. Best of all, Felix had promised to take her to his house on the dunes so that they could sit on the porch and drink mint juleps together.

She wasn't ready to break with the rituals of New York life.

She had grown used to Sunday evening sunsets on the promenade at Brooklyn Heights, the man dropping off laundry at ten o'clock at night, margaritas to make you fly. She would count the days until she could take the train and go and hear the Atlantic roar. She liked the fact that while it was hot it would soon be cold. She wanted to trudge through snow and ice and survive a winter.

No, it wasn't time to go.

"Girlfriend."

It was Goldie on wedge heels. She was sucking a lol-lipop.

"How you been? You know we've got Brooke running features. What a fucking drama queen. But we did that tranny story."

Utopia laughed. "Really?"

"December issue. Check it out. Where are you?"

"*Mille*. I find out tomorrow."

"*Mille's* cool. You can do some fun stuff there."

Miles appeared. He grinned and thrust both hands into his back pockets. His T-shirt read, *bleed me*, in red against white and he wore a leather thong around his neck. He looked like a star. Goldie clearly thought so.

"I hear you got a deal."

"We're recording up in Woodstock."

"Come up. We've got this house. There's a creek at the back where we swim," said Goldie.

Utopia found a pen and scribbled down her number on a napkin. They left the café. Utopia noticed that they were holding hands.

"Looks like love," said Marina, looking up from her paper.

"Easy come, easy go," Utopia heard herself say.


It was a fine day for flying kites. Tall and breezy. Dragging their heels down Prince Street, they glanced into windows at badly dressed mannequins. A woman was removing dog shit from the sidewalk with a plastic bag. Her golden retriever panted alongside. They watched a whippet-thin roller-blader collide with a cab at the corner of Prince and Sullivan. He folded himself over the bonnet with balletic grace.

"Fucking arsehole."

"Fuck you, fucking faggot."

"Charming," said Marina, as they emerged on the corner of West Broadway. "I'm going to pop myself into a cab and head up to Bergdorf's. Lingerie. Sure you don't want to come?"

"Positive."

They kissed each other goodbye and Marina's cab merged with the traffic.

Utopia welcomed her solitude. She needed a day to gather her thoughts and prepare for tomorrow. Packs of tourists herded past with cameras and rucksacks. Utopia pressed through and squinted at the naïve sidewalk art and cheap jewellery. A shoulder slammed into her. The force of delivery felt like a deliberate assault.

"For Christ's sake!"

Utopia stared.

"Jean?"

"Utopia."

"How are you?"

"Good, good. Yes, yes," replied the long-lost Jean Weiner in a white coat. It was embossed with hundreds of Chanel logos like a sea of sperm.

Utopia continued to stare. It was that dishevelled hair, those pale eyes, lipstick smudged as though by the back of her hand. For weeks she had found herself fantasising about this exact event as she strode through the city. She imagined bumping into Jean on the street and demanding an explanation.

So what the hell happened?

Jean had her home number. She could have called to say something, anything. And now here she was confronted with Jean and lost for words.

"I'm in meetings. I'm about to be set up with my own magazine."

"Right."

For some reason, Utopia didn't believe a word of what was being said. She had imagined that she would feel angry or at least resent Jean for leaving behind so much unfinished business and forcing her to fend for herself again. Instead she felt disappointment, sympathy even. Jean seemed unbalanced, her speech, like her make-up a scrappy façade.

"It's going to be an arts specific magazine for the more mature end of the market. The focus groups have found a core market."

"Great."

"I've got your number. Let's do lunch," she said and off she scooted before Utopia even had a chance to ask about the outcome of the court case or the fate of the Picassos.

Utopia watched her go, her shopping-bag swinging like a pendulum of mania from her arm. Let's do lunch. That same tired refrain. She was finally able to say goodbye. Turning in the opposite direction, Utopia shook her head.

It was over.

She crossed Broadway.

Sunday couples were hanging off each other's arms, necks and lips. She tried not to look but it was impossible, they were everywhere. She took a right on to Lafayette and the crowds dispersed. There above Little Italy was the police building and City Hall's clock tower in the distance heralded Broadway's descent towards the water. She was tempted to open her arms and start running so that she could feel the sidewalk pound beneath her feet.

Instead she stared up at the sky and tried to re-create the sensation of swimming under water, of silent immersion in distant blue. A motorised thunder detonated the peace as a helicopter flew overhead. It was impossible to pretend you were anywhere else. She should know that by now.

She reached her door.

She unlocked it and struggled to avoid the doorway stench of piss as she tried not to drop her Sunday paper bunched beneath her arm. She climbed the stairs. Her nostrils were attacked by a profusion of smells, ammonia cleaning fluid, spicy food, odours from rancid trainers left outside on landings.

One more flight to go.

The apartment door was unlocked.

"Johann?"

Silence.

She dropped her paper on the chair beside the telephone and walked into the living room. A pair of legs were jutting out from the end of the sofa. A supine figure lay hidden. She recognised the proportion of those limbs, the fade of those jeans and the scuffed black shoes with one lace undone.

She felt her jaw drop.

He sat bolt upright, his smile as broad as his face. "Ha!"

She stopped, frozen, before rushing to him to be embraced by his arms as though coming home. She was speechless. She felt numb. She needed to feel the wall of his chest against hers as proof of his being there. Her worlds now collided as she bit down on his shoulder and looked past his head at the wall beyond. She hugged him harder and harder, she couldn't breathe, didn't want to breathe until they were one.

She spied a ball of fluff skate across the floor and disappear behind a book shelf. She laughed. The vermin were taking over but she didn't care.

"What are you doing here?" she finally asked, pulling

back to see his face. She sketched it with her finger, around his eyes, along his cheeks, and the groove above his lip. She kissed him. She was shaking her head. She thought she might cry. If she did she would enjoy it. "You're a bastard for not telling me."

"I told Johann," said P, brushing her hair from her face.

She thought this was the best thing she had ever heard. It was brilliant.

"Did Johann let you in?"

"Yes. He seemed nice. Then he left. Off to meet some girl, he said."

She squeezed on to the sofa next to him. September rays spilt through the window to alight upon their faces and she wondered why they had never done this before. It seemed so obvious. She didn't know where to begin. She refused to let go.

"When did you decide?"

"Friday. I'd had enough."

She clasped her arms tighter around his neck.

"How are you? You look well. Tanned."

She laughed, pleased.

"I think Edward thought you ought to come home."

"Did you speak to him?"

"Yes, I rang to see how his visit went and see how you were. Did you have a nice time?"

"Yes." She paused. "We did."

P was nodding. His hair had grown. She had never seen it so straggly, with locks like wool. His skin was the colour of the back garden and Spanish sun and his eyes were so bright with their bottomless depth. She suddenly realised just how much she had missed him.

"A lot's happened, you know."

"Yes."

"I mean things, you know. All sorts of things. That friend who died." She hesitated.

But P was looking at her, an expectant smile shaping his lips. She wanted to tell him.

"We had a thing."

For some reason, it didn't sound as monumental as she feared. It sounded small, contained, over.

"You had a thing." He repeated it and chewed the inside of his mouth. "A big thing?"

"A New York thing."

He sighed then nodded. "Yes. Well, Christ. I don't know if I'm surprised. No, that sounds crap. I thought something might have happened. I didn't want to think about it. Fuck, it pissed me off."

She leaned back so that she was cross-legged on the sofa and facing him sideways. His expression was vulnerable and it made her feel afraid.

"Why did it end? Because he. . ." He was looking straight ahead.

"Before that."

He nodded. He was strong again. "What was his name?"

"Saul."

There was silence as Utopia leaned forward and took his hand. With every utterance came a sense of forsaking the small place she had inhabited alone for a place long-abandoned calling her back. It was an emotional exchange.

"What about you?"

He looked blank.

She had butterflies in her stomach. She didn't like it.

"Lou phoned. Someone saw you at Julian's party . . ."

He turned his head to face her confused. "And what?"

"That you left with someone."

"Sarah?"

Utopia shrugged.

He shook his head, disbelieving. He hated gossip. She knew that.

"What? Someone saw me talking to someone and then what? I'm meant to have fucked her? Jesus Christ. I give someone a lift home and . . . She's a friend of Julian's."

Utopia felt sick with self-loathing, ecstatic with relief.

P was shaking his head. He looked hurt. "Are you disappointed? D'you want some great fucking drama?"

"Of course not. Oh, P, I'm sorry. It's only because . . ."

"Exactly, I'm the one who should be angry. For Christ's sake." And he leaned forward and grabbed her, pulling her to him so that she tipped and had to uncross her legs for their faces to meet. "I'm not going anywhere."

"I kept wanting to phone and ask you to come."

They began kissing as he held her and made her come alive. It was a sensation of stillness that spread through her. P was the person who protected her from danger and from herself when her urge for self-destruction flared. But she had sought detachment because she needed to be responsible for no one but herself as her mother tried doing, as her mother was caught doing.

But the anger had passed.

She felt restored to the tide of life from where she had run. P was the person whose understanding of herself she sometimes felt outmatched her own. His grasp of the pain had so effectively cushioned her own that in the end she couldn't bear it. "Why do you always have to be so bloody understanding?" she had berated him. She had wanted him to betray her as she felt betrayed. It was her only wish he refused to oblige.

Things could be different. She knew that now. Her affection for him was the measure of her being. With her hands clasped in his, his breath seeking hers, she would take it slowly. Little by little.